A leap of faith . . .

Soon the distinct voices became an unintelligible thrum and I merged with the LINK. Images blurred together into a blinding white light. Though sightless and soundless, I could sense the LINK as it pulsed and breathed, enveloping me in its living warmth. I could have pooled there forever in the information flow, but Mouse pulled me further down, past the buzzing chatter of commerce and pleasure to something deeper, more basic.

Next to me, I felt him manipulate a password and trigger a response somewhere in the bowels of the beast. We snapped, with an almost palatable sound, into focus. The LINK glittered like the stars above. My consciousness felt anchored in something solid now. A definite here, yet its base was enormous, like a giant whose feet straddled the earth.

"My God, where are we?"

ARCHANGEL
PROTOCOL

Lyda Morehouse

RoC

A ROC BOOK

ROC
Published by New American Library, a division of
Penguin Putnam Inc., 375 Hudson Street,
New York, New York 10014, U.S.A.
Penguin Books Ltd, 27 Wrights Lane,
London W8 5TZ, England
Penguin Books Australia Ltd, Ringwood,
Victoria, Australia
Penguin Books Canada Ltd, 10 Alcorn Avenue,
Toronto, Ontario, Canada M4V 3B2
Penguin Books (N.Z.) Ltd, 182–190 Wairau Road,
Auckland 10, New Zealand

Penguin Books Ltd, Registered Offices:
Harmondsworth, Middlesex, England

First published by Roc, an imprint of New American Library,
a division of Penguin Putnam Inc.

First Printing, May 2001
10 9 8 7 6 5 4 3 2 1

To Shawn Rounds,
it is as much her book as it is mine

ACKNOWLEDGMENTS

I'd like to thank all the people who have helped me with the creation of this book, but especially my editor Laura Anne Gilman, my agent James Frenkel, and his trusted assistant Tracy Berg.

For all their support and belief in my ability, I'd like to single out for special gratitude Nate Bucklin, who first believed in me, and my mentor Eleanor Arnason (and Patrick Wood). Additionally, I should thank all the professionals who helped me along my way, especially, Anne Harris, Gardner Dozois, Pam Keesey, Peg Kerr, Laurel Winter, Terry A. Garey, John C. "Rez" Rezmerski, Robert Subiaga, Jr., Maureen McHugh, Scott Edelman, Angela Kessler, Philip Kaveny, Eric Heideman, and J. Otis Powell!

Thanks to present and past colleagues (and friends!) in: "Wyrdsmiths"—Harry LeBlanc, Naomi Kritzer, Doug Hulick, Rosalind Nelson, Bill Henry, Michael Belifore, Laramie Sasseville, and Ralph A. N. Krantz; "Karma Weasels"—David Hoffman-Dachelet, Kelly David McCullough, Barth Anderson, Manfred Gabriel, Kirsten Livdahl, Alan DeNiro, and Burke Kealey; The "Fierce Wild Women"—Terry A. Garey, Rebecca Marjesdatter, Ama Patterson, Eleanor Arnason, and Laurie Winter; The "Loft Group," including—William Stitler (and Lady Bird), Carole Ashmore, Bob Metz, Rachel Gold, John Burke, Jon Olsen, and Susan Hastings.

Friends and family who put up with boring writer stories, including William Laughing Turtle Bettes; Nick Dykstra; Julie Beale; Barb Bezat (and her family—Riley, my padawan William, and the Mah Jongg grrl Allie); the gang at "d'IHRC" (Susan Staiger, Jennifer Guglielmo, Todd Mitchney, Walter Anastazievski, Roman Stepchuk, Kristine Marconi, Joel Wurl, Judy Rosenblatt, and, the bodhisattva Timo Riippa); Gerriann Brower; Barb Mach; The Jacksons (John, Michele, Maggie and Jack); Michele Helen Morgan; Barb Portinga (and the rest of the TMF Folks); Ishmael Williams; Jules Raberding; Garry Kopp (and Samantha Rose); geisha-boy Nik Wilson; Paul E. "Theisenburger" Theisen; the best nephew in the whole world Jonathan Sharpe ("I know, you distract 'em, I'll rush 'em"); all the Rounds (Shawn, Keven, Pat, Margaret, Greg, and Barb); my cousin who taught me to play and gave me the heart of a writer, Laun Braithwaite; and, of course, my parents Mort and Rita Morehouse.

A special thanks to my last-minute proofreaders and fact-checkers: Robert Subiaga, Jr., and Rebecca Marjesdatter.

And, of course, to Shawn Rounds, who came up with the new title and so much more.

CHAPTER 1

My hairline itched where the dead receiver lay just under the skin. I reached up to caress the hard almond-shaped lump at my temple. Maybe if I squeezed just right, the implant would eke out some last drop of code, like a used tube of toothpaste. I stopped myself. Granted, since the excommunication, I no longer had to maintain the high standards of a decorated police officer, but you'd think I could retain at least some vestige of ladylike demeanor. The unconscious gesture made me look like a wire-junkie. My LINK access had been severed a year ago, but I tended to poke at it like a scab, especially when I was upset.

I picked up the note I found tacked to my office door again. Mrs. Rosenstone couldn't afford our barter anymore. She'd been using her access to the LINK to get my letters to the *New York Times* criticizing the presidential campaign published. In exchange, I did a little detective work into the death of her husband—she wanted more details than the "your husband died bravely" letter the government sent. Apparently, as of today, she decided the information wasn't worth the price. Her war-widow pension had mysteriously disappeared into the government's red tape for a second time in six months. Crumpling up her note, I tossed it in the garbage can. I could hardly blame the woman.

The office was as quiet as my empty head. Pools of light warmly mottled the hardwood floor despite the dirty windows and the layers of grime on the venetian blinds. Dust motes sparkled, illuminated by the stripes of soft light. As my gaze followed the specks swirling through the air, all I could think of was that I really should clean this place more often, especially since I all but lived here.

The broom closet held several changes of clothes. The cubbyhole beneath the window, designed for data chip storage, overflowed with coffee cups, plastic forks, and sundry dishes. Along the far wall, a bookcase of mail slots stood. In places you could still see remnants of labels that once bore the names of former office workers. Now the mailboxes were crammed with bills and traffic tickets, most of them past due. I was a pack rat; I probably had a better archive than the Vatican, if less organized. The only things that lent any style to the office were the big oak desk and the frosted glass door with my name on it: DEIDRE MCMANNUS, PRIVATE DETECTIVE.

Even after a year, it felt strange to be working alone, but Daniel was gone—and anyway, he would never have stooped to be a private eye, especially working for barter on the fringe. I snorted in contempt at my state. Solo, empty, alone: the story of my life.

It was a Saturday. I should be at home, but something about those block walls inhibited my thought processes. Maybe it was the way concrete muffled every sound, but whatever it was, I preferred to spend as little time in the apartment as possible. The sudden loss of steady income that the excommunication brought forced me into skyscraper living. Try as I might, I couldn't make that hole-in-the-wall feel like a home. Barring my bed, I moved everything I really valued to the office.

That was next. The rent for two places stretched an already tight pocketbook, and my supply of Christian Scientists in need of a private investigator was running dry. Despite their religious convictions against getting LINKed, the Scientists were, at least, respectable clients. More importantly to me, they could pay in credits rather than barter. The government recognized their objection as legitimate because it was based on religious belief against surgery. As conscientious objectors, they were allowed official external hardware.

Anyone else not on the LINK was either a dissenter or couldn't afford the process. America, as my letters to the editor often lamented, was no longer the home of democracy. We were becoming, instead, a theocracy, and had been since the last Great War, twenty-one years ago. Science, which had brought an ugly end to the fighting by producing and detonating the Medusa bombs, and the secular humanism that spawned it, had fallen so far out of favor that it was now officially a crime not to be at least nominally part of an organized religion.

Dissenters, mostly secular humanists and atheists or people like me, who were forced out of a recognized religion, made up the bulk of my clientele. However, as dissenters, they didn't have a citizenship card—no card, no LINK; no LINK, no access to commerce; no commerce, no credits. Not even my shady landlord would take home-brew or other barter in lieu of real rent. It was credits or the street.

People had suggested I simply convert to another religion and have done with it. There had been several offers. Still, my Catholic guilt told me I deserved to be punished for what had happened between Daniel and me. Moreover, the Pope had made things more complicated when he excommunicated me. Legally, I was still a Catholic, just an excommunicated one. So, if I tried to officially join another religion, it would be like trying to marry a new husband without being divorced from a previous one—not even Mormon women got away with a stunt like that in this country.

I sighed, then tapped the space key and watched half-heartedly as the *New York Times* scrolled across the antique monitor propped on the edge of my desk.

"Not even a graphical interface anymore," I muttered, waiting for the next article to materialize on the screen. I skimmed another op-ed page article.

Once again, the reclusive presidential candidate, Reverend-Senator Étienne Letourneau, took a firm position against "liberal" (read: all but heathen) Rabbi-

Senator Grey from New York. It took me two sentences
to realize Letourneau's rant was an obvious ploy to put
the fear of God into the opposition. This campaign was
such a joke. If you believed in what the LINK angels
had to say, and an overwhelming majority did, Reverend
Letourneau embodied the Second Coming of Christ. In
a theocracy, being God was a guaranteed winning
platform.

I had my doubts, and not just since the excommunication. One of my main arguments all along against Letourneau was that new messiah ought to have similar
basic tenets as Christ. A recluse holed up in the mountains of Colorado surrounded by all the fresh air money
could buy fell pretty damned short of my expectations.
Honestly, I'd sort of been holding out for a woman messiah this time around—or, at the very least, not some
nearly dead white guy.

My finger hovered over the reply key ready to fire off
another letter to the editor, when I heard a loud rap of
someone at the door.

"Later, Letourneau," I told the monitor, and hit save.
"Door's open," I shouted, twisting the chair to step back
into the leather pumps I'd kicked off earlier. I was still
adjusting the heel when he let himself in.

"Detective McMannus?"

"Not anymore," I corrected, without looking up.
"Door says private investigator."

With the shoe finally in place, I swiveled the chair.
Something between a gasp and a hiss came out of my
mouth.

Granted, masculine beauty has always been a weakness of mine, but this man literally took my breath away.
Olive-skinned, tall, broad-shouldered, slender-waisted—
he looked like he might have been sculpted from marble.
Unfortunately, this David remembered to dress himself
this morning. His fashion sense leaned toward urban
combat. Leather jacket and dusty-blue jeans hugged his
muscular frame. He looked like a warrior sheathed in
casual armor.

As I traced the line of his throat up to his face, a

smile captured my lips—a girl could cut herself on the angle of that jaw. His dark, curly locks were shorn above the ears in a martial style; gray eyes flashed from under strong, dark swatches of eyebrows.

"Are you Deidre McMannus?" He asked again, irritation marring his godlike brow.

"I am," I said, remembering to stand up and offer him a hand. Smoothing out the wrinkles in my blouse, I turned on my most charming smile. "And who might you be?"

He took my hand and I wasn't disappointed by the firmness of his grasp. "Lieutenant Michael Angelucci, Tenth Precinct."

"Oh. A cop." I dropped his handshake and turned my back to him. Not only a cop, but an angel freak. Since the appearance of the LINK-angels several months ago, thousands of converts changed their given names or surnames to include some form of the word "angel." More than half my client list was named Angelica or Angelo.

I sighed and sat back down. "Sorry, Mike, but I already bought tickets to the charity ball, so I don't think there's any more I can do for you."

Such a shame, I thought, allowing myself one last look at the way the stripes of sunlight fell across his chest. I should've figured him for a cop. My earlier assessment of his manly charms neglected to include the slight bulge of the standard-issue Glock tucked into the shoulder holster. With a clearer eye, I ticked off the other dead giveaways. The way he stood, all ready for action, held a certain flat-footedness that I should've picked up before. The biggest clue was the dumbstruck expression on his face. That said cop all over it.

Pressing the space bar, I retrieved the article I'd saved from the *Times*. I feigned an overwhelming interest in the screen, and added, "You boys should know I don't involve myself with police work anymore."

Michael eased his hands into the pockets of his jeans. He stood there, as if to tell me he had no plans of moving anytime soon.

Waving a hand in the air, I shooed him out of the

office. "Come on, Officer, you managed to find the door once."

He glanced at the door, then swung his handsome face back in my direction. A lesser woman might've swooned, but I just tightened my smile. I gave up on the *Times* with a sigh. "Let me guess this time is different: it's a matter of life or death."

"Actually . . ." Michael sauntered over to my desk and propped himself up on the edge. "It's more serious than that."

I laughed. Leaning forward onto my elbows, I rested my head on my hands. "What could be more serious than life or death?"

"Some things have eternal consequences." He smiled slightly, turning up the very edges of his mouth. The effect on his face was stunning. His eyes widened just enough to smooth the crease from the middle of his brow. Michelangelo eat your heart out.

"Some things do," I managed to say. "But I'm not running a church. You look like the football and Bible type. Why don't you try the Promise Keepers Church down the road? It's a drive-through."

"What they're selling can't help me."

I looked back at his face, trying to judge by his expression how he meant that. The tone sounded almost mocking, but his mouth turned down, and his eyes were serious.

"Yeah? But I can, eh?" I gave him a tired smile, "I have 'to warn you, I don't have any plastic figurines or Bible scorecards to offer."

"I'll have to make do," he said. Michael took my words as an invitation to stay and settled himself more securely on top of the scattered snail-news clippings and other clutter of my desk. His knee grazed the edge of a pewter picture frame. The back-prop folded and began to tip over, but Michael reached out to rescue it. He turned the frame over in his hands and glanced down at the photo. Something in the picture caught his attention, and his eyes flicked over it as if searching for some clue.

I leaned back in my swivel chair to observe him. The

springs of the chair creaked noisily. He showed me the photo, "Family?"

"Yeah," I admitted, wary of the direction this conversation was going. My personal life was off-limits. Still, I'd give him the benefit of the doubt. "My brother, the priest."

As he set the frame down near its original spot, his deep-set eyes searched out mine. I didn't like the intimacy of his gaze, so I found myself bristling and talking without thinking.

"So, what are you implying? My brother's a problem?" I scoffed. "Mike, I have it on good authority that Eion's nearly a saint."

"What? No, no, not at all. I was just . . . hmm-mmmmm." He paused, as if searching for the right words. Absently, Michael pushed at the glossy cover of the dog-eared paperback novel I'd been reading. His finger traced the edge of the design, skirting the hem of the heroine's ripped bodice. Slowly, along the embossed folds of the dress, his fingertip moved toward her bosom. Grabbing the book out from under his touch, I slapped the cover facedown on the desk, surprising both of us.

When he raised his eyes, I gaped at him mutely. I couldn't explain why I'd reacted that way. The feeling was silly, and I was losing control of this conversation. So, I grabbed the novel and tossed it into the bottom drawer of my desk. I kicked it shut with the toe of my shoe. "Bad habit." I shrugged.

Michael lowered his eyes. That slight smile turned up the corners of his mouth again. "Tell me something, McMannus. Are you still Catholic?"

"Does the Pope shit in the woods?" I fired back.

His gray eyes flashed up at my words, pinning me under a harsh glare. Determined to stay on top of the pecking order we seemed to be establishing, I stared back just as hard.

"So what does my faith have to do with anything?" I asked. "What? Are you one of the New Christian Righters out proselytizing for Letourneau? I always figured the force was crawling with Letourneau's minions. Listen, Officer, I have less than no time for you if . . ."

"I'm not," he cut me off. "Though in a way, it's Letourneau that brought me here."

"Well, if he's involved, I'm not," I bristled. "The good senator has caused me enough trouble."

"I know he has," Michael said quietly. He stood up, careful not to disturb the photo. Michael moved over to the window and looked out between the dusty blinds. He pushed the slats down with a finger. He had to be thinking hard about something, because the only view out my window was the unimpressive back alley of an abandoned Western Union. Truth was, most things were empty and derelict on this level, my office being one of the few exceptions.

"If not one of Letourneau's lackeys, then what are you?" I asked Michael's back.

"Just a messenger," he said absently, still watching the alley.

"Oh yeah? Well then, what's your message?"

"It's not for you," he said in a low voice. Michael squinted as though tracking the movement of someone outside. Pointing out the window and down toward the street level, he asked; "Is that man often there?"

"Who? A scruffy-looking soapbox preacher?" I asked. When Michael nodded, I checked my watch. Sure enough, the time read quarter to four. "Like clockwork. He's the only other guy besides me who works on a Saturday afternoon, I swear."

"Damn," Michael said through clenched teeth. Though he'd whispered, the curse cut through the still office air like a knife.

"Is that why you're here? The preacher? I can attest he's pretty harmless." Uncomfortable with the silence that had settled in the room, I asked, "So, if your message isn't for me, who is it for?"

"Why does he come to your office window? He's not going to get much of a crowd back there." Hooking his thumb toward the street, Michael turned toward me.

"He doesn't want a crowd. He wants me. When the

window is open, I can hear him harping about heretics and all that. He wants to save me, I think." I shrugged. "Nice thought, but it gets old, you know?"

Michael smiled.

I crossed my arms in front of my chest and let out a long breath. "Even though his rants sometimes irritate the piss out of me, I'm grateful for his persistence. At least someone thinks I'm worth saving."

"Why wouldn't you be?"

"You ever use that receiver in your head?" I asked him, tapping the hard, dead pellet at my temple meaningfully. I smiled to take the sting out of my tone.

"Martyrs and saints are rarely understood in their own time."

I sputtered out something between a choke and a laugh. "You're joking."

Michael shrugged and turned back toward the window. "Eternal consequences," he repeated.

I gave in to a chuckle I'd been trying to hold back. "Oh, I get it now. This is some kind of sales pitch. Cop salary is still that bad, that you have to work door-to-door for some shady 'indulgence' company, eh?"

He turned back to give me a patient smile. "No, but I am here on personal business. Listen, I'm willing to barter."

"Barter." I sighed. "Just what I need."

I shook my head and walked back behind my desk. I'd been excited at the prospect of a live client, but at the mention of the word "barter" the ache returned to my temple. I bit my lip to keep from scratching at the receiver.

"Maybe you can't afford me," I told him. "I only work for credits," I added to the lie with a flourish. "And, I mean Christendom credits, not the local variety Free State crap."

He looked around at my shabby office. "I think you might be interested in my barter."

"Oh yeah?" I sneered back, offended that my desperate straits were so blatantly obvious that he didn't even pretend to believe my lie.

"I can offer you the LINK."

I suddenly forgot how to breathe. Then, the insanity of his offer pushed a stream of words out of my mouth in a rush. "Impossible. No bio-hack in the world could bypass the meltdown trigger, and, if you're talking external mode, I'd be just as toasted. The feedback loop alone would kill me." As an afterthought, I added, "Not to mention the fact that it would be totally illegal."

"But if I could do it . . . ?" Michael's eyes twinkled.

"You'd be a god and I'd be your slave." I coughed out a laugh and dropped into the chair. I twirled a mouse-pen through my fingers. "But, you can just keep dreaming, big guy. You might as well offer me the moon."

"That would be a bit tougher," he admitted with a smile, but his tone was serious.

Michael's eyes still held that "I've got a secret" look, and my disbelief eroded. I dropped the pen and my flippant attitude. "You're serious."

"I am."

"Christ," I breathed, my mind reeling.

"It would be worth a lot to you, wouldn't it?" Michael asked quietly.

"You have no idea," I said. My voice sounded like sandpaper. The desperation in it reminded me of the urgent whine of the wire-junkies begging for access on Forty-second Street. I had to try to pull myself together; otherwise, this guy would think he could walk all over me. More than that, I hadn't seen the goods yet. I cleared my throat. "Presuming you can perform this little miracle, what exactly are you expecting in exchange?"

"A LINK-hack." Michael's eyes watched my face.

I looked over his shoulder to where the certificate of merit hung on the wall. I'd gotten that honor for successfully collaring a wire-wizard named Weasel, who was terrorizing the LINK. Michael was asking me to become what I used to hunt when I was on the Tech Vice Squad. He was asking me to break the law.

"Is that all?" I gave a relieved laugh. "Hell, I could

do that in my sleep. What do you want, Officer? Access to the department's slush fund? A peek at an Internal Affairs file? What?"

I tried, unsuccessfully, to keep my tone light. My finger stroked the lump of the receiver.

He scratched the short hairs at the back of his neck. "I want you to help me bring down the LINK-angels and expose Letourneau as a false prophet, a pretender."

His face scrunched up, as though preparing for a bad reaction.

I gave it to him. "What? Are you insane?"

"You heard me."

"The LINK-angels, fake? That's not possible," I told him flatly.

He nodded. I stared at him incredulously. The LINK-angels were a bona fide miracle. It wasn't just that they looked like angels. After all, anyone could assume any type of avatar out on the LINK. The thing that made LINK-angels different is they broadcast emotions, feelings. As a former tech-cop, I knew sending emotions via electrons was as unlikely an alchemist's attempt to turn lead to gold. The equipment needed would fill more than just one person's head. The human mind was still enough of a mystery that even if we had the technology to link to the emotional centers, sending something coherent was another matter. All that either party would most likely receive was a garbled jumble of images, sound and smell—as the bard might say, "full of sound and fury, signifying nothing."

Thus, all of the experts had agreed, secular and religious, what the LINK-angels did, no human could duplicate. The LINK-angels were what they claimed to be—a sign from God.

"Some people might say what you're suggesting is heresy," I told Michael.

"That's why I need you. You're already excommunicated. The Pope can't threaten you." Michael leaned against the windowpane and gave me a hard stare. "Besides, if Letourneau isn't the Second Coming, it's hardly heresy. Some might even consider a hack like that God's work. Anyway, why do you care so much about heresy?"

"I care. All right? I happen to care a lot. Despite what people say about me on the LINK, I don't take this sentence lightly. I lost my job." My fingers stroked the implant with an almost feverish desperation. "More than that, I lost a friend."

"Right . . . Daniel."

I wasn't surprised that Michael knew about my personal history. I had a fan-run site somewhere on the LINK, where people kept track of all my comings and goings. I was surprised at how much hearing that name out loud hurt.

"I apologize," Michael said. He dropped his gaze and stared at his chest.

"Forget about it." I shrugged. With some effort, I halted the rhythmical rubbing. To give my hands something else to do, I shuffled though the clippings and printouts on my desk. I couldn't look at Michael as I continued, "The LINK-angels are more untouchable than the Mafia, and they've picked Letourneau. The election is sewn up and people are roasting 'heretics' wherever they find them. A person can't even get a dissenting opinion printed in the *Times* these days without retribution." Thinking of Mrs. Rosenstone, I frowned and gestured at my monitor to empathize my point. "No. I'm truly sorry for whatever's happening to you or to whomever you represent, but count me out. I tried to go up against the New Right before and I lost . . . lost a lot more than I was willing to sacrifice."

"I'm certain Daniel's soul is clean," I heard him whisper.

Something in his voice made me search out his eyes. "Clean?" I repeated, "Clean of what?"

"Sin," he said simply.

I shook my head slowly. "I wish I could be so certain, big guy."

"So do I." His voice sounded heavy with defeat. Boots scuffed against the floor, as he turned to leave. "If you reconsider, my offer still stands."

I didn't look up from the clutter on my desk. In my attempt to straighten up the mess, I'd unearthed the article about Danny's trial. Damn filing system. Between my trembling fingers read the headline: "COP CONVICTED IN POPE'S MURDER." Despite everything, I should never have turned him in like that—never, I thought desperately.

"For him then," came Michael's voice at the door, startling me.

"What?" I quickly shoved the article facedown under a coffee cup. I couldn't stand the sight of Danny's accusing face. "What did you say?"

"If not for me, then take my case for him. It would clear your conscience."

"What makes you think it's my conscience that needs clearing?"

"Daniel is an innocent man."

"Everyone saw him shoot the Pope, Michael. Daniel's guilty. That case was closed a year ago. I want to leave it behind me."

"But can you?" Michael's eyes held me tightly, and my breathing became shallow.

My smile froze, and the room seemed suddenly smaller. Michael's eyes, with their molten passion, felt only inches away. I took in a deep breath to steady myself. I closed my eyes, not letting Michael's gaze drag me deeper into something I didn't want to do. "I'm not the hero you're looking for. I can't fight anymore. I'm spent."

Michael's hand gripped the doorknob. He looked out into the hallway. "Just consider my offer, would you?"

"I'm not taking your case, not for any price." It was a lie, but it was what a smart woman would say. After all, I knew nothing about Michael. This whole offer to reconnect me to the LINK could be some elaborate sting to try to entrap me into doing something really stupid. I looked up into Michael's eyes, which still watched me from the door. I wanted to trust those calm, gray eyes, but I shook my head.

When he turned to leave, I knew my false bravado

didn't really matter. For all intents and purposes, I was already on the case. I had to find out more about Michael and why he wanted the LINK-angels discredited. I had to know what he knew about Daniel. I'd take this job; I had to.

Excerpt from the *NY Times*, April 2075

COP KILLS POPE

Daniel Fitzpatrick, 33, of the New York Police Department was arrested today in connection with the shooting of Pope Innocent the XIV.

Ironically, Detective Fitzpatrick had volunteered to serve as crowd protection along the Pope's parade route. Witnesses on the scene reported that when the Pope's parade came through the pedestrian tunnel on the 50th level Broadway, Fitzpatrick moved in closely to calmly address one of the Swiss Guard, then pulled out his service pistol and shot the Pope dead. Fitzpatrick was wrestled to the ground immediately and taken into custody. [hot-link here for video and/or virtual reality replay]

The Swiss Guard who was approached by Fitzpatrick said, "I feel completely responsible, but I was fooled by the uniform. The police are supposed to be the good guys, right?" When asked what Fitzpatrick had said to the Guard, he replied, "Nothing, really. He was pointing out Muslim troublemakers in the crowd. We took him seriously, but I guess it was meant as a distraction."

However, police confirmed that Muslim extremists were spotted in the crowd. According to sources on the scene, the police had, indeed, requested via LINK that Fitzpatrick verbally inform the Swiss Guard of the possible danger, since, due to tradition, the Guard is not LINKed.

Police are suggesting that perhaps Fitzpatrick took advantage of a sudden possibility to get close to the

Pope, and that the murder, in fact, was not premeditated.

Yet, according to inside sources, Fitzpatrick had been acting strangely before today's events. "If you ask me," said an undisclosed source, "It was only a matter of time. He was a Protestant, you know. He was always going on about what would happen if the President made an alliance with Christendom." Though characterized by many as easygoing, inside sources said Fitzpatrick had been having angry outbursts. One report said, though no formal charges were made, Fitzpatrick might have attempted sexual assault on his partner mere days before shooting the Pope.

Rabbi-Mayor Klien demanded to know why the police officers assigned to the Pope's parade route had not been tested psychologically. To this accusation, Captain Allaire Morgan of the 10th precinct had no comment. The FBI has been called in to investigate this incident.

CHAPTER 2

The slam of the door echoed in my mind like the clang of bars closing a prison cell. I picked up the hard copy of the article from underneath the coffee cup and smoothed out the edges. The accompanying item about my excommunication showed a picture of me in a small box in the corner. I shook my head sadly. That was probably my least ladylike moment. The photo was a scan of the moment they announced the Pope's murder, and my hair was a mess despite the short cut I wear, blond hair twisted this way and that like a rat's nest. I hated that picture; I looked like a crazy woman. Somehow the photo had made the most of my least attractive features. My pug nose seemed even wider, and my lips were far too thin and pale.

I carefully folded up the article and wedged it under the desk blotter. My fingers grazed the letters Daniel had sent me from prison. Like so much in my office, I should have thrown them out months ago, but I just couldn't bring myself to do it. I felt guilty, I suppose, because I'd never opened them. I reached for them now, thinking I should finally read them. The envelopes were thin. The paper in my hands felt smooth. The computer-printed number with the address New Jersey State Penitentiary sent a chill down my spine. Danny always used to joke about hating New Jersey. I thought it was the final cruel twist of fate that he'd been sent there of all places.

It was no wonder I'd looked like hell in the photo. I

hadn't put in much sleep that week. Before the whole mess with the Pope, Danny and I were working on a hack-job case—a big one. We were spending later and later nights together hunched over code. I must have given him the wrong signals. It's not hard to see how it could have happened. He'd been changing so much since we started that case, growing darker, harder to reach. He'd had all sorts of strange outbursts—an anger that seemed to come from nowhere, and always right after a phone call or message. I figured that Danny, like most married cops, had troubles at home. We spent more and more time together, and I guess I must have crossed some line.

I found myself rubbing my hairline again. I pulled my hand away forcibly and stood up to walk over to the window. Outside, bathed in a ghostly green light, I saw Michael talking to the soapbox preacher. I shouldered the window open a crack as quietly as the old building would let me. Neither of them looked up.

"Stay away from that Jezebel." The preacher waved his arms in the direction of my window. Great, I grimaced, no wonder business dropped off so sharply. "Jezebel" was hardly the image I wanted to impart to my clients.

"She is unclean," the preacher continued to rave, ". . . unholy."

Michael's body stiffened, as if the insult were directed at himself and not me.

"No one is beyond redemption. That's the gift you give her. If it wasn't for the solace that brings, I'd . . ." His fists clenched at his sides and, for a moment, I thought he was going to punch the preacher right in the mouth. Then, with a snort, Michael turned away. Over his shoulder he added, "Try being the Christian you profess to be, and remember the phrase: 'Let him who is without sin . . . cast the first stone.' "

The preacher and I watched in stunned silence as Michael stomped down the alley toward the street. These days everyone used the Bible as a weapon, but usually to bludgeon, not to cut to the heart of the matter. Michael

impressed me. Either New York's Finest had raised their
admission standards, or this guy wasn't from around
here. That's when I decided to follow him.

Grabbing my keys from the hook by the door, I
dashed down the back stairwell. The preacher's eyes
were still watching Michael moving down the street, so
he didn't notice me slip across the street to the parking ramp.

My old beater was the only car at this level in the lot.
The lights in the parking ramp flickered meekly, reminding me that I needed to pay my electric bill in order
to keep the tube connection active. The car had a battery
for short-distance driving off the rail, of course, but gravity would be against me if I needed to go up a level to
get juice.

Since all cars were electric, all the major metropolitan
areas were covered in a gerbil cage–like maze of tubing.
Traffic Control, a huge hub of computers and sensors,
made sure that none of the millions of cars in the tubes
went barreling into each other. Control managed our
speeds and otherwise oversaw the difficult task of keeping up with city traffic. Needless to say, things did not
always run as smoothly as planned. Especially here in
New York.

I jumped in the car and, on battery power, maneuvered the car over to the tube-rail. With a spark, rail
connected to the car, and I lurched forward with sudden
power. The traffic tubes on this level were recycled plastic, and murky, but I was able to see Michael moving
on the street below me.

This far down, the shadows of the city were long, and
the light was hazy and greenish, as it was filtered through
more and more of the knotwork of traffic tubes and
skyways above. To my left, I could see three thin stabs
of pure light that had not been diluted by tubing. But,
mostly my world was cast in a perpetual greenish haze.

The car shook as I moved along. The tubing of lower
levels badly needed repair. The landfill-mined plastic had
worn thin in places, and I sped up, hoping to have
enough momentum to save me should one collapse

under the weight of my Chevy. At this level, there was no other traffic. The electric engine hummed quietly.

It was not difficult to follow the dark dot that was Michael's lone form on the cracked and ancient sidewalks below. Walking the streets of New York in the era of skyports and skyways was virtually unheard of and certainly not something for the faint of heart. If I learned anything about him, it was that Michael was braver than the average New York City cop. Not even a badge protected people on the streets these days. My grandfather remembered "beat cops," but these days that was an imperative sentence, not a noun.

Still watching Michael's leather jacket grow smaller as he marched into the distance, I punched the numbers for the Tenth Precinct into my mobile wristwatch-phone. "Yeah," I told the dispatcher that answered. "Get me Captain Morgan."

The image in the digital time readout window flickered, then morphed into a detailed three-dimensional image of an empty desk. Hard-copy files, photos, and data chips were spattered across the surface in seeming abandon. "All that's missing are the donuts, Chief."

"I thought that was the phone." I heard shuffling and continued muffled curses. He walked into view, and I saw the back of his head. Gray had completely overtaken the raven hair that impressed me so much as a rookie. Though, I was glad to see, he still seemed to have a full head of it. Taking in the rest of his trim form, it seemed he was still keeping in shape. A sweat-darkened leather strap of a shoulder holster contrasted with the starched white of his shirt. Even though his job confined him mostly to the desk and the rabbi-mayor's office, he wore jeans. Still as irreverent as ever. I smiled, but he didn't see me. He was still searching for the phone.

"Who even uses a phone?" He continued to dig under stacks of paper. When his search sent a row of data chips tumbling to the floor, I couldn't contain myself any longer.

"Behind you, Al, on your desk. The flat black box."

"Right." Finding it, he squinted into the monitor. "Listen, I'm going to have reception patch this onto the LINK . . ." Then, he recognized me. "Of course. You. Never mind, this is going to be short. What do you want, McMannus? I thought we had a deal. You stay out of police business."

"It's one of your boys that's come to me." I kept part of my attention focused on Michael as he trudged down the street. I'd slowed to almost a crawl to follow him and would probably end up with a ticket for going under the required speed limit. I glanced at my wristwatchphone. "Michael Angelucci. You know him, Al?"

"Know him? For Christ's sake, get your claws out of him; Mike's one of our star players."

"Yeah, I can see why." I spit out a bitter laugh. "He's got a heart."

My insult didn't even faze Al. He just narrowed his green eyes even further and glared at me suspiciously. "What's he coming to you for?"

"That's personal." I quickly turned down a connecting tube, as Michael rounded the corner in front of me.

Al drew his lips into a tight line and studied my face. "If he's bringing a case to you, I'll have his hide."

"He's not. I just wanted to make sure the guy was legit. He seemed awfully friendly to be one of yours."

Al barked out a gruff laugh. "Give him some time, McMannus. He's only been in the big city about a month. Transferred from Pennsylvania. Amish country. They're pretty cut off out there. No LINK."

I thought about my dingy office, and sneered. "It's a refreshing way to live. You ought to try it."

"I had so much hope for you, Dee. You were the best." His voice dropped to almost a whisper. When I looked down, his stony expression had cracked slightly. When he saw me looking at him, he pointed at me. "You were smart enough to know better than to cross certain lines. You don't fuck with loyalty and expect to stay in the force."

I shook my head. "Loyalty? That's what it was about

for you? Listen to yourself, Al. I notice you didn't mention justice."

"This is the real world, kid. You were too damned idealistic to survive on the force. Grow up, why don't you?" The finger that had been pointing at me now jabbed at the box. The time display scrolled across the screen, followed by caller ID, and then, finally, the fax light flashed. His frown deepened. Suddenly, his hand got really large and distorted, then the screen went dark. For a second, I thought he actually managed to find the off switch, until I heard him dejectedly mutter, "Aw, hell."

I realized he'd just flipped the phone over, so that the fiber-optic camera faced his desk. The line was still open, and I used the opportunity to foil his parting shot. "You were like a father to me, Al. A little loyalty from you might've been nice."

New York Times excerpt from 2075.

PARTNER EXCOMMUNICATED:
Pope likens McMannus to Jezebel

The Vatican issued a surprise announcement today excommunicating Catholic Deidre McMannus, former partner of Pope-killer Daniel Fitzpatrick. The brief statement from the newly elected Pope Elijah I said, "Statements made by McMannus at Christendom court have shown her to be a nonbeliever and a temptress of men." The statement included virtual replay of McMannus's admittance that she invited Fitzpatrick back to her place despite the fact that she knew him to be a married man, and her sworn testimony that she agreed with Fitzpatrick's controversial assessment of the invalidity of the LINK-angels.

Though absolved of any connection to the murder of the Pope, McMannus has been under heavy scrutiny in Christendom and beyond for her extraneous interviews and commentary. Vactian spokesperson Cardinal

Jacob Creed said, "I really doubt there's anything that woman believes in."

The *Times* caught up with McMannus at her apartment moments after the announcement was made. "Those bastards!" McMannus said. "Don't they know what this will do to me? How am I supposed to maintain religious accreditation?" [LINK here for virtual replay]

Religious scholar Dr. Jesus Martinez of the American Catholic university, Georgetown, was equally surprised at the Vatican's decision. "This is really not precedented," he said in a LINKed interview. "The Vatican rarely issues excommunication orders. As far as I can see, Deidre McMannus has done nothing that would normally call for excommunication."

LINK opinion polls, however, seem to think that the justice meted out by the Vatican is perfectly appropriate. "Let her rot, I say," harry11435@LINK.com posted today on the hot-LINK discussion group devoted to following the Pope murder trial. "She's a complete bitch."

On the same discussion group, Wiccan High Priestess Sapphire Whitewater publicly offered McMannus an invitation to convert. "McMannus is precisely the kind of woman my coven is looking for. Strong, self-reliant, and daring. Some might call those the qualities of a bitch, but I say they are the qualities of a witch."

McMannus has not yet replied to Whitewater's offer.

CHAPTER 3

The loyalty bit from Al really stung. Daniel shot the Pope in broad daylight in front of a thousand spectators. There was very little anyone could say in his defense. The prosecution was less concerned about the events of the shooting, since they were caught on 3-D cam and hardly arguable, but whether or not Daniel had premeditated the murder.

I was the character witness that backfired. My testimony proved that Daniel had been acting strangely, more secretive, before the murder, and though I'd made a case that I thought it had to do with problems at home, the prosecution could care less. For them, his odd behavior was enough.

Most damning of all was the fact that Daniel had hit on me, sexually speaking, the night before. His advances weren't entirely unwanted, but certainly out of character, not to mention a bit rough, for Daniel.

When the defense tried for insanity, I trumped them there as well. I pointed out that Daniel had been cognizant of right and wrong the night before—he'd stopped when I said "no" loud enough.

I shook my head. It was true that I was a liability to Daniel's case, but I didn't deserve to be branded disloyal to the force. All I had done was tell the truth. Then, when the Pope excommunicated me, he suggested that, by being attractive to Daniel, I was the seductress and somehow an instigator in the whole mess. The media immediately started calling me Jezebel. That was all the excuse the department needed to gather my walking papers. My infamy was a media nightmare for the force. Even now, a year later, my face never left the newscasts for long. In this era of religiously dominated politics, I'd inspired a strange, if loyal, fan base.

The tubes diverged as traffic detoured around the construction of a ten-story Jesus that would house the main offices of the Lamb of God church. Under the scaffolding, I could see the outline of Christ's features. It struck me how sad his eyes looked, staring out at the tangled skyline of New York. In his hands, a neon sign proudly proclaimed forty thousand served.

"McChrist," I muttered, pointing my car toward the down-ramp. I lost Michael for a second as he entered the service tunnel to the skyway. I quickly turned onto an up-ramp, and began to follow the tube circling the building. With my luck, Michael would hop an express to the hundred and fifty-first level; it would take me months to get up that far. Then, out of the driver's side window of my battered Chevy, I spotted him clearly. He stepped into the walkway and was making his way to Margie's, the local lunch counter favored by cops on this level.

I continued the circle around until I came to a car park across from Margie's. I waved my credit counter in front of the automated lot attendant. As much as that would hurt my pocketbook, I was glad to be on solid ground again. The shaky tubing had made my nerves raw.

When I reached a good spot inside the lot, I pulled out my binoculars. A couple of guys greeted Michael when he came in, but he sat alone at a table by the window. The waitress certainly gave Michael the once-over. I couldn't blame the girl. She didn't seem to treat him like a regular, however. Then, again, it could be her shy flirtation was just part of their weekly routine.

My stomach growled. I reached across the dashboard, and unwrapped a fat-free cupcake. As I bit into it, I tried to pretend it was the food being delivered to Michael's table. After two disgusting bites of the cupcake,

I had to give up. I tossed the sorry excuse for a pastry into the backseat, wrapping and all. Frustrated and wholly unsatisfied, I glared at Michael.

I rubbed the dust on the window with my sleeve, squinting at Michael through the smeared glass. I sat up sharply. Someone approached his table. Michael gestured at the empty seat. This guy didn't look much like a cop, although he was certainly wide and tall enough. I might've guessed him to be a soldier, but his coppery red hair was shoulder-length and unruly. Despite the warm weather, he wore a long brown trench coat, the kind under which a person could conceal almost any type of weapon. Beneath the coat, a smooth silk shirt peeked out. The whole ensemble would've made the Klein Fashion Empire green with envy. It was quite trendy-looking, although a bit upscale for a cop's friend.

It was times like this when I seriously missed the LINK. I might have been able to snag the stranger's retina, even at this distance. Then, I'd have a solid lead. Looking around the deserted car park, I sighed. This gig sucked. My stomach growled again and reminded me that there was, at least, decent food inside at Margie's.

"Screw subtlety," I muttered to myself, and reached for the door handle. "If he asks, I'll tell him I followed him."

Elbowing through the crowded walkway, I made my way to Margie's pink neon sign. With a grunt, I pushed the glass door open. The smell of potatoes and onions deep-frying in black-market animal fat filled the air. I love greasy spoons. It'd been over a year since I wandered into this particular joint, however. A few eyes checked me out. Over in the corner, Sergeant Dorshak gave me a hard glare, like I had no business in here.

I lifted my hand as if to tip a hat to him. Dorshak dodged my greeting by suddenly noticing the cooling food on his plate. With an unkind little laugh, I muttered, "Coward." In Dorshak's honor, however, I might order that oh-so-interesting blue-plate special myself while I interrogated Michael and his friend. After all, there was nothing like mixing a little pleasure with business.

"Hey, Mike." I clapped a hand on his broad shoulder. Sliding into the empty spot next to him in the booth before he could protest, I asked, "Who's your friend here?"

"Deidre." Michael looked surprised, but without missing a beat, he gestured across the table to the redhead. "This is . . . ah, Morningstar. . . ." Michael struggled for an appropriate description. "He's 'an old friend.' "

"How literary, 'Mike.' But, I believe you mean 'Arnold Friend.' " Morningstar chuckled.

Morningstar? I thought, with a surprised raise of my eyebrow. Going by the name of a fallen angel was a new twist on the whole naming phenomenon—very risqué. What kind of guy was this friend of Michael's, I wondered.

"Charmed, I'm sure," Morningstar nodded only briefly in my direction, his attention focused on Michael. "Love to stay and chat with your little friend here, but I was on my way out. Oh, and Captain? When you see the big guy next, tell it him he's got no business messing in my territory. Got it?"

Morningstar smoothed down the left side of his silk shirt with his right hand. It was the kind of gesture I'd seen gangsters use to imply they had the firepower to back up their threats. Even though it wasn't my fight, I casually slid my hand into the pocket of my suit coat and wrapped my hand around the butt of my Magnum. I edged away from Michael slowly.

Tension hung in the air, but Michael was cool. He smiled slightly, as if amused by Morningstar's display of bravado. In an even voice, Michael said, "This is hardly your territory."

The gangster sneered. Though he'd said he was leaving, he leaned back in his seat, considering it. "Yeah, yeah. Whatever." Morningstar sounded unconvinced. "It's not like the family's done much for the neighborhood lately, you know what I'm saying? If They won't do anything, it's up to me to take care of things, isn't it? I think of it as a kind of natural inheritance, kind of a survival of the fittest."

"What are you talking about? Fittest? You know which one of us is the favored son." Michael laughed unkindly. Something about his manner made it sound as though the implication was that Michael expected this "inheritance," whatever that was.

I looked at Morningstar with renewed interest. There was a bit of family resemblance in the face when I looked for it. Morningstar's features were thinner, but he and Michael shared a similar intensity. It was like they were cut from cloths of different colors, but of the same tone.

"Hmph." Something tugged at the muscles in Morningstar's jaw, as if trying to break through his facade of confidence. "Don't you forget that I'm older than you. I was first once."

"Not anymore," Michael said smugly.

"Look at you," Morningstar said. "Such arrogance."

"You would know all about that, wouldn't you?" Michael said.

The gangster laughed. "You're so fucking black-and-white all the time, brother. You have no idea what really motivates me, do you?"

"Of course I do, it's written all over your face," Michael said.

"Oh, and what's that, wise guy?" Morningstar asked. Pretending disinterest, he played with the saltshaker.

Love, I thought as I watched Morningstar.

"Jealousy," Michael said. "You want what I have. You always did."

Morningstar laughed, but it was a constricted sound. "Hardly. Look at you, you're a spoiled brat. You wouldn't last a moment without the family."

"I don't have to."

A sound, like the growl of a wildcat, emanated from Morningstar's throat. With no other warning, he lifted his edge of the table. The table separated from the floor with a loud rending sound, and the bulk of it bore down on me. I tumbled onto the floor as the plates slid off the plastic tablecloth and shattered.

Michael came down over the top of the still-moving table. I squinted, as my eyes registered only a blur of motion. An enormous blast of air pushed against me. The sound of a strong wind through trees filled my ears, followed by a deafening crash. My hair blew in front of my face and the plate shards on the floor rattled around. When I could see again, Michael had Morningstar by the scruff of his collar. The table was pushed against the seats Michael and I had been occupying. Wood splinters were spattered all over the floor.

Every head in the place swung around to see what was going on. Sliding the Magnum back into its hiding place, I picked myself off the floor and dusted off my regulation-length skirt. The gesture was purely for show since mustard dripped into my shoes. I picked my way around the splintered table and tried not to notice that it had once been bolted to the floor, though I could clearly see the holes in the floorboards.

"Take it outside, guys. Move it," I ordered in my best ex-cop voice. I sounded tough, but the truth was, their sudden violence scared me.

"No," Michael said in a commanding voice, still holding Morningstar's collar. "This ends here."

Morningstar loosened himself from Michael's grip with some effort. "Oh yeah, tough guy. You think you can take me on alone?"

"I will and I can," Michael insisted.

"But is it what the family wants?" Morningstar said, and Michael's resolve seemed to waiver. After making a grand production of shaking out his expensive suit, he squared his shoulders. "It makes you nervous doesn't it? Not knowing the plan. Let me give you a clue—you'll never know what They have in store for you until it's over. You're their puppet—body and soul . . . but wait, that's not right, is it? 'Body and soul'?"

With a quick glance around the room, I caught at least three cops with that faraway look that meant they were on the LINK. No doubt, they'd transmitted all the gory details to precinct headquarters by now. I was curious about this family squabble, but not enough to get arrested over it. I whispered to Michael, "I've got to get out of here, a squad's probably on its way."

"I'll come with you." Without removing his eyes from Morningstar, he added. "This is not the place or time for this kind of discussion, Morningstar."

"What, no reaction?" Morningstar smiled coldly. "It doesn't bother you? The difference between us and them?"

Suddenly, the red flash of my retina being scanned by three or more lasers blinded me. "Like any of you don't know who I am," I said, rubbing at my eye. "Come on, Mike, let's get a move on!"

Michael's eyes stayed locked on the gangster. Despite my insistence, he didn't budge. "They made their choice," Michael said grimly.

"Now that you're here in the Big Apple, what are you going to do? Maybe you've already bitten off more than you can chew."

Michael's eyes grew wide, and then he shook his head. "Lies."

I tugged his sleeve. "If you're coming, let's go. . . ."

Morningstar raised an eyebrow and gave a little laugh. "That's your best? 'Liar.' Whoa, big insult. I'm hurting. Hey, look, I don't care what you do. Just stay away from me, *capisne*?"

"Deus volent." Michael looked like he wanted to say more, so I tugged him on the arm. With that, he let me lead him toward the door.

"My car's this way. . . ." I pulled him in the direction of the car park. As the walkway's hustle and bustle surrounded us, I felt my shoulders relax. In a second we were at the car. "Get in."

The instant he closed the door, I started up the car. The engine sprang to life and I maneuvered us out of the car park and headed for the tollway. I glanced over at where Michael sat sullenly in his seat. He plucked at the peeling duct tape that held the glove compartment shut. Noticing my look, he said, "You followed me."

Just then, some Gorgon on a scooter cut across the traffic tube levels without so much as a "coming through" from Traffic Control, which was supposed to monitor all vehicles in the tubes. I leaned on the horn, and shouted after the punk.

"Stay in your own lanes!" I shook my head, and muttered, "Those Gorgons are going to give me gray hair of my own. What was he doing here anyway? It's not like there aren't traffic tubes expressly for bikes and boards."

"Hmmmm," Michael muttered, uninterested in my patter. His gaze tracked the scooter as it dodged around cars in the lower tube. "I know you followed me."

Before I could put on my "What, who, me?" face, he held up a hand.

"Don't bother making up an excuse," he said. "This thing is a relic, and anyway, you were the only car on the lower level."

I smiled, but wondered how he knew the Chevy was mine. Suddenly, I remembered: if he was a cop, then he had the LINK. "Yeah, I ought to get something built in this decade, I know. But, hey," I joked, "in another year this baby qualifies as a classic."

"Technically, sure." Returning my humor, he ran his hand along the scarred dash. "I doubt anyone'd mistake this for cherry."

The car in question hummed into the third level. I remembered gas-guzzlers from before the war. I'd been young, far too young to drive, but I had a strange nostalgia for them. Despite what it did to the classic status, I had it converted to electric years ago. It had cost me a month's salary to get a battery big enough to haul the Chevy's frame for more than a couple of kilometers, and to fit it to draw energy from the tunnel currents. I could've bought a newfangled, lightweight car for the same price, but I was a purist. I wanted a car to look like a car instead of the ugly, modern, supposedly aerodynamic things that passed for vehicles these days.

Following the entrance tube, we joined the line of cars that crowded on the seventh level. With one foot on the brake, I settled into the strangely comforting stop-start motions of a traffic jam.

"So . . ." Michael's voice was hopeful. "Does this mean you're considering the barter?"

"I'd like more information first."

"Of course," he said. "What can I tell you?"

"Interesting guy this Morningstar," I told him. "What's his story? He's your brother?"

Michael raised his eyebrows, then smiled. "I suppose you could call him that. We share a father, that much is true."

"I gathered." I watched the traffic with disinterest. The bumper sticker in front of me proclaimed its owner as a voter for Grey, Letourneau's opponent, in the upcoming elections. I glanced over at Michael, "So you and Morningstar don't get along, eh?"

He gave a disgusted snort. "Forget about him, will you?"

"Forget him?" I oozed sarcasm. "Big guy, you've got to be joking. You can't tell me he's not part of your problem."

"He's not." Michael sighed. "At least not right now."

"No?" I tapped on the horn. My noise started a cascade of beeps and blares from fellow frustrated motorists. I gave Michael's profile a cynical smile. "Okay, if you say so."

He shrugged, as he continued to stare out the window.

"So, your family is Italian? Your half brother is in the business?" I tried to gauge how he reacted to my innuendo about Morningstar's Mafia connection.

"Italian?" He shrugged. "I'd prefer Roman."

I glanced at him to check if he was being serious. "Okay," I murmured, not sure how else to respond. "Roman it is. So, what was it you said to him?"

"I see what you're thinking." He shifted his massive frame, so he could look me right in the eye. "Look, it's nothing like that. You have to believe me; Morningstar has nothing to do with you and me. He's right. This time things aren't so black-and-white, I'm afraid. We have to think beyond the dualism of me versus him."

"What does that mean?" I said in Michael's direction, my eyes on the bumper in front of me.

"Eternal consequences, but mortal players." He said as if that explained everything.

"Right. Fine." Traffic stopped completely. The tubes felt claustrophobic at moments like this. "What is the problem here?" I yelled out the window, though no one could hear me behind their Plexiglas shields.

Michael stared out the window at the business-district sprawl. Tubes covered the skyline like a chaotic ball of yarn. I could see lights blinking all around us, where several panels of the traffic tubes had been replaced with holographic advertising. Inching forward, we passed through the logo of cola being joyfully consumed by a drop-dead gorgeous Indian woman in a sari. The image stood partially over the stick shift. Michael's eyes were wide in wonderment, as though he'd never seen anything so fascinating. The advertisement faded as we moved forward another foot.

"You're not from around here," I said.

"Amish country," he murmured, looking out the rear of the car at the cola ad.

"Yet you're enhanced?" I asked, surprised.

"I'm sorry?" He gave me another one of his big, dumb-guy looks and a shrug.

"Cyberware," I supplied, with an arched eyebrow. What cop didn't know "enhanced"? Christ, half the guys on the force were ex-military, and those that weren't got special modifications under the table, or, at the very least, wore exoskeletons. With all the rogue wireheads out there, a cop couldn't be too careful. He still stared quizzically, so I added. "Your little dance around the table. The fight nearly broke the sound barrier. Impressive."

"Right," he said, as if reminding himself. "I wonder if that was a mistake."

I waved my hand to dismiss the idea. Then, I smoothly turned my momentum into a rude gesture as the woman in front of me hit the brakes for no apparent reason. I laid on the horn and repeated the gesture. I had to raise my voice to be heard over the responding traffic noise. "Don't worry about it. Almost everyone has some enhancement these days. It's not the sore thumb it used to be right after the war. So, what branch were you in?"

"Huh?"

Cute, I thought sadly, *but not very on the ball.* "You and Morningstar served in something together, I'm figuring the last big one . . . although you don't really look old enough. Anyway, he called you Captain. You're a lieutenant in the force, so you must've been a captain somewhere else. So, which branch of the military?"

"Army." He smoothed down the material in his jeans. It was the first time since he walked into my office this morning that he had answered my question directly. Fifteen years on the force taught me a lot about human nature, and it disturbed me that Michael chose this moment not to meet my eyes. Besides, Morningstar's references to "your boss" made me wonder if the title "captain" wasn't actually meant to imply *capo.* Still, for the moment, I let this lie ride.

"Yeah?" I continued to make polite conversation. "Did you see any action?"

He glanced up at me and gave me a weary smile. "Yeah. I suppose I did."

"Really?" I did some mental calculations, and gave him an appraising look. "I suppose you could have been a young man, say twenty or so, that would only make you in your forties."

He shook his head as if to tell me I'd asked him enough personal questions. The traffic was ridiculous, and I decided to get us out of this mess. I spotted a down exit moving at a quicker rate. In a second, I had us down on the sixth level and moving swiftly.

"I want you to reconsider taking the case," he said.

I nodded. "All right. Talk to me."

"Somebody's been using my name on the LINK to prop up Letourneau."

"Your name?" I asked. "What does Letourneau need with a cop's name?"

" 'A cop'?" Michael frowned, then, he said, "Oh, right. Me. No, not literally, more like figuratively."

"Someone's using your name, your LINK access, figuratively? How does that work?" I watched his face intently. I couldn't believe that a second ago he didn't realize I was talking about him when I said "a cop's name." Captain Morgan had confirmed that Michael was with the force, so what was up with this guy?

"Let me start again," Michael said.

"I think you'd better."

I decided that I needed to give Michael my full attention. I noticed a mostly empty parking lot and swung around to enter. I keyed off the engine and turned in my seat to look at Michael. He was frowning at the duct tape, as if trying to choose his words.

"It's not really my name I'm concerned about," he said finally. "It's more like my reputation and the reputation of some people very close to me."

"How is your rep tied to Letourneau?"

"To the LINK-angels." He corrected.

I studied his face. His lips were pursed and his expression serious. Glancing out across the car park, I could see a billboard with a beatifically smiling presidential candidate Letourneau. His arms were open and welcoming like the forty-foot Jesus. Behind him, in the 3-D space, hovered an image of a LINK-angel. The virtual artist had done a good job mimicking the experience of the angels. The apparition drifted in and out of view, like a dream: one time over Letourneau's right shoulder, the next second over his left. I shivered, then I shook off the feeling.

"I still don't see the connection," I said. "What do the LINK-angels have to do with your reputation?"

"Poseurs," he spit.

I laughed and shook my head. I pointed my finger at him in mock accusation. "Blasphemer."

"Heretic is more accurate, thank you very much." Michael's lips tightened like he was holding back something, and his face went scarlet all the way to the ear tips.

"That's a pretty fine line of a distinction."

"Not to me, and not to the law." He pointedly avoided my gaze and plucked at the duct tape. "Anyway, I don't buy the presumption that the LINK-angels have anything to do with God, nor are they inviolable. If I believed that, I wouldn't be asking for you to hack them."

"That's what I still don't get. Why bust the angels? Most skeptics have been convinced by them, even men of science. That the angels are genuine seems to be the only thing religious and secular leaders agree on. The LINK-angels' appearance was a worldwide miracle. . . ."

"I know all this," he growled. "That's why I need your help. You're the only one, Deidre. You know the truth."

"What truth?"

"I think you know." Michael's eyes were filled with an intensity that made me look away. I shook my head.

"I don't want to get involved," I said. "Besides, the truth doesn't count for jack, my friend; power and influence do. If I had either, do you think Daniel would be locked up right now? Do you think I'd be kicked off the force? Excommunicated?" I laid my hand out flat in the air between us. "No."

"Yet you can't let it go on the way it is, can you? You keep trying to print your letters to the editor, even though you know excommunication automatically bars you."

"I . . . I . . ." I didn't have an answer. "That's different."

"No, it's not. It's politics, just like this faux Second Coming, and it must be stopped."

"Now you sound like the Hasidic fanatics. They want my endorsement as a notorious LINK celebrity, too, you know."

"I'm not looking for votes."

"What are you looking for, Michael? You want the LINK-angels brought down, but why? What are they to you, really? What do you get out of it? All the LINK-angels have ever given anyone is a sense of peace. Why destroy that?"

Michael laughed. "As if that's all they do." He pointed his chin in the direction of Letourneau's smiling hologram. "You know as well as I that they're propagating the whole Second Coming myth."

"I know, I know. But what does it matter to you? Or is it who you represent, Michael? Who is this boss of yours? Is it in your father's interests that you've approached me?"

"No. I came to you on my own." He took in a long, steadying breath. "It matters to me because . . . it matters to me."

"That's not good enough."

Michael's gray eyes flashed up at me. "You don't need to know my reasons to do this job. Are you telling me you don't want the barter?"

"It's not worth the risk if I can't trust you. Why not go to the Hasidim or someone else?"

Michael shifted slightly on the vinyl seats. Creaking was the only sound for a few moments as he started to speak, but then stopped. Finally, he said, "I'll be honest with you, you weren't my first pick. I did go to the Hasidim first."

He glanced at me to gauge my reaction.

"The Malachim?" The Hasidic terrorists went by the code name Malachim Nikamah, the Angels of Vengeance.

He nodded. I raised my eyebrows, but held my tongue. It made sense. The Malachim were renowned hackers and the LINK was what they terrorized. They shared Michael's distaste for Letourneau's bid for messiah, and disbelief in the divinity of the LINK-angels.

"Things didn't work out with them," he said.

"And you think they will with me?"

Michael nodded.

"I don't know about this," I started. "People with past terrorist connections representing hidden interests don't exactly inspire trust, you know . . . it's not really my kind of thing; maybe you need the CIA or something."

"Do you trust your government, Deidre?" He gave me a knowing look out of the corner of his eye. "These are the same people who issued a life sentence for an innocent man."

"Daniel was hardly innocent, Michael. There is no doubt in my mind that he killed the Pope." I dropped my eyes and tried to keep my emotions in check. "It was a crazy thing that happened to Daniel, but sometimes people just snap."

"Is that what you really believe?"

"That's what I have to believe. The evidence is empirical."

"Maybe," Michael said quietly. "Maybe not."

"What do you know?" I demanded. "Is there something about Daniel's case that's changed?"

"The LINK-hack case you were working on has never been solved. No one has even touched it."

I hadn't thought about that case in over a year. With everything that had happened with the Pope, I'd forgotten about it. The details came back to me in a rush: "But, it was a smash-and-grab of bioware tech—hot stuff. The company, was it Jordan Institute? They hounded us every day to crack that case."

"Exactly my point," Michael said, turning to face me in the cramped car space. "Somebody's hiding something about Daniel's case."

"And, so, what are you saying? Do you think our old case is related to Letourneau and the LINK-angels somehow? That's kind of a strange leap in logic," I said.

"All I'm saying is that I just don't think you should count this case as closed just yet, Deidre."

Over Michael's shoulder, the billboard image of Letourneau caught my eye again, and I watched the angel drift around the board like a ghost. "I'd rather let the dead stay buried. I'm out of the force, and whatever stones they leave unturned are no longer my business."

Michael shook his head. "You might feel at the end, but there is still a lot to lose, Deidre. What if I told you I had proof that the Second Coming was a fraud?"

My eyes sought his. He met my gaze steadily. Could he be telling the truth? Excited, but cautious, I said, "I'd wonder why you hadn't gone to the media."

"The media haven't exactly been open to opponents of Letourneau."

"I see what you mean," I said, remembering the *Times*. "What do you plan to do then? And what's my part?"

"You have connections that I don't. I need to break into the LINK to expose the angels' fallacy."

"You'd have better luck hiring some crackerjack surfer, like the Mouse, or getting one of your pals in the Malachim to freelance. I'm not even LINKed anymore."

"If you'd take the job, I'd make the connection. You're a crack surfer in your own right."

My head itched. I ran my hands along the rough plastic of the steering wheel to keep from fondling the implant. He gave me a tight smile; I dismissed his sideways compliment by looking out the window. "It's not possible."

"The hardware is still there, Deidre," he said softly. "They couldn't take that away from you."

"Hmmmmm." I couldn't trust myself to speak. I had a white-knuckle grip on the wheel.

"My offer still stands. I can arrange to have your access reestablished."

His words hung in the air. I was acutely aware of the emptiness of my head and the silence in the car. There was no sound but my harsh, shallow breathing. The dead receiver near my temple felt heavy and cold. The itch had become a dull throb.

"Yeah?" I managed to scratch out of my dry throat. There was no lady in my voice, only junkie.

"Yeah." He sounded confident, and I so desperately wanted to believe in his ability to get me what I needed. "What I want to know is—will you help me?"

"You get me the connection," I told his reflection in the window, "and I'll do anything."

New Jersey State Penitentiary
Jan. 7, 2076

Dear Deidre,

Must have started this letter a hundred times. Had to give up on anything but voice-activated text, because I couldn't bear my pick-pecking on the keyboard.

(Not that they'd let me have access to anything with a motherboard. ~~Shit~~, they've sure got me figured wrong.) Anyway, I'm finding it easier to talk. Lessens the urge to re-write, you know?

Still don't know quite what to say. "Wish you were here" would get me a quick visit by the Morality Officer for a little attitude readjustment, and I've already been through that wringer once—thanks to a friendly round of fisticuffs that the wardens mistook for hostility. By the way, Oscar says "hi." You remember him, Dee. His page was called "Weasel." (What is it with rodents and those ~~damned~~ LINK-hackers anyway?) You know I wouldn't mean "the wish you were here" bit in THAT way, don't you? I know things got ugly there at the end, but we were partners for how long? Five years. You know me better than that. I just mean I wish to ~~hell~~ we could talk face-to-face, like the old days. I miss that. I miss you.

There's some things we need to talk about. Important stuff. Before we can get to that, I figure I got to clear some air. I know you were just doing what you thought was right, okay? I forgive you. All you said was that you didn't know what was happening to me and that I'd left early that night. . . . Ah. [PAUSE] Listen, about that night. I'm sorry. I should never have come on to you like that. ~~Shit~~, that's part of it. Part of this whole thing. I'm trying to say that I can see now that you were telling the truth on the witness stand. I'm not even sure I know what happened to me . . . what changed me. It's all seems different here. The whole thing seems clearer. Before . . . those things I said . . . I was angry. That wasn't me talking.

I forgive you, but I realize now there's nothing to forgive. It was your duty to tell the truth and you did it. I'm sure the guys on the force are hassling you over it, but don't let them. What do they know about it?

These ~~assholes~~ and their Moral Office know nothing about the complicated mess that real people have to deal with every day. It's easy for them. They've never faced a tough decision their whole life. You came through it, Dee. You're still on the right side. You just got to hang in there. Got to cut this off, but I'm going to write again. I hope you can find it in your heart to write back.

Daniel

CHAPTER 4

Ghosts. I frowned at the screen. There was no current LINK site listed for the company, Jordan River Health Institute, that had been so insistent that Daniel and I crack their tech-theft case. I keyed in a search of business archives for any listing of a merger, claim for bankruptcy, anything.

The processors started to whir, and I settled back in my chair to wait. I reached into the bottom drawer of my desk and pulled out my battered romance.

Even before I was cut off from the LINK, I had a yen for the luxury of a printed page. The smell of fresh ink on newsprint always sent a shiver down my spine. Though most people got their entertainment from the LINK, there were enough of us sensualists left to keep a few small presses in business. I flipped open the book and held it to my nose. As I breathed in the odor, I consciously tried to relax. I picked up the thread of the story easily, but my mind wandered.

Less than ten minutes ago, Michael took off to make arrangements with a contact. He said if things went well, he'd be back at the office by ten-thirty. Then, we'd go to this tech friend of his to get me rehooked. Just like that. I rubbed my head; the ache was back. My fingers traced the outline of the receiver. The flesh it raised was almond-shaped and about that size. From that hub, microscopic threads spun out deep into my brain. Though it was impossible, I swore I felt the throbbing pain begin to creep deeper, following that internal web.

Laying the book down, I rummaged around in my desk until I found some aspirin. I swallowed them dry, but they went down easily. *More junkie mannerisms,* I thought ruefully. Daniel would be horrified to see me now; there didn't seem to be much difference between me and the wireheads we used to bust.

I thought I'd get used to the emptiness in my head, but I didn't. I think that's part of why I loved this office. With the squeaky chair, the creaking hardwood, rattling windows, clanking of the radiator, and all the other tenants' muffled noises, it was never truly quiet here.

Sometime in the last hour it started raining. I strolled over to the window, my stocking feet sliding across the hardwood. The office was dark except for the clip-on desk lamp that hung precariously over the monitor.

After I'd been disconnected, it had been difficult even to find a desktop version of the computer. I'd had to construct much of it from scraps in the junkyard, rummage sales, and antique shops. I'd say I was lucky that the building my office occupied still had a hardwired data jack, but, the truth was, this place was so old it still had the remnants of the gas fixtures and a coal bin in the basement.

Human beings were funny that way: exceedingly inventive and lazy as hell. Old things remained—built over, built around. Living literally in the shadow and underneath the shiny new skyscrapers in Manhattan, ancient crotchety buildings like my office still stood, mostly unchanged since the nineteenth century.

While some technology raced ahead, like wetware, pockets of low tech survived all over. As a species, we tended not to clean up after ourselves. When we redesigned the LINK, we left vestiges of the old system to haunt the hard lines like cobwebs.

The war machine fueled most of the dramatic changes in tech. Wetware was invented so that we could have soldiers who could receive electronic commands sent from headquarters to the battlefield. The war had started in the Middle East over the shrinking oil resources, so in order to win, America finally implemented the electric-

vehicle plans it had kicking around since the last oil crisis. Of course, once the Medusa bomb got dropped, scientific advancement ground to a halt—except, of course,
in the area of entertainment. If there was a way to make
a holo-vid more virtually realistic, then the tech appeared overnight, only to be replaced by something better the next day.

I shivered and pulled my arms closer around my chest.
Despite the draftiness, there was a certain comfort in
the way the wind howled around the gables of the old
building. Reaching along the wall, my fingers searched
for the thermostat. When I found the ancient contrap-
tion, I lightly touched the wheel in the direction of
warmer. Not that it did much good in this rickety place.
I smiled and shook my head. Moving away from the
window, I felt for the coffeemaker in the dark. I fumbled
along the side of the smooth plastic until my fingers
found the switch and flicked it on. The orange brewing
light glowed. I waited for the telltale gurgling sounds
before I headed back to my desk.

With any luck, the information-retrieval programs
would have turned up something on Jordan Institute by
now. Scootching the chair closer to the monitor, I peered
at the message: "No matches found."

"Nothing?" I muttered out loud. I looked at my romance novel. I might be a sensualist and Neanderthal in
my attitudes toward the printed word, but at least paper-
and-ink information could not be altered. The LINK refreshed its information stream so often that archiving
became unmanageable. There were companies that tried
to save information, but, because of sheer volume, they
were forced to narrow their fields of interest. Most of
yesterday's news vanished into the ether.

I tried to recall details of the case. Blurred faces
floated in from the back acres of my mind. The sysop, I
remembered well: she was a skinny, nervous kid who
was frantic about losing her job. She kept offering Daniel and me coffee because that's what you did when detectives arrived on the scene in all the cops'-n'-robber
holo-vids. I'd liked her immediately. She'd had tight

braids of the deepest ebony tied off with those blinking beads that had been all the rage with the twenty-somethings.

The Jordan Institute's carpet had smelled new. The whole complex was part of one of those business-incubator buildings designed to accommodate rapid growth—or sudden collapse, as I suspected in this case. The product information that had been stolen had something to do with the treatment of mental patients. The sysop had said it was "revolutionary," but every new tech got that label these days.

There was nothing about the tech theft that had struck me as out of the ordinary. "Damn," I muttered. "If only I had access to my case notes."

When I was on a case, my LINK connection recorded all interactions: every interview, every debriefing with my partner, thoughts muttered out loud, everything. I occasionally kept paper notes, but after a case was finished, I shredded them. I had never imagined a time when I couldn't, with a simple thought, access all my stored information. The chips were on file, but, of course, the data for the Jordan Institute case had been seized as evidence in Daniel's trial.

As a cop, Michael had access to them. I could have him get a hard copy of them for me. A knot twitched in my stomach. Michael would be here in a couple of hours. The wail of a distant siren mingled with rolling thunder, and rain continued its steady barrage against the windowpane.

As much as I wanted it, I was crazy to agree to the re-LINK. For the right price, I could buy an external LINK on the black market, but as an ex-cop I had a certain number of strikes against me. First, despite everything, I still walked the walk. No illegal marketeer would come within ten feet of someone who could be a tech-vice cop in disguise. That was the other problem. I already had a reputation among the wireheads, and it wasn't the kind that got me an invitation to tea on a Sunday afternoon, much less a connection to pirated tech.

The biggest deterrent to getting a new connection to the LINK was the equipment itself. As Michael said, the hardware was still there in my head, microscopic threads running through my gray matter like a rabbit's warren. Even if I somehow managed to get the external stuff, the feedback loop alone would permanently crisp a few synapses.

God only knew where on earth Michael would dig up a bioengineer to do the reconnecting work. Sure, there were hack techs everywhere, but no one but a complete wirehead had the faith to go under their dirty scalpels. Even if I was that desperate, which I was, the LINK hardware in my head was restricted code; only a city-licensed biotech had the password. Rumor had it that there were booby-trap viruses ready to burn out the hard-wiring if anyone used the wrong pass code to re-activate.

My only hope was that Michael was part of some underground organization with connections to rogue cop-techs; otherwise, I was fried—literally.

Thunder clapped outside and rattled the window. I stood up and stretched. Despite its loud clanking, the radiator hadn't kicked in yet. It was still cold in here. After I'd poured myself a cup of coffee, I returned to my desk. Though the coffee was smooth and rich, my stomach fluttered.

When the phone rang, I was startled out of my reverie. "Damn." I flipped the receiver on and clicked it over to video. "McMannus here."

"McMannus? We didn't get much of a chance to talk at the restaurant . . ."

I smiled politely. It was my old pal Sergeant Dorshak. "Talk?" I laughed. "You avoided me like the plague."

"You were obviously busy."

"Yeah, yeah," I pursed my lips. "What can I do for you, Dorshak?"

"No. It's what I can do for you, Deidre." He pointed at the video.

"This ought to be interesting." I smiled tightly. I set

my cup down and stared intently at Dorshak's grizzled face. "So, what is this altruistic favor, Ted?"

"Angelucci. He's trouble. I hope you're not even vaguely considering working with that guy."

"I'm not," I lied. "You know I stay away from police business. Besides, I've already heard this tune from the captain."

His eyes narrowed, and he stared intently at my video image. *Dream on, Ted*, I told him silently, *the LINK won't help you over the phone. You need face-to-face contact to read an elevated heart rate.* "Right," he finally said. "Well, I'm glad you're not, because people here think he might be connected to leftist extremists in the Jewish community."

"Jewish community," I repeated, with a smirk. "I see you've been taking those sensitivity courses to heart. Last I heard you talk about the Malachim, the nicest thing you could call any of them was 'heathen.' "

"Yeah, well." He shrugged. Tugging at his collar, he added, "Promise me you'll stay away from Angelucci."

"Already done." I smiled. He looked unconvinced, so I added in what I hoped was a genuine tone. "Ted, seriously, do you think I want to deal with all that crap again? I'm already excommunicated. You think I'm going to risk losing anything more?"

My ploy worked, Dorshak looked really uncomfortable now. "Right. Well, just see that you don't. Maybe we'll see you around, McMannus."

"Sure." I took a long sip of coffee. Ted and I used to be friends. He used to tag along with Danny and me to pubs after hours. I always thought he had a crush on one of us. I used to think it was me, but after Daniel was arrested I began to wonder. Dorshak's accusations of my disloyalty were vehement, as if he took my testimony against Daniel personally. Given our history, it seemed odd that he would warn me away from potential trouble.

"Time to do some more digging," I said out loud. Reaching around the chair to my coat pocket, I rooted around for my credit counter. The flat plastic card was deceptively light. My life savings should be more substantial-feeling, I thought, as I bent the thin sheet with my fingers. I flipped the card over and touched the buttons in sequence. After taking a few seconds to think about it, the digital display told me my current balance. It was enough for what I was about to do, I decided, and slid the thin plastic into the slot on my wristwatch-phone. That was the other area in which technology advanced at lightning speed. If there were some new way to take money from you, someone would invent it. My credit counter could be used for anything, even phone-to-modem transfers to Swiss bank accounts, which was what I was intending, if Mouse took the bait. I dialed the numbers from memory.

He picked up on the first ring. Not many people had access to this particular phone number. "Mouse's house, Mouse speaking."

His page looked very dapper. Black hair short-cropped above the ears, which stuck out with trademark roundness. His face broke out in a wide, dimpled grin when he recognized me. "Deidre! Tell me you're back on the LINK!"

"Hey, 'home.' " I laughed. It was an old joke I shared with Mouse's page. I called him "home" as a play on the fact that he was a super-advanced version of a web home page. "If I was back on the LINK," I asked, "do you think I'd have to call you for information?"

"You break my heart, Deidre." Mouse's page feigned a hurt look. It was almost natural-looking, if you didn't know the telltale signs of digital imaging. There was only the slightest electronic halo. Damn, Mouse was one master surfer. If only he wasn't also a master criminal.

"I need intel, Mouse."

"And here I was thinking you had finally come to your senses and decided to move to Cairo and live with me in the sun forever. We could rule the world, you and I, Deidre. Tell me you will."

"I will." I smiled. "Soon."

"Ah, I know you. You might as well say never, McMannus." The page frowned. There was flickering on the screen, and the page gave me a worried look. "I have to reroute, catch a new wave. Someone's bagging your trail, girlfriend. Stand by."

I drank my coffee and waited. The thunderstorm rattled the window, and I found myself daydreaming about the hot African sun and a lithe, sun-browned young man. When I last saw Mouse real-time, he was begging me to spare his life. Not that I had that much power over his fate, as it turned out. The little con artist had weaseled himself diplomatic immunity, and the case Daniel and I had carefully built against him collapsed like a house of cards.

Sometime, during my pursuit of his case, Mouse decided my attempts to nab him were flirtatious. I did gain a healthy respect for his intellect and skill, but the rest . . . well, normally, I didn't go for his type. Clean-cut, barely legal boyishness was never that much of a turn-on for a meat-and-potatoes girl like myself. All the same, Mouse managed to grow on me; his relentless admiration was hard to resist. I was pleasantly surprised when Mouse himself, not his page, returned the call.

"Deidre." He smiled. The page was an almost perfect copy, but the original smile held a lot more snake-oil charm. "It really is you . . . and on something as crude and mundane as a phone line. Have you no sense at all? Luckily my page was able to reroute us to this complete relic of a pay phone. And, because I like you so much, I've got him running a boomerang trace on your trail. What can I do for you?"

Tousled black curly hair framed a youthful face. Two wires embedded in his temple were the only hint that Mouse was a heavy-hitter hacker. Despite the sun-drenched Cairo scene behind him, Mouse wore a leather jacket and a tee shirt that said LETOURNEAU IN '76.

"You support Letourneau, Mouse? You can't even vote in America."

"You'd be surprised what I can hack into."

I laughed. "And scandalized, I'm sure. But really, Mouse, you can't tell me you believe in the LINK-angels."

"Letourneau makes sense on the issues important to me, Dee. Expansion of the LINK and the preservation of America as a Free State. As for the rest . . ." He shrugged. "I'm reserving judgment about his divinity."

I nodded. I could understand why a hacker would want to keep America out of Christendom. Right now, operating as a Free State, an independent state, America was a chaotic jumble of companies and laws. Christendom imposed order wherever it went; hackers tended to abhor order.

"Say, Mouse," I said, "what do you know about a company called Jordan Institute?"

Mouse scratched his chin. "Some kind of loony bin, right?"

I nodded. "Mental-health technology."

"Okay. Is that what you want me to dig up?" Mouse asked. "Information on this company?"

"Yes, and information on two men, as much as my account will pay for."

He snorted a laugh. "Knowing you, that won't be much more than their social security numbers." He cocked his head at the video, as if considering something. Then, with a sigh, he added. "Listen, keep your hard-earned money. You're a hot item these days . . . we could"—an expressive hand waved about to feign embarrassment for the request—"barter. Give me some info to sell and I'll consider us even."

"I'm not sure that's a fair trade, Mouse. I haven't found anything about the company on the LINK at all. Could be a lot of work," I said.

"You're the P.I., Dee. I'm counting on you to do any real legwork. That's your specialty."

"Fair enough," I said. "But the guys might be hard to trace too. Angelucci's from Amish country . . ."

Mouse cut me off with a wave of his hand. "Stop haggling. I'm not talking a major trade; the color of your panties is enough to make me a small fortune."

I sputtered a laugh. "Color? Why not the brand, style, and cut as well?"

"I'm serious, Dee. If you'd consent to more than one

interview a year, you wouldn't be such a cult figure. You know you have your own bulletin board? I've logged a few hits there myself." I raised my eyebrows at this remark. It was hard enough for me to imagine Mouse condescending to surf a commercial board, but then to hang somewhere so kitschy truly surprised me. When he noticed my reaction, his smile broadened. "You've got some choice bytes. A boy can't help himself."

Heat rose on my cheeks. I leaned back in my chair, hoping the shadows would conceal my schoolgirl blush. "Mouse," I said sternly. "Business."

"What?" He shrugged with faux innocence. "This is business."

I kept my face stony and hidden.

"So serious all the time," he whined. When even this attempt got no reaction, he pursed his lips. Finally, he conceded. "All right, give me the names."

"Michael Angelucci, and the other is some Mafia tough going by the handle 'Morningstar.' "

"Oh, one of those," Mouse remarked with a quirky smile.

"What do you mean?"

"There's a whole cult of people taking fallen angel names, especially among criminals and rebellious kids. Although most of them aren't as biblically savvy as your guy. They're all calling themselves Lucifer or, even more creative, Satan." He wagged a finger at the screen. "You should know this stuff, Dee. It's part of your business. See, this is the problem with being cut off from the LINK and living in sheltered Christendom. . . ."

"Not yet, we're not," I protested.

"If you elect Grey, you will be."

"Grey is a rabbi," I countered. "He would never join Christendom."

"Grey is a wimp," Mouse said in disgust. "He'll do what the people want."

I laughed. "Isn't that what an elected official is supposed to do?"

Mouse gave me a grimace. "America is a sinking ship, Dee. You have never recovered from the war. What

America really needs is a benevolent dictator. Someone to guide wisely and steadily, not fluctuate with the tide of opinion polls."

"You're scaring me, Mouse. That almost makes sense." I laughed. "But, America is not Islam. We're kind of stuck on this democracy thing. Anyway, I'm surprised at you. How friendly would a dictator be to mouse.net?"

"Mouse.net is beyond single-country control."

"Ah-ha! Finally! World domination, eh, Mouse?"

He smiled, but there was a touch of sourness in his face. "You should give me more respect, Dee. I wield more power than you know."

"Enough power to get me information on two men sometime this week?"

Mouse blinked, then laughed. "All right, Dee. All right. Now then," Mouse said, with a wicked smile on his lips, "for payment . . . underwear. Confess. What kind?"

"Couldn't I give you some other information?" I stalled. It wasn't so much that I cared if the public knew this kind of detail, but that I was giving it to Mouse. "There must be something else you could sell?"

"Of equal value?" he asked. After I nodded enthusiastically in agreement, he smiled darkly. The lines of his face looked tighter, and, for a brief moment, he looked older—more serious. Squinting past the screen into the sun, he said, "Sure, McMannus. Tell me what really happened between you and Daniel the night before the Pope was murdered."

"White, bikini-cut, Hanes, size 6."

His gaze slid back to mine. There was something different behind his eyes, disappointment, maybe. Or, if I allowed myself the thought, hurt or rejection.

"Bikini-cut, no lie?" he asked, picking up his airy persona like a feather mask. "Kind of tawdry, don't you think?"

"I'm an eternal optimist." I shrugged.

My saucy comment was rewarded with a genuine smile.

"Someday, Dee . . . maybe you and I will both get

lucky . . . real-time." He wagged his eyebrows at me suggestively. "Got to run. I've got info to sell. I'll have the page ring you about the boomerang source, okay? Usual channels though, don't expect a telephone call. Sheesh."

After rolling his eyes at me, he was gone. When I found myself still smiling at the blank screen, I reached over and flicked the phone off.

Mouse's boomerang was my ace in the hole. The boomerang program was, as Mouse would put it, one wicked string of code. It followed a trace back to its originator, slammed them with a simple but irritating virus, and then returned with the information. Now, I just hoped Mouse would see fit to be generous with whatever information the boomerang provided; I was fresh out of good bartering material.

I smiled. Mouse was a paradox. With one hand, he raked in the dough through illegal, and often amoral, information brokering. Meanwhile, as if the right didn't know what the left was doing, the other hand busily redistributed that ill-gotten gain to the less fortunate around the globe.

Mouse provided wetware or exoware to anyone, anywhere, no questions asked. Also, he allowed free access to his shadow of the LINK—mouse.net. If people were as creative and devious as Mouse himself, they might hack their way onto regular LINK channels, but more often they were content to talk amongst themselves. This irritated the international governments and Christendom especially. Not only was mouse.net not regulated, Mouse's people also did their business with their own strange barter system, which operated independently of any economic system.

Fortunately for Mouse, he was clever enough to remain mostly harmless. Though many governments might prefer to shut Mouse down, his subscribers were mainly outcasts with little or no social, economic, or political power. Just to be safe, Mouse always buttered his bread on both sides. A great number of countries also owed him for information bought and traded.

The media tried to label Mouse a subversive rebel, but they'd misunderstood his motivations. From what I had learned when Danny and I pursued him, this generosity was a tenet of the Muslim belief in almsgiving. Though if the rumors were true about Mouse's misspent youth, almsgiving was the only part of his religion he followed with any kind of seriousness.

I pushed the chair away from the desk, and walked over to the coffeemaker. I poured myself another cup of coffee. Holding the warm mug in my hand, I breathed in the aroma. The coffee jock called it Sumatra, and next to romances, it was my other great addiction. Unlike any other coffee, it tasted just exactly like it smelled. The wind pushed a sheet of rain against the window. I took a long draught of my coffee and sighed contentedly. The old building's creaks and moans helped numb me to the silence.

I turned back to my desk with the intention of returning to my romance novel and letting the words fill my head for a while. Just then, a burst of lightning illuminated the office in a pale, bright flash. Against the wall, enormous wings fluttered. I cried out in surprise. The cup in my hand fell to the floor with a crash. The silhouette stretched from one corner of the room to the other. Before I could discern the rest of its shape, the shadow image vanished.

Black wings . . . black, like the ebony feathers that bore Phanuel through the LINK. He was the first LINK-angel to appear, like a shadow that crawled out of the world's collective unconscious. A dark, fluttering thing—his presence at a LINK node would cause mass panic. Unlike the others that would follow, Phanuel did not broadband. Instead, he chose to visit individuals and corporations separately. He never spoke; rather he was seen and felt. I was still a cop when Phanuel came to the police frequency. Though some claimed to, I had never seen his face, just blackness that danced at the edge of my consciousness and haunted me for a week—like a shadow on the wall.

The room was empty of illusions now, but I felt an

old chill go down my spine. I pivoted my head in the direction of the window, hoping to catch a reassuring glimpse of a fleeing pigeon. There was nothing I could see, so I moved cautiously closer to the rain-streaked window. Long lines of yellow-green light from the traffic tubes above made a crisscross pattern on the darkened windows of the rain-soaked buildings across the way. The storm-darkened skies heightened the oddness of the color of this near-street level, until everything seem bathed in puce.

I scanned the area, searching along the eaves for signs of a nest, but the shadows were long and it was impossible to discern much of anything. "Big crow," I told myself, though I hadn't seen a bird since the war thanks to the proximity of my office to the glass city that was once the Bronx, victim of the Medusa bomb. Still, I hoped aloud, "Or a raven." Anything but Phanuel.

My computer beeped. I scurried over to the desk to check my monitor, ignoring the broken mug on the floor. At the far right-hand corner of the screen, a mouse icon blinked at me. I clicked on it, and a window popped up. The text read:

Deidre, where on earth did you find this rust bucket? Man, it's no wonder you never hang ten out here anymore . . . can't be much fun surfin' without a decent 'board.

Boomerang came back empty-handed. Only happened to me one time before . . . when I tried to source a LINK-angel. Guess that means God is tapping your line, girlfriend. Seems like strange behavior for an omniscient deity, but, hey, I'm just a page. I'm not even technically sentient, why would I even pretend to understand the mind of God?

Allah akbar, the Mouse.

The window disintegrated pixel by pixel. Despite the holes, I read the words over and over again, until there was nothing left. My mouth felt dry. My hands shook. I turned my monitor off. The darkened office was becoming a tad too quiet for my tastes. What had seemed cozy now felt haunted. It was time to get out and walk around. Checking my watch, I decided I had plenty of time to spare before the meeting with Michael. I popped open the bottom drawer of my desk and grabbed my shoulder holster and, after a brief hesitation, the romance as well. With the gun safely tucked under my arm, I headed for the door.

Excerpted from the LINK-angel site, 2075

LINK-ANGELS, A BUDDHIST'S VIEW:

Buddhism demands that we have no blind faith.

Therefore, I think it unwise to dismiss the LINK-angels completely without first applying the tenets of wisdom and compassion. The term "angel" and their traditionally Christian appearance are somewhat disconcerting to many Buddhists. Yet their message, the idea of a Second Coming, is not unknown to our philosophy.

In the history of the Mahayana Buddhists there exists the idea of the *maitreya,* or "Future Buddha"— a second Buddha that would come and purify the world. It was also believed that the first Buddha prophesied the coming of the second.

Letourneau could be a *bodhisattva,* or even, one supposes, this Second Buddha. In some ways it is even easier for a Buddhist to accept the possibility of divine enlightenment to be bestowed upon a mindful individual. We do not have to believe that the man himself is a god, only that his ideas are enlightened. I am not suggesting that Letourneau is that man, however, only that is possible and certainly could fall within the realm of our belief system.

*   *   *

As to what the LINK-angels are, on the other hand, it is much more difficult to ascertain. Turning again to the Mahayana Buddhists, we find the idea of the Buddha as the manifestation of a universal, spiritual being with three bodies: the Body of Magical Transformation, *nirmanakaya,* the Body of Bliss, *sambhogakaya,* and the Body of Essence, *dharmakaya.* The angels could be a representation of the Body that exists in the heavens, the Body of Bliss.

"Bodhi" or *"budi"* means "to wake up." Perhaps the LINK-angels are a wake-up call to all of us to return to our more religious roots.

CHAPTER 5

Over the dissipating storm clouds, a blood-red moon rose low on the horizon and loomed large behind the city skyline. Through the plastic sheath of the walkway I could see it clearly. Full and round, it capped the rooftops like a bowl or, I thought with a shiver, the glow of an exploding Medusa bomb. From the elevation of the skyway, I could see the reddish glint of what had once been the Bronx, but was now a crystal necropolis.

It was that bomb, more than even the angels, that made converts out of a secular society. Though I was only a teenager, I was part of the youth war effort and had signed on to be in the cleanup crew at ground zero; our standing orders were to shatter anything on the streets that looked even vaguely human. Thanks to the Medusa, the Bronx was glass as far as the eye could see. Most people had time to evacuate, but hundreds were frozen as they tried to escape the blast. Crystallized faces, locked in silent screams, stared accusingly as if daring us to desecrate their graves.

"Would you like me to pray with you, sister?"

A voice at my side startled me. I shook off the memories that had flooded my mind. I glanced over at a short woman in the deep purple cassock of the Church of England. She stared up at the moon like I had. Auburn hair touched the tip of her shoulder and framed her round face like a lion's mane.

I smiled down at her, since she was several inches shorter than I. "I wasn't praying . . . just thinking."

She laughed softly. The corners of her eyes crinkled slightly. "There isn't a person alive who doesn't look at that moon without a little prayer in their hearts."

The newspapers had been heralding the blood-red moon as a sign of the Second Coming, of Letourneau's divinity. Quieter voices suggested it was simply the Canadian forest fires that caused this phenomenon.

"What if it's not a sign of the apocalypse? Maybe the moon is red just because of the prevailing easterlies?"

"Nature is part of God's plan," she said simply, as if people suggested heresy to her every day. "Nothing that happens is 'just' science, sister. All of it reveals the hand of God."

Her eyes flicked over my dripping raincoat. She started past my eyes to my temple. I flushed; I hadn't realized that I'd been rubbing the implant again. "Do you need a safe place to stay tonight?" she asked. "Maybe some access to a little white noise?"

White noise was a common treatment for info junkies, since it sated their need for constant input. I pulled my hand from my head and backed away. "No thanks. I'm okay."

She nodded at me as if she didn't believe me, but wasn't going to push it. The look in her eye begged me to take that first step and admit I had a problem.

"Before you go, Sister, may I ask you a question?" I asked. She looked puzzled, but nodded. "Do you work with the mentally ill?"

"Of course. It's part of my outreach."

"Ever heard of a company called Jordan River Health Institute? They're no longer in business, but they were a year ago."

She looked surprised, then said, "Actually, I have. Several of my parishioners were scheduled to receive some of their biosoftware. Jordan never delivered."

"Do you remember what the software was supposed to do?"

"I'm not entirely sure, but . . ." Her eyes looked up and off to the right as she accessed her LINK-memory. "I think it was supposed to help patients suffering

chronic pain. Somehow the software was supposed to
stimulate or manipulate the pain and pleasure centers of
the brain."

"Really?" Subconsciously I reached for pen and pad
then I realized I'd forgotten it. Since the excommunication, I'd been forced to take paper notes like my P.I.
ancestors. I'd just have to remember this bit of information. "Do you think they'd actually found the emotional
centers of the brain?"

"I doubt it," the nun said. "I mean, I guess I always
assumed that's why the orders were never filled. They
made promises they couldn't keep." She looked as
though she were about to go on, but then stopped.
"Why? Why do you want to know all of this?"

"Ghosts. I'm trying to put some ghosts to rest."

"Good luck." Her voice was quiet and, rather than
press me, she moved away. "Your church may have
abandoned you, Deidre, but God has not."

Startled that she had recognized me, I murmured,
"Thanks."

Watching her leave, I felt envious. She had capital
letter Faith. I always tried really hard in church to feel
the Holy Spirit in me. I never got even a tingle, except
when my feet went numb from sitting on them. Next to
me in the pew, Eion glowed. The only time I even came
close to feeling that kind of fulfillment was when Daniel
and I successfully collared a LINK criminal. Eion swore
to serve God; I swore to "Serve and Protect." It had
been a good balance.

My nose caught a whiff of something delicious. The
smells reminded me that my earlier attempt to eat had
been rudely interrupted. Following the odor, I made my
way to a bustling deli. The holographic marquee adver-
tised great food first in English, Hebrew, and then
Yiddish.

I went inside. The low-level conversation noise filled
my head, and I let out a long sigh. This was the perfect
place to relax until it was time to meet Michael. I ordered a couple of potato knishes from the counter and
jockeyed for a position at a table near the window. I

retrieved my paperback from my coat pocket. The older gentleman seated next to me raised his eyebrows curiously at the sight of a hard-copy book, but he smiled as if pleased that someone else still made the effort to bother with print. He toasted me with his coffee cup, and I reciprocated with a knish salute.

I fingered through the dog-eared pages searching for where I'd left the intrepid heroine hanging. Ah yes, I smiled, still arguing with the enigmatic, but darkly handsome hero. Deeply into the novel and just starting my second knish, I heard someone shout my name.

"Deidre!" A hand touched me familiarly on the shoulder. A dark-eyed woman with a crew cut stood next to me. A white patch of scar tissue interrupted an otherwise perfectly shaped eyebrow. It had been almost twenty years, but, despite the new haircut, I recognized Rebeckah immediately.

"I'd ask you to join me, Rebeckah, but . . ." I gestured helplessly at the crowd.

A meaningful glance at the man in the seat next to me was all it took for her to commandeer a place at the crowded counter. While her attention was elsewhere, I unobtrusively slipped the paperback into my pocket. Once she'd settled herself, she asked, "It's been a while. How are you?"

"Holding up," I managed to say around a mouthful of knish. "You?"

"Fine." She said absently, watching the door.

I thought about asking her if she was planning on coming to our college's next reunion, but even if there were going to be one, neither of us would go. Rebeckah was underground these days with the Malachim, and I was off the force, excommunicated.

She watched me eat in silence. After inhaling the rest of the potato pastry, I cleared my throat. "You've always been shitty at small talk, Rebeckah. This meeting isn't a coincidence, is it?"

"My mistake. I thought you came here to talk to me."

I raised an eyebrow and looked around the restaurant. Could Rebeckah be implying that this little deli was the headquarters of the Malachim? I decided not to ask. She might not appreciate us being overheard.

"Actually," I said, "I was just out wandering. Maybe it was psychic. I have been thinking about you."

"Oh, really? Decided to join us finally?"

"No," I said, "but I hear we have a mutual friend."

"Is that so?" Leaning back on the stool, Rebeckah observed me carefully. "Who could that be?"

"Michael Angelucci," I said. "Apparently he contacted your people before talking to me. Hear anything about him?"

"No," her mouth said, but her eyes were dark and guarded. "We've been keeping our dealings with the Italians to a minimum, you know that."

I laughed. "He'd prefer to be called 'Roman.' "

"A Vatican agent?" Rebeckah scoffed, jumping to a conclusion I hadn't even considered. "Thanks to that hotheaded ex-partner of yours we haven't had contact with Vatican City in over a year."

I started to chide her for being so public about her business, when the full impact of what she'd implied struck me. In a conspiratorial tone, I whispered, "Your people had a Papal connection?"

She laughed. "Don't look so horrified, Deidre. Historically, your popes have made questionable alliances with nastier folks."

"No, no, that's not what surprised me," I said. Picking at the crumbs on my plate, I tried to piece things together. "The Pope . . . he was, er, sympathetic to your cause?"

"To our methods, no," Rebeckah admitted quietly. "But our aims . . ." She shrugged.

"Your aims?"

"We've always been Free Staters. Even though America is a theocratic republic, at least there's still a pretense of the representational government model. Christendom is a badly disguised oligarchy."

"But isn't the Pope the leader of Christendom?" Rebeckah's political jargon made my head ache again.

"He is now. Innocent had a plan to decentralize his power and give it back to the people."

"I'll be hanged," I said. Putting my hands on the countertop, I leaned back on the stool. This information was a big hole in the case against Daniel. At the time, everyone claimed Danny had been motivated partly out of fear a presidential alliance with the Pope would bring Christendom to America.

Rebeckah nudged me on the arm. "I hate to cut this short because it's been a long time, but I have to go." Jerking her chin in the direction of the window, she frowned. "Seems like you were followed here, Dee. I can't risk another arrest right now. I've been compromised enough lately."

"Wait," I begged. "If you do hear something about Angelucci, will you contact me?"

Her eyes flicked about nervously, but she paused long enough for me to press my card into her palm. Glancing down at it absently, she sighed.

"Sure." She squeezed my shoulder tenderly. Reaching up absently, I placed my hand over hers for a second. Too preoccupied to make a more formal or proper goodbye, she headed for the door. My eyes were riveted to where she'd gestured out the window. I scanned the crowd for a suspicious or familiar face. When I found none, I found myself looking up at the evening sky searching for dark wings—raven's wings, or angel's.

I laughed under my breath. Rebeckah's paranoia was rubbing off on me. No doubt it was just some sleazy reporter or a remote cam; they were forever darting in and out of my peripheral vision. All the same, I decided to err on the side of caution. I relinquished my precious window seat to an anxious patron and headed for the bathroom.

The toilets, the sign indicated, were located down a narrow, dingy hallway. Instead of choosing the door clearly labeled, WOMEN, I took a detour. I boldly entered the one marked EMPLOYEES ONLY and found myself in a tiny kitchen. A half wall separated the cashier from the kitchen, but the noise from the deli could only barely be heard over the humming of several industrial-looking refrigerator units that flanked the wall closest to me. Vat-grown lettuce and other vegetable matter were strewn across a low metal table. Soy-salami and other meats hung in disarray on the far wall. Then, I saw what I was looking for. Over the head of a surprised chef glowed an exit sign.

Rapping the edge of the counter as I passed him, I said, "By the way, excellent knishes. Best I've ever had." My offhand compliment must have taken the poor man by surprise, because I was already at the door when I heard him shout in protest.

As the door closed behind me, I found myself in an old abandoned trade-way. Most restaurants and stores were connected by a set of delivery tunnels. As respectable businesses moved closer and closer to the top floors of the skyscrapers and began using roof access for delivery, the money for upkeep of the tunnels disappeared. Some places still used the trade-ways, but the farther from city center you got, the more likely that gangs of Gorgons had taken them over as private thoroughfares.

This one was clearly not in use. The smell of urine was close in the stale air. Graffiti dotted the walls. Some of the scrawl appeared to be a phonetic approximation of English, but mostly the colors bled together into a kind of urban artistic expression.

Someone was illegally siphoning electricity to power Christmas lights duct-taped haphazardly across the ceiling. The track of lights closely followed the strip where the train used to run. Apparently following someone's internal sense of aesthetics, the Christmas lights occasionally abandoned the linear and burst into starlike patterns. As I looked down the tunnel, I noticed the designs seemed to happen at regular intervals.

Curious, I moved to a spot directly underneath one of the starbursts and looked up. The lights danced around a shifting rectangular shadow. The object didn't look like any kind of conduit box I'd ever seen before. Also, maintenance crews tended to paint things like that with fluorescent yellow stripes, so that they were easily located in case of emergency. This box was a flat gray metal that seemed to absorb the light intentionally. If I could only get closer, I thought, I might be able to take the cover off to see what was inside.

Just as I was about to search for something to use as a stepladder, I heard a shuffling noise. I decided not to take any chances and headed for the exit. As I walked, I stepped over discarded fast-food containers. Finding a door marked EXIT, I quickly pushed through. As I expected, the doorway opened to the pedestrian skyway system, which roughly followed the same path as the traffic tunnels.

I hugged myself as a blast of air breezed through my damp clothes. The sound of my shoes scuffling against the nubby carpeting mingled with the noise of the other evening strollers. Strains of a rock tune wafted out of a pool bar. The green neon hanging in the window proclaimed that the tavern proudly served imported stout. Slowing my pace, I contemplated going in to sample the bitter, dark brew for Daniel's sake. He had loved the stuff, and often dragged me to similar smoky, raucous places for a "nip," as he called it.

A fond smile playing on my lips, I approached the door. Through the glass, I could see Celtic warriors posturing around the pool tables, holding their cue sticks like ancient spears. Daniel's broad-featured face and crinkle-eyed smile greeted me in every glance.

With my fingers still wrapped around the door handle, I froze. Suddenly, I remembered how rage had splotched Daniel's cheeks with purple. I squeezed my eyes shut, trying to stop the scene from replaying in my mind.

"You going in, then?" A lilting voice broke me out of my reverie. "Or are you just going to stand there gawking?"

"Uh." I looked up at the curious frown and backed away from the door. "No. No, I'm sorry. I can't."

"Suit yourself," I heard him murmur as I moved off.

Heat rose on my cheeks. I hurried my steps. Trying

to calm my jagged nerves, I took a deep breath. I crossed
another skyway toward the shopping district. A woman
walked by with an arm entwined around her lover. They
leaned into each other, laughing. Her mauve scarf
matched her shoes exactly. Her lightly colored hair was
coiled in a style I had attempted but could never maintain with such perfection. I imagined myself in her place:
1.3 kids and a condo in midtown. Despite my fierce inde-
pendence, some days I would kill for a warm, strong arm
to hold.

I paused to examine this week's haute couture as ad-
vertised by the mannequins in Bloomingdale's window.
The holograms moved in an alluring yet businesslike
way, skillfully showing off the cut with a swirl of the
skirts. The images behind the mannequins flashed scenes
of somebody else's affluent life. Without the LINK, it
was like watching a silent movie: picture, but no sound.

Pressing my fingers to the glass, I tried to feel the
pulse of information emanating from the display. I
touched my cheek against the cool, smooth surface. If I
shut my eyes, I could almost sense the barrage of advertising slogans and insistent sales pitches like the distant
thrum of a bass cord.

"Infoslut." A familiar rasping voice shocked me out
of my reverie.

I pulled myself away from the shop window and
blinked. "Oh, it's you." In front of me in a ragged, wet
coat, stood the Revelation preacher. It was strange to
see him out of context and at such close range. I almost
checked my watch out of habit. "What are you doing
here at this hour?"

The pungent odor that hung around him was intensified by the steamy wetness of his clothes. His eyes were
distant, but a shaky hand pointed unfailingly to my
heart. "Sin," he declared, his voice rising to a fever
pitch. "Sin flowers in you like a tainted rose."

I turned away. He was talking Jesus-nonsense again.
I don't know what I'd expected. Perhaps I'd hoped that
off duty he was a coherent, normal man.

"Cast out of heaven, driven from Sodom, thrust down from the tower of Babel . . ."

I stopped paying attention and walked back toward the office. Experience taught me it was best not to encourage him. Ignoring him, however, I discovered, was easier when separated by walls. The preacher trudged behind me like a faithful dog, his voice falling into the rhythm of our steps.

"Jezebel, Jezebel, Satan tempts you again, and again you fall. You would sell your soul for access to the LINK."

I spun on my heels and caught the collar of his coat. Shoving hard, I yanked him around until he fell against the bulletproof glass of the skyway window. We hit the surface with a muffled thrum. He was smaller than I was, so I pressed my full weight against his slender frame. "What? What did you just say?"

"Sin tempts you, but you should resist. The flesh is weak. Sin is always the path of least resistance. Fight him, fight him."

"Who sent you here?" I demanded.

His eyes rolled up into his head. "Thus is the word of our Lord. Thanks be to God."

"Amen," I said, continuing the service. I let go of his collar. The preacher's knees buckled and he dropped to the floor. The excitement taxed his already overworked neurons, and his head lolled against the glass.

A small crowd had gathered. Twice in one day I found myself fleeing the scene of, if not a crime, then, at least serious assault charges. Maybe it was the fear behind my eyes, but no one made a move to stop me.

New Jersey State Penitentiary
Jan. 12, 2076

Dee,

I feel like a blushing schoolboy. Every day at mail call I get hopeful that you've written, and I eye up all the packages in the screw's bag. Never anything

*for me. I'm not trying to guilt you, though I'll admit
to secretly hoping it might work. After all, I hear you
Catholic girls have an overabundance of guilt. Seriously, it's okay. There's a big chasm between us. It's
going to take some work to get across. I know that.*

*They had all the evidence against me, Dee. You told
the truth. There's nothing wrong with that. Sure, at
first I figured you should have more loyalty to me.
I'm your partner for ~~Chrissake~~. I was LINKed to all
the news coverage during the trial. There was a lot of
brouhaha about the fact you tried to finagle a secret
deal with the FBI: my premeditation for your anonymity. Of course, when Interpol seized jurisdiction
you had to take the stand anyway, didn't you? I
didn't think you'd really go through with it until I
saw you there. I felt pretty betrayed all right.*

*At the time, I figured you were still pissed off about
that night. I thought you were paying me back for
trying to . . . you know, get it on. Let me just say
again—I don't know what came over me. I completely lost it. I was just, just . . . overwhelmed by
lust. I know that really ~~fucked~~ with our trust. I never
had any feelings like that for you before . . . well,
no, that's a lie. Of course, I thought you were attractive, but that just means I'm a het, right? I mean,
half the straight guys on the force thought you were
to die for. It wasn't anything more than that ever,
Dee, I swear. That night came out of the blue. Scares
me to think about it, really. I'm sure it must've
scared you worse.*

*You never mentioned that night. You could have,
you know. It would've made things worse for me inside. Nobody likes a rapist. And an attempted rapist
is just some ~~prick~~ with no follow-through. Murderers,
I've discovered, command some respect, at least.
Without that reputation to hold people at bay, I'd
probably be a dead man for being a cop.*

* * *

I don't want to waste too much of your time, Dee. I just want to say, I don't harbor any of those resentments anymore. I know why you did it. You're a good cop. Telling the truth is what good cops do. Sometimes truth outweighs loyalty.

Daniel

CHAPTER 6

The rain started up again, and my hair was soaked by the time I got back to the office. Though much of the sky was blocked by traffic tubes, water found a way to ooze though the holes to reach the ground. Ten minutes to spare, but Michael was there already. He leaned casually against the door. The tip of his broad shoulder covered part of my name and title stenciled on the frosted glass. The moisture in the air made his hair curly, but otherwise he was dry as a bone. Either he drove, or he'd been waiting a long time.

"You ready? The LINK awaits."

"Deal's off," I growled as I stomped up the stairs. I muscled past him to unlock the door. "Somebody is on to us."

He sprang upright with the speed of a snake. "What are you talking about? Who?"

"I don't know, but the preacher seemed to know a lot of details, too many details. I can't risk it. Not even for . . ."—the LINK—". . . for Danny."

The key didn't seem to fit. I jangled it angrily, trying to force it. The lock finally clicked open. I swung the door wide, with the intention of slamming it back onto the hinges with a lot of force. Tracking my thought process, Michael caught the edge of the door with enhanced speed.

"Deidre, be reasonable." His fist gripped the door over my head. The muscles in his arms jumped at the constant pressure I applied. "I understand your fear.

You're taking a lot of personal risk, I know. But there's more than you at stake here."

"So you've said." I leaned harder on the frame. The door creaked, but his grip never wavered.

"You don't believe me."

"I don't even know who exactly you're working for, Michael. Why should I trust you?"

"Because it's the right thing to do," he said firmly. His gray eyes searched out mine. "And because I can give you what you need—access to the LINK."

My mouth went dry. Swallowing hard, I lied bravely, "That's not enough."

"So you're telling me if I walked away right now and you never got connected—you could live with that?"

"I'd have to, wouldn't I?" I said, but I couldn't look at him. I eased up the pressure on the door, then let my shoulders drop. "It'd be better than selling my soul."

"But would it be better than saving it?"

In his voice there was a whisper of something familiar: a warmth, a sense of rightness I hadn't felt since the LINK-angel Gabriel appeared on the LINK. The LINK-angels had appeared one by one, each bringing with it its own emotional aura. Unlike Phanuel, who appeared to people individually, Gabriel had been simulcast on all frequencies. Strength and power were the purview of this one. He was the enforcer. We felt the righteous burning of his sword as it bored through the LINK's collective consciousness. Every LINK-angel's eyes were molten cores of light and right. The face before me had a similar conviction. His eyes glowed with a shimmer of the fierce fire I had seen and felt in the LINK-angel's visitation.

After what I had learned about Jordan Institute, I was beginning to believe that the LINK-angels might not be the miracles everyone claimed them to be. I didn't really think it was possible, but Michael insisted that the LINK-angels weren't real, that there was someone, a human hand, behind their appearance.

I decided to play a game with him.

"You're a LINK-angel, aren't you?" I asked.

Michael jumped back as if I had slapped him

I'd hit a nerve. "Let me guess . . ." I was running with it now, hot on a hunch. "That's the connection to your reputation. If the LINK-angels are constructs like you say, one of them was modeled on you, wasn't it?"

Michael stood stock-still and didn't reply. Still, I felt encouraged to go on.

"That's why you're so certain that the angels are frauds," I said, "and why you won't tell me who you work for. It's him. It's Letourneau. You're ratting him out. That's why you want me to do it . . . because you can't without implicating yourself. No wonder pressure has been coming from all sides. So tell me, are all the angels cops?"

His face was wide with surprise. I couldn't tell if I'd played him right yet or not.

"No." He schooled his expression. "Definitely not."

"But, I'm right aren't I? You're one of them . . . an angel."

"I am the archangel Michael."

"What a coup." I beckoned him into the office. "I was never the best catechism student, but that means you're number one, head honcho, right?" He nodded. I looked him over. If he was the mastermind behind the LINK-angels, I'd have to reassess my impression of his intellect. Looking at his wide-eyed expression, I was having some trouble.

"So how'd you do it? I mean, to fake something like that has got to take some major equipment, major programming."

Michael hovered in the doorway and gave me an anxious look. "Do I have to remind you we have an appointment to keep?"

"Cool your heels, angel boy, I haven't decided anything yet." Walking past the broken cup on the floor, I deliberately hung up my coat and settled behind the desk. "Sit down. We have to talk."

"Is this really the safest place . . . ?"

I smiled patiently. "One of my best-kept secrets"—I pointed to the ceiling, and whispered—"Unitarians.

They have an office upstairs. The door says ANTIQUES, but it's a front. They've been running some kind of underground railroad for outspoken secular humanists, radicals, and scientists. They have more jamming devices and security taps than the FBI, CIA, and NSA combined."

He nodded, although he continued to look doubtful. Cautiously, he lowered himself into the seat across from me. He sat stock-still, but I could tell he was uneasy. Cop or soldier reflexes held him tightly under control. Like a mental fencer, he was trying to give me the smallest target possible.

Michael was smarter than he'd led me to believe, that much I could give him, but the image of super-hack still didn't fit him. With his fortysomething stability, he was atypical of the local variety of wirehead genius I'd busted down in my time. Arrogant, yes, but his was a physical prowess, not a mental one. Usually LINK-hackers couldn't keep the wicked glee out of their voices when they talked code. Michael acted like he barely knew it existed. More than that, he seemed embarrassed when I guessed he was augmented. If he was an ex-soldier, his hardware was the kind of equipment that gave pimply-faced netfreaks wet dreams.

"So," I had to ask, "you're the disc-jock behind the LINK-angels, eh, Michael?"

"No." he said slowly, as if carefully choosing each word. "Letourneau is the man you want."

"He's a wire-wizard, then? Are you saying the candidate actually got his hands dirty this time? I thought the only code Letourneau knew was the neo-Nazis' secret password."

Michael snorted. "I don't know about that. All I know is that I can't have other-Michael besmirching my name."

"The other Michael? Your replacement?"

"My nemesis."

"So . . . someone took your place on the project?"

"Something like that."

The muscle in his jaw flexed and his eyes narrowed. I

sat back in my chair. Over the pillar of my fingers, I asked, "So, this is about revenge?"

"No," he pronounced carefully, "vengeance."

"Okay." I stretched out the word to let him know I didn't agree, but I wasn't going to argue. Michael was a cop: it wasn't my place to remind him that it was a thin line he was walking. Besides, if he'd gotten mixed up with Letourneau, then he'd already crossed over once. He was trying to work his way back, and for that I had to respect him. "If you were replaced early on in the game, how much do you know? Can you bring Letourneau down with what you have?"

"I can, well, no I can't." He couldn't contain his energy any longer; standing up, he began to pace. "The question is subtlety. It must be seamless. The hand that guides shouldn't be seen—everything must appear to have cause and effect. It's the only way to change the popular view. People don't believe in miracles anymore."

"People believe in the LINK-angels," I countered. "Isn't pulling off miracles your whole gig?"

"That's exactly why I can't just pull the plug on them."

"You could do that?" My eyes were wide.

"Only the mind and will of Man is beyond my purview."

I sputtered. Now he was acting like the wireheads I knew, with their I-rule-the-world-by-my-genius-alone attitude.

"Right," I said sarcastically. "Come back to Earth, Michael. You're taking this archangel role too seriously. Anyway, if that were true, why would you need me?"

"I can't expose my involvement . . . not until the very end."

"I get it," I said. "If you're the first Michael, you can't afford to have Letourneau find out you intend to rat him out, not until showtime."

He nodded, and stopped pacing.

"Where am I at the end, when the curtain comes down, Michael? Center stage?"

He crossed his arms in front of his chest. He stood with his legs slightly apart, like an athlete. The line his body formed was arrow-straight. My mind returned unconsciously to the vision of the LINK-angel with the flaming sword. I swallowed hard. He said, "You think I'm looking for a scapegoat."

"I do," I murmured.

"I have no intention of making you the fall guy." His voice was assuring. "When this is through I promise you that you will be revered."

"More likely I'll be burned at the stake. Mike, you've got to respect my position here. I need something concrete, some proof that you really can bring Letourneau down before I invest in this caper of yours. If the LINK-angels are a fraud, and I help you expose them, I'm going to be one hell of a lot less popular than I am now . . . and I'm already as far down in official approval as I care to go."

"I can offer you two things, Deidre." Michael leaned over the desk. We were face-to-face. "First, the LINK." His gray eyes locked on mine, and I tried to keep the deep desire from surfacing. I quickly shut my eyes before he could sense my desperation. It was too late.

"I know exactly how much that means to you, Deidre. You've lived in silence a long time, shunned by the community you swore to serve and protect . . . a system that betrayed you and Daniel both. And, that's the second thing I can offer. If you help me expose the LINK-angels, I promise to use whatever power I have to help clear both of your names."

"The LINK and my reputation back." I opened my eyes slowly. "I guess you know how to make me an offer I can't refuse, don't you?"

"We can still make the appointment tonight." He held out a hand.

"Are you sure you're not the Devil himself come to tempt me?" I smiled weakly and took his hand. A brilliant warmth enveloped me. It was as if, outside, night had become day, and the sun had broken through the clouds.

"Yes," his voice floated into my consciousness, "of that I'm certain."

(excerpt from the *New York Times* multimedia, 3-D graphics interface, from April 1, 13:05:76, . . . text- or audio-only format available for the user-impaired.)

April 1, 2076
13:05:28
CHRISTENDOM NODE, PARIS. A real-time assault was carried out against the Paris node earlier this morning. Though hardware damage was sustained during the attack, emergency sysop crews from the French Christendom Commonwealth were able to reroute the systems through a provincial backup power source in a matter of hours.

The shock of the sudden loss of LINK functions sent seventy-two people into severe cyber-trauma. Hospitals are overloaded, but no cyber-related fatalities have been reported thus far (hot-link to continually updated hospital reports).

Traffic control also suffered during the LINK-attack. Twenty-three accidents happened as a direct result of cyber-trauma. Miraculously few people were seriously injured. French Traffic Control sysop, Andre Montenque had this to say, regarding the surprisingly low number of serious accidents, "The French, we're already crazy drivers . . . If nothing, we know how to drive defensively."

Experts have also reported surprise at the low number of cyber-trauma and cyber-shock victims. American biotech surgeon Christine Robinov, who was instrumental in aiding damage control during last month's attack in Helsinki, explained, "The only people affected dramatically by this kind of hardware terrorism seem to be those engaged in some form of multiprocessing. High-level system operators and LINK-maintenance workers—anyone who can't make a quick node transfer—are the ones we see most in the hospital.''

No group has claimed responsibility for the Paris attack, but Christendom spokesperson Shelia McEvers believes this to be the work of the LINK-terrorist group known as Malachim Nikamah. (hot-link here to discussion of the Malachim Nikamah, and their history of terrorism in Christendom and beyond.) ''The method is very similar,'' she said. ''Cruelty like this could only come from a non-Christian group like the Malachim shel Nikamah. Who else would do this kind of crazy, destructive thing?''

The Nation of Islam cautioned the Vatican regarding issuing broad statements against non-Christians, but joined in denouncing today's attack. Both superpowers donated extensively to the relief fund. (hot-link here to see actual donations sent.)

The French government has increased security around its hardware nodes and cautioned other governments in Christendom to do the same. Any citizen wishing to route through French nodes must follow the international law of full-disclosure. The French sysops have announced a radical change in its on-line policy: absolutely no handles will be accepted, even those with proper visa handshake packages. This new policy also disallows access from any addresses ending in mousenet. (hot-link to related articles, ''Commercial Handle-Users Outraged at French Node Policy'' and ''Russia Angry at Mouse.net Exclusion.'')

French president Anton LeLand told real-time reporters, ''This kind of terrorism is the work of agents of the Antichrist. They must be stopped.''

CHAPTER 7

Michael let us in the apartment complex and led me down a flight of stairs. I stayed two steps behind him. Parking up a couple of levels was my idea. Bad enough I had to park my classic in Hell's Kitchen, the least I could do was stow it in the slightly more affluent upper levels.

At apartment 301, Michael stopped and knocked once. Without waiting for a response, he entered. I hesitated only briefly before following him through.

"Gabe?" Michael called out. Water came on in the back of the apartment. Followed by the clinking sound of someone doing dishes. Michael headed toward the sound. "Gabe?"

Michael didn't invite me to follow him into the kitchen, so I closed the door behind me. I heard the lock engage automatically. A large tricolor flag spanned two windows. The top edge was held in place by several thumbtacks. It did double duty as a curtain, although not very well. Light from the passing cars flashed through the threadbare material, first brown, then yellow and green. The pattern seemed familiar, but I couldn't be certain. Pan-African or some such, I decided, as I scanned the rest of the apartment.

The walls were as thin as the cloth, and street noise filled the tiny apartment. Gaudy wallpaper peeled away from the edges of a water-stained ceiling, and a single bare lightbulb hung dangerously overhead. Despite the harsh light it cast, the apartment felt homey. Brick-and-board bookshelves lined most of the walls and under the windows. Five worn but comfortable-looking chairs circled about a battered end table. The smell of dark-roasted coffee wafted in from somewhere and mingled with the strong aroma of curry.

I snooped around for something that resembled biotech equipment, though I would have settled for anything made in this decade. The only thing I saw was dusty hard-copy tomes on Islam, the Baha'i movement, versions of the Koran, political history, and Malcolm X. Not one medical journal among them. As a roach scuttled along one of the bookshelves, my stomach fluttered. My only hope was that a sterile lab was hidden behind one of the bookshelves, like something out of James Bond.

An eruption of masculine laughter came from the kitchen. Through the rumble of their voices, the words were impossible to distinguish. The sound had an odd pattern and cadence. It was fast-paced and rose at the end of phrases—definitely not English.

Just as I was ready to burst in and introduce myself, a black man stepped into the hallway. His skin was a well-worn, walnut hue, so deep it almost seemed to glow. A dazzling smile still graced an open and expressive face. Dark, brown eyes twinkled when he saw me. Salt-and-pepper hair was cut short on the sides. He wore a loose-fitting, button-down shirt and jeans, and looked like the farthest thing from a biotech.

"I'm Jibril. You must be Deidre." He smiled again, this time just for me. He took two steps, closing the distance between us, and extended his hand.

"No, I must be crazy." I took his hand and pumped it once, grinning maniacally. I noticed a bright flash of something embedded in his forehead between the eyes. "You have one of those new microchip tattoos?" I asked.

Jibril nodded sagely. "Would you like to see it?"

I'd always been curious how those things worked, so I said, "Yes."

He closed his eyes for a moment, and the chip began to glow slightly. When I stared at it, I saw a swirling, gilded script moving from right to left between his eyes.

"It's beautiful," I said. "But I can't read the words. What does it say?"

Strolling out of the kitchen, Michael leaned against the doorframe. " 'There is no God, but Allah,' " Michael translated, " 'and Muhammad is the prophet of God.' "

"Heckuva statement," I breathed.

With a hardy laugh, Jibril clapped me on the shoulder. "You're right, Michael. Definitely refreshing."

"Didn't I tell you so?" Michael smiled. "Deidre is a regular firebrand."

Our brief dash in rain had soaked Michael's leather jacket. He stood so close that I could smell the musty, wet odor. The curls of his hair hung enchantingly over one eye. I wondered how it would feel to reach up and run my fingers through it.

I cleared my throat, and a soft punch to his arm hid my growing embarrassment. "You getting sweet on me, big guy?"

Jibril bright grin faded. "My prince," he said, arching his eyebrow.

"A discussion for another time." Michael glared at Jibril. Though his tone was light, the smile he gave Jibril held a trace of tightness.

"Of course, but . . . If you want to talk about it, I've been there, you know."

"Who could forget," Michael said with a smile.

"Yes, well." Jibril coughed out a little laugh. Turning to me, he brightened. "You came here for something. Let me get it for you."

I frowned. Jibril made it sound like the LINK was something he could just pull down from his bookcase and hand over. " 'Get it for me'? Shouldn't we prepare for surgery or something?"

"You'll see." He smiled cryptically. Jibril walked over to the flag-draped window. Kneeling next to the book-case underneath, he retrieved a small wooden box. It was plain dark wood, perhaps mahogany. There were no markings on it whatsoever, and it was about the size of an old cigar box. He pulled out something small and shiny. He replaced the box, and returned to my side. His hands enveloped mine. His skin felt dry against my sweating palms.

"What the hell is this?" I demanded, searching his brown eyes. He was focused on something far away.

"It is done," he said, pressing the hard, round object into my palm. He squeezed my hand tightly and shut his eyes.

A loud rap startled me. Still holding his hand, I felt Jibril jump in surprise.

"FBI!" An angry voice shouted from behind the door. "Open up!"

Michael looked at me. "Were we followed?"

"Oh shit!" I tried to squirm out of Jibril's grasp. Jibril held my hand firmly. I couldn't escape his grip without relinquishing my hold on the strange, metallic object he gave me. Despite the object's apparent uselessness, I couldn't bring myself to let go. I tried to will my fingers to release. My mind refused to obey. If that thing could somehow reconnect me to the LINK, I wasn't about to lose it—no matter what was at stake.

"Are you crazy or something?" I barked at Jibril, trying to catch his eye.

"It is as Allah wills it," he said as he watched the door with a dreamy expression.

Michael grunted. "God has chosen the FBI as Their agents? I'm in the wrong profession."

I squirmed in Jibril's grip. "Let go of me." I gestured with my knee.

Michael held up his hands. "Relax, Deidre. Don't do anything rash. We've done nothing wrong. What can they do?"

"It is as Allah wills it," Jibril repeated calmly.

"We're coming in!" A muffled command came from behind the door.

"I'm going to open the door," Michael said with a

quiet conviction. "Show them that we intend to cooperate."

" 'Cooperate'?" I repeated, stunned. "Good Lord, you are a country bumpkin, aren't you? You don't cooperate with the FBI. They'd just as soon shoot as not."

Michael stopped in front of Jibril and me. "What do you suggest we do? Run? I might have been a small-town cop, but I know enough to realize that if those agents are doing their job, every exit is covered. We wouldn't get far. Gabe is right. It's out of our hands."

"Not if I can help it." I slammed the flat of my foot into the most vulnerable part of Jibril's body: his knee. With a yelp, he let go of my hands.

The apartment door strained under the pressure of someone's body or a battering ram. Wood began to splinter. They would be through the door in a second. I pocketed the metallic object Jibril gave me and reached for my Magnum. Michael grabbed my elbow before I could even pull the gun out. "That would be really stupid, Dee. You know that."

"Let go of me," I demanded, sizing Michael up for my knee trick.

Following my gaze, he said, "Don't even think about it. What do you think you're going to do with that gun anyway?" His smile was as tight as his grip on my elbow. "You're one tough woman, Deidre McMannus, but not even you could hold an entire battalion of FBI agents at bay with a measly six rounds from an ancient projectile weapon."

The door slammed open so hard the doorknob punched through the thin plaster wall. A black uniform stepped cautiously into the room. Bright yellow block letters spelled out FBI on his ball cap. A badge was printed on the tee shirt underneath his heavy leather jacket. Seeing me, with my fist in my pocket, the agent raised his assault rifle.

"Play it cool," Michael whispered to me. "We didn't do anything wrong."

"I didn't, that's for sure. What about you? What about him?" I jerked my head in the direction of Jibril, who had propped himself up on the chair and was rubbing his knee. "What have I been aiding and abetting this time?"

Two more uniforms gingerly stepped around the shattered doorway. As I stared down the barrel of a gun, my feet felt rooted to the spot. Sweat pricked under my arms. Michael let go of my elbow, and raised his hands.

"I'm a cop," Michael said calmly, as if his announcement of that fact would diffuse everything. "Take it easy."

More black-and yellow-clad men streamed in the door, like a horde of wasps, followed by uniformed police.

When I saw the police, I relaxed a little. With effort I let go of the Magnum, and put my hands up. As a uniform passed near me, I asked, "You boys got a warrant?"

He looked over his shoulder at the FBI, then walked away. The police moved about the apartment. I could hear doors popping open as they methodically checked the other rooms. Someone grabbed Jibril, shouting, "Get your hands behind your head. Down on the ground. Move it!"

"Don't push me, man, I'm already wounded," Jibril protested, glaring at me. He complied with the officer's demands. "Yeah. Don't you people need a warrant or something?"

An FBI agent frisked Michael and took his badge and gun.

"And you wanted to cooperate," I sneered at Michael. I slowly pulled the gun out butt first, ready to surrender it. So far, however, the cops and the agents were ignoring me. They concentrated their testosterone-hyped bullying on the men. I scanned the uniforms for a woman. Without one, I might be spared the humiliating process of being frisked until we reached wherever they intended to take us. With luck, I could secrete the mysterious object somewhere before then.

"Get down on the ground," the FBI agent growled, infuriated that Michael continued to stand there—blatantly disobeying his order.

"Not until I know what's this is all about," Michael

said, his tone perfectly reasonable. "I'm not going anywhere until I get a little explanation here."

"Yeah," I piped up, finding my voice. "What exactly are the charges? What's the Bureau's business here, anyway?"

"Conspiracy to commit terrorism," a uniformed cop explained, since the FBI agent's eyes were locked on Michael. "The Bureau is always called in on terrorist charges."

A cold fear settled in my stomach. Conspiracy to terrorism was the same damn charges they'd tried to pin on me. Conspiracy was an impossible rap to evade because hearsay was admissible in court. America has always hated terrorists. I knew from my days in the department that when terrorism got pinned on some poor sap, he was going down, even if it meant doctoring a little of the evidence. I looked at Michael and saw a shadow of Daniel's face flit through my mind. We were completely screwed.

I held my breath. The fluorescent yellow on black of the FBI uniforms burned into my eyes. The apartment was filled with movement. Somewhere behind me, a bookcase was overturned with a crash.

"Get down!" The agent raged. I saw his grip shift, readying to strike Michael with the butt of the rifle.

"No!" I switched the Magnum in my hand, and my feet suddenly carried me forward. Michael twisted at my sound. The agent's swing whizzed inches from his jaw. Anger flashed in Michael's eyes, and he pivoted with enhanced speed. In one fluid motion, he backhanded the agent. Still in the follow-through of the missed punch, the agent's face collided with Michael's fist with a crack.

Someone tackled me from behind. I felt my legs swept out from under me. The nubby carpeting softened the impact of my chin on the floor. My body went limp. I didn't resist as the gun was pried out of my numb fingers. Turning my head, I squeezed my eyes shut. I didn't want to see the rest. I could hear Michael's shouts of protest mingling with Daniel's ghostly cries.

New Jersey State Penitentiary
Feb. 12, 2076

Dee,

I know it's been a month or more, but my head got really ~~fucked~~ with after the Moral Officer got ahold of the last letter. Guess suggesting their office was full of crap wasn't the smartest thing I've ever done. You know me, though, huh? Bullheaded as ever.

All the same, I don't know how many more of these I'm going to get a chance to write. I've got to tell you, every day I'm more convinced we were set up. But, listen, don't get me wrong. I'm guilty as sin. You know, I heard you don't think so. I got this new cellmate in here who tells me in your last interview you claimed you still felt I still could be innocent somehow. I appreciate the sentiment. It's essentially true, you know. Problem is, I was holding the smoking gun—literally.

This is going to sound like the Morality Officer knocked something loose upstairs, but . . . I know I did it. I killed the Pope. I didn't want to, but I did it. They made me.

Dee, you're the only one I trust to really listen. I notice you haven't written back, but I'm sure you've got things on your mind. Maybe you're still working out what to say. I know how hard it was for me to start. But if what my cellmate said is true, then I know you haven't given up on me. So, try to understand what I'm about to tell you: it was Them.

They got inside my head, screwed with my emotions, got me all ~~fucked~~ up, and by the time I was standing in front of the Pope I hardly knew which end was up. You said I was changing. It was true. They were doing it to me. Sending their little signals through the LINK.

You know what this means, right? It means they did it, Dee. They changed lead to gold. You'd better watch yourself . . . watch anyone who's LINKed.

Daniel

CHAPTER 8

The coffee was stale and the room smelled of old cigarette smoke. I peeled the edges of the Styrofoam cup and lined the pieces up in a straight row on the marred table. The clock on the wall read two in the morning. A headache hovered on the edges of my consciousness, while the shadows on dirty gray walls haunted me. The FBI agent who was playing "good cop" did not look happy. He glanced over at the one-way glass and cleared his throat. "Maybe we should try this again?"

It wasn't really a question I was expected to respond to, so I continued peeling. The line of white pieces was getting longer. I imagined them as lifeboats abandoning the tepid coffee. The wood of the table looked like an enormous dark sea. The white pieces were tiny by comparison.

"How do you know Jibril Freshta?"

I glanced up at the agent's deceptively soft green eyes and sighed. "I told you already. I don't. Until now, I'd never even heard his last name."

"What were you doing at his apartment?" He looked as impatient with this process as I was. "It seems rather coincidental, then, wouldn't you agree, Ms. McMannus, that you were with a known Muslim radical and a possible member of the Malachim Nikamah, at the time?"

"Malachim? You mean Michael?"

The agent nodded. "I've been told his precinct's Internal Affairs Department has had a close watch on him since his transfer from Pennsylvania."

"Gee," I sneered, "I wonder who told you that."

"Don't be a wiseass, McMannus," bad cop said from where he leaned against the wall. It was Dorshak. For effect, he wore just his shirtsleeves. The black holster was a dark contrast to the perfectly pressed white oxford. He'd been showing me that gun for hours. Instead of being impressed with the battered .45, all I could think was he must have gotten a raise finally, after all this time. His shirt was so white that under the harsh light it almost blinded me. I recognized his haircut from last week's issue of *GQ*. Too bad he didn't have the looks to carry it off. It made him look half-finished, as though he had all the right parts, but none of them fit.

"So," I said, leaning back in the chair. I held up my bruised chin with more confidence than I felt. "You've had me followed ever since our phone conversation, haven't you, Ted?"

"I knew you couldn't stay away from Angelucci." Dorshak squinted. He crossed his arms in front of his barrel chest. He used his fists to give his biceps extra bulk. "I tried to warn you this would happen."

I laughed. "Oh, yeah. Thanks a lot. You're a true friend."

"Don't act like any of this is my fault, McMannus. You're the one with the history of consorting with terrorists and murderers." Dorshak's tone was indignant and he wagged his finger at me. "Why don't you try cooperating with the Bureau for once, and answer this guy's questions, huh?"

"Why don't you answer a question of mine, Ted? Why is the tech-theft case with Jordan Institute still open?"

"What?" Dorshak looked honestly baffled by my request. "Who?"

"It's the case Daniel and I were working on before he shot the Pope."

He shook his head from side to side. "I don't know anything about that case. If you think that has anything to do with what's happening now, well, then you've been listening to those conspiracy theorists too long, Dee."

I swallowed the desire to rise to Dorshak's bait. My

instincts told me Dorshak knew nothing about the Jordan Institute mystery. I glanced over at the FBI agent, who watched our exchange patiently. He had a slightly faraway look in his eyes. Most likely he was recording the conversation and transmitting it to the Bureau's local office. There a team of agents deciphered my every word and gesture and relayed back the appropriate response to the field agent.

"What was it you people wanted?" I positioned my face dead center of the eye where the fiber-optic camera was hardwired. I resisted the urge to wave.

"Freshta. How do you know Jibril Freshta?"

He was like a bloody robot. "I don't. How many times do I have to tell you? I don't know him."

"What were you doing at his apartment?"

I studied the table, hiding my pupils from a possible scan. He'd probably register the elevated heart rate, but there wasn't much I could do about that. I let the air in my lungs come out in a slow breath and shook my head.

"If you roll over on them, you can still save yourself," Dorshak growled. "But, as you should know, the antiterrorist act is pretty strict. Keep this attitude up, and you'll end up on death row. Like Danny."

"Of course," reminded the agent, "the Bureau can be lenient. If you cooperate, things will go easier on you."

The threats were almost verbatim from the last time I sat in this hard plastic seat. I shut my eyes. It seemed like a thousand years since I was on the other side of this table, and Danny and I would argue over who was going to get to be bad cop this time. He always insisted a woman made a better good cop. To which, I countered, woman as bad cop had pure shock value. Besides, I would remind him, his warm brogue would melt even the hardest heart.

The FBI agent was trying out his version of the "comforting, trust-me" look right now. It just didn't have Daniel's style.

"Come on, McMannus," Dorshak snarled. "You know how this works. The cop is the one we want. He's already under Internal Affairs' watch since his contact with the Malachim. All we need is a little more proof that he's antigovernment. You of all people should know hearsay is admissible evidence in antiterrorist cases."

"I resent that implication. Daniel was no terrorist." I shoved my fingers through the perfect line of Styrofoam lifeboats. One of them capsized. I swept the rest up into my fist.

"He shot the Pope in cold blood, even he's admitting that now." Dorshak gave me a pitying glance. "But, I forgot, you're not LINKed anymore. You don't have access to the interviews he's given lately. Your partner is way over the deep end, McMannus—way over. He actually claims the angels told him to do it. They . . . what was it he said . . . ? 'Guided his hand.' "

"Wha . . . ?" I thought I'd hardened myself to any assault on Danny's character over the last year, but Dorshak's words punctured my resolve. Danny never believed in the LINK-angels. He always said if they were a sign from God, the true God, why did they only appear to the affluent—those connected by expensive wetware? Daniel convinced me, Jesus was a man for the poor, the outcast. Why would God only talk to the rich? It seemed like a major change in policy.

I took a deep breath. Dorshak had to be mind-fucking me. "Right," I sneered. "And you've got a bridge to sell me."

"You don't have to believe me." Dorshak forced a thin smile. "It's a matter of public record. Why don't you get your pal Mouse to bootleg a copy of it sometime."

That stung. Of everything Dorshak tried, suggesting that I needed to rely on others for info really hurt. I stuffed the wads of Styrofoam I'd been crushing in my palm into my pocket.

The FBI agent looked at me with renewed interest. Forgetting his "good cop" character, he asked, "You know the Mouse?"

My fingers stroked the edges of the hard shell of the implant at my temple to ease my headache some.

"They're lovers," Dorshak answered for me. "Deidre sleeps with anyone."

"Anyone except you, Ted. How does it feel to be the only man the 'whore of Babylon' wouldn't touch with a ten-foot pole?"

"Pretty damn good," he sneered. Dorshak put his hands in his pockets, and rocked forward on the balls of his feet confidently. I only knew I got to him because of the slight flush rising from his collar. It was bright pink next to the starched white of his shirt. "At least I know I'm disease-free."

"Are you so sure?" I purred. "Well . . ." I made a show of carefully inspecting his new shirt and designer tie, ". . . maybe you did get enough of a raise to finally afford 'licensed help.' "

My head snapped to the side. The pain from the blow to my cheek lagged seconds behind. Dorshak's enhanced muscles had ahold of my suit-coat lapels before I realized I'd been hit. He dragged me out of my seat. The plastic chair crashed to the floor with a hollow sound. I used his own hyped-up momentum against him and brought up my knee.

With a strangled moan, Dorshak let go of me. He stumbled back against the solid oak table. The look in his tear-rimmed eyes made me step back.

I cursed. From his reaction, I realized I only managed to graze his crotch. "Next time I'll get ahold of them, Ted, and I won't let go."

A growl came from deep in Dorshak's throat. The FBI agent was on his feet and between us with his arms outstretched. "Cool down, Sergeant," the agent said, reprising his good cop role. "I'm going to have to ask you to step outside. Take some time out."

With a hand protectively over his balls, Dorshak retreated. "You won't live through the next time, bitch," he spat.

The FBI agent carefully righted the chair. Dusting off the seat, he gestured enticingly. "Are you okay?" he asked. The soft, green eyes filled with compassion. "Can I get you something." He glanced at my mutilated cup, and suggested, "More coffee perhaps?"

"No." I eyed the proximity of his gun. Deciding

against a federal offense, I slumped down into the cool curve of the chair with a defeated groan. "Thanks, I'm fine."

"We're all tired," he said with almost genuine emotion. He half sat, half leaned against the edge of the table. I could smell his cologne. It was spicy and exotic— not what I would have expected from him.

"It would be nice to go home." He rubbed the bridge of his nose between two fingers. "We're not asking for a lot from you, Ms. McMannus, just enough to convict Angelucci. If you help us, we might even be willing to forget how you pulled your gun on a federal agent."

"I guess I lost my mind," I admitted.

"Your response was understandable, even forgivable . . ." The unspoken "if" was heavy in his meaningful tone.

"You want me to do it again," I said mostly to myself, "and get burned again. You know, the last time I trusted one of your guys all I got was kicked in the teeth for it. I was promised anonymity in exchange for information about Danny." My eyes sought out his, and I jabbed my thumb angrily at my chest. "I was never supposed to see the witness stand, and instead, not only am I there, but I'm all over every LINK frequency from here to Kalamazoo."

His green eyes looked distant. I must have really gotten the home office in a buzz. I glanced at the clock, timing them. It took three full clicks before the agent spoke.

"The Bureau wanted to keeps its promise to you," he said slowly. "But Interpol claimed jurisdiction. When the case went to Christendom's courts, it was out of our hands."

"I know that." My tone was flat. I wasn't going to give him an inch. "I was there."

"I think you're putting your faith in the wrong people for the wrong reasons, Deidre. All we're asking from you is a little information. In fact, all you have to do is tell us what the three of you were doing at Freshta's apartment."

When I found myself reaching up to caress the receiver, I jerked my hand away. I suddenly remembered the strange object Jibril gave me. I dug in my pocket for it. Of course, I found nothing except lint and Styrofoam pieces. All my possessions were locked in a safe box as part of the arrest procedures.

"Looking for this?" The agent held the mysterious item up for me to see. It was a short and squat cylinder, no larger than the spent casing of a .45. Smooth and silver it gleamed seductively in the harsh light. "Can you tell me what it is?"

"No," I said truthfully. I had to hold on to my own hand to keep myself from rubbing the implant.

"It's a hematite bead." He dropped it on to the table.

"It's a what?" I asked, stunned.

"A bead, for a necklace or something." The agent dismissed it with a wave of his hand. "Take a look."

With numb fingers, I picked it up to examine it. On the top and bottom were holes for a string. I turned it over and over in my hands and prayed its true nature would be revealed. It was just as the agent said: a bead, nothing more.

"Where's the real item?" I tossed down the bead hard enough that it bounced. "What kind of idiot you take me for?"

The agent smiled. There was gloating around the edges of his curled lips. The good cop persona was slipping. "I'm not sure. Maybe you should tell me." Crossing his arms in front of his chest, he continued, "Tell me something, Deidre. If I had the 'real' item, why wouldn't I use it against you? Were you after a data chip? Something else?"

I looked at the bead and tried to remember what Jibril had handed me. I picked it up again and pressed it into my palm. The bead was cool, almost as cold and heavy as the dead receiver in my head.

"Do you have any idea why Jibril would set up a clandestine meeting to pass you something so useless?"

"Fuck," I breathed. "It was all for nothing."

"So it seems," the agent said with a smirk. He moved

around the table. His hard-heeled shoes clicked on the linoleum floor. "Now why don't you tell us what they wanted from you, and what you thought you were getting in exchange?"

I gripped the smooth bead tighter. Did Michael intend to set me up? It seemed likely. Jibril wouldn't even let go of my hand as the FBI broke down the door. All he would do was talk about the will of Allah. Yet if they intended to be caught, why were they surprised? And, why did Michael resist arrest? Was it just a show for me? To make me think it wasn't a setup? It didn't make any sense. Dorshak said they didn't want me, but Michael. Otherwise, I might've believed Michael double-crossed me. But, why would the FBI want me? I had no real political power to wield against Letourneau or anyone else for that matter. I was a celebrity, sure, but without the LINK, I was a nonplayer.

I still didn't trust this FBI agent enough to tell him anything. There was something deeper going on here, and I wasn't going to give an inch until I found out what. Besides, I had an old score to settle. Looking up at the agent, I slowly shook my head from side to side.

"Look"—the agent sounded exasperated—"you were duped. Not only that, but right now you're facing a pretty serious charge of resisting arrest. You owe these people nothing."

No, I thought silently, *but I still owe myself some dignity. Last time, I chose to save myself, and I've regretted it ever since.* Michael might still be in a position to bring Letourneau down if he could get out of this somehow. For Danny's sake, I had to give Michael that chance.

The agent tapped his finger impatiently on the wooden desk. "Maybe you don't understand why we want Angelucci so bad. Let me tell you something about him. Angelucci is a vigilante." The agent pressed. "He's trying to take the law into his own hands. You and I both know how dangerous that kind of behavior can be."

I nodded despite myself. As much as I had loved Danny, that was what he had become. When he shot the Pope, whatever his reasons, he acted above the law, and

I had had a responsibility to the truth. Daniel had changed, had kept the passion I loved, but lost the sensibility. Worse yet, I saw the passion turning into something angry, something that verged on uncontrollable. I could have kept it to myself, stayed silent, but that was a sin. The sin of omission. And having denied truth, how could I sleep at night?

"If you have any feelings of loyalty to this guy, it's misplaced." The agent frowned. He stared at the one-way glass, considering something. Leaning closer, he continued in a conspiratorial tone, "He has more dotted lines to antigovernment groups than . . . I don't know what. Angelucci has his fingers in all the radical groups: Hasidim, Muslims . . . possibly other heathens as well. Not to mention the liberal fringe like ACLU, human rights campaigners—which we know is a front for queers—and God knows what else. He and his pals, like Jibril Freshta, have been stirring the pot of dissension for the last year. They're gaining ground, too. If left to their own devices, they could bring back an era of secular presidents. Think about that, McMannus. Do you want the return to the kind of government that fostered the science that brought us the Medusa?"

In my mind's eye, I saw the result of science's most horrible creation—a frozen form that was once human, now a statue of glass, in a silent, but deafening, scream. "No," I whispered, my voice hoarse.

"I didn't think so," the agent said softly. "But that's what Angelucci wants: a world without a moral backbone. A world like our grandparents and parents suffered through, when drugs and violence were commonplace, when children were raised in schools where religion was outlawed, when the world had no common spiritual view. . . ."

I nodded, but knew that the agent talked only about those who were LINKed. Crime still ruled my universe. However, I couldn't deny that the majority of the population lived better than ever since the war, thanks to the programs of the new religious governments. Despite the restrictions, the government worked, which was more than could be said for its last incarnation.

"Angelucci is a menace. I thought you understood that, Ms. McMannus. You have a history of being more reasonable than the rest, more honorable, more concerned with the truth."

That's what I told myself every day since Daniel's conviction: the truth was more important than loyalty. I took my oath to serve and protect seriously during my days on the force. That, to me, was the distinction between an honest cop and a dishonest one. Though the system became tougher and tougher to support in good conscience, I held on to the tenet that truth and justice were at the core of it all. Believing was how I lived with myself.

What if the FBI agent was right about Michael? I didn't know that much about his motivations. If I hadn't guessed that he was a LINK-angel, he would never have told me. My head ached.

"The LINK." I clutched the bead to my heart. "He promised me the LINK."

The agent nodded encouragingly. "Illegal biotech is an international offense. As a decorated tech-cop, I would've thought you'd know better. What on earth would make you cross that line, Deidre?"

I shook my head. The feds had more enhancements than the average cop, how could he know what made me consider it? He'd never lived without the LINK, in the dark, surrounded by the silence of one's own thoughts.

"What did they want from you?" he asked.

"Michael wanted my help. . . ." Looking into the agent's eyes, I stopped. If I told the agent that I suspected that Michael was a LINK-angel, what then? If they were true to their bargain, I might be let off. But, what would happen to him?

Letourneau would never let this go to court. He would use the same influence that got Danny into Christendom court to stop this one. If Letourneau was the perpetrator behind the angel hoax, then he surely wouldn't want to have Michael busted for LINK-crimes, because that would implicate him.

"Your help with what?" the FBI agent probed. He inched closer to me.

I looked down at the silvery bead in my hand. Something was screwy with this scenario. The uselessness of the bead seemed a clear indication that Michael and Jibril had set me up. If Michael was in cahoots with the FBI, then why did the agent keep stressing that they wanted Michael, not me?

"Deidre, you were saying something." The agent stood next to me. His shadow eclipsed the artificial light. In the sudden darkness, I shivered.

There was no way to tell what was the right thing to do. I had to act on my gut feeling. The question was: Did I betray Michael like I had Danny? Could I live with myself if I made the same mistake again?

"No," I said out loud. "Find another informant."

Excerpt from the broadband Associated Press LINKS, March 3, 2076.

SATANISM CHARGED IN SENATE RACE

The California Senate race eclipsed the presidential campaign briefly today when the incumbent Reverend-Senator Cliff Jacobs (New Right Collation) denounced his opponent, Raven Starwater (Earth Powers Collective) as a Satanist.

"The 'Earth Powers Coop' are a bunch of hippie-freak Satanists who smear the sanctity of this High Office," said Jacobs before a supportive crowd. "If Ms. Starwater looked into her crystal ball, she'd see who's going to win this election: good always triumphs over evil."

In a press conference at Earth Powers headquarters in the Haight-Ashbury district of San Francisco, Reverend Starwater denied allegations that her organization has ever tolerated an unrecognized religious group, such as Satanists. For her own religious beliefs, she said, "My citizenship card is valid. The United States Government has validated the nature of my 'goodness.' The Reverend-Senator is not qualified to judge the validity of my religion." (hot-link here to entire speech by Rev. Starwater.)

Earth Powers is a cooperative of New Age spiritualists. The organization achieved governmental accreditation only last year, thanks in part to the controversial Taft-Pallis Act. Taft-Pallis guarantees accreditation to any religious group, regardless of numbers of members, which can prove a long history of practice in America or a belief in one God. The Act was ratified due to pressure from the American Indian Movement (AIM), the American Civil Liberties Union (ACLU), and the American Catholics.

Despite the Act's stated favoritism toward Original American rights, it was the Wiccans of Massachusetts who were the first to register under this Act, claiming their history of practice in America can be substantiated by the Salem witch trials. As more and more formally outlawed groups discover ways to prove a history of practice, the Act has fallen under harsh criticism. Presidential candidate Etienne Letourneau (New Right) has vowed to find a way to "strike a blow against this regressive Act and make America safe from the lunatic fringe."

CHAPTER 9

The agent shook his fist in my face and yelled something threatening. At least, I assumed it was belligerent by the way his reddened face contorted. I should've heard shouting, but instead a melodic, disembodied voice seemed to echo: *By an act of faith, it is done.*

Stars of light appeared in my peripheral vision. Sound filled my ears, like a thousand voices talking at once. I thought I was about to pass out, so I waited for everything to fade. Instead of fading, suddenly things became super-focused. The room seemed brighter. The sensation was much as if I'd just removed sunglasses.

A digital time readout blinked into existence in the upper right-hand edge of my vision. To the left a visual, radio, data, and subvocal frequencies monitor winked. I could feel the pulse of the city again. Weather information appeared at a thought. The satellite traffic grids from six different cities spiraled into view. I flipped manically through all 327 video and entertainment bands. Light-headed with the bombardment of sensations, I gripped the edge of the chair.

Superimposed over the vision of the interrogation room, the words *Urgent Message* flashed. Atrophied mental muscles took over, and with a thought I tripped the go-ahead response.

Dee, it's me, Mouse's page overwhelmed my senses. I had to shut my eyes to get rid of the nauseating effect. The page streaked down a busy Cairo street on in-line skates, weaving around mixed traffic of cars, motorcycles, and camels. Dust flew everywhere. He looked sky-ward, as though my eyes were a floating camera. *You just surfaced like a fucking submarine. No, man, more like a goddamned armored U-boat . . . and the LINK is the Lusitania. You rock, girl.* Turning serious, he added, *"What's going on? Are you okay? A LINK break like yours is going to make some waves, if you know what I mean.*

With one part of my consciousness, I frantically began to sever newly formed connections to the LINK. The readouts vanished at my command. Sparing one thin ten-dril, I sent a real-time reply command to Mouse's house.

I opened my eyes and focused on the agent. He leaned over me, his fists pressed hard against the tabletop. "Do you understand what I'm saying to you?" he asked. "This kind of grandstanding will get you nowhere. Don't you understand? Angelucci and his ilk are dangerous."

I breathed a sigh of relief. The agent appeared un-aware that I was now fully LINKed. I opened my palm, and stared at the bead. A biochemical transfusion? Was it possible Jibril discovered a way to reopen LINK con-nections through skin contact?

"Maybe you don't grasp the seriousness of this situa-tion, Ms. McMannus?" the agent was saying. "If you don't cooperate, we're going to have to book you as an accomplice to terrorism."

Dee? A small, floating window opened up. Mouse's face was tight with concern. *Sorry it took so long to get back to you, but you're hard to trace. My page tells me that a second ago you were everywhere. But, now . . . poof!* He shrugged, *Anyway, thanks for leaving the line open, otherwise, I never would've found you.*

You're welcome. I switched to subvocal. *Michael Angelucci and I were picked up by the FBI. Have you heard?*

Mouse nodded. *Terrorism again?* His mouth smiled broadly, but his eyes looked worried. *Won't you ever learn?*

The agent rapped hard on the table. "Are you lis-tening to me?"

"You were threatening me with prison, I believe." I smiled sarcastically at the agent. "Do go on."

In the corner, Mouse's face scrunched up. *Ouch. I heard that. Do you think that was wise? The Feebs have got a serious case against you.*

How do you know what kind of case they have against me, Mouse?

"You're damn right you're going to do time. I thought you were reasonable, McMannus." The agent threw up his hands.

Mouse shrugged. *It's obvious you're in trouble, that's all. Hey, I did that search on this Michael guy, and let me tell you, he's no angel.*

Michael's not an angel anymore, you mean, I reminded Mouse. *Anyway, maybe the terrorists are the good guys this time.*

What are you talking about? Mouse frowned, drawing his eyebrows together.

I don't have time to explain right now. Mouse, when was the last time you browned out New York?

The Mouse's eyes went wide; he shook his head. *You're crazy. I can't do that again so soon. Besides, I'm sure they've got a tighter lock-down on the codes.*

I just want one city block. Any kind of distraction will do, really. Maybe you could tweak Traffic Control this time. I tried to put a smile into my electronic voice. *I thought you could do anything. Rule the world, you said. Are you going to disappoint me?*

My page said that, not me. Anyway, forget it. Mouse's head bobbed back and forth more frantically now. *Even if I was able to do it, you'd still be surrounded by armed cops, half of them ex-military. Besides, you can't afford that kind of thing. Remember, I saw your credit counter. I like you a lot, Dee, but not this much. No way. No. Way.*

The door flew open and crashed against the wall. In surprise, I pushed the chair away from the table. Dorshak rushed in and headed toward me.

"She's got a signal coming in, you stupid fuck," he yelled over his shoulder to the FBI agent. "Shut her down! Shut her down!"

Mouse!

Dorshak's targeting computer presumed I'd stand up, which was a fairly reasonable assumption. But instead, I dived under the table, and his arms grasped the empty space. I heard the chair catch his knees. Unable to stop, both of them slid into the wall with a crash.

From under the table, I saw the perfectly cuffed pant-legs of the FBI agent as he danced back and forth, unable to decide which way to go. I crawled toward the open door. The sound of the chair being tossed aside with a curse alerted me that Dorshak was hot on my heels.

Static assaulted my senses. The connection to Mouse was severed by some jamming device. Old reflexes kicked in, and I switched to the emergency police frequency.

Situation in progress in detention level three. Request backup immediately. It was Dorshak.

Belay that order. FBI in control of the situation. We have jurisdiction on all terrorist cases. We assume full responsibility for the situation, I sent via a satellite feed in Washington, DC. It was an illegal and obvious hack, but I didn't have time to wrestle up an official tag before Dorshak grabbed my ankle.

"Try to belay this," Dorshak hissed between clenched teeth. As he yanked me back, I wrapped my arms around a table leg and hugged it close.

Just then, the lights went out.

NY Times Opinion Page/Letters to the Editor; April 7, 2076

OPPOSITION TO LETOURNEAU

What bothers me the most about the New Right's presidential candidate Etienne Letourneau is that I've never met the man. Certainly, I've been present at his on-line rallies and seen his avatar debate Rabbi-Senator Grey on the entertainment band. I've even been on his virtual tour of the "Letourneau Future."

Yet, I've never seen the candidate in real time. Rabbi-Senator Grey hails from New York, and I've seen him talk, real-time, at the Temple Headquarters. I shook his hand. It brought me back to a time, before the war, when candidates were expected to go out and meet the people.

Letourneau sits on high, in his secluded Colorado mountain retreat, surrounded by clean air, and hand-picked disciples. Some of us might find that lifestyle enviable, but it's a sham. He lives only through the LINK, not on the real streets of America. Letourneau's "Future Tour," as slick and appealing as it may be, seems to completely ignore real-time problems—like wire-addiction, crime, and those hundreds of people who still live without the LINK due to poverty or religious persecution.

Rabbi-Senator Grey has a working plan to bring the LINK's wealth to real-time people. Because of this he seems cynical, dark, and negative, but, in my opinion, he's just the opposite. What Rabbi-Senator Grey represents is a positive change for real America, not more promises of entertainment bands for the apathetic and private financial bands for the rich.

—Mrs. Isaac Stone, New York

GRAY IS GREY

The Rabbi-Senator Grey is like a dark cloud rolling over America. His doom-saying politics are a drag on the spirits of the American people. What the world needs is a positive brilliance like Letourneau. The New Right is both New and Right. Letourneau has his finger on the pulse of this country. He's incredibly insightful into problems that the average American faces: the downward spiral of "Free Credits" in the World Market, which is vital to American economic survival; the need for faster processors and more frequencies for the continuing health of the entertainment band—still America's number one export industry; and a stronger taxation on outside "hits" so we can get appropriate payment for LINK-users outside of this country.

The Rabbi-Senator's insistence that we put a precedence on real-time problems shows how completely out of touch this candidate is with the needs of the average American. There are only 14 percent of Americans who are without LINK privilege, and most of those are simply too lazy or stubborn to convert to a real religion. Since Taft-Pallis, these degenerates only have to convert to some New Age religion to have full access to the LINK: why don't they just get off their butts and do it? The rest of us, who are productive and spiritual citizens, shouldn't have to shoulder the burden of this "intellectual elite" who already have the support of the ACLU and other fringe organizations.

Letourneau represents a step forward for decent, productive Americans. Bleeding heart liberals like Rabbi-Senator Grey will only bleed America dry. Let Letourneau bring money into American markets!

—Mr. David Boxeth, Brooklyn

CHAPTER 10

"What on Earth?" Dorshak cursed in the darkness. I wiggled experimentally in his iron grip. Despite the distraction, his hold remained firm.

The emergency police frequency erupted with noise. *There's been a massive power failure in Traffic Control grid numbers forty-five, sixty-seven. . . . Unconfirmed LINK-hack into police band . . . Power outage in holding cell locks . . . Get someone on that backup generator, for Chrissake! . . . We've got a riot down here, people. I can't stop them . . .* The dispatcher became overloaded. I switched off.

I flailed the pointed heel of my shoe in the direction of Dorshak's face. I battered at him blindly, until something soft gave way under my constant barrage. Dorshak howled in pain. I pulled my foot away, but the shoe stayed behind. Not sparing the time to imagine what had happened, I switched my concentration to navigating a way out from under the table. I scooted along on my knees, sliding on the linoleum clumsily. The rungs of the plastic chairs hampered my way. I shoved at them, sending toppled chairs skittering about. Their crashes added to the confused shouts of the FBI agent. Finally, my fingers closed around the far end of the table. I pulled myself up from my hands and knees.

The glow of the exit sign drew me like a beacon. Out of the corner of my eye, I could see the form of the FBI agent. We each took a step toward the door. I stopped. The agent advanced closer to the door. Behind me I could hear Dorshak moaning, his pain sharpened into anger. His curses became more specific about what he would do to me if he got his hands on me again. I doubted it would take more than a few seconds for Dorshak to translate words to action.

The agent twitched, as though weighing out a course of action. I grabbed ahold of one of the chairs. Before I could bring the chair around, the agent drew his gun. Red glowed in the pupil of his right eye as the targeting computer came on-line. Despite the danger, I had to laugh. Only a Feeb would need a computer's sights at this close a range.

As if to remind me of the real threat he posed, the agent's finger tightened noticeably on the trigger. "You know what they say, right?" His voice trembled with excitement. "The only good traitor is a dead traitor."

That wasn't what I expected from my green-eyed "good cop," and I told him so. "Aren't you supposed to ask me to surrender before you shoot?"

"Who's to say I didn't?" His lips stretched into a thin smile. "Dorshak?"

Dorshak just moaned, not making a good case either for or against me.

"What about our viewing audience at home?" I used the chair to gesture in the direction of his camera eye. "Don't they have something to say about this little first-degree murder?"

"Hmmmmm." He pretended to consider my words carefully, then said, "Golly, but they seem to have been blanked out like the rest of the precinct. I guess they'll have no choice but to believe my report."

"Jesus. You're sick." I grimaced.

The agent snarled, and I had a sinking feeling that quip was going to be the last one I'd ever make. Not clever enough to die for, I thought as I pivoted in a vain attempt to swing the chair around to block the blast. I knew it was useless—plastic wasn't much protection against a gun.

My peripheral vision registered the motion of the door opening. I watched the agent's eyes leave me for a sec-

ond. Wasting no time, I charged him. I heard the click of
the trigger being pulled, but somehow his gun misfired. I
propelled the chair at him with all my force. Chair and
agent clattered against the wall.

Pushing past them, I ran right into someone's arms. I
thrashed against the human fortress that held me, ready
to kick or bite my way out.

"It's me, Deidre." A smooth baritone tickled my
ear. "Michael."

"How did you find me? Wait. Tell me later. We've
got to get out of here . . . Dorshak, the agent, maybe
others . . ." My words came out in a breathless, incoherent jumble. "Go, go, go!"

It was too late. Behind us, the one-way mirror shattered. I turned in time to see muted red light glinting
on the explosion of glass. A dark form leapt through,
carrying the glass around her like a deadly aura. She
landed on the table with a thud. The glass slivers made
a plink-plunk as they fell away from her, seemingly ruled
by a gravity that she defied. She barely slowed her stride.
It was another FBI agent. I could tell by the red light
coming from her left eye: the targeting computer.

Michael pushed me behind him. On impulse, I accessed the LINK. The world fell away around me in a
starburst of light. At the speed of thought, I lassoed the
FBI frequency and hacked my way in. A wall of ones
and zeros scrolled passed my vision, stretching as far as
I could see in every direction. The wall seemed to ripple
as the numbers flashed through. I searched through the
binary for the key. Reaching into the tangle, I grabbed
hold of a back door and squeezed myself through.

Suddenly, my perspective switched. I rode piggyback
behind the charging agent's infrared filtered vision. Michael stood by the door, or, at least, what I assumed was
he. The readout was confusing. A bright light glowed at
the center of Michael's chest. It was like a hot coal,
almost white against the ghostly pale blue of the rest of
his body. The light was the size of a pinprick, but the
heat it radiated spread out in two massive triangular

shapes. Their apexes met at the core, and spread out like a bow tie.

"What the . . . ?" I heard the agent say from my vantage point on the LINK. She was almost on top of Michael. I began to panic. My mind sent out a single thought: *Stop!*

Enhanced muscles spasmed as the LINK connection between mind and body was severed. I was propelled back into my own consciousness with an almost physical snap.

"Grk," was the most intelligible sound that came from the mouth of the advancing agent. I shook my head to clear it and saw the agent stumble mid-stride. She plummeted facedown onto the floor. Dorshak and the FBI agent who had interrogated me were also silent.

I was stunned. That wasn't how the LINK was supposed to operate. Normally, it took several seconds, an eternity LINK-time, to connect two or three individuals to one agreed-upon frequency. Even cops and FBI agents usually operated on separate bands, while maintaining only a loose connection to the official channel. Not to mention the fact that my command was more of a desperate request than any real code. If something so simple as "stop" could do this kind of damage, I certainly wouldn't have been the first fugitive to use it.

"Did I kill them?" I whispered. I didn't trust my voice in the eerie silence.

Michael shrugged. He seemed uninterested, as if he were used to federal agents dropping like flies every time he entered a room. "Doubtful."

I looked to the fallen agent. Her eyes had rolled up into her head, and a string of drool escaped from her trembling lips. Her hands made useless grasping motions at the air. Breath came in ragged spurts, but at least she seemed to be taking air in on her own. Before I could get too close to the still-quivering agent, Michael laid a hand on my shoulder. "What have I done?" I murmured, horrified. "We can't just leave them here like this. They could die."

"They could live." Michael's voice was quiet.

"I can't take that kind of risk with people's lives."

"I understand. Call for an ambulance." He sighed. "But while we run, eh? Every second is costly."

I nodded. I patched into the emergency police frequency and sent out a code thirty-eight. I logged off before the dispatcher could capture my ID. When I returned my attention to the present, Michael was crouched over Dorshak. During the same blast that downed the agents, Dorshak slumped against the floor. Most of his body was still hidden by Michael or the table, but I could see his face.

No one would have ever mistaken Dorshak for a handsome man, but now his features took on a frightening cast. His face was covered in blood and gore. An eyelid drooped unnaturally over a damaged cornea. My heel had punctured his eyeball. Bile rose in my throat. I had seen violence in the line of duty before, but never anything this gruesome. "Oh, Ted."

Michael grasped Dorshak's trembling arm. Michael held Dorshak's wrist stiffly away from his side to expose the holster.

"What are you doing? Leave it," I heard myself say. "It's an old .45. He doesn't even have laser sights on it."

With his other hand, Michael quickly removed the gun. Then, unceremoniously, he released his grip, and Dorshak's arm fell to the floor like a deadweight. "We need a weapon, and the antique is the least likely to have a homing device. Your compassion is notable, Deidre, but there's no reason to be foolish."

Tucking the .45 into his belt, he said, "We've wasted enough time. Let's go."

I wanted to protest, engage in a philosophical discussion about compassion, but he was right. I grumbled a barely civil, "Fine."

I hadn't moved since downing the agents, so I took the remaining steps that separated me from the door. It opened to chaos. In the hallway, a leather-clad punk sprinted past, nearly knocking me backward. Uniforms followed close on his heels. "No good," I whispered, and shut the door. "Can't go that way."

I turned around and leaned my back gingerly against the door. I took a deep breath and tried to think. An agent quivered at my feet and Dorshak's dead eye seemed to stare at me. Tearing my gaze away, I looked up at the gaping hole in the mirror. The jagged edges formed an angry cavern of darkness.

Michael stared at me anxiously. I watched him track my gaze. "Through there? You know a way out through there?"

"Maybe," I murmured. Dorshak lay just under the window.

"Well, come on then," Michael insisted. Stepping over a chair, he made his way to the mirror. Glass crunched under his boots. Pulling the cuff of his leather jacket tight, Michael swept the remaining glass from the mirror's base. Glittering shards rained down on Dorshak, but he never flinched.

I did.

"I'm barefoot," I said, unable to drag my eyes away from Dorshak. My voice sounded distant and hollow in my ears. "I can't . . ."

Michael laughed unkindly. "A second ago you were fighting tooth and nail, now you're worried about your feet?"

I swallowed my disgust. I didn't want to say what was on my mind—how horrified I was at the terrible ease with which I destroyed the minds of the FBI agents, or how I couldn't stomach the idea of stepping over the cadaverous, blinded Dorshak. Instead, I just stared at Michael and said, "You're the one in a hurry. Cut feet will slow me down."

Reaching under the table, Michael found my bloody shoe. "Here."

I pursed my lips.

"Deidre," Michael insisted in a low voice, almost a growl. His face was hidden in the shadows, but the gray of his eyes caught the light. The hard lines of Michael's face, which I'd been so attracted to, looked menacing now. I wondered if I'd made the right choice, after all.

"I made a deal with the devil to bring these lights

down," Michael continued. "Don't make my sacrifice meaningless. Let's get out of here while we still can."

I grabbed the shoe. Wedging it on, I felt a sticky wetness curl around my toes. I was grateful for the darkness as I hauled myself into the maw of the anteroom. I slid onto a table headfirst and banged my already bruised chin.

"You know," I said loudly. Finding the edge of the table with my fingers, I pulled my legs around and felt for the floor. "I don't know what you're talking about sacrifice for. Mouse gets credit for this brownout, so don't go attaching your sig. file to it just yet."

I had just stumbled onto the floor, when I heard Michael vault easily onto the tabletop. He landed with a soft sound that belied his obvious mass. A quip about how much I despised his cyberware advantage died on my lips as I suddenly remembered the strange infrared I'd gotten from the FBI agent's vantage point. That image was nothing like the normal readout on a cyborg. Even the best shadow-ops hardware could only reduce body temperature a few degrees. Michael's body appeared as cold as the rest of the room, all except that strange bright center.

"You nuclear-powered, big guy?" I asked quietly.

I heard the sound of leather against leather as Michael moved around the small room.

"I found the door," he announced in lieu of a response.

There was a loud popping sound as Michael forced the lock. The hallway was illuminated by a thin string of battery-operated lights.

"If we get out of here, you'll tell me exactly what you are, Michael."

"If we stand here arguing about it, that isn't going to happen, now is it?"

Twisting my mouth into a grimace I hoped he could see, I pushed past him. "Follow me."

We were lucky that the door Michael found opened into a back hallway. Despite the evidence of Dorshak's raise, it seemed the police department never got that remodeling money they'd been begging for since my days on the force. It took me three seconds to remember the layout. I'd be more surprised at my ability for recall, if it wasn't for the fact I spent most of my dream time still walking these halls.

"This way," I told Michael. I slipped off my shoes and took off at a run. My pounding strides made a sharp slapping sound on the concrete floor. Over my shoulder, I shouted, "Let's take this deeper into the station. It should be deserted, what with most people trying to get out. Plus, it will give me a second to hunt up some files. From there, I want to find . . ."

The backup generator interrupted me. The machine groaned deep within the station walls. The lights flickered, then sprang back to life. In the brilliant electric flash, someone appeared in my path. I instantly recognized his coppery, shoulder-length hair and handsome, arrogant features. He still wore the Armani suit from this morning's escapade at the restaurant. A tiny dab of mustard on his lapel was the only sign of his scuffle with Michael. Otherwise, he looked impeccable.

"Morningstar." I slid to a stop. "Where the hell did you come from?"

"Exactly," he murmured with a laugh. It was a dry, feathery sound, decidedly unpleasant. Turning to Michael, he said, "You squandered the opportunity I gave you, Michael. I hope you don't think that nullifies our deal."

"He's the one you made a deal with?" I jabbed my thumb in the direction of Morningstar's chest. Michael didn't acknowledge me, but I could tell by the fierce way he stared at Morningstar that it was true. "Oh, Michael."

Now I understood. It was no wonder Michael had been acting emotionally closed off. He'd gone back to the "family." I only prayed, for Michael's sake, his deal didn't involve another job with the Mafia.

Though his expression was impassive, Michael's eyes searched Morningstar's face, "As long as Jibril is free."

"He proved much more decisive than you, dearest

brother, albeit not as much of a team player." Morningstar smirked. With a dismissive wave of his hand, he added, "Jibril has flown the coop. He's long gone."

Michael's jaw flexed. "Don't call me that."

"What? 'Brother'? We're made from the same stuff, Michael. You can hardly deny that."

I felt absent from this conversation, almost invisible, yet totally absorbed, just as I had at the restaurant. Michael and Morningstar dominated whatever space they occupied. It was as though the sheer power of their personalities muffled the very fabric of the universe.

I made my living noticing things other people didn't, but I never even heard the cops approaching until they were right in front of me. Even then, they had to shout in order to get my attention.

"You there!"

I jumped at the sound. Two plainclothes stood at the end of the hall. Their standard-issue guns already drawn, they stood like partners who'd been together for a long time. The older one stayed slightly behind and a little to the left, watching their backs, yet ready to cover the front.

Though they weren't in uniform, they might as well have been. They wore similar suits in that same rumpled cop way so many longtime detectives had. I didn't know their names, but I knew these guys. Even their crew cuts were identical.

Raising my hands, I put on a charming smile. "Hey, boys . . ." A sudden wind rushed past me. The gale ruffled my blouse and tugged at my hair. Behind me, the emergency lights blew out one by one. Glass showered down, flying toward the detectives. They raised their hands trying to ward off the shattered bulbs.

The instant their guns pointed away from me, I was ready to run. I turned around just in time to see Michael and Morningstar draw their weapons. Michael grabbed for the battered .45 with his right hand, as Morningstar reached for his weapon with his left. Their arms unfurled in perfect unison. They looked like deadly mirror images.

"No!" I screamed.

Explosions ripped through the tiny corridor. Searing heat pierced my shoulder, followed by a scorching pain that seemed to illuminate every nerve ending. Spun around by the momentum of the bullet, I bounced clumsily against the wall. Darkness tickled the edge of my vision. I groped at the wall and fought to remain standing. I clutched my shoulder, trying to staunch the blood flow.

Michael's arms were on my waist, supporting me.

"You've been shot," he whispered.

I pressed my lips together. The silence of the hallway rang in my ears. I turned my head, keeping my cheek to the cool plaster surface of the wall. The two detectives lay on the floor; neither of them moved or made any sound. The dark blue of their suits looked black against the gray tiles. My face contorted to a grimace as I noticed their bodies were sprawled at awkward angles. There was no blood.

"No blood?" I repeated out loud, my voice a harsh whisper. "No blood?"

"Untimely heart attack," Morningstar said, as though pleased.

"You bastard," I murmured, for somehow I sensed Morningstar was to blame for their "heart attacks."

Michael lifted me off my feet and took me into his arms. I groaned as he pried me away from the wall. The steady coolness of the plaster had been my anchor. Without it, I felt dizzy and, seeing the trail of gore I left behind, my stomach lurched again.

Wrapping his arms around me, Michael put a hand over mine where I pressed my shoulder. The coolness of his flesh was comforting and he added needed pressure to the wound. I laid my head against his chest and, despite myself, snuggled deeper into his embrace. Remembering the infrared, I hoped all the heat from the center of his body was enough to keep me from going into shock.

"Deidre?" Michael said softly, rousing me. "Can you tell us how to get out of here?"

I forced my lips into a sneer. I didn't want to help

them. Michael was no better than his Mafioso brother to let those detectives die. "Could have talked our way out."

"It's already done." He glanced over his shoulder at the smirking Morningstar. "The point is moot. If I have anything to say about it, they'll live. You might not. Tell us how to get out of here."

I shook my head.

"Oh, for fuck's sake. Leave her," Morningstar said. "We don't need her to get out of here. You don't need her."

"Deidre," Michael's voice cut through the fog in which my mind floated. His eyes drew me in, holding me firm. His gaze glowed with a deep, fearsome fire that seemed to reach out and physically warm me. Enveloped in heat, I floated, tied to reality only by those unearthly gray eyes. The cops survived. Somehow I knew what Michael said was true.

"Locker room," I said finally, my confidence in Michael renewed. "Through the office to the locker room. It leads to a parking lot. But, I wanted . . . I wanted to get files . . . Jordan . . ."

"There's no time." Michael's breath tickled at my ear, and I shivered.

"Very nice," Morningstar said warmly, as Michael started down the hall. "I feel you stepping just that much closer to me, dear brother."

"It was necessary," Michael said.

"It's also distinctly against the rules. And, here I thought you were so very 'by the book.' After all, you're always so careful to use doors and cars and all these earthly crutches. WE could just leave, you know. Speed would save her."

"I will not cheat, simply because it is easier. That's your way, not mine."

"Is it?" Morningstar said. "You're willing to ask me for a miracle you won't do for yourself. How is that different—besides being more cowardly?"

Michael said nothing as they walked on. Each step he took jarred me painfully where I was cradled against his shoulders. I shut my eyes. Fighting to remain conscious, I concentrated on the sound of their voices. I could hear the click of Morningstar's steps fall into rhythm with Michael's.

"You have forgotten the rules, haven't you?" Morningstar's voice was swelled with glee. "Or are you willfully ignoring them?"

Michael's grip tightened around my shoulders. He said nothing for a long moment. I must have drifted out of consciousness because the next thing I knew Michael was trying to rouse me. "Deidre?"

I opened my eyes to look around. Michael had brought me as far as the main hub of the station. People ran around us as if we were invisible. The room was a tangle of desks and chairs. Half-eaten sandwiches littered several tabletops. Every desk's monitor blinked in protest of the power outage. A hiss came from the main precinct hologram, and it flickered unsteadily. Hundreds of red dots littered the surface of the map, each indicating a reported crime in process.

The wide glass of the captain's central office reflected the chaos. Beside me, I heard Morningstar let out a satisfied sigh. "Beautiful."

"Behind the captain's area, there's a door," I said. "It leads to the locker room, from there you can get to the parking lot. But . . . there are security cameras . . . automated checkpoints . . . all these cops, surely one of them will stop us. . . ."

"Don't worry about that right now, Deidre," Michael said. "We'll take care of that."

"We?" Though I couldn't see his face, I could hear the smile in Morningstar's voice.

Michael grunted in response. He started toward the door, without another word. My head started spinning with the motion. I focused on the sight of my own shoulder. My fingers and Michael's were entwined. Blood outlined each digit of my hand, filling in the crevasses of wrinkled skin. Michael's hand was smoother than mine. I might have been beginning to hallucinate, but I swore the blood seemed reluctant to blot his perfection. Where my hand was blackened by the flow, his appeared nearly spotless.

I heard a door spring open. "After you, my dear Alphonse," Morningstar said.

Wordlessly, Michael descended the stairs. I reached up with my other hand and grabbed a fistful of Michael's jacket. I squeezed it at each step. It didn't replace a bullet to bite, but it helped.

"Don't get too familiar, Morningstar," Michael commanded. "You're mistaken if you think I trust you for a moment. For all I know, you set this whole thing up."

"Why would I do that?" Morningstar asked.

"To hurt Deidre. To separate Jibril and me. To weasel me into a position where I would ask for your help. Who knows? Maybe all this is just to aid Letourneau. He is one of yours, isn't he?"

"That would make things easier for you, wouldn't it, Captain?" Morningstar said. His voice had a seriousness in it I hadn't heard before.

Michael said nothing. The pounding of his steps was the only response he gave. The sharp echo in the narrow staircase sounded like a hammer. Each ringing blow felt like someone was driving a hot spike through my shoulder. My vision blurred from tears of pain. I held on to Michael's jacket, swaying on the fringe of consciousness.

"What if I told you Letourneau had nothing to do with me?" Morningstar said, when Michael didn't respond. "Maybe all of this is part of the plan. Did you ever consider that? What if you and I are still just puppets? It wasn't we who tasted the fruit of knowledge. It wasn't we They made in Their image."

"Your jealousy is so apparent, Morningstar." Michael's voice was a fierce growl in my ear. "You will not corrupt me."

Morningstar laughed wickedly. We had reached the bottom of the stairs, and Michael stood in front of the door. He tried to use the hand that held my legs to work the knob. His grip shifted me awkwardly; I cried out in painful protest.

"Allow me." Morningstar laughed again. This time the

sound was soft, but it was still as mocking. I heard the latch click and felt a cool breeze rush in. "As for your corruption, my dear, dear Captain, it's not up to me. It's you who will decide if the flesh will corrupt the spirit or make it stronger."

Michael stood in the doorway. His breath came in sharply. "Decide?"

"Yes. Freewill, Michael. It comes with the territory. I tried to warn you earlier. Spirit united with flesh, it seems, breeds it . . . like a disease. For once in your miserable existence, the choice is yours. You could make a mistake. Perhaps you already have."

"No," he whispered, still not moving.

"Yes," Morningstar said firmly. A small chuckle escaped his lips, "An interesting dilemma, isn't it? Your light has certainly shone brighter; will your darkness eclipse even mine?"

"You lie," Michael snarled.

"Sometimes Truth can be the greatest of Adversaries."

"No!" Michael shouted.

A strange sound tickled the edges of my consciousness. It reminded me of a sunny day, when my mother would hang the clothes out to dry. Eion and I would run between the sheets that flapped in the wind.

Darkness swallowed my vision; I felt myself floating away. From a distance, I heard a voice say: *Forgive me, Father. . . .*

LAW Chat, on the legal bandwidth of the LINK, October 12, 2075

KMarshall@LINK.com

"I'm from the District Attorney's Office in New York. I'm looking for advice on a very unusual situation that we've got here. A couple of our detectives actually put their hands on hard evidence linking a power reroute hack on the New York node to a perp code-named the Mouse. They nabbed him real-time here in New York. The case against him is pretty solid. That's not the problem.

"My problem is with his AI. As strange as it may seem, there don't seem to be any precedents on the books about the culpability of an AI in LINK crime. Mouse's attorney wants to make the case that since the AI did the crime, the AI should do the time. Any advice?"

SZien@LINK.com

"First of all, the AI can't do the time. There's no way to bind a free agent like an AI. The only solution would be to deactivate it, which would be tantamount to a death sentence. For a power boost that seems a little excessive, don't you think?"

AThomas@vatican.va

"If I may interject? There aren't that many true, operational AIs out there. Mouse's page and the Dragon of the East, the two notable exceptions. Still, there's no way to prove that the AI, even Mouse's AI, is truly responsible for its actions and not behaving according to some deeply programmed code.

"The Vatican policy is that an AI is similar to a soulless golem or an elemental [See the vatican.va file AI7-23.] under complete control of the wire-wizard. The wizard is ultimately responsible for all of the AI's actions."

SZien@LINK.com

"I am pleasantly surprised, (although I should not be, I suppose), to find my esteemed colleague at the Vatican familiar with the Jewish concept of a golem. Likewise, I agree with the bulk of his statement. There simply is no way of telling if Mouse's page or The Dragon of the East aren't just extremely detailed programs that are operating completely at the will of their makers, even if they appear to operate independently."

NIPetronenov@mousenet.com

"Russia, my proudly atheist country, runs almost completely via mouse.net. We recognize Mouse's Page as a full citizen and grant him all according rights, including that of asylum, which, I must inform you, he is exercising at this moment. Ms. Marshall, I suggest we continue this discussion on a private band."

CHAPTER 11

"Forgive me, Father, for intruding at such an early hour," a voice said as I opened my eyes a crack. Morning sun filtered through stained glass. Deep reds glowed in the tunic of the mosaic: Christ the Shepherd. Black lead outlined a clear piece of glass representing a halo. Unadulterated sunlight shone through it, contrasting the surrounding browns and blues. The lamb draped over Christ's rounded shoulders rested its head under the crook of Christ's jaw.

Like the lamb, I was being carried. My head was nestled against smooth, cool skin. The flesh was almost as cold as the air in the drafty cathedral. I looked around dreamily. Speckles of sunlight did their best to warm the wood of the pews, but the church felt distant and as empty as a tomb to me.

This is no place for refuge anymore. Not for my soul, not for my body. Surely the police will find us here, I tried to say, but my voice was too weak. All that came out was a helpless-sounding croak. I barely recognized it as my own voice. Cradled like a fragile doll, I tried to move. My body felt too heavy to lift. My left arm swung uselessly at my side. A heavy pain thundered in my shoulder.

"Shhhh," a voice cautioned. "Save your strength." His warm breath tickled my cheek. I could feel strands of his hair, feather-light against my nose. The sensation distracted me from the pain. I shut my eyes and held on to the softer feeling.

"I'm just vesting for Matins," a different, but familiar voice responded. "You'll have to wait, my son. I can't let you in. The church isn't ready."

"Hagia Sophia. She is always here, is She not? Besides, your sign claims twenty-four-hour service. I need your service now. I can't wait fifteen minutes until 6:00 A.M."

"Yes . . . but . . . that woman needs medical attention, not prayer."

A growl rumbled near my ear. "Does the parable of the Good Samaritan mean nothing to you, priest?"

"Of course! But, this is no place for the wounded. . . ." The priest's words ended in a soft, "oof." It was the sound of surprise, or of being pushed against a wall.

"Yield or I will destroy you." A blinding light penetrated behind my eyelids. I jerked open my eyes to the sensation of a sudden strong wind. The priest collapsed against the marble basin of holy water. His hands raised as if to ward someone off. The priest's face was turned away, hidden against the folds of his black robes, but I recognized the silver-in-blond hair.

"Eion," I whispered.

At my voice, Eion looked up. "Dee . . . Oh my God," Eion murmured, but was interrupted with a hiss. My head bobbed as I was carried farther into the church. Bootheels crashed against the stone floor, sending noise ricocheting against the vaulted ceilings.

The somber-colored banners that hung along the processional fluttered in the aftereffects of a sudden strong wind as I was marched toward the altar. I bounced painfully as he took the low stairs two at a time.

"No," I moaned weakly. My mind protested, *I'm bleeding, please, not on the altar cloths.*

"No!" Eion's usually commanding voice was tinged with hysteria. "You defile the church!"

"Blood is part of your covenant with Him, yes? Besides, in the old days They were quite fond of grand gestures like this. Remember Abraham and Isaac? Trust me. If anyone knows how to get Their attention—I do."

Reaching the dais, I was laid gently on the altar. I

looked up into his face. Chestnut brown eyes met mine, not the flashing gray I expected.

"M . . . ?"

"Morningstar, though I would prefer to have been introduced as Sammael," he said, with a slight upturn of his mouth. The expression was somewhere between a grimace and a smile. "Sammael was my given name. Michael likes to call me Morningstar to remind me of my little tumble from grace."

The church echoed with Eion's gasp. "Satan . . ."

"Satan . . ." Morningstar hissed out the name, savoring it. "Did you know that 'satan' used to be a generic term implying any adversary?" Morningstar asked me, ignoring Eion. "Now I'm the only one worth mentioning. Fortunately for you, priest," Morningstar said over his shoulder, "I'm arrogant enough to appreciate the compliment."

He glanced over at the crucifix suddenly, as if it had spoken to him. Auburn curls brushed the hard angle of his broad shoulders and fell loosely across his muscular back. Flecks of red-and-blue light speckled his black designer trench coat.

The hazy light of the cathedral seemed to illuminate a ghostly form underneath the image of Morningstar. It was as though his clothes were a thin gauze wrapping. Underneath another image glowed. A frayed tunic hung limply across his naked shoulder. It was pure white in places, but dark soot stained most of the fabric to a dull shadowy gray.

Hovering on the edge of consciousness, I could see a glimmer of enormous wings, the span of which must have reached twenty feet. Like the tunic, they were blackened and tattered. Almost completely featherless in most places, a few patches of white clung stubbornly to wounded flesh. The angle of one of the wings was askew, and the sharp edge of bone poked out, painful and raw-looking. He held the broken wing close to his body, as though it were still tender.

"You've been reading too much Milton," Morningstar sneered in my direction. Snapping back into focus, the trench coat solidified. Like a blanket thrown over a lamp, it blocked out most of the image, but I still saw a bright light glowing at the center of his chest.

"Don't fool yourself with such romantic images. We aren't even crafted from the same stuff as you. What I truly am you can't comprehend, just as you can't comprehend God." Morningstar's brown eyes bored into me. "Though in so many ways you are more like God than I will ever be."

My head felt light. I was hallucinating, clearly. "Michael?" I rasped, "Where is . . . ?"

"He's left you in my more-than-capable hands, Deidre." Morningstar dusted off the edge of the altar and sat on it. "It seems Michael needed some time to think."

"Get off the altar! Get out of my church!" Eion yelled, rushing down the processional toward the altar dias. In his hands he gripped a gilded cross like a spear.

Morningstar recoiled as though someone had slapped him. Heat rose on his cheeks. "Your church?" Standing up, he snapped his coat out behind him. "You would do better, priest, to remember by whose grace you were elevated from animated clay to the likes of gods."

Eion stopped at Morningstar's admonishment. His hands trembled, but he remained firm. "This is His church," Eion repeated. His unfinished vestments hung loosely around him like a dressing gown. The fire in his eyes contrasted the vulnerability of his undress. "If you are . . . what you say you are, you don't belong here," Eion commanded.

Morningstar's back straightened. I saw fists clench at his sides. Then, with a forced breath, his shoulders relaxed. "We are all God's creations. I belong here as much as any, perhaps more. I was the first, the best."

"Yes, you were." Michael stood in the doorway, silhouetted by the morning sun. His shadow stretched nearly the length of the processional, its edges protectively touching Eion's shoulder.

I tried to sit up. My shoulder came away from the altar cloth with a wet sound. I no longer felt any pain, or, rather, I felt as though the pain was distant from my consciousness. Morningstar's hand touched my chest, pushing me back down. The pressure of his hand seemed to anchor me in the present. I wrapped my hand around his and held on as though my life depended on it.

"I was and I still am." Morningstar sat back against the altar, his hand resting lightly on my stomach. "What you can't stand, dearest brother, is that even now, after everything, They still love me."

Michael's jaw flexed. Then with a shrug, he said, "Thank you for bringing Deidre safely here. I'll take over now."

"Dismissed with a shrug? Fuck that." The hand on my blouse balled into a fist. I was jerked upright. "I could kill her and destroy your plans."

I tried to pull away, but my body no longer seemed to be under my command. I could hear someone gasp and murmur a prayer. It had to be Eion, because Michael pounded toward the altar. A crackle like flame brushed my consciousness. I turned my head toward the sound.

Large pure, white wings billowed from behind muscular shoulders. The feathers were fanned out, completely obscuring the church from my view. Looking twice his size, Michael held a flaming sword in one hand—ready to strike.

"Sheathe it, Captain," Morningstar said with a smirk. "I have no intention of cowering like a snake at your feet."

"I'm willing to bet that I'm faster than you."

"You are?" Morningstar's voice was full of surprise. "That's an awfully devilish risk you're taking."

Michael said nothing, holding his position.

I groaned. Using all my reserve strength, I pitched myself forward, trying to distract Morningstar. My arms flapped against him uselessly. He laughed. Still gripping my blouse, he pulled me closer. The smell of patchouli and sweat overwhelmed my senses. It was a strangely appealing yet repulsive smell, and not at all what I expected from the dapper Morningstar.

"When this is over," Morningstar whispered, "remem-

ber me. Some things done in the name of love have a
bitter edge."

With that, Morningstar let go of my blouse. Michael's
reactions were fast enough to cradle my head before it
smacked against the stone. I felt so foolish being tossed
around like a rag doll between these two men, especially
in front of Eion.

"I hate it when you rescue me." I tried to prop myself
up by the elbows. Michael helped me into a more upright position. In his arms, the pain in my shoulder settled into a dull ache.

"I'll try to remember that next time," Michael said.

"Do."

From my elevated position, I looked around the
church. I was surprised not to see any trace of Morningstar. "Where did he go?"

"Disappeared," Eion said, his eyes wide.

I grimaced. A sharp jab of pain shot through my arm
when I tried to move it. The pain cleared my mind, and
I remembered last night. "Like someone else I trusted.
What happened to you, Michael? Why'd you leave me
with Morningstar?"

"I needed to know if Morningstar told the truth," he
whispered, not trusting himself to look at me.

"And, did he?"

"I'm afraid so," Michael said quietly.

I struggled to a sitting position. As I pulled my legs
down clumsily, the altar cloth came part of the way with
me. I reached out to straighten it. My body felt thick,
and I stumbled. Michael untangled the altar cloth from
between my legs. Eion rushed up the steps, trying to
grab the chalice and candles that I'd brought down with
me. The candles broke on the stone, and the chalice
rolled down the stairs noisily. I stared at them stupidly,
unable to do much of anything.

"I'm sorry, Eion."

Eion pushed the candle crumbs aside and sat down
next to me. "It's okay, Deidre. It's okay."

"Deidre," Michael said, laying my head against the
altar stone. The stone felt cool and hard against my

back. "I have a lot to explain, I know. You need to know the whole truth."

"Damn straight," I said. Then remembering where I was, I turned to Eion. "Sorry about the 'damn.' "

"Dee . . . don't worry about it, really." He patted my knee, then glancing over at Michael, he said, "I think she's delirious. You need to take her to a hospital . . . or do something." Eion accented the last words as if they held special meaning.

I looked at Eion. Despite years on the force, I'd never been shot. Maybe I was delirious. After all, just a second ago I swore Michael and Morningstar were talking as if they were real angels, and I thought I saw wings . . .

I shook my head to clear it and almost fell over with the effort. Michael reached out a hand to steady me. His hand was firm, solid, real. Yes, I told myself—the conversation, the wings—they were all part of some kind of fever-induced dream. That's all this was. After all, this was New York 2076, not some biblical backwater. Angels, real angels, didn't walk the Earth. Right?

"Something will be done," Michael said ominously.

"God's will be done." Eion kept his gaze slightly averted.

"There's the proof." I said, with a little smile. "I am dreaming. I think you're genuinely concerned about me, big brother."

Eion glanced up at me, and the corners of his eyes crinkled. "Of course I'm worried about you, Diedre. I always have been. I guess . . ." He looked over at Michael with an odd, almost worshipful look, ". . . I guess my prayers were answered."

"Right." I grimaced as pain lanced through my shoulder. I slumped back against the altar. Michael's hand rested on my shoulder, steadying me. I felt a warmth seeping through my limbs, and I breathed deeply and relaxed. My consciousness floated away from the pain. Looking at Michael, I saw his lips moving as he talked to Eion, but I couldn't make out any of the words. I wondered if I should be panicked at my sudden loss of hearing, but I felt at peace.

Around Michael's face, a thin bright light shone and illuminated the outline of his body. It was as though he were only a cardboard cutout and the prop had slipped, revealing what lay beneath.

"Deidre?" Michael's voice brought me back. "Eion is going to show us to the belfry."

"What?" I asked. I blinked. I felt like I'd just woken up from a dream. "Why?"

"We need a safe place to stay for a while. The police are looking for us." Turning to Eion, he added, "I hate to impose, but . . ."

"Of course," Eion said. Standing up, he gathered the bloodied altar cloth in his hand. "You can stay as long as you like. If we had a room free, I would offer it, but God has blessed us with a full complement of priests this year. I'm afraid that leaves the belfry or the basement for your accommodations."

"The belfry would be fine, Father. It would give us a good vantage point in case the police track us this far." Michael handed Eion the chalice and, for a moment, their eyes locked. "I don't expect you to lie for us, of course, but, if you could give us some warning. . . ."

"Leave things to me," Eion said. "You'll be safe here."

I stared at Eion in amazement. "Thanks for doing this for me . . . for us."

Eion just smiled, his eyes holding that Faith I'd envied my whole life. Instead of looking at the cross, Eion now stared at Michael. Behind Michael, a stained-glass window caught my eye. A white-robed angel stood with one foot firmly on a twisting, green glass shape of a dragon. The angel's fist gripped a fiery sword. The hand was outlined crudely in black lead, but the glass had been hand-painted to show each digit clearly. Though poised in action, the angel's face was frozen in a beatific gaze. He looked outward calmly, without the slightest hint of malice.

I let my gaze slip back to Michael. The leather jacket he wore was ripped along the sleeve, where he had brushed aside the glass. Dark curls spilled over his forehead. His eyes were hooded in the muted light of the stained-glass windows, but his long, dark lashes caught the light. Michael smiled at me, as if he knew my thoughts. His eyes glittered with fondness. I felt the flush of heat rising on my cheeks and remembered what he had said to Jibril about me. "A real firebrand"—it might've been patronizing, but the warmth and affection was clear in his tone. Anyway, I had known what he meant. A lot of men in my life didn't know how to express the combination of exasperation and attraction I seemed to inspire in them, especially since I lived my life outside the rigid bounds of "happy homemaker."

Michael continued to stare at me, his gaze becoming more intense with each passing second. I looked away, feigning bashfulness. I looked up at the stained-glass image of St. Michael again. Even destroying Satan, the saint's face shone with God's grace. When I looked at the stained glass, I felt nothing but reverence. Looking back at Michael, I felt something entirely different. I returned his intense stare and smiled.

Having finished putting the chalice and the cloth somewhere, Eion cleared his throat. "Let me show you to the belfry."

"I know you don't want me to rescue you, Deidre," Michael said, his eyes still glittering mischievously. "But, will you at least allow me to help you up the stairs?"

I pretended to consider his offer. "All right, but I want to go on my own two feet. You've played enough Rhett Butler."

Putting his arm around me, he helped me to my feet.

I squinted, ready for the jarring pain, but it never came. My legs were steady as we moved slowly toward the door. Pleased with the new strength flowing through my limbs, I felt buoyant, and laughter bubbled out of me.

"Deidre, are you all right?" Eion asked.

"I've never felt better." I said.

Eion frowned at me, as if, somehow, by convalescing, I had disappointed him. Turning to Michael, he asked,

"Will she be all right? I could call a doctor . . . unless . . ."

"She'll be fine with me, Father."

"Ah." Eion nodded, "Of course."

We stopped in front of the door to the belfry. The door was neatly hidden in the shadows of the confessional booths. It would be easy to walk right past it if you didn't know what you were looking for.

"If the police or the FBI show up . . ." Michael started, but Eion raised his hand to stop him.

"As I said before, leave them to me."

Michael nodded solemnly. "Very well."

"Thanks, Eion," I said. "This means a lot to me."

He shook his head slightly. "It's nothing. I'm just glad you're keeping better company these days."

"Hmph," I grunted, but held my tongue. I let him have a parting shot. If he wouldn't take my gratitude, it was the least I could do for him.

We turned and headed up the stairs.

The belfry was open to the air. The breeze across my face refreshed me. Standing there, supported by Michael, I almost felt one hundred percent recovered.

The bell tower stood in sharp contrast to the heavily Gothic influence of the interior of the church proper. The regularly spaced, glassless windows were square and fashioned of unadorned stucco. As we stepped up to one of the windows, the wind tugged at my hair. I gripped the edge and looked out.

The multilevel, concrete apartment complexes rose in heavy lines skyward, throwing lines of deep shadow across the red clay–tiled roof of the church. The after-church rush-hour traffic was just starting. Color and motion filled the tubing between the buildings, like an IV unit feeding an enormous sick beast.

Below, I saw a gravel lot. A few early-morning worshipers gathered at the front steps. A young man sat on the steps. He tapped the handrail with a stick in tune to an inner music. Two girls chased each other playfully through the car park, pausing occasionally to toss a piece of gravel and squeal with delight.

Suddenly, I noticed that the church wasn't attached to any skyway or traffic tubing. Eion's church was more cut off than my office. That meant Eion was a missionary to the un-LINKed. I was floored. I'd always assumed he preferred to work with the affluent churchgoers.

"We should duck down," Michael said. "Someone might see us."

"Sure," I said agreeably, since his arm still supported my weight. With a laugh, I paraphrased a passage from the Book of Ruth: " 'I go where you go.' "

"Wait," he cautioned. "The floor is filthy."

Like a perfect gentleman, Michael shrugged out of his leather jacket and laid it on the guano-spattered floor. I giggled again. "I guess Eion has bats in his belfry."

"And birds," he said, pointing his chin in the direction of a blob of straw and plastic wedged against the roof. "We should be grateful, I suppose. It means they're making a comeback after the war."

I nodded. Michael helped me down onto the floor. I leaned my back against the low wall. We sat facing the church's bell. Enormous and simple solid bronze, it hung from the center of the ceiling. Pulls disappeared into the floor, looking majestically old-fashioned. The heavy rope was for appearance; somewhere behind the pulpit was a digital panel that controlled the tolling of Mass bells.

The blood on my blouse was cold; the fabric was sticky. I told myself I should be feeling pain, but even by looking at the wound I couldn't conjure any. My head was remarkably clear.

"I should be dead," I said. As if to prove my point, I lifted the edge of my bloody blouse and showed it to him. "I've lost so much blood."

Michael nodded. "Are you in pain? I guess I should take a look at that, eh?"

He sounded so unconvinced that I shrugged. Then I remembered my shoulder and winced.

"I guess I should," he said with raised eyebrow. After moving so that we sat across from each other, he reached out to open the first button of my blouse. He undid the first two without thinking. By the third, his fingers hesitated.

I looked down at his hand hovering over my half-exposed cleavage. The look in his eyes was so far from a beatific grace that I smiled wickedly. Undoing the button myself, I shrugged my shoulder out of the blouse with a laugh. "Better?"

He neither looked in my eyes nor at my breasts. Instead, he made a big production of looking at the bullet hole. He laid his hand over my shoulder as he had in the church. I flinched, thinking it should hurt, but the pain didn't come. Instead, my body flushed with warmth. It was as though his mere touch could heal me. But, that, I told myself firmly, was impossible; it would take a miracle.

"Whatever you're doing, don't stop," I said with a contented sigh. I felt myself losing consciousness.

I must have fallen asleep because when I woke up, Michael was lying beside me, an arm thrown protectively around my waist. His chest pressed lightly against my breasts, and, with every breath, I was conscious of my half-opened blouse. Our bellies touched. My chin rested against his collarbone. Sometime during my nap, my skirt had twisted up around my thighs. My legs were entwined around his. Beneath the thin, scratchy barrier of my nylons I could feel the warm softness of his denim jeans. I slid my legs along the shape of his calves. My crotch inched closer to his.

"Are you awake?" His voice was loud in my ear and held no trace of grogginess. I could feel a blush burn the tips of my ears.

"Ummm." I started to pull away, but his arm tightened around my waist. A soft kiss brushed my forehead. That was all the encouragement I needed.

I grabbed the short hairs at the back of his neck and pulled his face to mine. I expected hot and hungry, but our lips met cool and gentle. My legs squeezed his thighs urgently. I pulled his hair roughly. "Michael . . ."

He seemed determined to drive me insane with slow softness. His lips moved deliberately down my neck to the hollow of my throat. His kisses were so feather-light they tickled. I squirmed against his touch, trying to force his lips to press harder and to move farther down. Through clenched teeth, I said, "Don't stop there."

Clutching his belt buckle, I pulled at him until he finally consented to roll over on me. I wrapped my legs around him, pressing into the bulge in his pants. I felt strangely grateful to feel that there. Angels, I knew, were supposed to be sexless. Desperate to feel his weight on me, I clawed at his back. Even though I felt the material of his tee shirt rip, my hands felt oddly empty, as though I were clutching at air.

"Wait," he murmured into my chest.

Strangely grateful, I let him pull away. "Michael, what's wrong?"

"I want to go slow. This is my first time."

I scooted out from under him so fast, I nearly kicked him in the groin. "You're a . . . vir . . ." I stumbled over the word, the concept, and then settled on, ". . . a really good Catholic?"

"I . . ." He dropped his gaze bashfully and shook his head. "I've just been really busy."

Too busy to have sex? I tried really hard not to laugh, but I could feel a giggle rising in my throat. I put my hand over my mouth to hold it back; I didn't want to embarrass him any further. It wasn't really all that unusual for man Michael's age to be a virgin.

These days preachers constantly rallied against the sins of the flesh, and the harsh penalties for being involved in prostitution were not worth the risk for most people. With the inaccessibility of birth control and abortions, the lack of treatment for STDs, the social stigma of being or having a child out of wedlock—well, honestly, I was in the minority. Many people took vows to abstain until marriage; many people kept them.

Undoing the last button, I let my blouse fall off my shoulders. A cold wetness slid down my arm, reminding me that I should feel something more than the ache between my legs. I did, but it was a hunger that burned me. I wanted, I needed, to know more about Michael as a man.

I touched Michael's chin, stroking the prickles of his stubble. I pressed both of my palms to his face. I let my hands trail down his body, touching, testing. A little laugh which I hoped sounded kind slipped out. I moved closer to him, snuggling back into our embrace. "If you've been too busy for sex, big guy, then maybe you deserve a nice, long vacation."

I kissed his forehead, softly, as he had kissed mine. "We can go slow," I said, even as I pulled at his shirt. My legs knocked against his desperately. "Or maybe we could just do it twice."

////READ.TXT only//// Dee, I thought you might find this interesting. I found it while doing a job for Mouse . . . I won't compromise your cop-honor by going into details about that. Sorry about the ding-bats. I caught it mid-hack, er, I mean, mid-JOB, so it's not in the best shape. Plus, your rustbucket of a motherboard isn't very forgiving. Anyway, looks like your old college roommate is having more troubles. Allah protect us all from the FBI.——The page P.S. [file follows]/////(*)**&)&^&*$%$%$#%$# !@$%^&*()(+ . . . . . protection program. All you need to do is give us just a little more information.

Malachim: Screw your witness protection program. I want an upgrade. I was told your office would be willing to provide me with what I need.

Agent Chan: What you're asking for is highly illegal.

Malachim: No upgrade, no info.

Agent Ramirez: Playing hardball with us isn't a very inspired idea, wirehead. You could spend the rest of your snotty little life in prison with zero access for the LINK-crimes the Malachim Nikamah have committed. As an admitted member of that organization, you're not in a position to bargain. Period.

Malachim: uh . . . What do you want?

Chan: Current location.

Malachim: They're already on the move, since I was . . . uh, expelled, I'm sure. I can only tell you where we were.

Ramirez: Why aren't you dead?

Malachim: What?

Ramirez: Why weren't you executed? Terminated with extreme prejudice. Silenced. Whatever you people call it. For your betrayal.

Malachim: I think you're projecting, sir. That sounds more like your organization than mine.

Ramirez: Why you impudent little . . .

Chan: Let's not lose our heads. I think Agent Ramirez has a good point. Our sources tell us that the leader of the Malachim, one former-Colonel Rebeckah Klein of the Israeli army has a very fierce and unforgiving nature. She's not known to give quarter.

Malachim: To the enemy.

Ramirez: Don't get all righteous on us, Malachim. You're the one who came to us. You're the one who named names.

Chan: If we've gotten the wrong impression, why don't you tell us more about her?

Malachim: She's a nice Jewish girl. My mother would have liked me to marry her . .))((^&^&^%

CHAPTER 12

Michael and I stood in an orchard. The heady fragrance of apple blossoms in the sunshine hung in the air. Swans floated on a lake nearby. Their passing caused the slightest ripple on the smooth glass surface. The water was as gray as Michael's eyes. He kissed me again. When he pulled away, I saw he was dressed in a crude tunic like the one the stained-glass angel wore. I was afraid to look at his face. Somehow I knew it held that same beatific gaze. "You're human," I tried to tell him, but it was like I was speaking underwater. The sounds distorted, and seemed to float away.

He offered me a white lily. The sheen of dew sparkled deep in its alabaster throat.

"Remember me. Some things done in the name of love have a bitter edge, Deidre."

I looked up to see the face of Morningstar superimposed over Michael's smiling face. I looked down to find the lily in my hands. I didn't remember taking it. A blast of wind fluttered through my blue robes. I looked up to see a wheel of six wings spinning through the air. It was monstrous. The apparition seemed to stare at me with Michael's eyes. URGENT MESSAGE. The sunshine disappeared behind a dark thundercloud. Lightning flashed. I saw a silhouette of an enormous wing across the office wall. URGENT MESSAGE. Locusts plagued the Nile Valley. A red mark turned avenging angels away from the door. Michael's voice echoed, "I am the archangel Michael."

URGENT MESSAGE. I woke up with a start. Running my fingers through my tangled hair, I yawned. The afternoon sun was hazy. Fishing for my blouse, I found Michael's tee shirt instead. I let my fingers caress the edges of a small rip in the material fondly with the memory of our lovemaking. *URGENT MESSAGE.* Pulling the shirt over my head, I mentally triggered the go-ahead switch.

Mouse was sitting in an Egyptian café. The setting sun bathed the whitewashed walls in a pinkish glow. The place was filled with smoke and conversation. Mouse's usually pleasant face was twisted into a scowling frown.

Well, good afternoon, I said, even though I knew it was late in the evening Cairo time. I wiped the sleep from my eyes, and stifled another yawn.

Cut the crap, Dee, he said. *You're holding out on me.*

Reducing his image to a small window, I mentally placed it in the right corner of my vision. I shifted part of my concentration to finding my underwear. *I don't know what you're talking about, Mouse.*

I'm not saying I'm not impressed, but I'm dying to know who've you got doing your hack work. You boosted Daniel from jail, right? Very clever. He smiled. The expression was eerie on the page; it was almost too realistic. I swear I saw a cold fire behind Mouse's eyes. Maybe I wasn't talking to the page after all, but the real McCoy.

Mouse, is that you?

What? Of course it's me. After all this excitement, I've given you your own dedicated line, girlfriend. My page is out of the loop. Anyway, he's got plenty to do running mousenet. Now tell me—where are you hiding Danny boy? When you see him, tell him his sig. file is all over this latest. Hot.

I missed something in the translation, Mouse. What are you talking about?

Well, someone must've sprung Danny out of the old loony bin. Who else could pull off a stunt like this?

I stopped my search and sat down hard on the cool

wooden floor. My heart was racing. I had to struggle to keep my voice subvocal. *Daniel escaped?*

Cute, but innocence never played very well on you, girl. Who else could it be? Mouse shook his head, tipping his teacup in my direction in a salute. *If it wasn't you, tell me who browned out New York?*

You did. Even my electronic voice sounded unsure, as I asked, *Didn't you?*

Fifty-three cases of severe cybernetic trauma, you think I did that? He jabbed his thumb at his chest to emphasize his point.

Fifty-three cases . . . I repeated, shell-shocked.

Traffic control blown, he ticked off the offenses on his fingers—*brownouts in seven precincts, including backup generator failure across the board; FBI headquarters in DC hacked, seventeen local bureaus down; and New Jersey State Penitentiary blacked out.* He waved his hands in exasperation. *Ah, the brotherhood of police . . . I never counted on Daniel still having loyal friends after all this time. I suppose you had someone in the prison system, maybe the warden, and then there was your grand escape. I was sure you were tapped out of friends on the force.* Mouse lifted the teacup to his mouth distractedly. A deep frown slashed his boyish face. *How many people are on your side anyway? Who's doing the coordinating of that army?*

Are they all right?

Mouse blinked. Setting his cup down slowly, he cocked his head at me curiously. *Who?*

The fifty-three cases.

Mouse's eyes scanned an invisible report. *Two reported heart attacks. Ten dead and several people wounded in traffic accidents. All fifty-three cyber-trauma cases reported in stable condition.* He pursed his lips, then a smile spread across his face. *You could have done that yourself, Dee. What is it about you that always makes me give you free intel?*

I shook my head mutely. My mouth twitched as I tried to smile back at Mouse's beaming grin.

Mouse stared at me, as if measuring me up. *So . . .*

he said slowly, *you scrubbed the agents, eh? The way you boosted onto the LINK was awfully powerful, now that I think about it . . . do you have some kind of new tech or something?*

"I don't know . . ." I finally found my voice. I also spotted my underwear across the room, but I didn't have the energy to retrieve it.

What? Subvocal, Dee. I didn't catch all of that.

Daniel . . . did he escape? I had to know.

Mouse shook his head slowly from side to side. *Barter, girlfriend. You already owe me for the hospital report.*

I got up and crossed the room. *You picked a fine time to start playing hardball, Mouse. Anyway, if I remember correctly, you still owe me. All I got from you about Angelucci and Morningstar was that Michael was no angel . . . and I intelled that one myself.* I glance over to where Michael lay sprawled. Definitely not an angel, I smiled. Before slipping into my underwear, I quickly constructed a mental image of them. I sent the visual to Mouse as an addendum.

Mouse raised his eyebrows appreciatively. *Bonus! Don't think I'm not going to post that to your bulletin board. You know, you really need to take some time to construct a page, Dee, or at least get a better camera eye going. I'm getting tired of this shoddy work; I'm used to better from you.*

You of all people know I don't have the time to devote to making an AI right now. Tell me about Daniel. You think he's out?

I don't know. The prison is still in chaos. Some people escaped, that much is certain, but nobody is making official reports on anything I can access. Frankly, Dee, I'm surprised you don't know. Are you saying you didn't black out the prison?

I thought back to how easily I hacked the FBI frequency. I'd blasted Dorshak and the FBI agents with barely a thought. Mouse was right. Jibril's tech must be more powerful than anything I'd ever seen or used before. "If I did, it was unconscious. Christ, what am I capable of?"

Mouse cursed in Arabic. *I heard something, but it wasn't clear. Repeat?*

*Sorry. I need to think about all this, Mouse. And—*I looked over at Michael—*there's a lot going on this end. I need to call you back, okay?*

No, wait, Dee. . . . I'm on my way there. I need to talk to you.

It has to wait. Sorry. I broke the LINK connection and mentally turned off the urgent message override command. I needed some time for uninterrupted thinking. Looking over at Michael, I smiled. He moaned and rolled over. My eyes followed the muscles as they rippled along his body . . . just as they should. There was nothing unearthly about the man lying here, no. I shivered and hugged my arms around my waist, feeling the firmness of my hips.

I shook my head, brushing aside the eerie feeling creeping across my skin. The strangeness of my dream still haunted me, no doubt. I stretched my arm experimentally. I could've sworn I'd been shot last night at the police station. There was no sign of a bullet hole, not even a bruise. I pulled back the fabric of the tee shirt and touched the flesh of my shoulder tentatively, as if it didn't belong to me, or as if I expected mere contact to dispel the illusion and reveal a horrible wound. There was nothing. My skin was unbroken. It was a miracle. I looked over at Michael. His penis twitched in a dream, and a smile touched his lips.

"I must have dreamed the wound," I told myself in a voice that sounded unconvinced. "I must've dreamed it. I must have." A six-winged creature with Michael's voice flitted through my mind, dream words echoed: *I am the arch . . .* "No," I stopped myself. "No."

Reaching out, I grabbed Michael's leather jacket. It was solid, not an apparition. "See," I whispered. "Real."

Michael stirred at the sound. With a groan, he stretched. The noon sun spread across his body as he unfurled. Seeing me, he smiled. "Morning."

"Hi." My voice sounded small. Looking at my hands, I realized I was still clutching his leather jacket. Even though I knew I must look foolish standing there with his tee shirt on, stroking the contours of the soft leather, I couldn't quite bring myself to relinquish my hold on the jacket.

"You okay?"

I glanced up at him. He had propped himself up by the elbows to take a better look at me. Even in his nakedness, his pose held the relaxed confidence of a statue of a Roman god. I laughed nervously at the thought. Michael's association with divinity was hardly in the small "g" category, I reminded myself . . . or was it?

"Deidre?"

"When you said you were too busy to have . . . um, when you said that earlier, what were you too busy doing? No, uhm, that didn't make any sense, did it?" I suppressed a nervous laugh and clutched the jacket. My stomach lurched. "Michael, are you . . . Michael, what are you?"

He scratched his chin, considering. Then, he stood up and walked over to where his jeans and underwear were wedged into the corner. Stomping into them, he said, "I knew I should have told you before."

He glanced up from buttoning his fly, and his eyes locked on mine. The sound of torrential fluttering of six powerful wings filled my ears. A monster with Michael's soft gray eyes said, *I am the arch . . .*

I shook my head. "You know what? I changed my mind. Maybe I don't want to know." I jettisoned the jacket and started frantically gathering my remaining clothes. "In fact, I really have to go. I talked to Mouse a second ago and found out that Daniel escaped. I don't know what Danny's planning on doing, but I can guess his target. I think I need to intercept him before he goes after Letourneau. I mean, who knows what kind of mental state he's in? The last letter of his I finally read . . . man, he sounded a few bytes short of RAM, if you know what I mean. Daniel could be a real liability. He could damage our ability to have a little surprise on our side— not that we have any real plan, which is something else we have to . . . Oh."

My breath caught in my throat as Michael slid his arms around my waist from behind. His arms were strong and solid, but the center of his chest burned with that strange warmth I had felt in the police station. I remembered the vision from my piggyback into the FBI agent's eyes: a glimmering bow tie of heat radiated from a molten center. It was as though what seemed to be Michael's body was a shell, and the real beast lay under the surface.

"I've never been a LINK-angel, Dee."

His arms around my waist squeezed me tightly, but comfortably. I squirmed in his embrace. "Michael, I really don't want to know this." I whispered. "I'm afraid it will change things."

"Like what?"

I turned around to face him and put my hands on his smooth chest. "Like this." I stroked his rib cage with my fingernail. He shivered.

"Why would that have to change?" He smiled, tightening his grip around my waist. "I kind of like that new development. It was nice . . . twice."

"Michael . . ." I was dumbfounded. I searched his face for some comprehension, but he just smiled rakishly. "What about chastity and celibacy?"

"What about them?" Stepping back from our embrace, he frowned. He looked me up and down. "Are you telling me you took a vow of celibacy? Deidre! This is a fine time to tell me that."

"No," I started pacing and was on the verge of shouting. "Not me, you. You're the one who's supposed to be chaste, pure . . ."

"Why? Says who?"

I stared at him. Despite the sun, the wood floor felt cold. I was uncomfortably aware of my body: the heaviness of my breasts; the feather-light touch of the oversize tee shirt against my nipples; and the empty ache between my thighs.

Standing there in just his jeans, he reminded me of so many of my lovers. The dark mass of his hair was tousled, and his underwear peeked out of where he'd left the last button of his fly undone. The sun highlighted the wisps of hair on his arms.

I slapped his face with my open palm. The connection was solid, and I was rewarded with a satisfying tingle in my palm. Staggering back in surprise, he cupped his chin in his hand.

"Deidre! What possessed you to do that?"

"I just wanted to know."

"Know what?" Michael rubbed his chin. From an unreadable face, his gray eyes watched me intently.

"I just wanted to know if you could see it coming." Relieved, I took in a deep breath. I let the tension drop from my shoulders.

"What do you think that proves?" Michael asked, buttoning the last of his fly. Not waiting for a response, he continued, "This is exactly what Morningstar has been trying to remind me of since I got here."

I stared at him. "What?"

"This level precludes predetermination. Here, the apple has been eaten, as it were."

He leaned against the narrow wall space between the windows. His tall body was cast in shadow, and the light streaming in formed bright semioval shapes on either side of him like wings. From the shadows, his eyes seemed to glow with an inhuman light. I gasped and shook my head.

"This is all crazy. Listen to you, you're spouting nonsense like the Revelation preacher."

"Am I?" Michael crossed his arms in front of his chest. Though most of his body was still shrouded in shadows, the sunlight outlined the muscles of his arm. Only a few hours ago, those arms held me. Looking at the hard lines of his body, I desperately wanted to believe he was a solid, normal man. I tried to deny the truth, but I knew.

I remembered the moments he was on top of me. The usual comforting feeling of being held down by another's weight was missing. First time, I'd tried to pull him tighter. I could feel the outlines of his flesh, but without the mass. Later, I'd rolled us over, trying to banish the feeling of being alone, only to have that horrible sensation replaced by something worse. When I was atop him, it had felt as though I were floating on air.

Now, it was my head that felt light, and I swallowed hard. "Michael, I'm not ready for this."

Michael stood very still, as though afraid that with any sudden move I might bolt from the room. He chose his words carefully, slowly. "I think you've suspected for a long time, Dee."

My fingers brushed the live connection of the LINK implant. What was once dead, had been revived . . . resurrected . . . and with such strange timing. It was almost as if, the moment I chose not to betray Michael the way I had betrayed Daniel, it came alive. No, I shook my head mutely. It couldn't be.

Pulling my hand away from the implant, I flexed my fingers and felt the strength in my muscles move all the way up to my shoulder. "Miracles."

"Yes, miracles," Michael said quietly. He turned to look out the window at the smog-shrouded city. "So incredibly precious. So costly. Every time I come, I'm given a purpose and allowed one miracle to use to that end. One. It irks me, you know? Morningstar is right. I should have trusted you to make the right choice. Jibril trusted you. But, I didn't want to risk it. I have been trying to stack the deck, and very ungenerously, I might add. I used Morningstar, I used Jibril, because I didn't want to tarnish myself. You see, a miracle is a manipulation . . . and when you manipulate the universal fabric like that, you take the easy road, you turn away, *yetzer-ha-ra,* sin . . ."

"Sin?" I asked. "As in fallen angel? Like Morningstar?"

"No," Michael shook his head. "Morningstar is different—an angel of darkness. He is night to my day. And, like the daylight, we wax and wane in our strength, but in the end there are never more of them then there are of us; it's an eternal balance."

Michael turned to look at me. Seemingly unaware of my stricken look and the cold, hard feeling in the pit of my stomach, he continued, "I've been trying to do the right thing, the slow and hard way, yet I've probably botched the whole operation. Making a deal with him was stupid, but I needed an ace in the hole. We were trumped. It could have been the end of the whole thing. So, I used my one phone call, and I called him. I'm in danger of embracing darkness; I could lose my high place . . ."

Michael looked out the window at the bright sunlight. "But to truly fall is to die. To never return to the other place."

"Other place?" I asked, then shook my head. I didn't want to hear him say it. He looked as though he would answer me anyway, so I quickly added, "What makes you fall?"

"I don't know; God decides."

"God . . . uh-huh." I ran my hands through my hair. With the simple gesture, I tried to ground myself. The belfry seemed too airy all of a sudden. I felt too exposed under its vaulted ceiling. The coldness in my stomach crept outward toward my limbs. "Michael . . . what you're saying . . . what you imply . . ." I stopped, then restarted, "I mean, what about us?"

"Oh." Michael shook his head, as if to get back on track. "The whole thing about women needing to cover their heads in church so as not to tempt us—that's totally a myth. It's the abuse of power that corrupts, not flesh itself."

It finally broke. A wave crashed over the shoal of my reality.

"Thanks for the clarification," I said suddenly, with more sarcasm than I intended. "Look, I've got to go. Take a walk or something; clear my head. I've got to figure out what to do about Daniel. I've got to figure out what to do about you."

Michael's eyes were on me, burning through to my soul. "You can't. The police are looking for us. It's dangerous out there."

"It's dangerous in here." I gave him a weak smile. I turned on my heels to go, afraid of what I might say if

I stayed. My hand on the door, I said, "I need to sort some things out on my own, okay? Just give me ten minutes. We can talk about it then."

As the door swung shut I heard him say, "I love you, Deidre."

Eion met me halfway down the stairs with a smile and a tray of fruit.

"I was just coming up to check on you and Michael," he said cheerily. Then, his face registered the fact I was wearing Michael's tee shirt and not much else. Eion looked at my bare legs and blushed.

Under normal circumstances I might have enjoyed taunting Eion, but with Michael half-naked just beyond the belfry door, I froze.

"No!" I shouted. "Don't go up there! Michael is . . . Michael is . . . sleeping."

Eion stared intently at the grapes and oranges on the tray, a strange smile playing on his lips. "Okay," he said to my surprise. Clearing his throat, he added, "Maybe you'd like to come down to the rectory, have some lunch . . . or take a shower or something?"

"Yeah," I said. "A shower would be nice."

The shower restored my sanity. My fear gurgled down the drain with the warm, reviving water. Relaxed, I joined Eion in the refectory. Wrapped in a black terry-cloth robe with the papal heraldry of Saint Denis embla-zoned over my heart, I sucked orange juice from my fingers. Eion sat across from me, his hands folded neatly on the wooden kitchen table. A few curious priests poked their heads in, but before I could even wave "hello" they disappeared.

"Probably don't get a lot of women in the rectory, eh?"

"Of course not." Eion sniffed with a practiced offense. "We're Roman Catholic, remember, not one of those heathen American Catholics."

I laughed, flicking an orange peel across the table.

"No, Eion, I can't exactly see you as the handing-out-condoms type."

"Dee!" Eion lifted the peel out of his lap gingerly. He placed the offending item on the tray. "Please remember where you are."

"I'm in the lunchroom, Eion. This is hardly sacred ground. Condom isn't a dirty word. Besides, I've got it on good authority that sex isn't a sin." My smile faded. I wondered what possessed me to say that. I could feel my carefully constructed world rock just a little. I gripped the edge of the table to steady myself.

"Forget I said that," I told Eion's shell-shocked expression that I was certain mirrored my own.

"I think I'd better," Eion said.

I shook my shoulders out and let go of the edge. I lined up another bit of orange rind between my fingers. "Come on, be the goal."

"No, now stop it!" Eion waved his hands. "I have something serious I want to talk to you about."

The peel was aimed perfectly, my fingers poised to deliver a hard flick. "I don't think I can handle any more seriousness right now, bro. Come on, play with me instead, huh?"

"Deidre, I had a vision."

I sputtered at his words. The orange peel bounced off the fruit tray. I straightened the collar of the robe and gave Eion a hard look. "What do you mean, like another LINK-angel?"

"No, Dee, nothing like that—it was beautiful. I was in the middle of Matins when it came to me." The lines on Eion's face smoothed out, reminding me of the stained-glass angel's peaceful gaze. "It wasn't at all like the LINK-angels . . . it was less clear, more like a dream—very symbolic."

I nodded. Everyone around me had gone completely insane. "Okay," I murmured. "What did you see?"

"You." Eion's fingers reached out to recover the out-of-bounds orange peel. He placed it on the tray with the others.

"Me?"

I watched him in silence. Finally, he looked up at me. "Yeah, isn't that odd?"

"I'd say," I agreed. I ran my fingers through my damp hair and rocked back in the wooden chair. "When you say 'vision,' you're not talking about, like, a daydream. You mean something more biblical, right?"

"I'm quite certain it wasn't a daydream. And . . ." His eyes slid away from mine again to stare at the fruit bowl. "With our visitors, and, well, everything that's happened today, I'm sure it is some kind of portent."

"I don't want to hear this, Eion. Things are already too weird."

"Nothing like this has ever happened to me, either, Dee," Eion said. "None of this. I'm afraid if I tell my colleagues about this, they'll think I'm completely insane."

"Maybe you are," I said quietly. "Maybe we all are."

"You're wrapped up in something big, Deidre. I know I haven't been supportive during all of your trauma. But . . ."

I snorted, "That's an understatement."

". . . But," he continued, ignoring my jab, "this vision . . . I saw you in an apple orchard with a seraphim. You were holding a lily."

"I am the archangel Michael." Another voice, chiding me: *"Remember me."*

I tasted citric acid in the back of my throat. "A lily?"

"Um?" Eion looked at me, as if suddenly realizing he was talking to a layperson and not another priest. "Oh, well, it's an old-fashioned icon, but standard enough. Old hard-copy of images of the Visitation always show the Virgin Mary holding a lily. A dew-draped lily represents an active male . . . well, you have more experience with that sort of thing than I. Surely, you can see the resemblance."

"Some things done in the name of love have a bitter edge."

"The Visitation," I repeated. My stomach flopped. "Eion, you can't be serious."

"I don't know what else to make of it."

I stood up so suddenly that the chair crashed to the floor. Eion jumped.

"I need to borrow some of your clothes," I demanded, my voice thin with hysteria. "Where's your room?"

"What?" Eion started at my sudden change of mood. "Why . . . ?"

I was close to grabbing him by that little white collar and shaking him. Instead, I balled my fists at my sides.

"Eion!" I cut him off. "I have to get out of here right now. Show me your room, or I swear I'll rip those clothes right off your back."

"Going?" Eion's eyes glittered with panic. "Where?"

Morningstar had said in the church: "I could kill her now, ruin all your plans. . . . Your plans." So, I thought with a sneer, it was determined all along.

"Dee?" Eion's voice was thin. "What should I tell Michael?"

My lips pressed into thin, hard resolve. "Tell him I've left him in your 'capable hands.' "

LINK site path—LINK-angels, what are they, what are your experiences with them. . . .//

The nature of angels, a Unitarian perspective: by Darcy O'Donnell

Like everyone, I experienced the LINK-angels on a very personal level. Phanuel appeared to me while I was out in the "back-forty," as I like to call the far end of my urban garden, picking aphids off my William Baffin roses. I'd been absently listening to International Public Radio via the LINK, and suddenly, the angelic visage peered at me between the slats of my wrought-iron fence. We stared at each other, me with my crushed-aphid carcass-encrusted gloves, and he with his absent, worm-eaten eye sockets. Then, like any good Unitarian Universalist minister, I attempted to engage him in a philosophical debate.

It's the oldest joke about Unitarians, of course. When faced with the diverging paths on the road to enlightenment, one with a sign reading, "This way heaven," and the other with, "This way to a discussion about the existence of heaven," the Unitarian always picks the latter.

So, although I stared right into the face of a LINK-angel, possibly a portent of the empirical existence of God, I said to it, "If you're a real angel, why do you only appear on the LINK? Why, when I see you, is my heart filled with dread? Shouldn't even the angel of death fill me with radiance?" Then, true to my doubting nature, I attempted to touch it, and it faded away.

Since then, I have been thinking about angels. I dusted off my King James version of the Bible, my copy of the Torah, the Koran, and a whole slew of other religious books, and went looking for passages and information about angels. What I found surprised me. The first biblical mention of angels is in Genesis 19:1–3, "The first time angels appear in the Bible, they are fully human. The two angels arrived at Sodom in the evening, and Lot was sitting in the gateway of the city. When he saw them, he got up to meet them and bowed down with his face to the ground. 'My lords,' he said, 'please turn aside to your servant's house. You can wash your feet and spend the night and then go on your way early in the morning.' 'No,' they answered, 'we will spend the night in the square.' But he insisted so strongly that they did go with him and entered his house. He prepared a meal for them, baking bread without yeast, and they ate."

Here are angels acting like men. They argue, they eat, they need a place to spend the night. Later in Genesis, Jacob also greets angels of the Lord as if they were men and invites them to stay in his house. The Hebrew word for angel, *"Malach,"* means, simply, "a messenger.'' In the Koran, though the angels are clearly spiritual beings early on (we see them in The Cow 2:3 at creation speaking directly to God), in The Family of Imram 3:39, they act as messengers to Mirium for Allah. It has been postulated by more learned scholars than I that the Israelites were influenced in their thinking about the spiritual nature of angels when they intermixed with Arabic peoples (see Jeffrey Burton Russell's series about the history of Satan.)

The Septuagint renders the Hebrew into *aggelos* which also has both significations—holy and secular messengers, as the original was written. By the time the Bible is translated into Latin, however, the divine or spirit-messenger is separated from the human, rendering the original in the one case by *angelus* and in the other by *legatus* or more generally by *nuntius*. Even if you believe the hand of God inspired the Bible, the division between these concepts was created wholly by human decision-makers.

As a Unitarian, I have always believed that if there is a God and he does directly influence Earth via messengers such as angels, he would probably do so through real people, like Sojourner Truth, Martin Luther King, Jr., etc. So why electronic angels, why such an obvious move from God. . . .

CHAPTER 13

The shoes were too big for me, and they rubbed the backs of my heels raw. As I'd left the church, Eion had reminded me that impersonating a priest was a federal crime that carried the death sentence. I didn't care. Each jab of pain kept me anchored—kept me from thinking too hard. I was too angry for rational thought, anyway.

I leaned up against a wall. My fingers scraped against the concrete for support. The smell of urine and rotting garbage wafted on the breeze. Picking up my head at the odor, I began to wonder where my feet had taken me. Suddenly, I realized I was walking on the street and not in the skyway.

Less than two blocks away loomed the glass city. I could see the outer rim of a blast line. The skyline glittered like a forest of crystal. Straight edges of buildings, windows, and high-rises burst with prisms of color. Thanks to the traffic tubes, it had been a long time since I'd seen unfiltered sunlight. Here, in the old city, there were none. The apartment complexes, once gray and drab, now reflected the blues and whites of the sky. Only a hint of color could be seen under the sheath of the Medusa bomb's glass, unifying everything in a shimmering whiteness. Hulks of ancient cars stood like enormous jewels in the glassy road.

I gave up standing in favor of slumping against the wall. No wonder my feet were sore; I must've walked for hours to make it as far as the glass city. Pulling off

Eion's shoes, I tried to rub some life back into my toes, then took a long breath—probably my first calm one in hours. I pulled up my knees and wrapped my arms around them, hugging myself. The crumbling asphalt warmed the soles of my feet.

Too bad the sun did nothing for my soul. I rubbed at my shoulder, willing it to hurt. Despite my efforts, the pain refused to come. The miracle stubbornly clung to my body like a parasite.

I shook my head sadly. So much for going for a short, ten-minute walk. Michael would have to wait. I wasn't ready to talk to him yet. I wondered if I ever would be.

My thoughts ground like gears. Michael couldn't leave me with child; his body was a shell of air, impotent. Eion hallucinated the connection to the Visitation; or maybe the fact that we dreamed the same thing was coincidence. Anyway, if I recalled my Sunday school lessons correctly, it was the archangel Gabriel who spoke to. . . .

A gear derailed, crunch. I hid my face in my hands as I remembered Jibril, rather Gabriel, offering Michael advice about me: *"I've been there, you know."* Michael responding, *"Who could forget."*

"Jesus Christ!" Then, to banish the thought, "No! No. No."

Despite my protests, my mind conjured an image of a black Madonna and the chocolate-skinned Jibril naked and sweaty. I wondered: did she have to coax him?

The engines came back on-line with a lurch. These weren't biblical times. I was certainly no virgin, nor especially worthy. I was excommunicated, a disgrace to the Church. What Michael and I did back in the belfry was not sacred. It was good sex, but hardly miraculous.

My shoulder twitched. Okay, maybe there was a miracle involved, but it still bore little resemblance to the holy virgin birth. Besides which, I didn't want the job. I've never been exactly maternal. I didn't own a dog or a cat, not even a goldfish. I wasn't responsible enough to raise any kid, much less the second . . . an angel's kid.

Moreover, I couldn't afford it. The price of raising a child was enormous. If I didn't get some new clients soon, I was going to have to live in my office. I was still excommunicated, even if I did have access to the LINK. That meant I didn't have health insurance. What, was I supposed to have this child in a . . . "Barn?" I groaned. "Oh, God."

I pulled my face out of my hands with effort. The sun glistened across the rooftops of the glass city. The black of Eion's robes absorbed the warm light. I frowned. There wasn't a cloud in the sky. Yesterday's storm had purged the air of much of its usual foulness.

Rubbing my aching feet, I felt a blister on my heel. This wasn't how things were supposed to happen. Angels didn't walk around in painted-on jeans. But then, what did I know? Most of my images of angels had come from artists' renditions, stained-glass windows, Sunday school, and the LINK-angels. I tried to remember angels in the Bible, and all that came to me was lyrics from the Christmas song, "Hark, the Herald Angels Sing." I could no longer distinguish between folklore and fact, and probably even the "facts" of the Bible had been diluted.

I sighed, and leaned my head against the warm bricks of the crumbled warehouse. A fishy river odor drifted above the smell of garbage and human waste. Letting the warm sun batter my face, I shut my eyes and tried to think.

I might not be pregnant. I played "Vatican roulette" with Michael, but I'd been lucky before. I knew my body pretty well. Still, the child could be Michael's one miracle. It was possible that his purpose here was to impregnate me. All the contraceptive planning in the world couldn't stop a cosmic plan.

Michael told me that he kept running afoul of the concept of freewill. Presumably that meant that I had a choice in all of this. Perhaps there was something I could do about it. Thanks to the New Right, abortion was considered murder, and, if convicted, I could face the death penalty. That was only if I was convicted. I used to be a cop; I knew how to avoid detection. I could do it, and I could get away with it.

But, if Michael risked turning to impregnate me, then

he would certainly risk more to see me take the child to term. I could probably avoid secular detection, but could I run away from God?

"You're a long way from the nearest mission, priest lady."

I started at the voice. Dirty, ripped jeans hung loosely around a thin waist. The heavy-duty flak jacket still held someone's name and rank. I would've mistaken the man before me for the original owner if it wasn't for the shoulder-length silver hair and matching eyes. I was face to face with a . . . "Gorgon." I whispered.

Gorgons were possibly the ugliest by-product of the Medusa bomb. Once human, they had lived too long in contact with the glass city. The Medusa bomb worked by beginning an organic-like chain reaction of crystallization that moved through physical objects. Even though the blast had occurred twenty-one years ago, the reaction was still "hot" inside the transformed glass, and anything or anyone that touched it was infected. That residue "radiation" caused tissue damage and mutation. Gorgons were that mutation—each generation being born, maturing and dying in the span of a few short years. They had a culture that was both childlike and brutal.

The Gorgon crouched down to take a better look at me. He sniffed the air like a wild animal testing my scent. He smiled, showing me his sharpened incisors. "Insults are hardly necessary . . . Human." He mocked my horrified whisper.

"Your English is very good," I told him, hoping to appeal to his childlike nature. All cops were trained in the language the Gorgons used among themselves, but it changed every generation. I was out of touch, and Gorgons didn't live particularly long. "Are you a passer?"

"I'm as much of a passer as you're a priest." He tossed his silver mane about his shoulders. " 'Fraid the hair is a giveaway. It went some time ago. That ended my passing quick." He poked me in the shoulder playfully. "You smell like a Joey."

"Still?" I smiled, willing myself to take deep, even breaths. "I left the force over a year ago."

"Gun oil," he explained. Then, cocking his head at me quizzically, he pointed to my forehead. "What are you doing here if you have a map in your head?"

I touched my temple reflexively. The receiver's lump was warm beneath my fingers. I could almost imagine the thrum of activity dancing beneath my skin. "I turned it off."

"Not very smart." The Gorgon eyed me suspiciously. Not many turned off all of their LINK functions. Most people stayed in constant connection with the weather and directional satellite. When I shut down the urgent message override command, I'd also disconnected minimum service.

After all, Mouse was the best hacker there was. If he wanted to bounce a message through the weather channel relays, he could find a way, and if Mouse could do it, someone else might be able to follow him. With the cops and the FBI on my trail, I couldn't take that risk.

The Gorgon sniffed the air. I wondered if he could smell my fear. "You're running away," he pronounced. With a cock of his head, he changed his mind. "Or are you hiding like the others?"

"What others?"

He shook his head. "It's a secret. They give us outside food if we keep the secret. What we hunt here just makes us sicker. Of course"—he gave me another toothy grin and a tenderizing poke—"your meat isn't contaminated yet."

"Oh." My smile faded. Curiosity had momentarily suppressed my fear. At the Gorgon's veiled threat, a lump returned to my throat. "Um, I thought that was an urban myth."

"Depends on how you define cannibalism. We don't eat our own kind . . . Human." The silver in his eyes glittered menacingly. He licked his lips for effect. I heard a faint whoosh; then, suddenly, a spring-loaded stiletto appeared in his hand.

The Gorgon waved the weapon inches from my face

so I could get a good look at his handiwork. Crudely fashioned from glass rather than steel, the blade's tip appeared sharp enough to puncture armor. Tattered scraps of fabric served for a functional grip. There was little doubt in my mind that the glass stiletto was as deadly as the look in the Gorgon's eyes.

I lashed out a foot. I aimed for his knee with my best police-training karate kick. The Gorgon absorbed the blow and rolled easily to his feet. Barefoot, I scrambled to mine with less grace.

"You don't want to fight me," I shouted with as much bravado as I could muster.

"Kill her and our deal is off," a voice said just above my shoulder. I swiveled my head at the sound. The sleek barrel of an H&K fléchette rifle, a PT37 to be exact, lowered until it rested an inch above my left shoulder. The deadly click of a safety being released echoed strangely in the surrounding glass. The red dot of the laser sight glowed pink against the Gorgon's pale skin. "Drop your weapon, 'Tober."

The Gorgon shrugged. The stiletto disappeared into his jacket. "Fair 'nuff, 'Becka. Didn't know she was your girlfriend. Don't eat girlfriends."

A throaty laugh barked behind me. "Good policy."

The weapon disappeared. I heard rather than saw the figure come around from behind me. The rifle was a dark spot in front of mirror-camouflage. With a ripple of movement, she exposed her face. A hairline scratch on the mirrored goggles connected to a scar above and below the left eye. In sudden recognition, I shouted, "Rebeckah!"

"Every time I see you, your clothes get less and less practical, Dee." She gave me a crooked smile. The butt of the gun gestured at Eion's robes. "Please tell me you haven't joined some crackpot religious order and taken a vow of celibacy."

"That's the second time someone's asked me that." I looked down at Eion's cassock, reminded of everything that happened in the Church. "Although I'm beginning to think maybe I should."

"Don't you dare." Rebeckah smiled, her eyes unreadable behind the goggles. At a LINKed command the holographic armor changed to nil, and her suit became blue-screen blue. Her hand rested lightly on the handle of her fléchette rifle, nonthreatening, but ready.

Turning to the Gorgon, she said, "Go back to the command center, 'Tober. Tell them I'm bringing a guest."

'Tober shrugged for a response, then scampered into the glass city. We watched his lithe form jog away.

"He works for you?"

Rebeckah shrugged. "Sometimes."

"Is he reliable?" I couldn't help but ask. In the distance, the Gorgon vaulted over one of the frozen car-shapes playfully.

Considering my question, Rebeckah clicked the safety back in place, and let the rifle dangle on its shoulder strap. "As a rule, Gorgons' priorities are askew, but 'Tober and I are friends. He'll do what I ask because he likes me, and because, right now, there isn't anything more interesting going on."

I scoffed. "Rebeckah, you don't ask—you command. Who said I was going back with you anyway?"

"The longer you stay here the more likely you are to be infected." She looked at my bare feet, mere inches from the glass. "The command center is well shielded."

It was neither an apology nor an excuse, just a statement of fact. My smile broadened. "All right. Lead on."

We passed through a glittering gully. Mountainous apartment complexes cast shadows across the glass street in long, dark stripes. Last night's rain made parts of the street almost impossible for me to navigate in Eion's shoes. Rebeckah steadied me with a hand around my elbow.

"Do you believe in angels, Rebeckah?" I asked without preamble, shattering the silence in which we'd been walking.

"What kind?"

"You know, Old Testament kind. Oh, sorry, I mean

like in the Torah. . . ." Then I stopped, failing to find
words to describe Michael and my dream. Rebeckah's
firm grip steadied me as I slid on the street as though it
were a sheet of ice.

"Of course. The first time the Torah talks about
angels, they're just 'messengers.' They come into the Is-
raelite camp and have food and drink, like regular men.
I think those kinds of angels exist. I might even be an
angel like that to someone sometime. You never know
when you're doing God's work."

"Trust me, sometimes it's painfully obvious," I
sneered.

"You sound bitter." Her voice was soft, concerned.

Pretending I hadn't heard her comment, I continued,
"But, what about the other kind of angel? The ones the
LINK-angels are based on—with big wings, and flaming
swords, and all that?"

We reached dry ground, and she let go of my arm.
Readjusting the rifle's strap on her shoulder, she turned
her head away. "I've never met any like that."

"You've met Michael Angelucci."

"I have." She spoke slowly, her tone dark.

"I thought so," I murmured, adding a mental check
mark next to my suspicions. "So, Rebeckah, what'd
you think?"

I left my question purposely open-ended, and she
chewed on her response for a long moment. Wind blew
through the glass-encased leaves of a lone tree-shape on
the boulevard. Instead of the rustling I expected, the
breeze whistled and moaned through the unmoving
glass. Finally, Rebeckah turned to look me in the eye.

"Your Michael knows how to cause a shake-up, that's
for sure."

My anger flared up. "He's not 'my' anything."

Rebeckah shrugged off my outburst. "I lost several
good soldiers after his brief stint with us. We've always
had spirited debates in camp about LINK-angels, our
work, and whatnot. His philosophy was . . . disturbing."

"Yeah, that's an understatement," I said with a low
whistle, reminded of my conversation with Michael in

the belfry. I shook my head, banishing my growing dread. "Do you believe him?"

"He gave very persuasive proof to back up his arguments."

I didn't have to ask for details to know what Rebeckah meant. The look on her face told me she knew exactly what Michael was. Fear pulled her face taut, and I could feel a chill returning to my stomach.

We turned the block. A chain-link fence surrounded what was once a playground. Though the barrier had probably been forbidding in its earlier incarnation, the Medusa-glass gave it a delicate appearance, like crystal lace. The sun danced along the symmetrical curves, catching my eye.

"For myself, I decided that it didn't matter," Rebeckah said. "The Talmud is filled with conjecture about the nature of God. Thousands of scholars have wrestled with the question since the beginning, each of them claiming the others were wrong. It shouldn't surprise me that no one got it right. That's the reason the name of God remains unpronounceable . . . to keep us from trying to define, to limit, that which is undefinable, unlimited. As for the rest, we do what we do because it's a good way to live. The laws we follow are sound. Whatever might be decided about the nature of God has very little effect on the truth, the goodness, of those laws."

The chill I felt disappeared. I smiled at Rebeckah. Even though our beliefs were worlds apart, her faith steadied me. "You're good for me, you know that?"

Her lips turned up in the slightest of smiles. "Anyway, I have to believe in angels."

"Why's that?"

"I'm a Malach Nikamah, an avenging angel, after all."

I had heard the Hebrew translated when reports of LINK-terrorism first broke in the news, but had since forgotten the irony. Rebeckah and her followers purposely chose to name themselves after angels to challenge the LINK version and to remind people of the possibility of hoax and of a human hand behind the stir.

The glass-encased buildings grew denser as we ap-

proached the center of the city. The city was deadly
quiet. No pigeon coo or insect buzz broke the unearthly
silence. In the warm afternoon air, I imagined I felt the
deadly chain reaction reaching up to grab me from
every surface.

"We're here," Rebeckah announced, jumping down
into the window well of a basement-level apartment.
Over flash-frozen marigolds in a window box, I could see
the dark hairs of her flattop. She knocked three times on
the bottom pane. After a few seconds, someone on the
other side removed the false glass. Rebeckah crawled
through, motioning for me to follow her.

Gingerly, I lowered myself. It was tempting to use the
fire escape for leverage, but I wanted to avoid as much
direct contact with the Medusa glass as possible. I
crouched, ready to take the awkward plunge and crawl
through, when a hand from inside offered a pair of armored gloves.

"Thanks," I said, pulling them on. Ducking my head,
I scrambled through the narrow opening. The Medusa
blast had entered the apartment the same way I did,
through the open window, freezing everything inside.
The new occupants had removed most of the walls that
were glassed in the explosion, including the ceiling. The
same armored fabric that comprised Rebeckah's camouflage suit draped the outer wall and the floor. With the
false glass in front of the opening, the danger was effec-
tively minimized. Even so, the four guards wore fully
operational combat armor.

One of them waved the tip of his fléchette rifle in my
direction. His eyes were locked on Eion's vestments. His
voice held a thin, incredulous tone when he asked,
"Your guest, Commander?"

"Yes, and see that she gets outfitted with armor
pronto, soldier," Rebeckah said. Acknowledging his
"Yes, sir," with a brief nod, she gestured me farther into
the complex. "I'm afraid I can't give you the full tour,
you understand, but let me show you to the mess hall.
We can get something to drink while you wait for some
decent clothes."

"Sure," I murmured, willing to be led anywhere, especially since the action didn't involve any thinking on my part. I stripped off the gloves and looked around for a place or a person to return them to. One of the other guards took them from me wordlessly.

"Thanks," I murmured.

I followed Rebeckah into the bowels of the apartment complex. The hallway was dark, except for a string of Christmas lights running along the seam between the wall and the ceiling. The light was weak, but steady. The apartment was too deep inside the glass city for the Malachim to be easily siphoning power from the main grid. I deduced that they must either have their own generator somewhere or a really good LINK-hacker on their team. Knowing Rebeckah, it could be both.

The number of people we passed surprised me as I shuffled along the nubby carpeting. Occasionally, wild silver locks interspersed among the dark, militaristic haircuts. Rebeckah must have noticed my eyes following a pair of silver heads as they disappeared up a flight of stairs, because she said, "The Gorgons lived here first. It didn't seem right to oust them. Besides, they've proven to be excellent scavengers . . . and surprisingly willing to barter."

"Politics and strange bedfellows." I shrugged. I was intrigued by the alliance between the Malachim and the Gorgons, but too tired to pursue it. My eyes were distracted by the soft colors of the Christmas lights. Someone had made a Star of David at the intersection of two hallways. "Nice decorations."

Rebeckah laughed and held out her hand to indicate the direction I should go. "The Gorgons," she explained. "They must have found a warehouse full of the lights. They string them up wherever they go. Some of my boys augmented their haphazard design and siphoned a bit of power for them. The light is strange, but I've gotten used to it."

"I've seen something like this in the abandoned service tunnels in Manhattan."

"I'm not surprised." Rebeckah nodded. "The tunnels are a great way to get around unnoticed."

"For you or them?"

"Both," Rebeckah said, as we headed up a flight of stairs. The stairway was too narrow for us to walk side by side, so Rebeckah took the lead. Over her shoulder she asked, "Why?"

"Do you have your own generator, or do you boost the city's power?" I asked. My fingers brushed the handrail. Red lights looped around the rail, giving the shadows of Rebeckah's armor a purplish cast.

"You didn't answer my question, Deidre. Why do you want to know if we use the service tunnels?"

I waited, saying nothing. I hoped she'd drop her question, but I knew I'd never win a game like this one with Rebeckah. At the landing, I paused to catch my breath. Rebeckah turned to regard me evenly.

"All right, all right." I gave in. I smiled, because I knew I'd be the first to break. "I only ask because I saw these strange boxes set at intervals throughout the tunnels running along the old cable-car power lines. They didn't look like maintenance units; they were too purposely concealed. In fact, I wouldn't have noticed them at all if it weren't for the Gorgon's lights. Are they yours?"

Rebeckah looked genuinely surprised by my information. "No. Manhattan, you said?"

"Yeah, not far from the deli we met at, actually. I guess that's why I suspected they might be your power siphons."

"We have our own generators."

The stony look on Rebeckah's face made me realize what I'd implied was very definitely against her code of honor.

"I'm sorry, Rebeckah. Of course, you're not thieves. I didn't mean . . ."

Rebeckah cut off my lame attempt at apology. "Whose are they, I wonder."

"I don't know. I suppose it could be the Unitarians' underground railroad."

Dismissing that idea with a shake of her head, Rebeckah smiled. "They're not that organized—too much infighting. Besides, it's summer."

I laughed. The Unitarians were notorious for closing down their churches in the summertime. At Rebeckah's nod, we started back up the stairs. After my long walk in ill-fitting shoes, I had to ask. "What floor is the mess on, anyway?"

"It's the top floor. Back when this was a condominium it was used as a 'party suite,' a common room for the residents."

"Great," I grumbled, hoisting myself up more steps. The red lights changed to a bright white at the next floor. "What about the Gay Liberation Ecumenical folks?"

"Most of their energy is concentrated on repelling the gender-bending fashion restrictions. Even the extremists in Vulva Riot and Act Up's LINK protest have been confined to newsgroups—very much within the letter of the law. The most they do is run under handles to protect their identities. The ones with resources to pull off a siphon are under too much scrutiny." Ahead of me, I saw Rebeckah's proud shoulders droop just a fraction. "I wouldn't rule them out, but it's unlikely."

"I heard the Black Muslims were organizing around this guy Jibril Freshta," I said, hoping to slide past Rebeckah's iron defenses. "Could it be them?"

Either I was sly enough that she didn't catch it, or she gave it to me. "From what I hear, Freshta is a pacifist and very law-abiding. So far, his people seem to prefer peaceful demonstrations."

"Then why are the police after him?"

"Nobody likes a troublemaker in an election year . . . even a peaceful one. Besides, he's been an easy target. Unlike us, he operates a hundred percent in real time. That means no handles, no quick reroutes. The cops know what he looks like and where he goes. Brave guy."

I remembered Jibril's broad smile. "Yeah. He's got the kind of face you remember. You ever met him?"

"No." Her tone was even. I couldn't tell if she felt

anything more than a passing respect for Jibril's message or not. Black Muslims had an unfortunate history of being anti-Semitic. I couldn't imagine Jibril as one of those, but I could understand her caution.

"I hope he's okay," I said mostly to myself. We continued climbing. After passing a level of yellow Christmas lights, I asked, "Have you heard anything about me on the LINK? About Daniel?"

"I heard you were plugged in again," Rebeckah said, as we turned the landing, moving up to a stairwell draped in blinking pink lights. The shadows fluttering along Rebeckah's suit looked lavender now. "There's an APB on the police frequency about how dangerous you are."

I chuckled. "Dangerous? I guess I'm giving your reputation a run for the money, eh?"

"I'm not feeling my reputation threatened just yet," she said with a wink, as we finally came to the party suite. I was out of breath.

Leaning against the doorframe, I looked in. The suite had not made the conversion to cafeteria very smoothly. The ghost of a once-swanky apartment party room hung around the edges of the mess hall. What was once a wet bar now served as a buffet line. None of the furniture matched; soldiers sat on sofas and on the floor around end tables.

The only lights in the room were eerie shafts of muted sun that penetrated the Medusa-sheathed penthouse windows, and, of course, the ubiquitous Christmas bulbs hanging in great profusion from the ceiling.

Despite the awkward accommodations, the mess hall bustled with activity. Men and women sat scattered about the suite in clumps of conversation, laughter, and heated debate. Silver hair was mixed liberally among the Orthodox men wearing *payot,* the side locks, and military buzz cuts. The smell of beef stew simmering in a Crock-Pot made my mouth water. Rebeckah headed into the room, amid many waves and shouts of greeting.

Grief tugged at my heart. Watching Rebeckah move easily through this band of LINK-terrorists and Gorgons,

I envied her. It seemed strange. This woman was public enemy number one, constantly on the run, forced to live in the glass city and risk infection from the Medusa biovirus or worse, but at this very moment I wished I were she.

I had no one like her comrades in my life. Since the excommunication and all that came with it, I'd been alone—without even the ethereal community of the LINK in which to find comfort. My lover was an . . . no, I didn't even want to think about that. With a shrug, I pushed away my darkening mood as Rebeckah waved me over to a central table. For the time being, I was given a respite from a loneliness I hadn't even fully realized I felt. I might not be able to have Rebeckah's life, but I could pretend I did for as long as I was a guest here.

Rebeckah introduced me to our tablemates. I forgot most of their names the instant she said them. I nodded politely all the same. It wasn't like me to be so distracted—my police training made me an expert at keeping names and faces sorted—but my attention focused on an intense-looking soldier. He was frowning suspiciously into his coffee cup, his head tilted to the side. He was powerfully built, but the line of his neck was as graceful as any dancer's. The short hairs of his military cut only served to heighten the effect.

"Raphael," Rebeckah repeated, "meet Deidre."

Our eyes met. The noise of a subway car—the sound seemed to rush toward me, bringing with it a strong wind.

"Dee?" It was Rebeckah. She stood next to me, her hand soft my shoulder.

"Sorry," I mumbled, leaning into her to steady myself. "I've been having trouble with visual feedback lately," I lied.

Concerned eyes slid away from mine. Feedback was a common problem of those who had their LINK connection severed. The subject was too close to home for LINK-hackers, who could face a sentence of disconnection if caught. I took the opportunity their discomfort provided to take another look at Raphael.

With a sheepish grin on his face, he lifted a hand in a brief wave. The look on his face seemed to say, "You caught me."

I snorted a laugh and shook my head. He slid over, offering me a seat. Rebeckah helped me into it and sat down beside me. Once I settled, I whispered to Raphael, "You people are everywhere. Can't I get away from your kind?"

He turned his head to inspect me with the same intensity as he had inspected his coffee cup earlier. Then, he smiled. "My mistake. I thought you were one of 'our kind.' "

"What?" I exploded, my voice a little louder than I intended. Everyone put their spoons down and stared at me. Rebeckah frowned, her eyebrows crinkled with concern.

"Dee," she asked, "you okay?"

"Sorry. I'm a little on edge. I guess I could use that drink you promised."

"I'll get it," Raphael offered. "Apple juice okay?"

"No, wait. . . ." I'd wanted Rebeckah to get it so he and I could have a chance to talk, but Raphael bolted out of his seat and was halfway to the bar before I could stop him. I frowned at his retreating form. I didn't even get a chance to tell him I preferred something stronger— like coffee.

"You guys know each other." The way Rebeckah spoke, the phrase was more of a statement than a question.

"Not really." I looked her in the eye, hoping she'd see the truth.

"Hmph," Rebeckah said. "Well, Raphael has that effect on people. When we first met, I thought I'd known him. I spent months wracking my brain, trying to remember if we'd ever served together in Israel. . . ." Rebeckah looked as if she were about to say more, when a soldier approached. "Yes?"

"A word, Commander?"

Rebeckah nodded, standing up to move a short distance from the table. "Excuse me."

I looked away, not wanting to intrude on her business. My eyes strayed back to the table full of strangers.

"You're an American Catholic, then?" A bearded man to my left asked politely. Ringlets of brown hair fell down either side of his face.

"Oh." I forgot what I must look like to them. "This is borrowed. I . . ." I couldn't think of a simple way to explain how I ended up in Eion's vestments, so I just said, "My brother is a Roman Catholic priest."

"I see." He smiled, sensing my discomfort with the situation. "Well, any friend of Rebeckah's is a friend of mine."

"She's not just any friend. That's Deidre McMannus. You guys remember all the stink when the Pope was killed last year," a woman said at the end of the table. Underneath a leather vest, she wore a black muscle shirt with a picture of a rodent chewing on coaxial cable. Tattooed barbed wire and fiber-optic lines wound like Celtic knotwork around her biceps. The uniform of a LINK-hacker, if I've ever seen one.

"She's that Deidre McMannus," the wire-wizard continued with a touch of awe in her voice. Her eyes snaked over to mine cautiously.

I gave a weak smile. I couldn't get away from my reputation anywhere, it seemed. "Yep, that's me."

"Ironic choice in clothing, then, eh?" Raphael said with a wink, as he returned to the table. He shoved a plastic glass of apple juice in front of me.

"I was in a rush." I cupped my hands around the sweating clear plastic—though it wasn't what I'd wanted, at least the juice was icy cold. I took a long, refreshing swallow.

"I hear you've never been much of a slave to fashion, anyway." The hacker at the end of the table gave a hearty laugh. "Hanes, bikini cut? I would have thought you a boxer shorts type."

I blushed. Mouse, the stinker, had actually posted the information about my underwear. "Well, uh, they're cheap."

The people around the table laughed, and not un-kindly. I found myself smiling warmly.

Raphael touched my elbow. "We should talk." His breath tickled my ear.

"I don't want to know you, Raphael," I said firmly. I stared into the remains of the apple juice. A yellowed reflection of my stern expression glowered back at me. "I don't want to know any of you."

"Too late for that," Raphael said, taking a sip from his coffee mug. I could smell the rich aroma. I stared furiously at my juice.

"It's not like there are hundreds of us running around," he continued. "If you've met even one other—you're already in the thick of things. In the center of the storm, as it were."

"Story of my life," I muttered. My breath rippled the surface of the juice, fracturing the image of my face into abstraction. "Only this time, I'm going to walk away."

"You don't seem the type." Raphael's voice was low and sincere. With a shrug, he added, "But, it's your choice."

" 'Choice,' why is it always about 'choice' for you peo-ple?" I slammed the plastic cup down with such ferocity that juice sloshed onto my hand. "It's like you're ob-sessed with freewill."

Raphael arched an eyebrow, and his mouth drew into a thin line. His eyes scanned the table, but the others seemed engrossed in their own conversations. Turning back to me, he shrugged. "We don't get out much."

"There's an understatement." I laughed through my fingers, as I sucked the spilled liquid from my palm.

Turning back to his coffee mug, Raphael took a long sip. His Adam's apple bobbed up and down, but his face betrayed no emotion. Sliding his gaze back to mine, he asked, "May I ask who you met?"

I stifled the urge to say no because I wanted to see how he reacted when I dropped the names. I started at what I presumed he felt to be the bottom of the list, and worked my way up. "Morningstar, Jibril, and Michael."

Raphael set his cup down gently, and his brows drew

together. He ran a callused thumb along the rim of the mug. Corded muscles jumped on his powerful forearms as he crossed his arms and balanced his elbows on the edge of the table. Steepled fingers lightly bounced against his lip, the only sign that what I'd said disturbed him. Finally, Raphael spread his hands in a gesture of acquiescence. "You really are in the center of things."

I laughed. Unbidden, my mind flashed to an image of Michael naked. I remembered his smooth, cool skin under my fingers and the smell of his sweat. The dream-image of the thundering of six wings of a monstrous seraphim broke my pleasant reverie. Shaking my head, I grumbled, "I'd really rather be somewhere else."

"I'm sure you're where you're supposed to be," Raphael said gently.

"I'm not sure of anything anymore," I countered. Rebeckah touched my shoulder, interrupting my train of thought.

"I've got some news, Dee. Come with me."

She pivoted on her heels and began heading out of the suite before I could even acknowledge her command. As I stood up to follow, I leaned close to Raphael and whispered: "We'll talk again."

He smiled. "I don't doubt it."

I would have taken the time to come up with some parting shot, but Rebeckah was already to the door. If I didn't hurry to catch up, I'd lose her. I scrambled out of my seat.

"Hey, McMannus!" I heard from the table. Glancing over my shoulder, I saw the hacker at the end of the table give me the "thumbs-up." I returned a smile and a wave.

"A contact of mine has seen Daniel," Rebeckah informed me when I caught up with her in the stairwell. "Apparently, some of your fellow officers helped him make a break for it when the power blew in New Jersey."

I let out a breath I didn't even know I was holding. "Where is he?"

"My contact saw him in the underground heading into

Manhattan. I have a feeling he's looking for you." She looked at me sideways, judging my reaction. My mind was already meeting with Daniel. I wondered what he looked like after all this time, what I would say to him, and how I could explain why I never answered any of his letters.

Rebeckah's firm voice cut through my jumbled thoughts. "You shouldn't even risk it, Dee. It's going to be quite a trick to get ahold of him without alerting the syscops."

"You know where he is?"

"Not exactly, no," Rebeckah said patiently. "Just that he's on the move and headed into Manhattan. It's possible you could intercept him before he gets too far. But, it's dangerous right now—"

I cut her off with, "I have to try."

Rebeckah nodded grimly. "Somehow I knew you'd say that."

We stopped in front of one of the apartment doors. She took a key card out of one of her belt pouches and swiped it through the lock. The door popped open. "There's armor in there. I had to guess at your size." A slight blush rose on her cheeks, but she cleared her throat, and added, "If we get caught trying to contact Daniel, I don't want you to get busted for impersonating a priest."

"Thanks, Rebeckah." I reached out and captured her hand. I gave it a quick squeeze. "I owe you."

"If you think I'm not keeping score, you're mistaken," she said gruffly. "This is barter, not charity."

"Still." I smiled. "Thanks."

I shut the door behind me. The clothes Rebeckah referred to were laid neatly at the foot of a narrow bed. A footlocker, a desk, and several bookshelves were placed squarely along the walls. The interior design evoked a certain *je ne sais quoi* or perhaps a *dorm du college*.

I inspected the armor on the bed. Picking up the undershirt, I turned it over in my hands. The fabric was heavy, some kind of blend of super-thin fiber-optic cables and cotton. Its blue-screen blue shimmered in the

ARCHANGEL PROTOCOL

muted light. The only window was covered in a film of
Medusa-glass; the light that eked through had a hazy
quality. Heavy-looking curtain material hung on either
side of a small window. I got up and pulled it shut, even
though I doubted anyone would be passing by, or, if
they did, be able to see through the waves of the
bomb's sheath.

Shrugging out of Eion's cassock, I let the vestments
slip to the floor. I pulled the armor's undershirt over my
head. The material was heavy and slick against my skin,
like a scuba gear. Though a bit small through the shoulders, the suit stretched to cover my body snugly. The
neck of the undershirt came all the way to my chin; the
sleeves extended well past my wrists. Rebeckah had
made a pretty good guess at my size.

I stepped into the pants and wiggled the tight material
over my hips. As I buckled the armored sections onto
the leggings, my fingers fell into routine and my mind
wandered. Right now Daniel was heading into Manhattan, looking for me. Despite his letters' assurances that
he'd forgiven me, my stomach knotted at the thought of
facing him again. I sent him to prison. The words spoken
in the courtroom maligned his character, and I was part
of all of it. Captain Morgan hadn't forgiven me for that
betrayal of partner loyalty. Truth be told, I hadn't forgiven myself. It seemed insane to expect that, after everything, Daniel would welcome me with open arms.

Then there was that small problem of Daniel's guilt.
He'd killed the Pope. Nothing I'd heard or seen since
changed my mind. Daniel's last letter sounded like the
ramblings of a madman—with all his talk of "them,"
and how I shouldn't trust anyone on the LINK.

I hefted the heavily armored jacket onto my shoulders.
Connecting the two edges, I ran my fingers along the
seam. At my touch, the jacket automatically clicked together, guided by a strong magnet. The instant all the
pieces were in place the uniform hummed to life.

Israeli technology was top-of-the-line. The uniform existed as a walking LINK connection, holographic armor,
and as a cybernetic exoskeleton to provide physical pro-

tection. I ran my fingers along the surface of the armor, impressed with all the bells and whistles.

Only the helmet remained. The Israeli insignia had been scraped off either side and replaced with a crudely stenciled image of a black wing. In indelible marker someone had carefully scripted the word: "vengeance."

Sitting down on the small bed, I put a hand on the pitted surface of the helmet. Michael corrected me when I speculated that his involvement in bringing Letourneau to justice came down to revenge. No, vengeance, he said. Vengeance.

I shook my head. The only thing vengeance had going for it was a healthy dose of righteousness; and, when it came down to mortal affairs, the whole notion seemed like an arrogant shifting of the blame for any bloodshed to a higher authority. Yet, the Malachim fought against oppressive injustice, and Michael, too, in seeking to expose Letourneau, sided with what I could consider goodness. Perhaps "vengeance" was correct in their case.

Despite my rationalization, I shivered as my fingers traced the raised surface of the black wing on the helmet. There was nothing I would kill for. It was my profound lack of Faith that kept me from the kind of commitment to a cause that the Malachim, Michael, and even Daniel had. My experience as a street cop taught me that justice, like truth, mutated and changed. What I'd seen of Michael and his ilk cast doubt on the infallibility of even the divine. That only served to solidify my distrust of absolutes and people who espoused them.

Picking up the helmet, I tossed it from hand to hand. Raphael had me pegged better than I cared to admit. Though I tried to let those with convictions fight in my stead, I found myself again and again in the center of the storm. More than that, I pushed actively against the winds, as if I had the power to turn nature from its course.

Caressing the stencil of the black wing, I put the helmet on. I searched through the lining of the hood for the tiny filament connecting the uniform to the LINK. Finding it, I spit on the tiny rounded pad at the end of the wire and stuck it to the panel in the helmet above the almond-shaped lump in my temple that housed my LINK receiver.

Ones and zeros flashed briefly as the uniform's computer calibrated to match my LINK connection. Once the systems meshed, a window popped up in the right corner of my field of vision. A two-dimensional box scrolled pertinent information, and certain files automatically downloaded in the memory system of my LINK. I still couldn't see through the helmet's armored face shield. Mentally, I toggled the view option. My vision unfurled to a complete 360-degree view. The experience disoriented me, until I focused on one thing. Holding my gloved hand up in front of my face, I tested the holographic defense.

On, I subvocalized. I could hear a faint hum as holographic imagers came on-line. Tiny lights, like pinpricks, broke out on the surface of the gloves. Seconds later, my hand disappeared. Almost. When I wiggled my fingers, I could see the mirroring camouflage struggle to re-form a reflective surface. The imagers lagged a fraction behind the movement, giving the illusion a rippling effect. When I moved slowly and precisely enough, I was virtually invisible.

Off, I commanded. My glove returned to blue-screen blue. *Hey, partner . . . it's me.*

New York Times, April 4, 2026. Text only file follows.

"FLAME" DISRUPTS GREY'S VISIT TO WIRE TREATMENT CENTER

The presidential candidate Rabbi-Senator Chaim Grey's visit with patients at the Lou Dameshorey Wire-Addiction Treatment Center today was interrupted by public outcry during his on-line address. The "flame war" was so massive that it caused node static for nearly two hours. The situation was remedied when the candidate narrowed his speech broadcast band to members of the press.

The controversial sound bite follows. [The *New York Times* requests all responses be directed to editorial.link, and not the main frequency.] ## "These are the forgotten ones; the ones to whom the current administration turns its back. Wire-addiction is the epidemic of modern times. Never, since the AIDS crisis have so many people been so neglected by a United States government." ##

Immediately following the above statement, a flame war began. Grey's campaign managers were unable to reply fast enough to the LINKed responses and the node overloaded. Grey's campaign spokesperson, Augustino Sanchez, explains, "People were cranked that the Rabbi-Senator paralleled the current administration with the outlawed secular government."

Many of the flames have been lost, but Grey's campaign managers say they are carefully sifting through the undamaged responses in order to understand what touched the public's nerve.

"There's more than the secular analogy going on—it's the queer thing," an anonymous representative from the illegal organization ACT UP told this reporter. "First of all, no one likes to be reminded of the 'gay plague.' And then, for Grey to say that queers weren't deserving of their fate is like admitting he likes the sin and not the sinners, if you get my meaning."

The ACT UP spokesperson's comment may have some merit, as a large percentage of people polled since the flame war agree that it was the reference to AIDS made them the most angry. [To see survey methodologies and results—hot-link here.]

"Wire-addiction is nothing like AIDS," said Gail Beckmen from Brooklyn. "I know some good people who have had trouble with the wire."

Reverend-Senator Etienne Letourneau was notably silent during this controversial event. His office has made no response, except to say that the Reverend-Senator's "heart goes out to all those who suffer."

CHAPTER 14

Hey, partner . . . it's me. I jumped at the sound. I turned to look around the room, even though my brain instantly registered the voice as subvocal.

An image wavered into existence, like a ghost given form. His face, as always, looked as if it had run into too many fists over the course of his forty years. Wild black hair had been tamed by a prison buzz cut. His features were thinner, hungrier, but his dark eyes still flashed with mischief. The smile he bore was the roguish grin of a wolf.

With a cluck of my tongue, I admired his craft. He had taken the time to construct an image, as well as preempt the LINK's usual command routine. No incoming message warning, just Daniel, standing there like he'd never left. Although, not quite. The facial image was recent, as the buzz cut attested, but it was evident he cobbled the body together. Crackling with energy, the picture refused to stay still beneath the perfectly replicated face. I imagined he hacked the image from the prison camera, maybe even during the breakout to cover his tracks.

Lagging behind, came the LINK's response: *MESSAGE, recorded 4:59 pm EST, source unknown.*

"Some help you are," I groused to the LINK. Smiling, in spite of myself, I added, "Anyway, I know who it is. Hi, Danny."

The image of Daniel was frozen in space, waiting for a go-ahead command. I shook my head. Only a social miscreant like Daniel would program a message to appear without the usual warnings and then bother to have the politeness to wait for a response.

Go ahead, I sent, then added out loud, "You old fox. You've only gotten trickier with age."

Sorry for the crudeness of this message, but I needed to get your attention, he said, his eyes apologetic. *Friends of mine tell me you're back on the LINK. I'd like to know how you've managed that, Dee. Maybe you could hustle me a reconnect after things settle down? I'm jonesing bad.*

I looked at the image of Daniel with renewed interest—he was hardwiring this? Not possible, I told myself, he wouldn't have the time, and, besides, he could hardly run with a board and key-in at the same time. This was someone else's LINK connection, then.

Anyway, the image continued, *I hope the rumor is true; otherwise, I have no idea when you'll get this message . . . It's being transmitted through a friend's access, and I don't know how long he can keep it bouncing around.* The image shrugged, sending the image of the body into a sizzling chaos. *If you haven't already heard— I'm out. We need to meet, to put our heads together, like the old days. I've got some crazy ideas about Letourneau I need to bounce off your superior brain, old friend.* Danny threw me a wink. *Contact me any way you can. My friend will be listening for you.*

The three-dimensional image became flat. The pixels separated, raining down to disappear into the floor.

"With a performance like that, you should've been a wire-wizard, Danny," I told the empty room. Daniel must have had the message bouncing around the LINK waiting for me to surface again. When I plugged into the uniform's LINK connection, I broadcast my location, giving the message an in.

Shutting the holographic armor down, I pulled the LINK filament from my head. The uniform still hummed with power, and all of its other defenses would remain functional as long as I wore it. Putting the helmet under an arm, I stepped out into the hallway. Rebeckah leaned against the wall waiting for me, her arms crossed in front of her chest. When she saw me, she smiled. "I started to think you'd given up on the idea of chasing after Daniel, and all this foolishness."

"Yeah. Well, no luck. I got a message from Daniel." I tapped the helmet. "I just hope I wasn't LINKed long enough for anyone else to get the drop on our location."

Rebeckah's smile broadened, as she used a booted foot to push off from the wall. "I'm going to make a Malach Nikamah out of you yet. I appreciate your concern, Dee, but we're covered. All the uniforms' LINK connection have been modified to bounce through random LINK nodes. If the cops are watching for your frequency right now they think you've hopped a plane to Tokyo or Paris or God knows where."

I let out the breath I was holding. "Of course," I muttered, embarrassed I hadn't thought of that. "Otherwise you could never use the LINK without the cops finding your hideout. I should've figured."

"Forget about it." Rebeckah indicated the direction we should walk with a jerk of her head. "What did Daniel have to say?"

"You were right. He wants to meet."

"I still say it's crazy." Her lips tightened to a thin smile, then she let out a breath in a snort. "But, there's no stopping you, is there?"

"He says he has information about Letourneau."

"I'm already in for a pound, Dee, you don't have to entice me." Rebeckah turned a corner down another dimly lit corridor.

"What do you mean?"

Rebeckah said nothing, staring grimly ahead.

"No, Rebeckah," I protested, "you've done enough for me. Like you said, it's a fool's errand. I can't ask you to come along. . . ."

"I didn't hear anybody asking." Rebeckah stopped suddenly and turned to face me. "And, I'm not taking any argument. We're backing you up, Deidre McMannus. You're going to owe us, big-time, but you're not traipsing off to your little rendezvous without our firepower covering your fugitive ass. You can just forget any ideas of Lone Ranger heroics. We're going in with you. End of discussion."

It was. My mouth hung open, and I couldn't formulate any coherent or rational objection.

"Good." She pivoted and headed down the hallway. "I've got my people working out a location for the meeting," Rebeckah continued, her voice matter-of-fact. "We need something defendable, out of the way, and not too close to the glass city. I want to have a safe place to retreat to if something goes wrong." She looked over her shoulder to make sure I was following both her and the conversation. "You, get in touch with Mouse. Sharron is capable of running the LINK end of things, but I'd rather keep her sig file off this operation. I'm supporting you as a friend, not as part of the cause. You understand?" I nodded. "When you call Mouse, make it quick. Even with the armor's built-in loop, I don't want to give the authorities any trail they could follow."

"Agreed," I said, because there wasn't much else to say when Rebeckah was in command mode. Absently, I groped for the filament in the hood. "I'll meet you in the dining room in—what? An hour?"

"Give us two."

By way of agreement, I stopped moving. Rebeckah's powerful strides carried her off, moving deeper into the apartment complex until her blue uniform was swallowed by the cavernous darkness. I turned back in the direction of the stairwell, intending to make my way upstairs to the mess hall.

My fingers found the thin connection wire. Still moist, the pad stuck easily to my receiver. I jacked in. This time, I carefully monitored the routing patterns scrolling past my vision: through Detroit to the Vancouver node, from there to Juneau. The signal never stayed with any one node for longer than a microsecond. Satisfied with the process, I reached for Mouse's address.

The page appeared in the uniform's LINK window at the upper right corner of my vision. The image assumed receptionist mode, being little more than a headshot and sporting an old-fashioned telephone headset. *Mouse's house, Mouse speaking.*

Hey, 'home,' I recited, and smiled to myself, never failing to find our old joke funny even after all this time.

Solid handshake, Dee. Sweet system. I see we jettisoned the bucket of rust. Good call. The page smiled broadly. The eager smile made him look even younger than usual. *Man, you move fast. Yesterday it was a slow surf on a mundane phone line, then you blow the top off the LINK, and now you've got me chasing you through sophisticated LINK hops. You never cease to impress, girl.*

Thanks, Mouse, but before you get all excited, the hardware is on loan. Listen, I'm sorry but I can't hang long. Reaching the stairwell, I began to pull myself up toward the mess hall. I nodded politely to two Gorgons who were galloping down the steps. *Where's your alterego? I thought he had a line dedicated to me.*

We do, but he's on a plane, marooned in real time. Eight hours, poor guy. But, don't diss me, Deidre. With a shake of his head, the receptionist headgear disappeared, winking out of virtual existence. The page metamorphed his shirt and tie into a more streetwise costume of a leather jacket and black tee shirt. The change of clothes made the page look remarkably more like his real-time alter ego. *I've got full authority to run all the operations until he can get back on. Only thing I can't do for you is hardware work.*

Mouse is on a plane? Where's he going?

Somewhere eight hours away. How should I know? I don't care where the body goes.

Mouse . . . I said, while stopping on a landing to catch my breath. Though ten times more comfortable and more maneuverable than Eion's vestments, the armored uniform weighed twice as much.

Deidre. No. I'm not trailing my own credit line just to tell you where the body has run off to. That's like spying on myself. Anyway, it's nothing to flake out about. We've been off-lining a lot lately, on business trips. I figure it's best not to know what the left hand is up to, you know?

Despite his breezy manner, the space between the page's eyebrows creased. It was strange to see an unconscious, human gesture on a construct, even an AI as sophisticated as Mouse's page.

A passing soldier frowned at my apparent inability to walk and LINK, so I started up the stairs again. *Listen, I can't stay out here much longer. Do you have any secure place we could go?*

Why are you so worried about time? Your system's loops are hard for me to keep up with. I doubt the cops are running anything more sophisticated than mouse.net.

I smiled at Mouse's bravado. Though I'd never seen the hardware mouse.net ran on, Mouse had always impressed me as the cobbled system in the basement of Mom's place type.

Right, I sent. *You Überphreeking on me, boy?*

Mouse frowned at my jibe. *You'd be surprised at the tech we can pull off. Speaking of, and since you're so wigged about tails, why don't you follow me to our main address.*

I'm honored, I said, and this time I meant it. The hub of mousenet, like Xanadu or Camelot, was a place out of legend. Theories about it raged in the LINK-cop community. Most doubted its very existence. *How many jumps away is it?*

The page shook his head, as if disappointed that I hadn't guessed his secret. *Close, but so far away. One, Dee. It's only ever one jump away.*

One? The LINK, though in practice more like radio waves, used power nodes to boost the bioware's ability to store and send information. I'd always assumed that Mouse's closest power center was Cairo, and that was at least twenty jumps from New York's central address. *Where is it?*

Well, it's not exactly a where. Getting you there is going to take a change in mind-set, girl. Maybe you should sit down—literally.

Okay. I'd reached the party suite. I spied an empty seat on a couch at the far wall.

Ready? The page asked. *It's going to blow your mind.*

I plopped down on the couch. In preparation, I squeezed my eyes shut. *Hit it.*

Despite Mouse's warning, I still expected to be raced along a series of connections in electronic space at the speed of thought. Instead, I felt something far more disturbing. Following his lead, my LINK consciousness expanded in all directions at once.

My real-time stomach dropped, giving me a phantom feeling of falling through the floor. Tightening my grip on the arms of the couch, I tried to remind my body that I was safely sitting in the mess hall.

The sensation of moving all at once like that, like the blast ring of a Medusa bomb, had my internal processors struggling to make sense of the shifting waves of information. Thousands of images flipped through my mind as I extended farther out. Unable to completely abandon linear thought, my mind groped to make sense of snippets and pieces and parts. *Twenty percent chance of rain tonight . . . Il y a une f . . ."* Holo-visuals of the entertainment frequency flashed through personal conversations and meshed with Traffic Control. *Coordinates: 55 degrees latitude, by . . . Oh, Trent, I can't live without you . . . Wei. Joe sun! . . . your very own, buy now!* The jumble of voices and images threatened to overwhelm me. *¿Quién sabe? . . . first level . . . oh yeah? . . . set alarm for . . .* I felt my real-time stomach tighten at the prospect of becoming indistinct within the greater universe of the LINK.

Soon the distinct voices became an unintelligible thrum, and I merged with the LINK. Images blurred together into a blinding white light. Though sightless and soundless, I could sense the LINK as it pulsed and breathed, enveloping me in its living warmth. I could have pooled there forever in the information flow, but Mouse pulled me farther down, past the buzzing chatter of commerce and pleasure to something deeper, more basic.

Next to me, I felt him manipulate a password and trigger a response somewhere in the bowels of the beast. We snapped, with an almost palatable sound, into focus.

The LINK glittered like the stars above. My conscious-ness felt anchored in something solid now. A definite here, yet its base was enormous, like a giant whose feet straddled the Earth.

My God, where are we?

MOUSE.SYS. The page's voice was flat and emotion-less. Mouse hadn't programmed any company manners into his secret base to impress visitors. No doubt he'd never anticipated having any guests in his hub.

I can't stand talking to a disembodied voice, Mouse. This is disorienting enough as it is, I said, tapping my foot to test the virtual landscape. My construct relayed no messages to my senses, and, although I saw a horizon, I felt disconnected, floating.

Humph. For my benefit, the white light of the page solidified into a construct. Long colorful robes billowed in an imaginary wind. The only part of his skin that was exposed were his hands and deep, black eyes. Gesturing wide with his hands, the page asked, *Better?*

Much, I said, grateful to have something besides the unending plane on which to focus. The page's costume reminded me of the Muslim women in New York. Red satiny material draped across his face and down his shoulders, mingling with a wild assortment of colors and patterns of turquoise, gold, and orange. It was not the kind of outfit I could see the real-time Mouse adopting, so I asked, *Page, is there another name you would prefer to be called . . . besides Mouse?*

The nebulous light of the space intensified for a mo-ment, reflecting twin silver disks in the page's eyes. *Mouse is fine . . . but thank you for asking. Sometimes Mouse calls me Mickey, but, honestly, I'm not fond of that.*

'Mickey Mouse.' I can see why not. I stared out into the endless horizon. *What is this place? I mean, real-time.*

Everywhere. We're in the directory of every hard drive in existence. The world's databases are still stored on hardware, every old PC has a mouse or mouse-pen, mouse-drivers, and mouse directories. We spread the mouse.nest virus via the LINK and took up residence. That's where we are. Nowhere. Everywhere.

No wonder we could never find you, my subvoice translated oddly, sounding tinny on my electronic ears. The atmosphere of the directory felt at once both expansive and close, as though we were adrift in a monotonous ocean of black and white surrounded by a fine fog. *To think, you were right below our feet. Now I understand how you could perform such seamless hacks. I always said every one of your info boosts smelled like an inside job. I can't believe I never saw the mouse/Mouse connection before.*

Well, we count on people not getting it. Don't kick yourself. The billowing robes shrugged delicately.

Cut off from the LINK operating functions, I wondered how much time passed. Even here in the secret hub of mouse.net, I felt unsafe.

Page, I called you because I need your help again. I have to set up a real-time meeting with Daniel.

Daniel? The page's eyes were round. *Mouse warned me that he was out.*

Warned you? Why?

The page's colorful robes flapped in a warm breeze. The endless landscape rippled, like wind over dunes in a desert. *Daniel is a liability,* the page said finally. *A loose cannon.*

I nodded, wondering what Daniel could possibly know that would make Mouse nervous. *How about I barter what Mouse wanted last time . . . your help for what happened the night before the Pope was murdered.*

There was a long pause. The flat, gray, opaque directory surrounded me, oppressive in its endlessness. I glanced up at the sparkle of the LINK above, waiting.

Deal, the page said finally. *But this sucks, you know? I have no idea if other-Mouse still wants this information.* His flippant tone seemed incongruent with the traditional clothing he had chosen. *I might get my code in big trouble for agreeing to this.*

Far away, I could feel a smile form on my face. *Thanks, Mouse.*

Yeah, well, before you get carried away with gratitude, maybe you'd better explain to me how you figure I can help. Mouse gestured for me to follow him. As we walked I felt as though we were passing through thin curtains as directories flipped past. *Every syscop in virtual space is after you or Danny. Even my genius has its limits.*

I doubt it. I conjured up an electronic laugh, which bounced hollowly in the expansive space. *I just need you to provide a distraction. I'll do the real work.*

Oh, I get it. I put my tail on the line and do some outrageous hack, so when the heat is elsewhere, you slip through to Daniel. Nice. If your info isn't really hot, real-time Mouse is going to be pissed when he on-lines, girl, and not just with me.

It is. Satisfied that the deal was struck, I readied myself for off-lining.

Hold on, dear heart. His words were like a hand on my arm, holding me in place *We struck a barter. Half now, half on delivery.*

The page's voice hung in the space a moment longer than was necessary, insistent. I swallowed a hard lump in my throat. I hadn't counted on having to tell my tale, even part of it, right away. Steeling myself, I took a long, slow breath real-time.

You're stalling, Mouse noted. *Spill or the deal is off. You can find some other LINK-rodent to risk his code for you.*

Not wanting to lose him, I started. *Fine. But, only half now, got it?*

Mouse nodded. Taking a deep breath, I launched into my tale.

Daniel and I were at Kick's, at our table in the back, talking shop. I remembered the crowd was thin for a Friday night, but Danny was in good spirits. He thrived on the intensity of a challenging case. The one we had in front of us was a doozie. "What I can't figure is how the hacker got through the city's defense grid." Daniel's voice still rang in my ear. "The syscops said they didn't have a log-on all night."

So focused on imagining the perfect crime, Daniel blindly lifted the Guinness he'd been nursing all night to his lips and half of the sip splashed his shirt.

I laughed, handing him a napkin. "I swear, Fitzpatrick, the way you get into a good hack, you'd think you were a LINK criminal in a past life."

"I must have some heavy karma to work off, if I'm a cop now." He daubed at his shirt halfheartedly.

"That I don't doubt."

He feigned protest. "What are you saying about me, McMannus?"

"I'm saying you're a rogue, Danny boy."

"Well," he admitted, with a half smile he knew made him look devilish, "true enough." After a more careful sip of his drink, he tipped the glass in my direction. "Have you worked out our problem yet?" Tapping his watch, he noted, "It's been half a minute already. I'm surprised at you."

I laughed. Daniel always told me he was the team's PR man, I was the brains. This time, however, I was stumped. "Best I can do is state the obvious: smells like an inside job—or a mouse."

I had the idea that the hacker might have slipped into Jordan Institute under a maintenance sweep. Danny logged on to check. Even though I could reach out and touch him in real time if I wanted to, I always felt alone when Danny surfed the LINK. He wasn't any good at multiprocessing, so he just stared blankly into space. His usually handsome face grew slack, and, with a smile, I wondered how he ever got through academy training without walking into walls.

His face grew noticeably paler. I sat up, thinking he might have found something. "You pick up here." Daniel waved in the direction he'd been staring, "I just got an urgent call from the big guy."

" 'The big guy'?" I asked him, but he didn't hear me. With a shake of my head, I accessed the LINK. I jumped to where we kept the syslog for the Jordan files, looked

for Danny's bookmark, and started combing the records
for a tiny extra power surge that would betray the hacker's entrance. I had been at it for only a few minutes
when Danny interrupted me with a touch on my arm.

Logging off, I gave him my full attention. "What's
the matter?"

That's when things got strange, in retrospect. He got
all anxious, and he said we should leave—go somewhere
more private. Since it was late anyway, and the bar
would be closing, I suggested my place.

We got into his car. I could still smell the leather
upholstery. Danny drove the slickest thing on the market. Nothing but the top of the line for him. His car
screamed "new and improved." I couldn't stand the
thing. I ran my finger along the slippery smooth surface
of the monstrosity, a creature of chrome and steel. Anytime I was forced to ride in his car, I had the same
complaint, "No fucking character."

"What are you saying about my girl? She's got plenty
of character . . . like a refined lady—elegant, distin-
guished. Anyway, what's more important—she's got
power." Reaching over to pat my knee, he smiled into
my face. "Which is more than I can say about your
floating boat."

"Boat? I'll have you know my Chevy is a classic. Not
like this dime-a-dozen clone." I huffed in mock indigna-
tion as I buckled in and relaxed into our familiar routine.
"Besides, power is overrated."

"Hmmmm, I don't know about that." He murmured
low and sultry. "Power is awfully sexy."

I looked over at him, surprised at the tone of his voice.
His gaze swept the line of my dress. Suddenly self-
conscious, I felt naked.

"Yeah, right," I said. My voice sounded stilted in the
close atmosphere of the car's interior. I covered my embarrassment, and myself, by tugging on the buckle that
crossed my breasts. As the motion of my hands drew his
eyes, I reached up and ran my fingers through my hair—
willing him to look at my face.

Smiling a wolfish grin, he turned the ignition. The engine sprang to life with a healthy purr. His eyes stayed locked intensely with mine for a strained moment, then he turned his attention to the car.

I rolled my shoulders, relaxing them forcibly. Our teases bordered on the sexual in the past and had never bothered me. We'd been working on this case for too long and in too-close quarters. The nightlong brainstorming exhausted me; I wasn't reading him right anymore. He was in a strange mood, that was all, and I had mistaken the tone in his voice.

As if in confirmation of my thoughts, Daniel gave me a familiar wink. He patted the smooth control panel lovingly, and said, "Listen to that, will you? Just like a kitten."

The near-silent hum of the car's engine made a pleasant change from the sputtering of my Chevy, but I wasn't about to admit that to Danny, "Sure, if you like 'em quiet and unassuming. I prefer the ones with a little more spirit, more gusto, more character."

"Hmmmm, feisty." The look in his eyes told me he wasn't talking about the car anymore. "I'm beginning to see your point."

I'd walked right into that one; my attempt to lighten the mood and return to our old camaraderie ended with another awkward sexual innuendo. I batted at the air between us, trying to dismiss the entire conversation. "Oh, Danny, knock it off. Keep your mind on business, will you?"

"It's hard." In the semidarkness, the black iris of his hooded eyes caught the light of a streetlamp. His handsome features appeared, momentarily, quite feral. "You look sexy tonight."

"You've obviously had too much whiskey, big guy. Maybe I should be driving."

"Okay," he said, "I prefer my women in the driver's seat, anyway."

I'd never seen Danny like this—it was as if he were a totally different person, and not one I trusted. "Pull this car over, right now."

Normally my partner had no trouble recognizing the

seriousness of my tone. Instead, Danny just smiled devilishly. He slammed his foot down on the accelerator, and the car leapt forward. Just when I thought he would collide with the cab in front of us, he pulled up into an up-ramp and hit the sirens.

At that point, I realized he intended to scare me. Not willing to give him that satisfaction, I slid into cop mode. Taking a deep breath, I forced myself to relax. That's when I noticed his face. His mouth hung open slightly, the way it did when he was on-line and concentrating.

I looked at Mouse, and said, *Daniel was jacked in the whole time.*

The page's tone was as inscrutable as his expression. *Do you have any idea who he was talking to?*

For all I know he was accessing Traffic Control.

The end of Mouse's embroidered shawl flapped noisily in the virtual wind. *But you doubt it.*

I did. I was beginning to believe that whoever stole the biosoftware from Jordan Institute was the one responsible for Daniel's shift in emotions. It was possible that Jordan's R&D had discovered more than just a way to access pain and pleasure, but other emotions as well, and that's what the tech-thieves were after.

Why is Mouse so hot for this story anyway? I'm sure he could read all the details on some bulletin board of mine.

The page watched me intently; his black eyes flicked over my avatar's form. *Mouse is curious about who you think did it.*

What if I told you I thought it could be Mouse, I said. After all it was possible, especially with what I now knew about mouse.net.

Do you?

The page seemed to want affirmation, but I decided to hold what few cards I had close to my chest. *The barter was for half now, Mouse. I've got a date to keep.*

I sent the image of my arms crossed in front of my chest. The page's black eyes held mine for a long moment.

All right. I'll cause your distraction. Give me twenty minutes from NOW.

A digital countdown appeared in the corner of my vision. *How will I know when you've done what you plan to do?*

You won't. You're expecting me to trust you, aren't you? Before I could comment, the image shifted. The page discarded the feminine costume for the receptionist gear he wore when we first connected. *I hate to be a bad "host," but . . .*

With the intensity of one of his boomerang viruses, the page snapped me back into real time. The ground rushed away from my feet, and I fell upward through the jumble of the LINK with blinding speed. The information stream crackled lightning-bright behind my eyes. I snapped them open to see Rebeckah kneeling in front of me.

My fingers fumbled for the filament in the helmet. Reaching out, Rebeckah popped the panel on the helmet and grabbed the connection. "You off?"

I nodded mutely, shutting the connections as quickly as I could. With the filament disconnected, Rebeckah gently lifted the helmet from my head. My hair was a mat of sweat, but the fresh air revived me; I took a deep breath.

Rebeckah watched me intently. Her usually controlled face showed a hint of concern.

" 'M okay," I croaked. All the liquid in my mouth had evaporated, and my tongue felt heavy and clumsy.

Rebeckah pointed to one of her comrades. "Water," was all she had to say. He returned with a brimming plastic cup before I could even protest.

"Where were you?" Rebeckah's expression hardened now that it appeared I was going to live. "Sharron couldn't finger your ID on the LINK."

"Mouse's hub," I managed around a gulp of water. The muscles in my neck shot pain to my shoulders when I tried to move.

Rebeckah glanced at Sharron. Following her gaze, I could see the disbelief in the hacker's eyes. With another swig of water, I swallowed the urge to pout, "Was too!" Instead, I said, "It's all set. Mouse will provide a LINK distraction in"—I checked the display still floating in the corner of my vision—"fifteen minutes, thirty-one seconds and counting."

Rebeckah's eyebrow raised. "Sharron, could we pull off a simultaneous attack? Keep the boys hopping?"

"You got it, Chief." Sharron smiled that gleeful grin every LINK-hacker flashed when plotting a job. It reminded me of Daniel. At the thought of seeing him again, panic crawled along my extremities. I shook my shoulders before the feeling reached my heart. Far too late for regrets or second thoughts, I told myself. Rebeckah and Mouse's page were in on the fiasco now, and I could hardly let them down.

As the crowd dispersed, I stretched my leg out experimentally. Cramped muscles protested with every minute movement. "Man, I must've been completely zoned," I grumbled. "How long was I out?"

"Only twenty minutes or so," Rebeckah said. Standing up, she dusted her hands on her thighs. "But you were in it deep. In a few more, I would've called a paramedic."

I raised my eyebrows.

She shrugged; her eyes left mine. "Even the best of us fall into old habits."

I let out an irritated huff; she figured I was off on an info-bender unable to resist the slick tech of the uniform and my new LINK connection. "I was a cop, Rebeckah, not a wire-junkie."

"Oh, really?"

I could feel my jaw working, but decided against defending myself. Rebeckah was part of a time in my life I left behind when I joined the force. She never saw my transformation. When she looked in my eyes she remembered a strung-out college girl, away from home for the first time, and lost in the LINK. I had to earn Rebeckah's respect; no amount of explanation would substitute. I kept my tone light. "Are you sure you still want to jeopardize your people in this venture?"

Hefting my helmet under one arm, Rebeckah sat

down next to me on the battered plaid couch. The tired springs let out a creaky sigh. Raking her fingers through her flattop, she smoothed out her frown. "We're old friends, Dee. Besides, you're going to owe us one when this is done."

"So you've said." My face scrunched up in a lopsided grin. "Funny, I'm a junkie until you need something, then suddenly I'm a wizard, eh?"

Rebeckah's eyebrow arched at my words, then she let out a laugh. "That's about right. So, what's the plan?"

"While Mouse and Sharron are running distractions, I'm going to try to locate Daniel's buddy,"

"Hell of a plan, Dee. There are over six billion users. You plan to ID each once until you find someone who might be a friendly? You'll be collared in under a millisecond."

I leaned forward, resting my elbows on my knees. My head pounded like a killer hangover, but, perversely, I enjoyed the feeling. Every corner of my brain felt filled with an ache. No more emptiness. The pain felt good. Like an athlete returning to the game, the headache reminded me I was alive, using nearly atrophied muscles. If that made me a junkie, so be it. With a weak smile, I said, "I know where Danny will go, virtually speaking."

Rebeckah shook her head in disbelief. "I hope you do."

The digital readout continued to count down in the corner of my eye. Ten minutes and counting. There was no point in discussing the consequences if I was wrong. Leaning heavily on the couch, I stood up. "Do you have a meeting location figured out?"

"Come on." Putting an arm around my waist, Rebeckah supported my weight. "We've got transport waiting."

Transport turned out to be a rusty pickup truck from the turn of the century. As I stood staring at the antique, five of Rebeckah's soldiers filed in around me and methodically piled onto the flat bed of the truck. They all carried rifles and wore full combat armor. After stowing their guns in a tool case, they turned their armor's holographic defense on. One by one, the Malachim shimmered, then disappeared before my eyes.

I pulled myself into the truck and felt my way into the middle of them. Surrounded by limbs I could feel but not see, I settled in as best I could. I hugged myself closely for fear of accidentally touching a stranger. Rebeckah stepped in last and pulled the truck's gate up behind her.

With ten minutes left on the countdown, I jacked the armor's filament into my LINK receiver. Rebeckah squeezed my hand reassuringly. I flashed her a confident smile, but, truthfully, I had no idea if I could find Daniel's ally.

I nearly jumped out of my skin when the combustion engine sprang to life. Turning around, I looked in the cab. Raphael, who sat behind the wheel, didn't seem alarmed by the rumbling explosions coming from the truck, so I presumed all was normal. Listening to the popping and wheezing, I suddenly had respect for how quietly my Chevy ran.

"Oh damn," I said. Rebeckah looked up expectantly. "My car is in Hell's Kitchen. I'm never getting it back."

Rebeckah grimaced. "Are you still driving that thing you had in college?"

I nodded.

"Good riddance," she said.

"That poor car gets no respect."

"You should keep your mind on the task at hand. Time?"

"Six minutes, ten seconds."

Rebeckah looked at Sharron who sat in the cab next to Raphael. "Sharron, you set?"

"Ready to rock and roll, Chief." Sharron held a deck on her lap. That impressed me; only truly serious hackers augmented the LINK with hardware. Staring at the board, I thought of mouse.net and whispered good luck to the page. I prayed he would get away with whatever he was planning. The page was quickly becoming my favorite version of Mouse, even over the real boy. Seeing me, Sharron gave me a wink. Raphael tossed me a salute and a broad smile. Neither of them wore any armor. I presumed they were meant to be in disguise, although as what, I couldn't tell. The antique might attract some attention, but, no doubt, the Malachim were relying on the fact that most New Yorkers were self-absorbed enough not to look down at the streets while driving in the skyways. Even if someone did notice us, locals were notorious for not getting involved.

At Rebeckah's nod, I powered up my suit. Tiny pinpoints of light blinked on, then my legs disappeared. Looking up just in time, I saw Rebeckah fade away. A crackle in the helmet's intercom preceded Rebeckah's calm voice. "Let's do it, people."

Two guards removed a false-glass garage door, and the truck bounced out of the underground car park and into the glass city. The setting sun turned what was once the Bronx into a blazing jewel of colors. Every crystalline edge reflected rosy sunlight. The combustion engine's noise puttered strangely through the glass streets and alleyways. The exhaust fumes added to the acrid, smoggy taste in the evening breeze. I was grateful for the radiation shield provided by the armor I wore. We drove in silence for a while, until only a few seconds remained on the clock.

"Ten." Sharron started the countdown. "Nine."

Her deck lit up as her fingers flew across the pad. I shut my eyes.

"Eight . . . seven . . . six," she intoned. I could feel the bounce of the road beneath the truck, but I let the rest of my senses be enveloped by the LINK. "Five . . ."

"Here we go," I said out loud.

New York on-line was a maze. Taking a moment to orient myself, I found the entertainment stream. Three jumps away lay Kick's café, where I hoped Danny's friend would be waiting. I held my breath as I approached the jump.

In real time, Sharron continued, "Four . . . three . . ."

The feather-light ID check of the sensors brushed my consciousness. I waited for the green light. Though less than a hundredth of a second passed, it felt like an eternity. Finally, the node opened; the uniform's LINK connection's constantly shifting home address fooled the access guardian.

"Two . . . one!"

As I stepped through the queue at the node, I felt a ripple along the wire.

What the heck was that? An untagged broadband crossed through the LINK.

"Yahoo!" Sharron shouted through the cab's open window. I opened my eyes to see her waving a fist in the air. Before I could congratulate her, she said, "Mouse rocks. Alarms are clanging from here to Timbuktu! I don't know how he did it, but it looks like hackers are popping up on almost every node."

Thanks to the confusion, I slipped easily through the next node. I was one step from Kick's. I slitted my eyes to concentrate, but I couldn't keep a grin from my face. As impossible as it first seemed, I might get away with this.

"Hold on to your avatar," Sharron beamed, "because here goes nothing."

She punched a key on her board triumphantly: I felt the LINK's power dip again.

Fuck! A collective swear slipped through the system's censors. A full-fledged smile took over my face, as I passed through the last jump. If the broadband profanity censors had crashed, then the syscops had abandoned their posts. All I had to watch out for was the local patrol now.

Another terrorist attack, I think, someone said nearby. As I made my way along the entertainment band, snippets of conversation washed past me. The syscops weren't maintaining line privacy; chatter came from several users at once. *I narrowly escaped Mexico City's node./I was hardbooted out of my game./Cairo is suffering some kind of brownout, I guess, because I just lost the signal./Where the hell are the system controllers?/ Someone call the cops!*

I slid out of the main byways to Kick's on-line café,

a stationary and private spot on the usually fluid LINK. Despite the uniform's shifting ID pattern, my heart raced as my entry was automatically registered in the café. Though heads popped up to check me out, no one was interested enough to offer chatter. I let my breath out in a long sigh.

I feigned casualness as I checked the café's menu for the list of users. If my hands weren't virtual, they would have been shaking. Scanning the names, I noted several regulars from the days I used to frequent the real-time version of the tavern. Among the usuals, one name jumped out at me: John Kantowicz. Per LINK protocol, along with his name, a badge number appeared. Kick's had a long history of being a cop hangout. It could just be a coincidence that an officer with a traditionally Jewish name was hanging out here at this time.

"You got a guy named Kantowicz?" I asked Rebeckah out loud. "A Lieutenant John Kantowicz?"

"Not that I know of, but that doesn't mean anything necessarily. We organize in cells. I only know the ringleaders."

I glanced at the other names one more time. Like a tap on the shoulder, I felt my icon being chosen for chatmode. *Deidre? Is that you?*

I turned to see the image of a police shield floating in front of me—no fancy, handsome avatar, just a shield. It could only be one man: Captain Morgan. *I'm sorry? I'm afraid you've mistaken me for someone else.*

It was a lame lie, but I prayed the armor's defense would keep the captain guessing. I hung up quickly, then selected Kantowicz's name from the menu. I had to act quickly. If I knew anything about my former captain, it was that he was very by-the-book.

Are you Danny's . . . ? I started to ask Kantowicz, but, before I could get more out, I was interrupted by a loud click. A larger version of the New York police badge floated in front of the café's logo. The captain worked fast, I thought ruefully, and you've got to admire that.

A synthesized female voice calmly intoned, *This is the*

police. We have secured a warrant, and are initiating an address lock-down. Please stay on-line until your identifications have been processed. Any attempt to disconnect at this time will be considered a hostile action. We are authorized to use deadly force. Repeat. We are authorized by the warrant to use deadly force. Do not disconnect or your LINK connection could be irreparably damaged. Your cooperation is appreciated.

"Shit," I shouted over the roar of the engine. "I was IDed. The cops just crashed the party. Sharron, are you off?"

"Powered down and out."

"Dee," Rebeckah's voice was urgent with concern, "you've got to get out of there. Drop the contact. We'll find another way to get ahold of Daniel."

"No. They've already got a lock-down—I'm busted either way. I might as well try a little evasive maneuver. Hang on."

Rebeckah yelled something, but I switched my concentration back to the LINK. I used the fact that Kantowicz and I were still connected by virtue of the chat volley and mentally pushed his avatar down on the floor of the club. I extended my senses outward.

What are you doing? Kantowicz shouted in protest. I could feel him resisting dissolution.

We're going under the door, like a mouse. Trust me.

Trust you? Who are you? Your ID keeps shifting.

A friend of Daniel's. I continued to pull him down, underneath the LINK the way Mouse had coached me earlier. We dropped through the floor easily. When we came to the police lock-down barrier, I felt a slight electric shock as we squeezed under it. Kantowicz and I got as far as Mouse's door before I realized I didn't have a key or a password.

Glancing back up at Kick's, I knew we couldn't go back. If the cops arrested my LINK address, I'd be a comatose homing beacon until they found my body. Rebeckah would keep me moving for a while, but she was a practical woman; she'd have to abandon my body eventually. I'd wake up in a holding cell, where I'd rot until they could prosecute me for what I did to Dorshak and the FBI agents during my grand escape from the precinct. Arrest now would mean the end of everything. No chance to see Daniel again. No chance to fix things with Michael, if that's even what I wanted. The rest of my life would be nothing but regrets.

There was no other option; I had to try to hack mouse.net.

//This electronic story, can be viewed either in full virtual reality LINK-interface, or is available in faux leather-bound hard copy for only 100 Christendom credits.

How the LINK-Angels Spoke to Me: A Collection of Personal Stories

A Boston Activist

Tony Delapalana, of Boston, who refers to his former life as that of "your average delivery guy," used to spend much of his time in the service tunnels delivering goods and removing garbage from the city. Since receiving a personal message from the archangel Phanuel, he now devotes his time to caring for the dead.

"It was like this," he explains. "A lot of people are afraid of death, but I'm a good Catholic boy, see? So, when Phanuel started haunting my dreams—being all spooky and that—I figured it was like Scrooge, you know, in that Christmas story: the ghost was trying to tell me something. For all my catechism, I never even heard of this Phanuel character before, but a miracle is a miracle, right? Anyway, I keep having these dreams where Phanuel is crucified. Only, instead of being nailed to a cross, he's, like, hanging from this big redwood. There aren't that many of the big trees left, so I figure this must be really important.

"So, I'm really wracking my brains: why is the angel of death the first guy to show up? Why am I dreaming about trees? So I start LINKing to all the sites about what the Church is saying, and my priest starts this whole study group and, anyway, it all sort of gels for me. It's about the apocalypse. It's coming soon. And, then I remember how on the Last Day, we're all supposed to rise up bodily, like Jesus. This realization freaks me out, right? It occurs to me that people aren't getting buried anymore because there ain't no more room in the inn, as it were. Only Orthodox Jews get to be buried, because they all seem to got the land somewhere . . . maybe in Israel, I don't know. Then, I realize that this is what Phanuel wants me to do: take on those crazy Earth Firsters and reclaim the forests so people can have good Christian burials. So, I get on the shuttle to Oregon, and I start kicking tree-hugger butt.''

Mr. Delapalana is personally responsible for starting the ''Last Day'' movement, which has wrestled 5% of the national forest lands out from under the secular ecoterrorist's control. His organization sees to it that anyone who wants a traditional burial can now have a plot set aside for them. Many consider the rough-and-tumble Mr. Delapalana a wild-man figure, like John the Baptist. By resanctifying burial, as John did for baptism, Mr. Delapalana has proven to be a prophet for our times.

CHAPTER 15

We're going in, I told a shell-shocked Lieutenant Kantowicz.

Going in where? he protested. *Where are we?*

Uh . . . I realized I just took a total stranger to Mouse's front door, and cop no less. So, I lied, *My secret hideaway.*

With my avatar extended, Mouse's doorway blended into the surrounding chaos. The door shifted around packets of information and strings of code, disappearing and reappearing like a cave beneath a waterfall. Blindly fishing through the wavering stream, my fingers swept over the smooth surface of the door. I needed a portal of some kind to access mouse.net, a keyhole or command line. I wished I'd been paying more attention to the page when he brought me here the first time.

Where are we? Why do I feel so weird? Kantowicz asked.

It's the undercarriage of the LINK, I explained, not thinking. *This is mouse.nest. Mouse's house.*

So, Kantowicz said appraisingly, *you're the Mouse?*

I was so absorbed in finding the lock, Kantowicz's question threw me off guard. *Oh, damn. What? No, he's just a friend.*

Interesting friends you keep.

The same could be said for you, I said, as my hands continued to grope for the keyhole. I dared a glance up at the LINK, but the whole datastream flowed into one glittering mass; it was impossible to distinguish Kick's from any other specific address. I had no idea if the police could pursue us here.

Even though I knew that only a few minutes had passed in real time, I could feel myself starting to panic. This was taking far too long. We would have to return and give ourselves up for arrest if I didn't find that command line soon.

Beside me, Kantowicz strained against our enforced connection. *Why not just off-line here?* His electronic voice crackled with distortion. *We're out, aren't we?*

Not really, no. We're in between. I extended us "under" the door, but we're not inside yet.

Can't we just log off?

Kanowitcz's questions were driving me buggy. I didn't really have time to explain all the nuances of how mouse.net worked, especially since I'd only recently understood it myself. I was tempted to let him go, let him fry his receptors, but I needed him to survive—if only so that he could get word to Daniel. *Sure, you can log off if you want,* I said; though I made no move to let him go. *But I don't want to be there when they find your body. Your internal LINK processors are already overextended. Tell me, Kantowicz, what are you seeing right now? Is it clear? Even our avatars have mostly dissolved. What do you think a hardboot is going to do to your brain right now?*

He was quiet as I continued my search. Lines of information slithered between my fingers, making it difficult to latch on to anything solid. Mouse was no fool. It was not going to be an easy task to break into his hub. My fingers connected with something, only to drip through my grasp. *Damn it,* I said, *almost had it.*

Kantowicz twitched nervously. I tried to shut him out and concentrate on finding that slippery line. I wished that I could call up a real-time clock, but since I'd have to be a registered user to log a request to the atomic clock, I left that option behind when we sank beneath the floor of the LINK café. I reached once more through the waving waterfall in front of Mouse's door. I connected. Before I could lose it again, I wrapped my fingers tightly around the command line.

Got it! The distortion that flowed around us disappeared. My vision became black and white. Looking above, I could no longer see the glitter of the LINK. Kantowicz's avatar vanished completely, although a line of text informed me that we still had a solid handshake. We were in a kind of nebulous space that was neither LINK nor mouse.net.

Now entrance was a matter of a password or a key of some kind. On a hunch, I threw the standard battery of words in the direction of the keyhole. It would be very Mouse to protect the most precious hub in the world with something so simple as the phrase, "God," but, after trying all the typical passwords I knew, I came to the sad realization perhaps Mouse preferred safety to irony.

This is crazy. White words appeared against the blackness surrounding me. A whisper, like wind through trees, hissed in my ear. *Cracking Mouse's house is the quickest way to a blank slate.*

I wasn't sure if the words came from Kantowicz or were a part of a security program Mouse installed; either way, I ignored them. Even though I doubted they would do any good, I tried a few more words and phrases associated with Mouse: Koran, alms, Cairo.

The door stayed closed.

We should give ourselves up. God only knows what's happening up there, the haunting, electronic whisper tickled my senses again.

I stared angrily at the glowing words and entered a command to check on the status of my connection to Kantowicz. I still held him firmly. My action jogged an idea loose in my mind. As I grimaced at the glowing text warning that hung in front of my face, I suddenly knew why this place felt familiar. It was like my computer screen.

Thanks to the excommunication, I'd been using the same kind of computer terminal that, according to Mouse's page, made up the ground floor of mouse.net.

My stubborn refusal to be completely isolated from the LINK had led me to ferret out and use an antiquated read-only process called "ftp." I'd only used ftp to connect to the main LINK nodes before, but, if memory served, the process was supposed to open directories of any sort to one another. If this didn't work, I'd have to surrender myself to the police or fry my brain with a violent off-line. Neither option was very pleasant. I steeled myself for failure, and entered the anonymous user password.

The blackness remained unchanged.

Damn it all to hell. I sighed. Just as I was about to send the release command to Kantowicz, a gray light appeared on the horizon. Like a sunrise, it seeped slowly over the darkness, until it warmed the entire space. Above, pinpricks of light widened until I could, once again, see the LINK. Next to me, Kantowicz's avatar shimmered like a ghost, then, solidified. The image of thin features and round, vanity glasses was a welcome sight. I'd done it. I could've hugged him, but we still had work to do.

Okay, we're in. Here's the ground rules, I said. *It's bad enough that I've exposed my friend's hub to an outsider, so we're only staying here long enough to slide out from this address, got it?*

Kantowicz frowned, obviously curious about the hub, but he didn't protest. I continued to hold his hand as we stepped through to the next directory. The cobwebs brushed my face as we moved easily over the boundary. I saw Kantowicz's eyes widen, as mouse.net's true nature dawned on him.

This is like the old web, he said, the glee of a brilliant hack illuminating his face.

I smiled in acknowledgment and wondered if all LINK-cops had such an appreciation of the criminal mind.

Our avatars reached a spot clear of directory threads. Though a roiling mist hung in the gray space, I could see the LINK without obstruction. We would have a safe reentry from here. Schooling my avatar's expression, I warned, *Just remember I saved you from arrest. If you use this against my friend, I'll find a way to tell your captain that you're associated with the Malachim.*

Disappointment showed on his face, but he nodded gravely. It was the first real indication that I'd nabbed the right guy.

I pointed to the twinkling river above. *Once we get back there, tell Danny to meet me at Yankee Stadium.*

It'll take us some time. We're still in Manhattan, and moving slowly.

I can wait. I wasn't sure why, but I felt the need to remain a bit cagey. I didn't want to tell Kantowicz that the Malachim's firepower was backing me up. *Just be safe.*

Danny gave me a message for you. Kantowicz grimaced and coughed, as though he found the role of errand boy distasteful. *He said: "Sancte Mìchael Archángele, défénde nos in prœlio."*

My heart skipped a beat at the familiar, yet alien name: Michael Archángele. Unbidden, the memory of Michael's naked body flashed before my eyes.

Are you all right? Kantowicz peered at me over the rim of his glasses. *The image of your avatar shimmered. I thought for a second you were going to yank me out with you.*

Oh. I looked down at our hands, still joined together, symbolic of our systems' connection. I released him. *You should probably go.*

I'm sorry. I didn't know it would bother you so much. What's it mean?

I shook my head. *I'm not sure exactly. Don't worry about me. I don't know why I reacted that way,* I lied. *It was thoughtful of Danny to pray for me, really. I didn't know he knew Latin. Tell him thanks.*

Sure. Kantowicz looked doubtful. *Daniel wants to meet at Yankee Stadium.*

I smiled at that. How like Daniel.

Kantowicz gave me the time and other particulars. Then, with a nod good-bye, he jumped back toward the information stream. I watched until his avatar melted into the entertainment traffic of the LINK. Part of me knew I should be heading back, but I stood there thinking about Michael. Of course Daniel had given me a prayer about the Archangel Michael—after all, he was the patron saint of cops. But the mention of his name made me wonder where he was and what he thought of my sudden disappearance from Eion's church. Michael might even be looking for me. I should find a way to call him or drop him a message to tell him that I was all right, physically, at least.

Psychologically was another matter entirely. Rebeckah's steady faith and calm pragmatism kept me from dwelling on the rift in my sense of reality that Michael's presence had caused. Rebeckah's wisdom had reassured me that, on some day-to-day level, defining God didn't matter; I still had to face the unsteadying concept that Michael's presence meant there really was a God.

I shook off my growing terror. I had too much to do to waste time worrying about religion. Rebeckah and her team were waiting for me.

I jumped, but was rebuffed by something solid. My avatar landed, sprawling from the impact. I picked myself up and tried to examine what had happened. Reaching out with a tentative hand, I touched an invisible barrier. I frowned. In read-only mode I shouldn't be able to affect anything in the directory, nor should anything be able to touch me. I pushed against the barrier. It stood solid, like a pane of impenetrable glass. It must be a kind of directory guardian, I figured, though I was still at a loss as to why it could affect me.

I sent a message into the hub. *Mouse, it's me. Deidre. Call off your guardian.*

Mouse is unavailable at this time.

Page? Are you out there? Call off your guardian.

Mouse is unavailable at this time.

Great, I muttered. As I moved to try to feel my way around the mass, it began to shift under my fingers. Hard, but liquid, the guardian moved like muscle beneath my palms. I tried to keep ahold of it, but tiny electric shocks quickly discouraged me. Pulling my hands back, I watched an inky darkness coalesce in the fog-draped, gray expanse of mouse.net. Swirling, the blackness grew until it filled the space above me, obscuring my access to the LINK.

The guardian bobbed overhead strangely, as though mimicking the movements of a blackbird caught in an updraft. Dread filled me. I'd seen a shadow of this creature before.

Phanuel.

The LINK-angel's glossy black feathers materialized in full detail. Black, like raven's wings, they swallowed the light rather than reflecting it. In the center of the dark plumage floated the hooded figure of a man. The tattered cloak hugged his bony frame. I could see the sharp points of his hipbones standing out against a shrunken stomach.

Something moved beneath the robe at his abdomen, and I gritted my teeth at the thought of maggots devouring his exposed entrails. He lifted his head, and I stepped back, unwilling to look into the face of the Angel of Death. Despite my best efforts, I caught sight of thin lips pulled back in a skeletal grin. A spider crawled out of his nose, and I watched in horror as the arachnid scuttled across his cheekbone to disappear into the folds of the hood. After that I kept my eyes focused downward.

A pale, bone-thin hand pointed at my avatar. *You do not belong here.*

I would have pulled the wire from my receiver in a New York minute if I hadn't thought the shock of resurfacing from outside the LINK would kill me instantly. Despite my fear, I frowned: that was another inconsistency. Mouse.net was outside of the LINK. No LINK-angel should be here, much less acting as a directory guardian.

Dark wings fluttered loudly as Phanuel moved closer. I could smell the odor of funeral incense and freshly upturned earth. Involuntarily, I looked up into his eyes, mere inches from my own. The sockets were bruised and sunken, and I could see something white squirming in their depths. I gasped and stumbled backwards. Cobwebs licked at me, and I swam frantically through their gossamer threads.

Phanuel did not follow.

When his shadow no longer blocked me and the shine of the LINK appeared overhead, I realized I'd escaped. I'd fallen into another directory, one that, apparently, Phanuel didn't guard. Quickly, before some other apparition could appear, I leapt out of Mouse-space onto the LINK.

Something tingled in my stomach, like nerves. I shivered, and tried to relax, but I felt the eyes of Phanuel on my back. There was another presence here, something alive. Perhaps it was Page coming back or even Mouse logging on, no doubt alerted by whatever breach in security had triggered Phanuel. I was curious, but I resisted the urge to look back, afraid I'd see the apparition on my heels.

As the babble of commerce surrounded me, I let out a relieved breath. I was safe in the crowd. The pulse of buying and selling that flitted through the virtual air energized me. Real time was a window to the right. Before I succumbed to the temptation of a new car, I dived through the gateway and off-lined.

The sun had set completely. Despite being encased in the uniform, I swore I could feel the coolness of the evening kiss my shoulders. As a full moon shone through a hazy sky, the truck rumbled through the glass streets on its reinforced tires. No sound echoed above the explosive engine. There was something peaceful about the night—I could almost imagine the call of a bird or buzz of a cicada. A pleasant thought, but I knew the city was dead. The Medusa-glass shimmered in the moonlight as a deadly reminder.

After my adventures on the LINK, my head thudded dully. I breathed in deeply, savoring the exhausted feeling that cramped my limbs. The armor felt heavy, and the LINK connection buzzed with spent energy, like muscles twitching after a long walk.

I rolled my head to one side, to work out the kinks

in my neck, and felt the give of something soft and yielding. I was cradled in someone's lap.

"She's awake, Commander," an unfamiliar, masculine voice said through the helmet's intercom. "Or, at least she's moving."

I sat up, pushing blindly against the soldier for purchase. Having been without electricity since the war, the Bronx was preternaturally dark. Here and there a light twinkled and refracted prismlike from a Gorgon's flashlight or campfire. Even through the uniform's filters I could smell an odor of urine and rot that signaled a nearby Gorgon encampment. Down an alley, I glimpsed the retreating silver of Gorgons scattering at the sound of the truck's explosive engine.

"Dee?" It was Rebeckah.

I yawned as I switched on my intercom. "Present and accounted for. Sorry about the little nap. I ran into a bit of trouble and had to go deep."

She had no sympathy. "Deep? I'd say you went deep. You were totally unresponsive. You're damned lucky you didn't wake up in a Dumpster, Dee. I thought you were arrested."

As if in response to the tone in her voice, all the aches and pains of deep LINK work suddenly assaulted me. Sweat tickled the short hairs at the back of my neck. I desperately wanted to pull off the restrictive helmet and grab a breath of fresh air to clear my pounding head.

"Mouse has an angel infestation." I stifled another yawn. "What do you make of that?"

There was a beat. Rebeckah's voice was tightly controlled, as she asked, "Is the meeting set?"

I nodded. Then, I realized Rebeckah couldn't see me; I was still invisible. Despite the fact that my mouth felt filled with cotton, I managed to say, "Yeah. All set."

"Good. Now, I'm warning you. If you fuck around like that again, Dee, that's it. You understand me? We pull out; you're on your own."

"Got it," I said. I heard a soft click in my left ear as Rebeckah changed to a private channel. I ground my teeth in anticipation. I was about to get my head served

to me on a platter. I cringed, waiting for the scathing
words.

Instead, Rebeckah's tone was soft, almost tender.
"You've got a serious problem with the wire, Dee."

"What? Fuck you," I said through clenched teeth.
"Just what the hell you do you mean by that,
Rebeckah?"

"You know what I mean." Her voice was a hoarse
whisper. "When this is done, I want you to see someone.
Join a twelve-step program or something. Promise me."

"I'm not a junkie."

"Most people can handle it, Dee. They can walk
around, live normal lives, all the while hooked into the
LINK. Why is it you come out loopy every time you
LINK up? Why is it you pass out cold?"

"It's not every time . . . only Mouse's—"

Rebeckah cut me off before I could continue. "I'll tell
you why," she said. "You're too into it." She jabbed her
finger too fast for the holographic armor to keep up,
and a wave of rippling skyline punctuated each word.
"Too into it. You get wrapped up in every sensation;
you have to follow every info stream. You always had
that tendency—hell, I'm sure it's part of what made you
a great vice cop, but now it's out of control. You're out
of control, Dee."

The truck's engine rumbled and sputtered like my
mind. I looked around the truck, searching to connect
with her invisible eyes. I needed to see if she really
meant what she said. Futilely, I scanned for a trace of
her face in the emptiness.

I had to admit that Rebeckah spoke some truth, but
the LINK wasn't the cause of that slow, twisting feeling
that haunted the back of my mind lately. It wasn't the
old desperation to know everything—to be a part of it
all—that drove me away from reality this time. Now it
was the complexity of real life that scared me.

My mouth worked as I tried to find a way to explain
everything, to absolve myself, but no words came. I
frowned at the corner where I imagined Rebeckah sat.
Something more than her fear of my old habit was eating

at her. I pressed the switch in my glove to hail her on the private channel again. When I heard her connect, I asked, "Have you lost people to the wire lately, Rebeckah?"

The line hissed quietly.

"You have, haven't you?" I said. "What happened?"

"It was ugly. I don't want to talk about it."

"Ugly?" I repeated, surprised. When I was on the LINK–vice squad, I saw all of the worst forms of wire-addiction from blank coma cases to fried burnouts. Drooling, shivering, emaciated, unwashed junkies were unattractive, sure, but so ugly that Rebeckah, woman of steel, didn't want to talk about it? "What do you mean, 'ugly'?"

"I said no, Dee."

I sat up straight. My palms pressed into the uneven surface of the truck bed as we bounced down the street. Old cop instincts tingled. Somehow this rash of wire-addiction among the Malachim was connected to something bigger. Despite her adamancy that I leave her alone, I had to press her for details. "This is important."

Rebeckah's voice was as brittle as ice. "We had to put him down."

"You're saying you killed a man?" I repeated stunned.

"Yes." Rebeckah's answer was simple and to the point, and gave away nothing.

The intercom crackled as I waited. Smog hung thickly in the air, and no stars were visible. The black of the night sky reminded me of Phanuel's wings—dark and impenetrable.

"There was no other choice," she said, finally. "I should have thrown him out the door when it started. Kicking him out would have saved his life, but I screwed up. He was a good hacker once, a good man, and I wanted to respect that. I thought the way to do that was to let the decent man inside fight his demons. I should have known that with a junkie, that's a fool's hope. He became obsessed. First the lying, then, hiding his use . . . the list goes on. Typical, really. Finally, he crossed the line. He came to me, demanding an upgrade to feed his addiction. When I refused, he threatened to expose us all. I thought he was bluffing. Two seconds later, he hot-LINKed our location to the police frequency. When he started naming names, I shot him."

"Jesus Christ."

"My mistake cost a man his life. I'll never tolerate a wire-head in my ranks again, you got that?"

"Got it." A sane person would have stopped there. After all, my college roommate had just admitted to murder. Instead, I added, "How many others did you expel after him, Rebeckah?"

"Two more, all in a matter of months."

"Huh." I'd asked the question mostly out of the old habit of leaving no hunch untried. "Do you think maybe they came across something on the LINK that changed them, infected them?"

"Like what?" Rebeckah's voice was curious.

"This is totally off-the-wall, but Daniel and I were working on a tech-theft case involving software that manipulates the brain's pain and pleasure centers. I've been thinking . . . maybe whoever discovered those parts of the brain came across others, like: obsession . . . lust . . . maybe even the awe of seeing an angel."

"I don't understand," Rebeckah said. "What are you saying exactly?"

"I'm not sure yet, but I think there's a connection between the tech-theft case and the LINK-angels. Maybe the person who stole from the Jordan Institute is using the emotional aspect of the tech to cause the mass euphoria . . . or the fear," I added, thinking of Phanuel, "that the angels cause. Maybe this person can also heighten other emotions, like the ones that cause wire-addiction."

"How is that possible?"

"That's the part I'm not sure of yet. I'm just running on a hunch right now. And, I suspect the angels are a construct"—I smiled although I knew Rebeckah couldn't see it—"just like you always thought they were."

"So, you think my hackers ran afoul of the LINK-angels?"

"If they're not for real, it'd make sense that they'd target you," I said. "After all, that's part of what you do, isn't it? Debunk their magic?"

The truck rumbled to a stop. Unprepared, I slid into an invisible Malachim. The toolbox opened up seemingly on its own. Rebeckah said, "We'll talk more about your theory later. On the belt pack there's a sonar. It's approximately two fingers from the buckle on your left. You might want to turn it on; otherwise, you'll lose us when we enter the stadium."

I mumbled a thanks, feeling for the switch. A loud ping sounded in my ear when I found it. The helmet's visuals sprang to life, widening to a 360-degree view. At every ping, a ripple of light moved around me, illuminating the shadowy figures of the Malachim.

A queasy disorientation threatened to blur my vision, until I noticed the glowing crosshair moved as I moved my head, distinguishing "ahead" from "behind." Despite the focus point, I nearly stumbled when I took my first hesitant step. This was going to take some getting used to.

Rebeckah's voice startled me. "Raphael and Sharron will check in every half hour from a nearby hideout. If something goes wrong, they have instructions to abandon us, and we'll be forced to make our way back to headquarters on foot. If the FBI or anyone else has followed Daniel, it's likely they'll have sonar and infrared. Don't assume you're invisible standing in center field. Always have good cover. Copy?"

"We copy, Commander," the team leader said for the Malachim.

"I understand," I said.

As the truck pulled away, I stood before a partially crystallized Yankee Stadium. The next ping of my sonar showed the Malachim moving toward the service entrance. I followed them.

The Medusa-glass had drawn an uneven slash in the center of the stadium, dividing it almost perfectly in half.

In places, the deadly crystal escaped its bounds and seeped under the folds of the curtain facing that decorated the upper rim of the ballpark. Glass crackled in the mortar between stones.

I followed the Malachim around the stadium until we reached the section of the arena that remained mostly untouched by the Medusa bomb. Moving cautiously into the building, the Malachim set up guard posts at every entrance as though following a predetermined plan. I stumbled less gracefully behind, admiring their cohesiveness and trying not to destroy it.

My body still felt heavy from my adventures in mouse.net, and my brain struggled to make sense of the wide-angle view the helmet provided. Just when I felt I'd gotten used to aiming for the crosshairs, we encountered stairs. The Malachim moved easily up them and took positions on the landing. I stood motionless at the bottom of the concrete-block obstacle as my resolve wavered.

Seeing the stairs and the wall behind it, the floor and the ceiling simultaneously, my eyes didn't know where to focus. I flailed my hand out until I connected to the railing. Once my hand wrapped around the solidness of the rail, I felt my center of balance returning. I shut my eyes and made my awkward way up the stairs.

The Malachim waited patiently, but I felt like a rookie again—I was obviously slowing them down. When my shuffling feet encountered no resistance, I opened my eyes, sighing in relief. I'd reached the landing and looked out an opening that led into the ballpark's central space.

I stood in position. The blip of the sonar steadied as the last of the Malachim settled into their places. Through the mesh of the fence, I could see the remains of the field. Years of neglect had sprouted tall grasses and a flowering tangle of weeds. A frozen crescent of shorter bluegrass, frosted by the bomb blast, stood in testimony to the original glory of this place.

I sat on the bleacher and waited. The smog had cleared somewhat, and I could see a hazy moon. As a thin cloud floated by, I thought of the Sunday school image of Heaven's cotton-candy landscape. Angels, real angels, were nothing like those harp-strumming, navel-gazing, billowing-winged clichés. No wonder Michael was pissed at the propagation of the LINK-angels myth. I tried to imagine the Michael that I knew sporting a halo and strumming a golden harp. My mind refused to see him that way. Instead, all I could visualize were narrow stripes of sunlight across his bare chest. I remembered the brightness in his eyes like molten steel. There was a majesty about him, but it was nothing Sunday school had ever prepared me for.

I stretched my toes, anxiously watching for a sign of Daniel's approach. A sound at the gate broke my reverie. I sat up and strained against the darkness to see any sign of Daniel. The shadows confounded me. Though I wanted to shout, I kept my voice a soft whisper of hope: "Danny?"

Rebeckah's command crackled through the intercom. "Front gate, confirm."

"Bogey confirmed, Commander. One man in a trench coat headed to the bleachers."

"Track him, front gate. It could still be a ruse."

When I saw a form coming up the stairs, I stood up. He wore a trench coat, but, even in the pale moonlight, I could see the brilliant orange of prison trousers beneath.

"It's him," I said, as I made out the black buzz cut.

"I've got him on scope," Rebeckah said. "I'll track him from here, front gate. The rest of you, keep your eyes open for others. If it's feds, they could also be in armor, so keep your infrared and sonar on."

I touched the button on the inside of my sleeve. "I'm decloaking."

"Keep your com connected, Dee. If you remove the helmet, take the external wire that fits in your ear, all right?"

"Got it, Chief," I said, as the helmet came off. I tossed it on the bleacher. The holographic defense returned to blue-screen blue. As I tucked the com in my ear, I waited for Danny to notice me.

He was leaning over the edge of the fence, looking out at the wild weeds of the former ballpark. The coat hung loosely on him, making him look thinner. His hair was a close-cropped helmet, and the ears he normally kept hidden stuck out. Even from behind, the haircut made him look vulnerable.

Finally, he turned toward the bleachers where I stood, my arms out. His eyes widened as he took in the Israeli uniform; then, finding my face, he smiled.

"Hey, Danny boy," I said, my voice catching in my throat.

"Dee." He took the stairs two at a time, and nearly bowled me over as he wrapped me in a crushing bear hug.

He smelled strongly of antiseptic, and my cheek prickled where the short hairs of his neck scratched me, but I held him firmly, until my ribs ached and a tear squeezed out of my eye. "Danny."

"Dee." He murmured in my ear, "You look good."

I pulled out of the embrace. Tugging the collar of his trench coat, I gestured at the orange of his prison clothes. "I wish I could say the same about you."

He laughed deep in his throat. "We're both dressed a bit different than the last time we saw each other." His fingers brushed imaginary flecks off the shoulder of my uniform. "So, what? Your old roomie finally talked you into joining her crazy rebels?"

"Oh, and what about Kantowicz?" I said, smiling. "You must have made some Malachim friends inside."

"My cellmate had the connections," Daniel said with a crooked smile. "I just took advantage of an opportunity."

"I'm glad you did," I said. "It's good to see you."

"Really?" In his voice, I heard all the same doubt and anxiety I had felt when anticipating this meeting.

"Yeah." Though my tone was light, I realized I still gripped his jacket. I felt a bit awkward holding on to him so tightly, but couldn't will myself to let go. I was afraid that if I loosened my hold on him, he might slip back into the ether. "Jesus, it's good to see you."

"Hey." He stepped away, and I was forced to let go of his jacket. He cautioned, "No cursing now. God has spoken to me, you know. I'm one of the chosen."

Archived excerpt from www.vatican.va, from July 7, 2075. Appears here in translation from the original Spanish.

The Papal Position on LINK-angels

The appearance of the LINK-angels is to be regarded as a miracle and a direct sign from God, Our Heavenly Father. As the biblical flood warned the Children of Israel of their arrogance and sin, so the LINK-angels warn all of God's Children that we have strayed from the path of righteousness. Secular governments have led only to chaos and wars. The Revelation of John says, "Blessed and holy are those who have part in the first resurrection. The second death has no power over them, but they will be priests of God and of Christ and will reign with him for a thousand years. When the thousand years are over, Satan will be released from his prison and will go out to deceive the nations in the four corners of the earth—Gog and Magog—to gather them for battle." The Medusa bomb, the hydrogen bomb before that, and all the engines of secular war were clearly designed by agents of the Prince of Darkness. A God of Love does not condemn his children to a death so vile as that of the Medusa bomb. The dead shook the very heavens with their silent cries, and the archangels have responded.

To paraphrase Jesus, "When in Rome do as the Romans do," but we are not in Rome any longer. Just as the Vatican became its own country, so must other concerned and righteous peoples separate themselves from the corruption of secular governments. We will shelter any who request asylum in the name of Christendom.

CHAPTER 16

"What did you just say?" The spell was broken. Just as I feared—the Danny I'd been hoping to be reunited with slipped out of my grasp.

"God has spoken to me," he said. I searched for the glint of madness in Danny's eyes, but only his familiar green eyes greeted me. Dorshak's words in the interrogation room came back to me: "*Your partner is completely off the deep end. He thinks the LINK-angels guided his hand.*"

I shook my head, as though trying to will the words back into Danny's mouth. "No, you don't mean that."

Ignoring the tremor in my voice, he smiled crookedly. "Yeah, I do. I've received an answer from the Almighty . . . a sort of peace."

I pushed away from him and sat down on the bleachers. I squinted up at him. "What are you talking about, Danny?"

He sat down next to me. The long-unused plastic creaked in protest at the added weight. Danny reached into the pocket of the trench coat and carefully laid a Bible on my knee.

I stared at the scarred and battered book, as though it might be a carrier of his insanity.

"I smuggled this out for you," he said, patting the book. "You'll find it illuminating."

"I'm a Catholic, Danny. You know we never read that thing," I said, pushing the Bible back at him.

"Maybe it's time." Firmly, Daniel placed the book

back in my lap. He looked deeply into my eyes. "I've been thinking about that night. All my notes are in there."

I looked at the Bible with renewed interest.

He shrugged. "It was the best I could do. It's the only paper the Moral Office allows besides toilet paper. But I could hardly have kept notes on that stuff, now could I? Keeping a Bible is expected."

I nodded, not sure what to make of this new development. "Danny, you haven't become a New Right convert, have you?"

"Hell no!"

"Why all this God-talk, then?"

"I told you, Dee. I've been chosen. God has spoken to me."

"Sure," I said hollowly. His shoulder touched mine, and we stared out at the ruined ballpark. The glass field glinted like a multifaceted diamond in the silvery moonlight. I put my hand over his where he pressed the Bible into my lap. His knuckles were dry and his fingers thin. As I caressed his hand, I noticed the absence of a band on his ring finger. "She divorced you?"

"Wouldn't you have?" His face scrunched up in a grimace.

"It's illegal. How could she possibly have gotten . . ."

"It's not illegal in cases of adultery, remember," Daniel said. "And even though you were acquitted of the charges, by the time the circus was through the press painted you a total nymphomaniac. Barbara didn't believe me when I told her I'd stopped before . . . well, you were there. You know the truth."

I pulled away at the memory of that night. In my mind, his hot hands, so unlike the gentle ones resting on the Bible now, pawed at my dress like an animal. "Yeah," I said hoarsely, "I was there."

He removed his hand deliberately, conscious of me staring at it. He folded his arms across his chest. "Dee, about that night . . . Did you get my letters?"

I nodded, returning my gaze to the glass-shrouded arena.

"It's important, Dee. This is why I wanted to meet. I need you to understand it was . . . Them." He unraveled one hand to jab a finger at the Bible. "Them, not me, who were in control that night."

I shook my head. He was completely delusional. "Oh, Danny."

"No, you've got to listen to me. The therapist at the psych ward told me to take responsibility for my actions, but he didn't understand me. I know I did it; it just wasn't me that did it."

"Do you know how crazy that sounds?" My voice took on the same tone Rebeckah's had when she begged me to join a twelve-step program, sympathetic yet tinged with hopelessness.

His eyes locked on to mine, asking me to trust in our partnership, to remember who he used to be. With a nod, he said, "I know how crazy it sounds, Dee. I think sometimes that I have gone off the deep end. But, you were my partner for five years. Was I really capable of any of it?"

"Sometimes we don't know what we're capable of." My voice sounded mechanical, harsh. "Danny, you have to face facts. They caught you with a smoking gun. You killed the Pope."

"Right. Right," Daniel said, impatiently. "I've seen the tapes. The whole world has. It was me, but who pulled the strings?"

"I don't believe in fate." The open air of the stadium robbed my words of their impact. I shook my head and muttered, "Freewill down here, my friend, freewill." I could feel my throat constricting, and tears burning behind my eyes. "Danny, maybe that doctor was right."

To have come so far only to find him so changed. It was almost more than I could stand. A tear slipped down my cheek, and I touched his back lovingly. I could feel his shoulder blades tremble beneath my fingers. He looked up at me, finally, his eyes so full of pain that I pulled away.

He looked up at me, his face puzzled, lost. "I thought you would understand."

"I'm sorry."

"I know I fucked up your life," Daniel said. "Believe me, where I've been I've had just as much time to think about it as you have—maybe more. But, I'm trying to talk about what really happened that night."

Daniel's eyes danced with that same excitement he used to have when we cracked cases together. His mood was infectious. He shifted his body to address me directly. I found myself mirroring his posture. "It was tech-telepathy, Dee," he said. "Don't you see? It was me doing all that stuff, but it was Them pulling the strings. I was a puppet."

"Except there's one big hitch," I said, articulating my biggest stumbling block to completely believing that the LINK-angels were man-made. "Tech-telepathy is fool's gold, Danny, and you know it. And what you're talking about is not just mind-to-mind communication—it's much bigger. Even if it were possible to send a mental image through the LINK, there's no way anyone could control your actions—make sure you do it."

"True. Okay, let's back up a second," Daniel said, waving his hand. "Maybe I used the wrong word. What I'm talking about isn't exactly tech-telepathy. It's more like sending an emotional command over the LINK. Hate . . . Rage . . ."—He dropped his eyes—"Lust . . . blinding emotions. As if someone could electronically transmit that very moment you 'see red' and lose all rational thought."

"Like the Jordan Institute's tech," I agreed, suddenly excited. "I've been thinking about all this. I thought, maybe . . . well, until recently, I never really connected it with what happened to you. Do you remember what we were working on, the tech-theft from the mental health biotech people?"

He blushed. "Not well. When they pulled the strings on the LINK I lost a lot of my memory files. I guess my brain wasn't used to storing things the old-fashioned way anymore."

I nodded. It was true for me as well. "Well, I've been piecing it back together. Jordan Institute was developing emotion-manipulating software—it was supposed to help people with chronic pain, or other emotional problems. Something that could touch those parts of the brain— pain, pleasure—who knows what else. But, I don't know, Danny." I shook my head. "It's a big leap from masking the pain centers to killing the Pope."

"Have you ever had an out-of-body experience, Dee?" Daniel said suddenly.

I gaped at him.

"Neither have I," he said to my stunned silence. "And, that's what makes me so certain that I was possessed by something."

My mouth still hung open, but now for a different reason: it made a kind of twisted sense.

"Okay," I said hesitantly. "Go on."

Danny's eyes watched mine intently. "Both times that *it* happened, there was a brief moment, before the emotion overwhelmed me, when I felt separated, floating."

"Separated from what? From yourself?"

Daniel nodded, then frowned in disgust. "Of course, the doctor at the psych ward told me that was just me disassociating from the horror of the event, but, Dee, it wasn't that."

"How can you be so sure?"

"Just before I . . ." He fumbled for the right word, then settled on, ". . . attacked you, and just before I shot the Pope, I was LINKed."

"LINKed where?"

"Nowhere in particular, I think I was just taking a call."

"From whom?"

Daniel shook his head. "I don't remember."

"You said hello to the 'big guy,' that night we were together."

"Did I?" He looked genuinely puzzled. "Who the hell would that be?"

Considering Daniel's earlier assertion of being chosen, I feared suggesting what I suspected: that the big guy was either God or Satan. Instead, I said, "Probably whoever stole the tech from Jordan Institute. Letourneau? Mouse?"

"You and Mouse are the ones in phone contact, not me. And I think I'd remember a call from the presidential candidate."

"True." I rubbed the back of my neck and took a deep breath. "So, what happened after the phone call? You said you thought you were LINKed during the entire time?"

"It was the strangest thing, Dee. I could see everything I did. Hurting you . . . shooting the Pope, but it felt like my consciousness was projected somewhere else. Somewhere surreal. I have the vaguest memories of it—a blank space, wide and open like the prairie, yet confined. I was certain I was on the LINK . . . but not . . . exactly."

"Mouse.nest," I whispered.

"Sorry?" Daniel looked expectantly. "What did you say?"

Glancing into his green eyes, I decided to trust him. I took a deep breath. "What you're describing sounds like Mouse's hub."

"You've been there?"

I nodded.

He laughed out loud and clapped me on the back. "Ah, Dee. Good thing I'm crazy, because otherwise I'd suspect it's you who's gone off the deep end. I thought Mouse's hub was pure fiction."

"It's not. And, he's got angels there."

"LINK-angels?" He asked, and when I nodded, he said. "So, aren't the LINK-angels everywhere on the web?"

"That's just it," I explained. "Mouse.nest isn't on the net, it's under it."

"Now you do sound crazy," Daniel said with a smile.

"Yeah, it's amazing, kind of far-out, but Mouse's house exists inside the old hardware that's supporting the LINK. Seems Mouse built himself a cozy little nest inside the nodes, the hardware, deep in the walls of the LINK—just like a real mouse would."

Daniel's face grew serious. "No shit?"

"I always wondered how mouse.net got its power," I said, "He really is just a parallel operation."

"Cool." Danny nodded. "But what does this have to do with the LINK-angels?"

"I don't know yet, not one hundred percent, anyway. All I know is that I ran into Phanuel inside Mouse's house," I said.

"My God," Daniel whispered. "Do you think he's the one. . . ."

I shook my head. "I don't know. Mouse isn't really big enough for this; he doesn't have the tech. Not even all the nodes on the LINK are big enough to hold the code it would take to do all that. I mean, what you're suggesting is that someone took over your body, moving your consciousness out of it. No one knows how to separate the mind from the body . . . or even if such a thing is possible."

Daniel shrugged. "What if what I felt was pure un-adulterated emotion, something so strong it blotted out everything else and gave the impression of pushing me out?"

"I suppose if Jordan Institute had found the pain centers, maybe our emotions are constructed the same way . . . or whoever stole the tech figured out some way to augment it. Still, it would take a lot of power."

"But the LINK-angels do exist. They can manipulate emotion. It's clearly possible, don't you think?" The way Daniel asked, it sounded more like a statement than a question. Inwardly, I smiled, his old cop-talk was coming back to him.

I shook my head. "Everyone says the LINK-angels are a miracle."

"You don't really believe that."

I swallowed a laugh. I didn't, but I still couldn't recon-cile what I knew about tech with what the LINK-angels had done. Plus, I felt the need to play devil's advocate; I was enjoying the sense of our interplay too much.

"Let's say for the sake of argument they were mira-cles? You're the one who's born-again. Are you telling me you don't believe in the LINK-angels?"

"You know I never did. And, I'm not born-again. Chosen by God. Big distinction." Daniel frowned at me as if he were the one trying to gauge my sanity, instead of the other way around. "Okay, all I'm saying is that the experience I had felt similar."

He gave me a weary look, and I remembered what Dorshak had said about Daniel: *"Daniel said the LINK-angels guided his hand."* Daniel chose his words carefully, as if he'd had this kind of discussion before. "Can we agree that technology of the LINK-angels is similar to what I'm claiming happened, at least?"

I nodded. "Although Phanuel operated on the individual level, Gabriel was sort of a group emotional experience. If the LINK-angels' appearances aren't miracles, and, in fact, are human hacker genius, or the product of Jordan Institute's research—then it is technologically possible. But, who has that capability? Or that kind of firepower?"

"Government."

I sputtered out a laugh. "Government? Now you're telling me you think it's a government plot?" Daniel didn't even crack a smile at my teasing, so I continued, "This is all hypothetical since I still maintain all the nodes in the world couldn't pull it off, but why would the government do it?"

"Letourneau clearly has motive," Daniel said grimly. With patient deliberation, he was building his case. Motive and opportunity, the standard requirements in any homicide.

"Letourneau isn't government yet—not until after the election anyway," I reminded him. "What about Mouse? He has the same access. And the angel in his hard drive could constitute evidence."

"True. Mouse could be working for Letourneau."

"Why would a Muslim work for the New Right?" I asked.

"Mouse is a terrible Muslim," Daniel reminded me. "He's far too interested in worldly goods."

I nodded. "He told me Letourneau stood for things he believed in—especially the LINK expansion."

"Makes sense. He wants to keep America out of Christendom, keep the LINK more chaotic, a hacker's paradise."

I started to nod. Then I stopped, suddenly conscious of what Daniel and I had been proposing. "Wait a minute. Letourneau? What made you suggest it might be Letourneau?"

"Haven't you been listening to me, Dee? The LINK-angels. They were what made me kill the Pope."

"The LINK-angels, yes, that's what I thought. But no one has ever connected Letourneau to the LINK-angels." *Besides Michael,* I added silently. "Except that they say Letourneau's the Second Coming."

"I'm making the connection."

"Okay," I said, "let's hear it."

Daniel took a deep breath, and said, "God told me the LINK-angels were false prophets."

I blinked.

It was the kind of statement I expected the Reverend-Senator himself to make during a press conference, not my ex-partner. I stared at Daniel. He stared back. His face betrayed nothing but absolute seriousness. Of course, truth was, an angel told me the same damn thing.

"God didn't happen to give you any hard evidence by chance, did he?" I asked.

"God doesn't need evidence, Dee," Danny said, exasperated. "God is God, for Chrissake."

"True." I smiled. Despite myself, I was starting to enjoy this conversation. "But he's not being very considerate of his humble servant, is he? It would help our case a lot if he'd deigned to leave us something that would hold up in a court of law."

Danny smiled back, but shook his head. "Don't make light of all this, Dee. I'm serious. This sounds even crazier than anything else I've said—but an angel came to me in my cell. A real angel."

My smile faded. The evening breeze felt cold against my cheeks. "An angel."

Daniel watched my face intently. "An angel. A real angel. I never told that doctor about this. I know exactly what he'd have thought of this new development, but, yeah, it was a real angel."

"How do you know? What did he look like?"

"Well, that's the strange part. He didn't look at all like what I expected. He . . . well, I guess 'she' . . . was a Chinese-American drag-queen. . . ." He laughed, and looked away self-consciously. "A drag-queen angel. Man, now that sounds crazy."

I touched Daniel on the arm gently. "No, it doesn't. In fact, that's the most sane thing I've heard you say all night."

He looked relieved, but skeptical. "Why do you believe that, of all things, Dee? That's the last thing I thought anyone would believe."

"I've met an angel, too." It was the first time I'd admitted that out loud, and I surprised myself by saying so without hesitation. "He's an Italian cop with a fondness for leather and blue jeans."

He laughed. "Mine preferred sequins."

"I'm sure the two of them would look great together."

"Heaven must be one strange-ass place." Daniel shook his head, giving me a ghost of a smile. A familiar twinkle lit his eyes.

"Neither of us is likely to find out."

"Hey, I might," he said. When I shot him a look, he added, "Well, I'm trying to change my life. I mean, for once, I think heaven might be my kind of place. I always thought heaven must be boring—perfect peace and all that. But, if drag queens and cops are angels, hell, it almost makes me think I might actually enjoy eternity up there."

"I don't know," I said, thinking of spending forever with Michael. I shook my head to banish the thought. "What did the angel tell you besides the fact that Letourneau wasn't the Second Coming? Anything?"

"Lots of stuff. We had long talks. Ariel, his . . . or, rather, her name was Ariel, was convicted for gender bending. Ten years she got for that, can you believe it?" When I looked at him quizzically, he explained. "She was my cellmate. Anyway, I took notes. It's all in here."

He pressed the Bible into my hands. "I knew you'd understand, Dee. I . . ."

His words were drowned out by the thrum of helicopter blades springing to life. Four sleek, black government stealth helicopters rose over the rim of the stadium, throwing beams of bright light down on the stadium.

"Scramble, Malachim!" Rebeckah's voice sounded far away coming through the thin thread in my ear. "Cover them!"

TXT transcript from McMannus Fan interactive 3-D BBS 2/25/76

kid@LINK.com
   "Did anyone (beside me) catch the HardLine LINK broadcast last night? The skycams caught a glimpse of our girl. You should've heard the commentary. Twenty-seven seconds of wild conjecture of why, who, and where. I figure she was out and about trying to sneak into church. It is Lent, you know."

justin@LINK.com
   "We agree on many things, my friend, but in this case you're dead wrong. Deidre is tougher than that. She doesn't even miss the solace of the church."

kid@LINK.com
   "Justy my man, you're so unplugged. Get a grip. McMannus is tough AND sensitive. Run archived interview10/11/25 on the main fan node if you need a refresher."

shelia@LINK.com
   "You guys need a life. Like any of us know her well enough to talk. 'Kid,' what I want to know is what did HardLine say? What was she wearing? (More illegal pantsuits, I hope. That girl's got rocks!)"

manny/BBSsysop@LINK.com
" 'Kid,' what I want to know is how you keep getting on this BBS with a handle. LINK protocol demands full disclosure. If there is a LINK hack in progress, the Tech-Squad will shut us down so fast it'll make our heads spin. This BBS is unlicensed enough as it is—the last thing I need is a spike sent right to the cop shop every time your unregistered name pops up. Shut down or uncloak!"

mouse@mousenet.com
"RE-lax, Mr. Martinez. Ain't no pansy spike built yet that could tag this rodent's code. But out of the goodness of my heart, I'll decloak. Shelia, dear, to answer your question <visual file attached>: Sorry, no pants. According to the scuttlebutt, Dee's been slapped with too many gender-bending injunctions from the Klein Fashion industry. Apparently her 'rocks' can only support so many lawsuits. As you can see, Hardline featured our girl looking smart in a forest green blazer and matching **regulation**-length skirt. Notice her hair is looking better than usual, still a little windblown, but not the fashion faux pas we've seen before."

shelia@LINK.com
"Thanks, Kid . . . Mouse! You're the coolest! Hey, speaking of gender-bending injunctions, can we start a thread on how low-rez the gender-bending regulations are? I swear, I'd kill to be able to go outside in a comfy pair of jeans."

CHAPTER 17

Spotlights danced through the stadium as the copters encircled the ballpark. The blades chopped at the night sky. A metallic voice rang out, "This is the police. Lay down your weapons."

"Weapons? I'm unarmed," Daniel said, as we ran for cover. Giving me a sidelong glance, he added, "And it's not like you could hide anything under that skin suit."

I ignored his implied question. If things got worse, Daniel would realize that the Malachim were here and armed to the teeth. I was more concerned about how the police found us so quickly.

"I can't believe it's the cops again," I shouted, vaulting over the bleachers in a mad dash for the entrance to the interior of the arena. "Someone must have betrayed us."

"Don't look at me. I sure as heck don't want to go back to prison," Daniel said between breaths.

The deafening noise of air through blades precluded further conversation. I stopped running and looked up to see the shiny black belly of a helicopter looming directly above us. That the police had pulled a gas-guzzling beast out of storage just for us was a bad sign. The spotlight was aimed beyond my shoulder, so I could see someone leaning out of the door of the car. The figure was dressed in black and was difficult to distinguish against the night sky. He had something trained on us, possibly a scope of some kind, because only half of his pale face was visible.

"There is a US Marshal here," an amplified voice said.

And a police sniper, I thought to myself, looking up at the helicopter. The machine bobbed up and down in the air, as though agreeing with my unspoken thought. Hot wind blasted down, ruffling my hair. Daniel's coat snapped in the mechanical breeze.

"Surrender the prisoner," the voice commanded.

"I'm not going back there," Daniel said from where he stood, just behind my shoulder.

"Don't worry, Danny," I said, squaring my shoulders. "I'm not giving up without a fight. We have to make a break for it," I told Daniel. My eyes stayed locked on the figure in the helicopter.

"Ready when you are, partner," he said, a familiar tone in his voice.

The instant my feet moved, a red light flashed from the helicopter. I barely formed the word, "laser-sights," when, I heard a deafening series of explosions. Daniel cried out. I spun on my heels. Daniel crumpled in the spotlight, clutching his chest. Hundreds of fléchettes had buried themselves in his flesh. The rapid fire of the gun was so fast that, as Danny had moved to protect his chest, his hands had become pinioned there. "Oh, Danny! No!"

I dropped to my knees beside Daniel just as the spotlight blew out with a crash. Glass showered down on my head. Then, something dark and heavy fell out of the sky with a wet thud. A strangled moan came from the bleachers only a few feet from me. I saw a police sniper's body sprawled awkwardly on the plastic seats. Pale fingers twitched in the moonlight.

"Shit!" I heard a Malachim exclaim over the intercom. "Commander, I've got fléchette rifle signatures on scope. Someone on the ground brought down. . . ."

"The kill was mine, soldier." Rebeckah cut him off sharply. Then, after a click to broadband, she intoned, "On my order the Malachim Nikamah will engage the New York Police Department and the US Marshal. Return defensive fire only. Repeat: We are firing in self-defense only." With a click back to the Malachim's private channel, she added, "Get those spotlights out of commission, boys and girls. Let's keep it clean."

Dots of light twinkled silently in the arena, as the Malachim engaged their laser sights. I turned my attention to Daniel. I rolled him over. I could see a widening, wet spot near his shoulder. The strong smell of blood and gore made me gag. Choking back the bile that rose in my throat, I put my arms around Daniel. "Come on, Danny, we've got to get you to shelter."

His fist clenched on the chain-link fence, and he dragged himself upright. Tears of pain glittered in his eyes, just as tears of desperation threatened to fog my vision. I held him tight around the waist and pulled him slowly toward the stair opening. I repeated words of nonsense, words of encouragement. "You can make it. Come on, partner, just a little farther."

Daniel's body was awkward and heavy in my grasp, and he crawled forward, hand over hand, with maddening deliberation. The constant rapid-fire explosions surrounding us made my skin crawl. Phantom sensations of tiny barbed arrows whizzing nearby jerked me this way and that, as though I might be able dodge something moving so fast.

Searing pain grazed my ribs, but I wasn't sure if it was a stitch in my side from exertion or the touch of a fléchette. I didn't stop to look. If it were a fléchette, I would know soon enough. Most of the barbs were programmed to start digging the second they hit something soft like flesh. I stayed hunched over Daniel, shielding his body as much as I could, as we crawled toward the doorway. "It's going to be all right," I kept saying.

"The Bible," Daniel said through clenched teeth. "Do you have the Bible?"

My helmet and the Bible were somewhere back on the bleachers. "I'll go back for them," I told Daniel. "Once you're in the doorway, okay?"

He clutched at my shoulder, his grip surprisingly strong. "Promise me you'll go back for the Bible."

"I will," I said. I needed to go back for the helmet anyway. Without that helmet, the armor was useless, and

I was cut off from two-way communication with the Malachim.

Finally, we reached the arch of the doorway. I pulled Daniel as far into the shadows as I could. He leaned heavily against the wall with a grunt. In a widening circle, wet blood shimmered beneath his trench coat.

"Oh, Jesus, Danny, I don't think I should leave you." I looked around frantically for something to help staunch the flow of blood.

"The Bible," Daniel insisted. "Please."

I frowned at him in concern; he stared at me imploringly. Finally, I nodded. Balling up an edge of his trench coat, I pressed the material and his hand to the wound. "Hold this," I instructed, though I knew it wouldn't do any good. "I'll go back for the Bible."

Looking out into the arena, I could see red dots of light on the bleachers. The hulls of the stealth helicopters were smoking from the continued barrage from the Malachim. The helicopters careened wildly, diving this way and that around the ballpark. Spotlights illuminated retreating shadows of Rebeckah's soldiers.

With a quick prayer to Jude, the patron saint of lost causes, I crawled back out into the bleachers. I pulled myself along on my stomach by my elbows. A scream rose above the din as someone's mark hit home. I winced, not sure who to be rooting for; I wished no one dead. Police or Malachim.

"Oh, God," I muttered, as I inched along. "I'm so sorry."

A spotlight illuminated the space in front of me and headed in my direction. I started to squeeze against the bleacher, but quickly realized the inch overhang wouldn't protect me. When the spotlight reached me, I scrambled to my feet. Adrenaline rushed through my body, and with a whoop, I sprinted the distance to the helmet and the Bible. The spotlight stayed on my heels.

Skidding to a halt, I grabbed for the Bible and the helmet. I stopped to turn around, and looked up into the bright light. A helicopter hung in the air directly overhead. It would be impossible for a sniper to miss.

A shadow, like a soap bubble film, appeared between the helicopter and me. Then, the spotlight blew out with a deafening crash. "What the hell are you standing there for, girl?" Rebeckah's disembodied voice shouted. "Run!"

As with all of Rebeckah's commands, I followed it without a second thought. Footsteps echoed behind, following me to the shelter of the doorway where Daniel slumped against the archway.

Kneeling beside him, I said, "Hang on. We're going to get you out of here."

The intercom crackled as Rebeckah sent out the fall-back order to the Malachim. To me, she said, "I'm going to stay and make sure everyone gets out. Get him to safety."

Daniel's face looked ashen. Covered in sticky blood, his hands trembled where he grasped at his wound. There was a thin whistle in his breath and a wet, sucking sound in his chest. I looked up to where I imagined Rebeckah was standing and shook my head. He's not going to make it, I tried to say. Instead, what came out was, "I can't carry him alone."

"Did you get the Bible?" Daniel's cold hand covered mine imploringly.

Tipping the helmet so he could see the Bible nestled inside, I nodded. "It's safe."

"Do you think they'll let me in?" His voice was a whisper.

For a moment I didn't understand what he was talking about. "Heaven?" I pulled out a courageous smile. "Nah, Danny, Saint Peter will stop you at the front gate. I keep telling you: God is a Catholic. You Protestants have got it all wrong."

"We'll see." He smiled.

"Not soon, I hope," I whispered. I looked at the entrance, toward Rebeckah, then down the stairway. Maybe I could carry him out, I thought, if Rebeckah or another Malachim helped. As I glanced back and forth, my gaze strayed past Daniel. Daniel met my eyes and held them. The look he gave me told me he knew; he knew he was dying. "Oh, Danny."

The air shook as one of the helicopters slammed into center field. A fireball illuminated the stadium. I threw myself protectively over Daniel's helpless form. When the debris settled, I still held him close.

"That night—" Daniel's words came out through great effort, close to my ear. "—I wanted to say I was sorry . . . really, sorry. Why me? Who had to gain from the Pope's murder?"

I shook my head. I'd asked myself those questions a thousand times over the last year. I had partial answers only—nothing I could give Daniel. "I don't know."

"You remember . . . that night?"

"Of course."

"What if . . . what if . . . that Jordan data . . . tripped someone's alarm?"

Daniel had gotten that phone call from the "big guy" right in the middle of searching those files. "A trigger. Of course," I said. "That's the connection Danny. Whoever stole that tech for Letourneau had a trigger planted as self-defense. You stumbled onto it, and it possessed you. Maybe the same thing has been happening to the Malachim."

"Malachim . . . Angels," Daniel's voice broke my excited ramblings. I looked down into his eyes; they no longer focused. Like his gaze, his mind wandered. "Surrounded by angels."

"Oh, Danny." I tugged on his trench-coat collar lovingly, as if to beg him not to go. "I want you to know: I believe you; it wasn't your fault. None of it."

"Hmmmm," he said, and I prayed to God that he heard me, because the next thing that came from his mouth was a dry, unearthly rattle.

Still rhythmically smoothing the collar of Daniel's coat, I shut my eyes and bowed my head. It wasn't right; I'd just gotten him back. He couldn't be gone.

"Danny?" I whispered, even though I could smell the loosening of his bowels. "Danny?"

I opened my eyes, only to see death's touch relax and

blur the features of the face I knew so well. It wasn't fair, I fumed silently, as tears rolled down my cheeks.

But, like so many things I tried to deny over the last few days, my protests failed to change the truth: Daniel was dead. With a trembling hand, I closed his eyes.

Police lights flashed against the wall of the stadium, red and white. The glare reflected by the glass hurt my tear-tired eyes. Footsteps echoed in the stairway. The police would be approaching soon, now that the Malachim had retreated. Touching Daniel's chest, I whispered, "I have to go."

I pulled on my helmet and tucked the Bible under my arm. As I stood up to leave, I took one last look at where Daniel lay. He slumped against the wall like a sleeping drunk. His ill-fitting prison trousers and ratty trench coat only added to the illusion. Such an ignoble death for such a brave heart, I thought, as I headed down the stairs. "Maybe I was wrong," I whispered. "Maybe Saint Peter will let you in, after all."

I burst into the open air. The parking lot appeared deserted, except for a lone, crystalline streetlamp. I felt horribly exposed; I could hear the distant whir of a helicopter's blades. The muscles of my back itched with the expectation of a fléchette sting. I concentrated on putting one foot in front of the other and ignored the rest. My vision focused on the alleyway in front of me, and I headed for the relative safety of the glass buildings.

Adrenaline propelled me deeper and deeper into the glass city. At random intervals I turned corners, hoping to shake any possible pursuers. The pads of the armored boots made a sucking sound as I ran, the soles automatically adjusting to give extra traction on the slippery glass surface.

Rebeckah had instructed us to regroup at Jerome Avenue near what was once Highway 87. From there, the survivors would make their way back to a new Malachim headquarters. Though the original HQ had not been compromised that she knew of, Rebeckah was unwilling to take the risk of leading someone there. Given the ease with which the police had located me, I had to agree with her logic. However, that meant if I didn't make the rendezvous, I'd never find them.

The moonlight threw brittle shadows at my feet that mocked my sense of direction. I looked around for street names or landmarks, but I didn't recognize any of them. I was lost.

This place was a ghetto of radiation for the Gorgons; most humans, even the police, stayed out. Thus, I wouldn't know a landmark if one hit me in the face. Even the shapes of the buildings seemed strange and squat to me. The Bronx was a city from another lifetime, preserved forever in glass.

I'd slipped on the helmet before entering the city, wanting protection from any surface radiation. My breath came in ragged spurts and my side ached. Daniel's Bible felt heavy in my hand. The deserted emptiness of the glassy streets was eerie. I missed the usually pervasive hum of traffic. Leaning against the hulk of a glittering taxicab, I gulped the night air. Though my hair itched horribly under the helmet, I didn't dare take it off, as that would disable the radiation armor.

The squatness of the Bronx disturbed me. Unlike Manhattan, moonlight fell easily to the streets here, unobstructed by traffic tubes and mile-high buildings. Tubing became popular after the war, as a solution to the continuing problem of the city's expansion, and the borough seemed foreign with only one level for all modes of traffic. Next to a Chevy decades older than mine, a glass-covered bicycle rested against a lamppost, secured for all eternity with a glittering, icy chain.

I began to realize that I was very, very lost. I couldn't even LINK into a global locating system, since I was afraid that I'd tip off the police

At the sound of a howling yell, I dropped to my knees. Peering over the hood of the cab, I searched for the source of the yelp. I heard nothing over the short, ragged huffs of my breath, which were amplified in the helmet. The street remained quiet and empty. Glass brownstones glinted dully with reflected starlight. I waited.

When the howl came again, I instinctively hunched lower and clutched the Bible to my chest. A series of short, staccato yelps echoed through the glass valley. The noise was joyful and defiant, like a Rebel yell. Then I saw them coming around the corner—Gorgons on the prowl.

Mutated by generations of radiation and inbreeding, the Gorgon temperament was considered unstable at best. As a cop, I had been instructed never to engage them hand to hand or when they were in a pack. I had seen the body of a fellow officer mauled by Gorgons: he was hardly recognizable.

The boisterous pack moved closer until they were nearly to the edge of the cab that I was crouched behind. I felt over the armor for a weapon, anything I might be able to use against them if need be. My fingers found a thigh pocket. Clumsily, I ripped open the flap. My hands closed around ten small coins. Through the gloves, I could feel their distinctive size and shape. I had an idea.

I hesitated only a moment before pressing the OFF switch on the armor. Despite my bravado, my knees shook as I stood up, and I nearly dropped the Bible.

It was a crazy gamble. I knew that Rebeckah kept Gorgons in her employ, but even if these particular ones knew where the new headquarters was, they could just as easily lead me into a cul-de-sac and rend me to pieces.

I tossed the coins at the Gorgon's feet. With a clattering, the copper skidded along the smooth glass street in all directions.

"There's more where that came from if one of you is willing to lead me to the new Malachim headquarters."

Four pale faces stared at me. White hair shone in the moonlight, giving the Gorgons an ethereal quality. None of them moved. I thought for a second that maybe they were ghosts or a mirage.

One of them, his greenish blue eyes locked on me, dropped to a crouch slowly. His body flowed like quicksilver along a tabletop, beautiful and chaotic. When his fingers brushed the coin, things exploded. In a flurry of fangs and sharpened fingernails, the rest of the pack launched themselves at him and the remaining money.

The first Gorgon hit the pavement with a smack. Straddling him, his attacker elbowed his face into the street. Glass shattered. Blood seeped into the cracks on the street. A groan of pain mingled with a growl of violence. In a smooth recovery from the blow, the first Gorgon drew his hand back into a fist and undercut the jaw of his attacker. One of the remaining two Gorgons collected coins. Seeing that, the two who had been fighting each other descended upon him.

Like a mirror image of myself, a female stepped back a pace from the others. Her eyes were also riveted to the savage tangle of men, but, unlike me, she smiled to herself like a child enjoying a game.

Noticing my stare, she said, "If this is the beginning, what's the rest?"

Blood spotted the street as the Gorgon's blows continued to break the glass sheathing of the ground beneath them. "I don't know," I said, my voice wavering in shock.

"You don't know? How come you said there was more where this came from?" she asked calmly, as her friends fought each other between us.

"Oh." I shifted my focus to her eyes. I concentrated on ignoring the sounds of battle around us. "I meant credits."

She nodded pleasantly. This conversation was surreal. I could see the three men in my peripheral vision. The first one's face was crisscrossed with bloody slashes where his face had hit the glass. I tried to stay focused and not to jump at every growl. Indecision or fear would kill any deal, and I knew it. I stared at her, unmoving, as she weighed the merits of my offer.

"How much?" She sounded interested.

"Fifty." I had at least that many credits in my account. Of course, I had no idea how I would get hold of my debit card. It was back in Eion's church with the rest of my things. I'd figure out the logistics if she accepted.

One of the Gorgon men escaped out from under the

other two and bolted into an alleyway. With a joyful yelp, they leapt after him.

"Christendom?" The female asked.

I shook my head, hoping this wasn't a deal-breaker. "Um . . . no, US."

We watched each other. A strangled cry in the distance made me jump.

"Okay." The female Gorgon shrugged. "I'll take your fifty."

She gestured with her head to follow her. I nodded in agreement, but my feet were rooted to the spot. I'd thought I'd been cool through the whole fight, but I noticed I held the Bible to my chest like a talisman. I took in a ragged breath.

"Come on," she insisted. Looking me up and down, she added, "You don't want to be here when they come back, do you?"

I shook my head. Gingerly, I stepped across the chasm of blood and broken glass to join her.

"Are you a girl?" The Gorgon asked as I fell into step beside her. Her hand reached out to investigate my arm, but quickly retracted when I turned sharply to look at her. "Like Rebeckah?"

I consciously reminded myself to breathe in and out. My frantic heart rate dropped slowly.

"Um . . . you can't tell?" I asked, but then realized the uniform hid what few curves I had.

The Gorgon shook her head. "I thought you might be, but wasn't sure."

I pulled my helmet off. It seemed disrespectful to keep it on while talking to her, despite the radiation threat, like wearing sunglasses indoors. After putting the Bible inside, I tucked the helmet under my arm.

She watched me curiously, her head tilted to the side like a dog. I felt foolish, but I held out my hand to her and introduced myself. "I'm Deidre."

She took my hand and gave it a shake—a weak attempt, barely brushing my fingertips. I had the sense she had never engaged in the custom of handshaking. She said, "They call me Dancer."

I doubted the reference was intentional, but there was something about the Gorgon that reminded me of Degas. Though unadorned, her features were delicate, like the deceptively simple-seeming brushstrokes. The long lines of her body held majestic grace. "I can see why," I said, relaxing.

"You can?" Dancer smiled. Self-consciously, she ran her fingers through her short-cropped silver hair. On me such an action would have done further damage to a haircut already resembling a rat's nest, but Dancer's hair mussed pixielike and adorable. "Really?"

"Yes, really." Her charm was infectious. The strangeness of the Gorgons' fight seemed like years ago. Though the woman before me was clearly capable of survival, I found myself wanting to take care of her. "Dancer, where do you sleep? Are you getting enough to eat?"

Dancer smiled. "Oh, sure. The service tunnels are a great place to eat. Restaurants throw away all sorts of good stuff. You'd like it," she said.

I made a face. "They're supposed to compost."

"Yeah, but Kick says that compost chutes cost money, and people don't like to spend money, which I don't understand because I love to spend money." She shot me a hopeful look, under a veil of silver eyelashes. "Fifty credits is a lot of money."

"I guess so." Though part of me knew I was being conned by a master, I resolved to find a way to make sure she got more than fifty once we got back to headquarters. "What are you going to spend it on?"

"Oh. Lots of stuff. Candy bars and Christmas lights— blue ones, I like the blue ones best. Yeah, I'd buy a whole string of dark blue lights. Or maybe something plastic, or . . ."—her eyes sparkled at the idea—" . . . a shirt that no one else has ever worn. But, you know what I'd really like to do?"

I couldn't help but encourage her. "What?"

"Walk in the front door of one of those tunnel restaurants."

I held on to my smile, even as I felt the edges twitch. One look at that silver hair of hers and the manager of the place would call the police; she'd never get served. She'd end up spending my fifty credits for bail, or they'd confiscate the card as stolen property.

"Don't look so sad, De . . ." Fumbling with my name, Dancer accidentally made it more personal. "Anyway, it's okay. I know I can't go in the other tunnels, the outside tunnels. It's just a dream."

"I'm sorry," I said. "That's a good dream."

Dancer nodded vigorously, but her face was scrunched up. I left her to her own thoughts. As we walked along, my armored boots made a soft squishing sound. Dancer, I noticed, wore heavy-traction mountain-climbing boots. She must have picked them out of the trash or stolen them.

"Do you spend a lot of time in the service tunnels?" I asked.

"They say it's better for us than the glass, but I don't know." Dancer was still brooding. As we walked, she stared at the ground. "The tunnels are all cramped and dirty. At least here there's sky."

"Is that what the Christmas lights are? Like stars in the sky?"

Dancer brightened instantly. "Oh!" She beamed up into my face and took my hand. I tensed, but I made a conscious effort to relax. Her invasion of my space was innocent. I let my hand be held. She continued to smile at me. "Yes! That's what they are—stars!"

"And those black boxes?"

"Are stars," she said again, as though testing the sound of the words together. "Are stars."

Dancer was too excited by my metaphor to concentrate on where I wanted the conversation to go next. I let it go for the moment. She continued to mutter about twinkling stars and Christmas lights. She led me down a narrow alleyway. Someone had made a fire in a glass-sheathed garbage can. The flickering flames threw long shadows around the narrow space. The contrasts of deep darkness and glittering glass were arresting; it was almost beautiful.

"We can't take down the boxes," Dancer said suddenly. "Even though they get in the way of the pretty light. The boxes are Mouse's. He gets really mad if you mess with them. So, we just go around them."

"Mouse's?"

"Uh-huh." Dancer nodded, letting go of my hand to wipe her nose. "Kick says he remembers when Mouse paid a bunch of us to put them up. I say he's lying; Kick's not that old."

"How old would you have to be to remember that?"

"Way older than Kick," Dancer asserted with a little pout. "Way. You'd almost have to be one of the first ones."

"You mean one of the first Gorgons?"

Dancer stiffened. She stopped walking and looked into my face, searching. I could see tears starting to form in her eyes. "I'm not a Gorgon. I'm not so ugly that I turn people to stone, am I?"

"No," I said. "You're beautiful."

She blinked back her tears. "Oh."

"If not . . . that . . . then what should I call you?"

She looked confused and vaguely frustrated by my request. Finally, she said, "Dancer."

Shaking my head, I smiled. "Okay, Dancer. I'm sorry I said that."

"Okay," she said, and we started walking again. We left the maze of alleyways to turn onto a main street. Dancer trudged along, lost in her own thoughts. Then, she peeked up at me, curiously. "You're funny, you know? Sometimes you say the prettiest things. It's kind of like a riddle, but it makes more sense. I wish I could talk like that."

"Where did you hear the story of Medusa and the Gorgons, Dancer?"

"One of you. A Malachim." She gestured at my armor. Then noticing the helmet tucked under my arm, she asked, "How come the black wing? What does that say?"

"Vengeance," I read, showing her the helmet.

"Sounds bad." She said seriously. "What's the book?"

"It was a gift from a friend. It's a Bible."

"Oh," she said, but I doubted she understood the significance of the book. Then she stopped suddenly and stood more erect. Her whole body seemed to quiver, like a horse testing the wind. Her head snapped up, as her eyes scanned the sky.

"Helicopters?" I whispered. Perhaps Dancer's hearing was better than mine and she could sense the whirring motors where I heard only our tense, short breaths. "Should we look for cover?"

She said nothing, just continued to stare at the sky. I followed her gaze. The flat roofs of the glassed buildings cut sharp edges into the night sky. The earlier cloud cover had lifted somewhat, and I could see a few faint specks of stars.

"Someone on the roof?" I asked, growing uneasy.

From absolute stillness, Dancer collapsed to a crouch. In the sudden movement, the metal buckles of her combat jacket clanged against each other. Her attention focused on the corner. A knife appeared in her hand.

"Someone's coming," I narrated for the still-silent Dancer.

excerpt from LINK discussion alt.religion after the LINK-angel's first appearance:

o'malley@vatican.va:
"Emotions aside, there is something seriously wrong with the LINK-angels. For one, despite the fact that most people have come to believe it to be true, there is no biblical evidence to support the idea that angels, particularly archangels, have wings. Wings were based on a medieval presumption that heaven was up, à la Dante's Celestial city, and that in order to travel back and forth, angels needed wings."

Antitov@mousenet.com:
"A clear thinker in the Vatican? Father, I'd watch your broadcast were I you. You're not likely to keep your collar at this rate."

Bryson@LINK.com
"Doubting Thomases! How can either of you deny what all of us experienced? It was a miracle—plain and simple."

Gross@LINK.com
"Bryson is right. The angels are what they are. The time for arguing is over. Anyway, it's just as likely that the angels showed themselves the way they knew they'd be accepted."

Antitov@mousenet.com
"Oh just admit it, padre. You don't want to deal with the fact that your assumptions about God were WRONG. God is everything the common, unschooled, unwashed masses always thought, and that sticks in your pompous educated craw."

Bryson@LINK.com
"Hear! Hear! Jesus was a champion of the common man. It's very possible that he would come back the way the common man would prefer to see him."

goldman@LINK.com
"Pardon me, but I don't think that Jesus has anything to do with angels. I have to agree with the Father. Angels have existed in traditions other than, and older than, Christian. But, what I'm most shocked to discover, if the LINK-angels are a true sign from above, is that they're all so white. The neo-Nazis and white supremacists are going to have a field day with this little tidbit. Made in His image, eh?"

CHAPTER 18

I tossed the Bible at my feet and jammed the helmet down on my head. I touched the ON button at my wrist to engage the holographic armor. The pinpricks of light came to life with an ozone crackle just as Michael stepped around the corner.

I was stunned to see him here, of all places. I wondered if he had somehow followed me in the ethereal plane or used a miracle to bring us back together. Despite everything, I was glad to see him.

"Michael!" I shouted. Michael turned toward the sound of my voice, but froze when he saw the Gorgon crouched in the middle of the street. I quickly powered down the suit. The hologram disappeared with a sizzling snap. I pulled off the helmet to show him my face.

"Deidre!" Michael started to step toward us, but stopped at the low growl in Dancer's throat.

"Dancer, he's a friend," I said. "It's okay. Relax."

The knife vanished. Dancer straightened slowly, with a careful precision that reminded me of someone uncocking the hammer of a gun. Michael came forward, and she backed away. "What's wrong with you?" I asked her. "I told you it was okay."

Dancer shook her head. "He's come for me already?"

"Who?"

Dancer pointed at Michael. "The angel of death."

The darkness shrouded Michael's features and gave his silhouette mass. The glass behind him glowed coolly.

I put my hand on Dancer's shoulder. "No," I said, "this one came for me."

"Okay. Good. But, can I have my fifty credits before you die?"

"Sure." I turned to Michael. "Pay the woman."

Reaching into his leather jacket, he pulled out a credit counter. He held it out for Dancer to take. She stared at his hand for a long moment before snatching the card. I never saw anyone run so fast. Before I could say good-bye, Dancer melted into the warrens of the glass city.

"Poor girl," I said to the space where Dancer used to be, "You sure spooked her, Michael."

"With such a short life span I imagine they try to avoid angels." Reaching down, Michael picked up Daniel's Bible and slipped it into his pocket.

Stepping nearer to him, I scooped his hand into mine. His skin was cool and dry. I rubbed his knuckles with my thumb, trying to impart my warmth.

"I suppose they do," I said quietly, a tacit acceptance of all that he was. "Michael, Daniel is dead."

I half expected him to say "I know," but he just nodded slowly and squeezed my hand. He murmured, "I'm sorry."

"Did an angel come for him?" My voice sounded much smaller than I intended. "Tell me Danny is in heaven."

Michael hesitated. I saw the muscle in his jaw flex, but then he looked down at my hopeful face. His eyes softened, and he whispered, "Deidre . . . of course he is."

I didn't ask Michael how he found me, or if he knew where we were going. We started walking, and I held on to Michael's hand as tightly as I held on to his lie.

The first silver light of morning was breaking the night sky as we reached Malachim headquarters. I didn't ask Michael how he knew where the new headquarters were or how he even knew that I'd been heading there. If it was one of his angelic powers, the truth was, I just didn't want to know.

The Malachim had regrouped in an abandoned warehouse at the edge of the blast line, on the far side of the glass city from the stadium. The efficiency of Rebeckah's people amazed me. In the time it took us to engage a US Marshal and the cops, the rest of the Malachim had gutted the old headquarters and moved everything to a new location.

As Michael led me deeper into the complex, I saw the hollow sadness I felt reflected on the faces of Malachim passing us in the hallways. Soon I found myself avoiding people's eyes, afraid of the accusations I might find there.

"As soon as everyone gathers," Rebeckah said coming up beside us, "there will be a memorial service. Probably this afternoon." I almost didn't recognize her voice. Her usual commanding tone was worn and scratched.

"Rebeckah," I said looking up. Without invitation, I stepped forward and wrapped my arms around her stiff shoulders. "Thank God you're okay."

Over my shoulder, she said to Michael, "It's been a long time, Malach."

"Rebeckah, I . . ." Michael started.

"Lots of people lose the faith. I understand. It's never easy to decide to die for a cause." Rebeckah's jaw muscle twitched. "Deidre, I have a lot to do, you understand. This memorial . . . it's for Daniel, as well. I hope you'll stay."

"I will. I can never repay you. Thanks."

"We knew the risks," Rebeckah said. I could see a tear forming in the corner of her eye.

My mouth opened, but I wasn't sure what to say. I intended to start talking anyway, to try to bridge the gulf between us with nonsense, babble—anything was better than the nothing that hung in the air. Michael put his hand on my shoulder, and the half-formed words evaporated. Rebeckah turned and walked away.

"Was all this pain and death part of the plan, Michael?" My voice was hoarse from all the unspoken words. I turned to glare at him, anger rising in me. "I mean, is the end going to justify all of this?"

Michael looked me in the eye, his gaze steady. "I pray it does."

I shook my head. "But you don't know, do you?"

"No." Squinting at me, he looked as though he expected an explosion.

I dropped a bomb of a different kind. "Michael, am I pregnant?"

His mouth hung open. He looked stunned.

"You can't be surprised. You can't be." My eyes narrowed. I looked him up and down, searching for some clue that he was faking his astonishment. He just stood there in the hallway, looking stupid. "You set everything up. Morningstar implied that he could ruin your plan by killing me, remember? He meant us, in the bell tower. The dream. The lily. Are you with me, Mike?"

"You're pregnant?" Michael asked, a stupid grin forming at the edges of his mouth. "Really?"

I stared at him, my mouth twisted in something combining a grimace and slack-jawed confusion. I couldn't believe he didn't have anything to do with the dream I'd had or the vision Eion had seen.

"Well," I muttered, "all the 'signs' seem to indicate I am."

Michael nodded appreciatively, not getting my reference.

"Hey," I offered sarcastically, "we could name him Emmanuel."

"What if it's a girl?" Michael looked genuinely hopeful.

It was my turn to gape stupidly into his face. "What do you mean, 'What if it's a girl?' "

"You already know its gender?" Michael shook his head in disbelief. "People certainly move fast these days. So, you've been to the doctor?"

"No, I haven't been to a doctor," I found myself shouting. "I had a fucking vision!"

The Malachim stopped to stare at us. The far-off banging of construction was the only sound in the hallway. When I looked to Michael to make our excuses, I noticed all the blood had drained from his face. When our eyes met, I saw sudden realization dawning there. I nodded my head. "Yes," I said. "Eion had the same vision."

"Oh." His voice was nearly a whisper. "Oh."

I grabbed his sleeve and pulled him out of the middle of the hallway. Blindly pushing the nearest door open, I all but shoved Michael into the room. It was a control booth for a theater. I could see a glass-sheathed stage through the window.

Ages ago, someone had converted this warehouse to a small theater. Rows and rows of empty seats glittered like ice-covered headstones. Fortunately, there had been no audience when the bomb hit. The stage was empty, the set only half-started or half-struck. I imagined somewhere in the cavernous backstage there was a frozen body of the technical director, caught working overtime to finish scenery for a play that, now, would never see opening curtain.

"I don't think we need worry," Michael said. "It might not be what it seems."

At first I thought Michael was talking about the theater; it took me a second to regroup. "Oh, yeah? And what makes you say that?"

"This is not the usual route. . . ." Michael cleared his throat noisily. "Um, Jibril is the usual herald for these things."

" 'Herald'?" I laughed. "Is that a euphemism?"

"Yes. . . . No. Messiahs are complicated. Some are born, but most are made."

I nodded, agreeing to myself that I didn't really want to know how messiahs worked—not right now, anyway. I had more pressing concerns. "I don't want this baby, messiah or not."

Michael chewed his lip. Noticing the Malachim working in the theater, Michael walked over to the control panel and looked out over my shoulder at them. "Okay," he said.

His hands rested on the edge of the board, and he peered intently into the theater. Hunched over the panel like that, he looked like a director—anxious, but con-

trolled—watching every move of the actors on opening
night.

My peripheral vision caught movement in the theater.
Malachim in armored suits were hauling flat cardboard
boxes to center stage. Though I couldn't see their faces,
they moved with a sad, slow precision. Watching their
work, I suddenly knew that the theater would be where
the memorial service would be held.

Michael was close enough to touch. The smell of him
drifted in the space between us. I breathed in deeply the
aroma of leather, and something else, like heavy incense,
frankincense, perhaps. The smell reminded me of
church . . . and sex.

"Michael, what about the baby?"

His gray eyes stayed riveted to the action on the stage,
as if he were afraid to look at me as he spoke. "I love
you."

"You're an angel Michael. You have to love
everybody."

"No, I don't." He grimaced at the Malachim in the
theater. Then, he swung his gaze to mine. Our faces
were inches apart, close enough to kiss. "I'm not talking
about godly love, platonic love, or anything like that. I
love you in the romantic sexual sense, Deidre, like a
man loves a woman."

"You love me; I see." Despite my earlier talk, I had
to keep reminding myself that Michael was an angel.
When I wasn't touching him, there was nothing about
him that seemed supernatural—no nimbus of light or
billowing wings. Instead, he stood there in his leather
and denim like any man. The light from the theater fell
across the lines of his face, illuminating shapes and contours. Yet, his solidity was an illusion, and I had no idea
what really lay beneath the airy shell he carried with
him: was it something I could love, or was it a monster
with six feathered limbs and a voice like thunder?

"Michael," I said, "show me your real face."

His gaze, which had been focused ahead, dropped to
his chest. "I can't."

I nodded. "Because I couldn't handle it?"

"Because I don't have one."

"I don't understand."

"When I'm not here, I'm nothing . . . everything. I'm in stasis, yet not. I'm not even a distinct me, but part of a bigger thing." As he searched for words, he scratched the back of his neck. The gesture seemed distinctly human. "It's hard to explain because it's nothing like here: there's no physical body to anchor the spirit to place and time."

"And yet you think you could love me like 'a man loves a woman'? Michael, we can't. We're not even the same species."

His eyes found mine. His dark eyebrows twitched as he searched for the right words. Finally, he said, "I haven't been back."

"Back where? Heaven?" He nodded. Though I didn't understand what he meant, the ashen cast to his face told me he was confessing to something serious. "Why not?"

"I'm afraid."

"Of what?" I tightened my grip on his arm. "Of God?"

He looked back over my shoulder at the Malachim. "I'm afraid of losing what I've gained here: a sense of self, apartness—and all that worldly life entails: having friends, enemies, lovers . . . a family."

I let go of his arm, and backed away. " 'A family'?"

He smiled. "It was just a thought."

"Well, forget it. Michael, you're an angel. I'm not."

"Deidre"—his eyes pleaded with mine—"I could stay."

"Stay? What does that mean 'stay'? For me? That's a sweet sentiment, Michael. Really." I patted his arm gently. "But, I'm not sure I want to go down in history as the woman that Saint Michael the Archangel, Defender of the Catholic Faith, Host of Heaven, and God Incarnate quit his job for."

"I'm not God. Others can take my place."

I shook my head. "But you're the best."

He frowned, turning back to watch the Malachim preparing the theater. "That gives me less solace than it once did. The best; the best at what? Vengeance? Now you tell me I may have helped create life. Creation . . . 'Who is like God?' indeed."

Michael's gaze returned to mine, and his eye glowed like a proud papa. My stomach soured. "Michael, I don't want this baby."

"You're not ready to be a mother?"

I hugged my knees. "I don't want to be the mother of a new messiah."

Michael turned around and propped himself up on the control booth. He watched me with concern, as I rocked back and forth. Finally, he said, "Okay."

"Okay? You said that before: okay what?" I stopped the rhythmical movement and unfurled my legs.

"I told you, messiahs are tricky things. My parentage doesn't guarantee anything."

"Uh-huh. I see." I tugged at the short hairs at my forehead in exasperation. "Michael, doesn't it seem a tad coincidental that I should become pregnant now, when Letourneau is claiming to be the Second Coming?" I hopped off the control panel and started pacing. My stomach felt like a spring unwinding. "When you first came into my office, you said you had proof Letourneau wasn't the new messiah, but I've never seen or heard a word of it. That's because this baby is the proof, isn't it? You said I would be revered for my role in all this when things were done. No wonder you could promise me that: I'm going to be worshiped as the holy mother."

"Sex was your idea, Deidre."

His voice was calm and almost emotionless, but the impact of his words burned me like a sword of flame. I stopped pacing to stare at him. The whole thing was my fault, just like with Daniel. When I could speak, my voice sounded like a little girl's. "I thought you said sex wasn't a sin."

"It's not." Michael leaned back against the console. "I'm just saying, it's impossible for me to have planned this pregnancy. I never intended to go to bed with you."

He smiled up at me. "I don't regret it . . . I just never intended it."

"You really believe this is just a happy accident?"

He shrugged. *"Deus volent."*

I let out a short, exasperated huff. " 'God willing,' Michael?" My head hurt. "Shit."

Michael stared innocently at me. I couldn't even begin to formulate words for my feeling. So, I resorted to my favorite trick during emotional crises—I turned on my heels and fled.

The wood door made a satisfying slam against its frame. I could almost pretend my action had solved everything. I started walking. It felt good to be moving, doing something. I didn't really care where my feet took me, as long as it was away. I focused on movement. The feeling of my weight shifting from foot to foot, the hardwood floors under my boots, my breath coming and going—all served to center me.

"Deidre, wait!" Michael's voice followed me down the hallway.

I stopped and let him catch up. As Michael continually proved, I couldn't run away from an angel of God.

"I'm sorry," he said. To my surprise, Michael took my hand in his. It was an intimate, loving gesture, and the first touch between us that I remembered him initiating. "I'm still learning how to . . . be with people."

I stared at his cool, dry hand. Squeezing firmly, I wondered if I could alter the sense of emptiness that surrounded my palms. The feeling was like clutching a hollowed-out eggshell—tough yet fragile.

"I need more than this," I said, as I let go of his hand.

"Michael?" A young man in uniform had approached us. He stood just close enough to be seen, but far enough away not to intrude. "Is that you?"

Michael clearly wanted to continue our conversation. His eyes danced back and forth between us, then finally settled on the Malach. "Matthew. Good to see you again."

Matthew looked me up and down, measuring. "I hope I'm not interrupting anything."

"Actually . . ." Michael started.

"No," I finished. I reached out my hand. "I'm Deidre McMannus."

"Matthew Mahaffry." Two pumps. It was a strong, confident handshake.

"Mahaffry?" I smiled. "Irish and Jewish?"

He returned my smile with a dimpled one of his own. "It happens, but I'm not. I've got a different kind of 'family' connection to the Malachim, if you get my meaning."

I shook my head.

"Girlfriend." He smiled. "I'm gay."

"Oh." It was rumored that Rebeckah sheltered gays, lesbians, and other sexual deviants unwilling to renounce their lifestyles, but I'd always thought the rumors false, a smear campaign to destroy the Malachim reputation further.

"How have you been, Michael?" Matthew asked politely. "Maxine told me you'd left in the middle of the night. What happened?"

"I ran afoul of Rabbi Feinstein."

"Theologically?"

Michael nodded.

"I guess I did hear about that. Your little display was quite the talk." Matthew shrugged. "I'm surprised you left . . . without saying good-bye."

As they continued to renew their friendship, I found myself staring, searching for clues. I'd never met an admittedly gay man before. If Matthew hadn't told me, I doubted I could have guessed. There was nothing about him that seemed feminine in the least. He held himself arrow-straight, none of the "warning signs" of unmanly posture. His body was slender, but not unmuscular. Matthew wore his uniform well, and I wondered if he did any actual soldiering. Most likely he did, as I doubted Rebeckah would allow anyone to tarnish the Israeli insignia by not doing their part for the Malachim cause. Rebeckah had an interesting sense of irony.

A ban of gays in the military was the first battle cry of the New Right's campaign against the Queer Nation.

The New Right claimed that the mass destruction of the war came down to a secular president's leniency toward gays during the "Don't Ask, Don't Tell" years. If we hadn't left the protection of the country in the hands of a bunch of fruitcakes, they claimed, none of this would have happened—"this" meaning the Medusa bomb. And here stood Matthew in the center of the glass city wearing a uniform.

"So, Michael," Matthew was saying, "maybe I'll see you later tonight? We could go dancing like we used to."

Michael's eyes slid over to mine, which were wide in surprise. "Like we used to?" I mouthed.

Michael blushed and turned back to Matthew. "Uhm . . ."

"You're welcome to come too, Deidre," Matthew said. Then, he added, "As long as you're willing to share." With a wink to Michael, Matthew waved goodbye. Over his shoulder, he said, "I've go to run . . . guard duty. It was nice meeting you, Deidre."

As Matthew moved off, Michael said, "Your mouth is still hanging open."

"What?" I hadn't realized I was still staring. I tried to stop my analysis of Matthew's walk before Michael noticed, but when I pulled my eyes away, I knew it was too late. Michael grinned at me. I blinked innocently up at him. "What?"

"You're terrible." Michael shook his head, still smiling.

"Me?" I said, still reeling from the shock of Matthew's parting shot. "You're a flirt."

Michael shrugged. "Matthew appeals to me. He's very funny and sharp. He was one of the most interesting people I used to hang out with when I was here before."

"Were you lovers?"

"No," he said quietly, almost regretfully.

"Are you bisexual?"

Michael grimaced. "You say that like it's a dirty word."

"Are you?"

"Gender is a human notion. Flesh is a costume I wear. My insides are male and female—in God's image."

I looked at Michael's broad, masculine form, and said, "So . . . God is okay with . . . It's not a sin?" I could still see Matthew moving through the hallway. "What about, what is it, Deuteronomy? 'Two men shall not lie down together.' "

"There are hundreds of laws in that book. Do you follow them all?"

"No, but Rebeckah's people do."

"Yes, and Rebeckah has no trouble reconciling it."

"What are you saying?" I asked, even though I knew. Rebeckah was a lesbian. I'd suspected for a long time. She was discreet; I never saw a lover. Since she had never confirmed or denied it, I'd figured it was none of my business. Mostly, I tried not to think about her sexual preference, because politically it was a liability, and a doozie at that.

"You're the detective, Deidre. Have you missed all the clues, or just ignored them?"

"Rebeckah is smarter than to be obvious."

"So then, you knew," Michael said. "Why do you do it? What's the point of denying the truth about people?"

"To protect myself from entanglements . . . and pain."

"More like just delay it." Michael grimaced.

"What would you know about it? Your life is pretty simple, Michael."

"Not anymore," Michael snarled.

It was true, so I held my tongue. Michael started strolling down the hallway, toward where a crowd was gathering. I followed to what looked like the main entrance. I could see the box office jutting out of the center of the wall, framed on either side by two double doors. Cracked projection squares, filled with holographic stills of actors in costume, spotted the walls.

The crowd of mourners snuffled quietly, waiting for the doors to open. Though a couple of people waved at Michael in greeting, he made no move to join them. We stayed in the back near a wall of holo-photos. In the dim light, the holographs flickered solemnly. Shielding my eyes from the pulsing light, I turned to face Michael.

More people had gathered, and the sound of soft sobs drifted through the hallway. "What's death like?"

He shrugged. "I wish I knew. I don't know what happens to you. I was born of pure spirit; you were forged between, a mingling of heaven and Earth. You are something less than me, yet something far greater. You are who They made in Their image. That's something I'll never comprehend, as my existence is a shadow of your own, a half of the whole."

Though his body seemed like a shell to me, it meant more to him. His body was his connection to godhood. I could see the desire in his eyes. "That's what you don't want to give up."

Michael nodded, but said nothing.

I stared out at the crowd. People held each other and wept openly. Daniel was dead. I tried to feel angry or sad, but nothing came. I had reconciled myself to his loss a year ago, when we were separated by his prison sentence. This was different, more permanent, but I couldn't dredge up any feeling. That scared me.

"Was it all an accident?" I wondered aloud. Hugging myself, my eyes stayed riveted to the grieving Malachim. "Or destiny?"

Michael was quiet for a moment. Then, looking up from his brooding, he said, "Her thoughts translate into my action. But, I'm like an arrow shot into water. She can see Her target through the ripples, but the water is deep and the current strong. The arrow doesn't always stay true to its course."

I shivered. Michael didn't usually talk like that. His eyes seemed unfocused, far away. To break the spell, I forced out a chuckle.

"Yeah, right. What is this, 'Zen and the Art of Mastering Freewill'?" More seriously, I added, "But since we're on philosophy, riddle me this, Michael: what's with the He, She, They business?"

Michael shrugged. "God is difficult to describe in

human terms. I use what feels appropriate, whatever fits the situation."

I grimaced at Michael's inability to give a straight answer. "But which is correct?"

"All of them. None. How should I know?"

I let out an exasperated snort. "But, you've met God."

"Not the way you're thinking." Michael smiled sadly. "I am God taken form, but then, so are you."

"You seem different, Michael. Are you okay?"

"I've been thinking about the end. I don't think I'm really ready. I . . ." His gaze flicked over to me, then out to the crowd. "After you left the church, I spent a lot time waiting for you to come back. It was the first extended period of time I spent here alone, just thinking—testing out my own feelings, my own motivations."

Before he could continue, Rebeckah entered the hall. The mood of the crowd shifted with her presence, like light coming into focus through a lens. Things began to happen. People wept more openly. As Rebeckah moved toward the doors, people touched her and held on to each other. They pressed closer, and Michael and I were swept into the center of bodies. I floated in a sea of embroidered yarmulkes and covered heads. I felt exposed and disrespectful.

Seeing us, someone handed Michael a skullcap and a scarf for me. He put the cap on deftly, as though he had done it many times before. I had expected him to look silly—the formality of the yarmulke clashing with the leather jacket and jeans—but he didn't. It transformed him into something even more beautiful than the Italian cop who disrupted my Saturday, what seemed so long ago. Before my eyes, Michael became a kind of Jewish prince. He was one of them, and I was suddenly the only outsider.

"Michael," I whispered, as we moved through the doors, "I'd like Daniel's Bible."

"Of course," he said. Reaching in his pocket, he handed it to me. "I'd forgotten all about it."

I nodded. The weight of the Bible in my hands wasn't nearly as substantial as I'd hoped. Prison issue, the book was small enough to fit in the back pocket of Michael's jeans. A greenish brown recycled plastic cover bent easily in my grip, and I tugged at its edges as we made our way into the theater proper with the others.

The Malachim had draped the room from floor to ceiling with protective material. A musty smell hung in the air, like the dust of an old library. Some raw glass was still visible, but the protection would be sufficient for a short ceremony. My fingers brushed along the fabric as we walked down the aisle. Soft, it felt almost like satin—smooth and cool.

Michael and I stood where directed. Even the seats had been draped with the armored material. I looked up at the stage, which had been left untouched and glittering. Its brightness was strangely compelling, perhaps because the dark cloth made the place seem smaller. The theater held us closely, like the walls of a womb.

Rebeckah came in carrying Torah scrolls. At least, I assumed it was Rebeckah by the way she walked. In full uniform, including the helmet, her features were obscured. I assumed she wore the helmet in order to keep her head covered; the uniform and a scarf would probably look odd.

All eyes followed her as she climbed the half-finished set to the second tier. There, she sat on a frozen chair in full view of the auditorium. She cradled the scrolls in her arms lovingly, her head bowed. A rabbi came in next. Suddenly people were sitting down; a beat behind, I joined them.

"*Yis-ga-dal v'yis-kas-dash sh'may rabo.*" The Hebrew sounded like nonsense to my ears. Next to me, Michael followed along flawlessly. "*B'ol-mo dee-v'ro chir u-say . . .*"

I let the sounds wash over me. I looked down at Daniel's Bible in my lap. My hands, in their usual way, smoothed and tugged at the book, as if of their own accord. The plastic frustrated me. Encasing a sacred text in the waste from a thoughtless generation offended my sensibilities. It was too close for comfort, reminding me of my own false faith.

I'd asked for the Bible with the hope of feeling less like a stranger, to find some comfort in what was supposed to be the center of my spiritual life. Looking at the book now, I knew I'd feel even less at ease in Eion's church . . . my church. That an angel of God sat next to me did little to bolster my faith.

Michael's existence should be proof positive that God watched over us and that what many believed about the universe was true. It was not enough for me. I felt as though there was something missing, something deep inside me that remained empty.

Tears surprised me by splattering wetly against the Bible. Even my tears were a sham. There was no grief for Daniel in them. I cried for myself, for my own death. Tears I should have wept a year ago rolled down my face in an unstoppable tide.

A part of me died when the dark veil of excommunication fell, shroudlike, over my days. Yet, even before that, I was never whole. I forever sought to fill the void in my heart with action or distraction. First, by immersing myself in the LINK, almost to the point of addiction, and, then later, by throwing myself into my career. My life was the opposite of Michael's: only marking time and place, a heavy, slogging clay bereft of the lightness of spirit.

People were standing again, and I struggled to my feet. Daniel's Bible slipped out of my lap, but I caught it before it landed on the floor. I leaned heavily on the cloth-draped chair in front of me. Under my weight, the Bible bent to the contour of the seat.

Like the Bible, I lacked a hard back or something in me that would not bend under pressure. I lost Daniel the first time because I didn't have anything solid to hang on to—no faith, no trust. Instead, during the trial, I relied on the facts, and what I so nobly believed to be the truth. The truth, I was beginning to understand, was more than just the sum of the facts. If I'd had faith, I could have made the leap beyond the facts, to something solid, unchanging.

When I chose not to betray Michael and Jibril to the

FBI, the LINK had miraculously reactivated. *"By an act of faith, it is done."* Too bad my act of faith had come too late for Daniel.

Michael tugged on my arm. I looked up from my reverie to see that I was the only one still standing. I quickly dropped into the seat. I considered LINKing into a translator so that I could better follow the service. My fingers touched the filament, but stopped. Like Michael, I rarely allowed myself the luxury of uninterrupted thought. I consciously resisted the urge to plug in and lose myself in the motions of someone else's ritual.

Instead, I flipped open the Bible, hoping to find something Daniel had marked as meaningful. Being a Red Letter version of the New Testament, all of the words of Jesus were highlighted in the text. Parchment-thin, the pages were made with low-grade recycled newsprint. I flipped randomly, hoping to find the notes Daniel had promised were inside. There was nothing except the printed word. I flipped more frantically, but still found nothing.

Rhythmical sounds of Hebrew drifted through the auditorium. When Daniel told me he had notes hidden in the Bible, I'd hoped for a journal of thoughts in the margins, or even cryptic, insane scrawl. There must be something I wasn't seeing. Then I noticed dog-ear folds marked certain pages. Maybe, given time and energy I could put together Daniel's puzzle.

"Faith," I whispered to myself. "Have faith."

The service had apparently ended, as people were standing up and quietly making their way out of the theater. I cradled the Bible in my arm. Even though I suspected it was useless, it was all I had left of Daniel. I followed the others numbly, letting the tide of people push me along. I wasn't even conscious of Michael following me until he took my hand.

"You okay?" he asked. "You look shell-shocked."

I gestured weakly with the Bible. "Do you believe in the idea of a holy madman?"

"Why?"

"Daniel's Bible. He seemed so lucid when we met,

but . . . just look at it, you'll see." I offered the Bible
to Michael.

Pulling away from the shuffling crowd, we stopped
near the holo-pictures again. Michael leafed through the
pages. I scanned the room, as I waited for Michael's
solemn agreement of Daniel's insanity.

"This is a great gift," Michael said, handing the Bible
back to me.

"Yes, yes. But there were supposed to be notes in
there from Daniel," I said, flipping the book open again
to show Michael the empty pages.

"Have faith." Michael put a hand on my shoulder.
"Things may yet reveal themselves. We should join the
others and give Rebeckah our condolences."

"Sure," I said, though I didn't really feel like being
with other people. I followed Michael through a series
of smaller and smaller hallways that snaked toward the
back of the theater. As we passed an open door, I
looked in. Piles of material and rows of finished cos-
tumes hung on racks, untouched by the glass. That not-
unpleasant musty smell hung in the air, as we continued
through to the back stage.

The Malachim had transformed the prop shop into a
reception area. A couple of Gorgons were still setting
up chairs and smoothing out tablecloths. There were others, like Matthew, who were non-Jews, but friends, and
part of the Malachim cause, all doing their part. Rebeckah had gathered a family around her, and I suddenly realized the depth of her sacrifice.

The smell of roasting potatoes made my mouth water.
I hadn't realized how hungry I was. I settled into line
behind Michael to get some food. Once my plate was
full, I continued following him to a table. I was so anxious to eat that it took me a beat to recognize Raphael
as he stood up with open arms to greet us.

"Rafe!" Michael said, putting his plate down to clasp
Raphael in his arms. As the two men held on to each
other, the world seemed to stop. The sounds of the gathered Malachim hushed, and a noise like wind around
gables whispered in my ears. A welcoming feeling crept

through my toes, warming me. When they separated, my heart ached almost physically. The room filled with the echoes of chatter again.

A chirping noise broke my concentration. At the second ring, I realized it was my phone. I put my plate down.

Over Michael's shoulder, Raphael eyed me curiously. Very few people used phones anymore. "Excuse me," I said, turning away to answer it.

A hand on my shoulder prevented me from moving away. Michael asked, "Are you sure you should?"

"This thing is a lot less traceable than a LINK-up. Besides," I said, as the phone rang again, "I'm curious."

He raised his eyebrows at me, but let me go.

Pushing the video and voice button, I said, "Hello?"

"Hey, Dee, it's me." Mouse's voice was almost a whisper, and he gave a little embarrassed wave to the screen. The video was a grainy black and white. On the wall behind him, I could see graffiti splashed in a crazy conglomerate of halftones.

"Are you in a public access booth?" I was startled, I didn't know any of those were still functional. "How?"

"Hot-wired." He shrugged, as if it were something he did every day. Ironically, the image chose that moment to waver. "I'm embracing my roots: phone phreak."

I smiled. "I'm impressed."

With a nod of agreement, Mouse took the compliment in stride. "Nice uniform. You convert?"

I shook my head. I opened my mouth to explain how I ended up with the Malachim, but when I thought of Rebeckah, no words came.

"Uh-huh," Mouse said, interested, but not pushing it. "So, did you ever catch up with that escaped fox?"

Danny. Of course, Mouse wouldn't know. "Have you talked to your page yet?"

"No. And, that's the other thing: I come back on-line, and everything is in chaos. No page in sight. Worse, someone breached my inner sanctum. My hub, Dee, my hub. I swear, if some two-bit hacker spiked me, I'll burn him."

I mustered all my courage and said, "Maybe you should send Phanuel after him."

The card I played made an almost audible snap hitting the table. Mouse's expressive face turned to stone. The only part of him that moved was his eyes, and they danced. Letting out a long, thin breath, he said, "I see." His voice was even and measured. "We should meet in person, don't you think?"

excerpt from the *New York Times,* August 23, 2076

Grey demands REAL-TIME

NEW YORK NODE. The presidential campaign reached a fevered pitch today as Rabbi-Senator Chaim Grey demanded a real-time debate with his opponent Reverend-Senator Etienne Letourneau (New Right).

"If the public is as willing to elect Letourneau as the polls show," Grey said during a regularly scheduled virtual debate at the New York node, "then they should demand to see how he reacts in real time. Though it is true that Letourneau could perform most of his presidential duties via the LINK, it is equally true that he might be called upon to act as an ambassador to a country that has no LINK access, or that an emergency situation could arise where LINK access is damaged to a certain section of the population. If Letourneau is the man you want, then call him down from the mountain to face me."

In a bold move, Grey, who had previously been unwilling to sling mud, continued to hammer Letourneau's reputation by saying, "Look at his track record. Letourneau has never shown up at a single session of Congress in real time."

Letourneau responded by reminding the Rabbi-Senator that thanks to the progressive and populist Gates Act from the turn of the century the question of residence was determined both by real-time address and electronic. Letourneau assured the gathered crowd that he qualified as both a resident of Colorado and of Washington DC.

He finished his remarks by saying, "Rabbi-Senator Grey continues to show what a Luddite he is. He doesn't stand for LINK progress. He stands for a regression into a Stone Age era."

However, in opinion polls taken after the debate, Letourneau dropped in popularity by twenty percent. Grey and Letourneau are now almost evenly matched. (Hot-link here for exact numbers and methodology.) The pressure on Letourneau for a real-time debate has escalated rather than diminished.

Shelia Brown, a longtime supporter of Letourneau, logged on to the post-debate to say, "I just want to see if Etienne is really as handsome as his avatar." Brown's post touched off a flurry of spam, all of it echoing similar thoughts. The responses ranged from strong Grey supporters to the most rabid New Righters. One respondent, who asked to remain anonymous, asked, "What if Letourneau looks nothing like his avatar? It's, like, totally possible he's a woof-woof, you know?"

Many Grey supporters raised the question of honesty. Joss Feinstein said: "All this resistance to a real-time debate makes me wonder what Letourneau has to hide."

So far, there has been no response from Letourneau's office.

CHAPTER 19

Mouse's black eyes bored into me. I found myself shaking my head. "No, I don't think so."

The shadow of a smile on Mouse's face held no warmth.

"No, really," he said. A shaft of dusty sunlight illuminated the access booth, and Mouse's smile transformed into something light and feathery. I was almost seduced.

"I think we should," Mouse continued. "It'd be fun. I'm in New York, as it turns out. I'd love to see where you live. Sounds like there's a party going on." He craned his neck, trying to see around the edges of the view screen. "Celebrating Daniel's return?"

"Something like that," I muttered. I'd have to get rid of the wristwatch phone. If Mouse knew enough about old tech to hot-wire a public access terminal, he'd be able to trace the satellite signal. The Malachim had just relocated, and, besides, I'd already brought enough hardship down on Rebeckah. This one I'd do alone. "I'm reconsidering, Mouse. Let's meet. My office is in Manhattan, Lower East Side. Give me a couple of hours. I want to say good-bye to Daniel."

"Okay," Mouse said, a frown pulling at his brow. "How about noon?"

High noon? Noon seemed far too much like a showdown at the OK Corral.

"No," I said, giving in to my superstitious instincts. "I need more time than that. How about one?"

"I guess I can waste time in the city. I've got some

friends to check in with. Hey, then," he said, continuing the pretense of pleasantness, "I'm looking forward to it, girlfriend. It's been a long time."

"It has." Genuine feeling crept into my voice. Though he was never exactly a friend, I was fond of Mouse. Now, I wondered how long he had played me, and how much of the game he was into. "See you."

"*Ciao,*" Mouse said, disconnecting the line.

When I turned back to the table, Michael was watching me suspiciously. I squeezed in between him and Raphael. Michael handed me my plate of food.

Raphael saluted me with a glass of milk. "As you prophesied, we meet again."

"I told you I was in the center of things," I said, stuffing potatoes into my mouth. "Where do you people get this great food?"

"We have a strong and supportive Diaspora."

"So it's not manna from heaven?" I said around another mouthful.

Raphael breathed out a short laugh. "We should get rid of her, Captain." Over my head, he said to Michael, "She knows too much, and she's far too cheeky."

"I happen to like it." Michael smiled, but imitated Raphael's clipped, military tone.

"You would," Raphael grunted. "As I recall, you were fond of Morningstar."

"Were? I still am." Poking my elbow, Michael asked, "Deidre, who called?"

"Mouse." I tried to sound casual. "He's in New York."

"Mouse? The Mouse?" Michael asked. "What did he want?"

"Nothing much." I shrugged. I wanted to do the Mouse meeting on my own, so I said, "He can't find his page and he wanted to know if I'd seen him."

"Uh-huh." Michael sounded unconvinced. "When we parted ways, you said you were going off to think. I take it you did more than that?"

"Tons." I gnawed on a carrot stick. "I'm not sure I believe you have no idea what's been going on here,

Michael. I mean, don't you two have some kind of angelic network to keep up on each other's activities?"

Michael blushed.

I set the carrot down half-eaten. "Don't you?"

Eyes downcast, he whispered into his chest. "Deidre."

There was accusation in his tone; I'd said something wrong. I shook my head in confusion.

Michael's jaw flexed. His eyes snaked over to Raphael, then back to his plate of untouched food. Through clenched teeth, he said, "I told you I haven't been back."

Raphael cleared his throat noisily. "If you need a report, Captain?"

"That won't be necessary." Brisk, Michael's real command voice reminded me of Rebeckah.

"Sir?"

"If you'd excuse us, Raphael."

"Yes, sir." Raphael took his plate and stood up. I watched openmouthed as he did as Michael directed.

After Raphael found another table to join, I said, "I don't get it. What on earth was all that about?"

" 'What on earth'? No, not about earth." Michael grimaced at his cup of coffee. I had yet to see him actually ingest any food. Snapping his head to the side to look at me, his eyes flashed with anger. "I thought I explained things to you, Deidre. Now Raphael knows."

"Knows what?" Facing him, I scooted my chair into the space Raphael had vacated. "That you haven't been back? What difference does that make?"

"I have never once strayed a single iota from the directives God assigned me. Since Morningstar left us, I have been Their right hand, the arrow most likely to hit the mark." His words pounded me almost physically. "I spent the last twenty-four hours doing nothing—a delicious, precious nothing, but a nothing all the same."

"But, I mean, doesn't God already know that, Michael?" During the barrage of Michael's words, I'd backed the chair up until the legs tangled with Raphael's empty one. I couldn't retreat anymore, so I added: "Isn't He all-knowing? It's not like you can lie to Him, is it?"

Piercing me with a fierce gaze, he said, "It is, if I never go back."

"You would do that? Michael, what's happened to you?"

"I . . ." The hard cast of Michael's face melted a little. Then, pushing his elbows onto the edge of the table, he frowned into his clasped hands. "You wouldn't understand."

"You're right." I settled back to my food. Picking up a hard roll, I bit into it. "I don't get what's so great about being human. What do we do, but mark time until we die? Doesn't seem worth coming to blows with God over, you know?"

"It is," Michael said grimly. "It wouldn't be the first time heaven was rent in two over humanity."

"Hmm, I suppose not." I chewed thoughtfully, and washed the bread down with a sip of Raphael's abandoned milk. "But, while you've been plotting the second war in heaven, I may have figured out who the LINK-Michael is."

"What?" The fork that almost reached his lips came down with a slam. "When? How long have you known?"

"Mouse has a copy of Phanuel in his hub."

Michael's eyebrows raised expectantly.

I shook my head. "I suspect that Mouse boosted tech from an outfit known as the Jordan Institute to create the LINK-angels." I thought of the phone call. Mouse had seemed so pleasant, so nonthreatening. I could still be wrong about him. "But we shouldn't jump the gun."

Michael snorted. "But why else would he have a copy of an angel in his hub?"

"To scare off other hackers?" I suggested.

"Doesn't that seem a bit excessive?" Michael asked.

"It does. And, as far as I know Kantowicz and I were the first-ever uninvited guests."

"But you suspect Mouse is the originator of the LINK-angels?"

I nodded.

"This is great." Michael smiled, relaxing. Finally, a forkful of peas made it into his mouth. "You're really on to something."

I shook my head. "I'm not so sure. Some things don't quite sit right for me. What bugs me about my theory is that the page said he tried to boomerang the LINK-angels. Why would he do that if Mouse is the originator?"

"Maybe Mouse doesn't know what the page has been doing—or vice versa."

"The page is Mouse's construct. How could he not know?"

Michael snorted a sad laugh. "A parallel situation jumps quickly to mind."

"Michael, you're completely different from an AI."

"Am I?" His face pinched up, and he looked away. Picking up his fork, he poked at the potatoes on his plate. "No, I'm exactly like the page. A program with sentience. A construct of a higher being. A messenger; an 'errand boy,' just as Morningstar said."

His shoulders scrunched, and his face tightened even further. I put my hand on his shoulder. "Isn't being an angel much more . . ." I searched for the appropriate word, "I don't know . . . glorious . . . than that?"

Michael's voice was soft, but I could hear a distant thunder in his words. "When I threw Sammael out of heaven I was filled with a holy passion. I shouted: 'I am Michael, who is like God!' " His eyes sparkled with the memory. Then, he laughed and dropped his head slightly. "Sure, there were moments of glory—if war and carnage can, in fact, be glorious. I've tasted the other side now and find I'm tired of carrying the heavy sword of vengeance."

The word "vengeance" reminded me of earlier conversations with Michael. "But you came here on your own this time, you said, to stop Letourneau from using your name."

"That's not entirely true." Michael sighed. "I find the sin of omission easier than lying."

"Don't we all."

He rewarded me with a tired smile. "Yes, I guess we do. Truth is, I came to you on my own, but the Four were deployed to infiltrate the believers—to bring the truth to light."

"The believers? The Four?"

"Archangels." Michael's attention drifted away, then, he laughed. "You know, I might feel badly for straying, but Uriel has really missed the mark. Last I heard from him, he was embracing our dual sexuality and calling himself by a woman's name."

"Ariel."

"That's it exactly. How did you know?"

"Daniel met an Ariel in prison."

"Indeed." He shrugged. "I guess I'm the only one off the mark."

"You found me." I asked, "Wasn't that your assignment?"

"My assignment was to find the perpetrator of the LINK-angels myth. You've done that for me."

I rubbed his shoulder. There were things I wanted to say to comfort him, but instead what came out was: "Does that mean Ariel's assignment was Daniel? But why?"

He shook his head sadly. "The plan is only clear to me above, or as it reveals itself, not before. I have a murky sense of the bigger picture, but the longer I'm away—the more it fades. I would tell you, Dee, if I knew."

"I know."

Michael's eyes searched mine, but I had nothing to say. I couldn't understand what he was going through. It was well out of the realm of my experience.

Over Michael's shoulder, I saw Raphael in the buffet line. He had one hand on the arm of an older man, a rabbi it seemed to me, supporting him. They were engaged in an animated conversation, and Raphael's strongly lined features broke out into a kind grin. The strength Raphael exuded warmed me even from this distance.

"Michael, maybe you just need some time with Ra-

phael to get back on track, you know?"—I hated myself
for lying to him—"I need some time to say good-bye to
Daniel in my own way. Let's plan to meet up in a couple
of hours at my office, okay?"

"Where are you going?"

"Nowhere," I said lamely. It was such a bad lie that
I couldn't look Michael in the eye.

"I'm coming with you." Michael's voice sharpened
with determination.

"You don't even know where I'm going," I protested.

"Last time you said you were just going out for a
walk, I had to go looking for you."

Mouse would bolt if I brought Michael along to the
meeting, but I didn't really want to be alone right now.
The funeral had left me feeling drained and, despite his
tendency toward unnerving conversation, Michael's presence comforted me.

"I just got you back," Michael continued. "I'm not
willing to let you out of my sight just yet."

"Can you be invisible?" I asked. "I mean,
angelically?"

He shook his head. "Only at great cost. Why?"

"You can come as far as my office, then I need to be
on my own for a little while. . . ." I sighed. What was
the point of keeping the truth from him? "I'm meeting
Mouse. I need to do that alone."

He brightened at my words, and nodded. "Okay.
Should you need to get ahold of me after we part,
though . . . take this. . . ." From the inside pocket of his
jacket, Michael pulled out a scrap of paper. "Earlier, at
his apartment, Jibril gave me some numbers. He said
you would understand how to use them."

I looked at the crumpled piece of newsprint. A LINK
address, phone number, and access pass code were
printed in a swirling, flourished hand. "Where did you
get all of this?"

Michael shrugged. "Jibril is the patron saint of
telecommunications."

I blinked. I looked back at the numbers, then up at
Michael. Patiently, I waited for Michael to start laughing

and to let me in on the joke. When he started picking at the peas on his plate, I cleared my throat. "No, seriously, where did you get these? Are they safe?"

Michael's eyes roamed my face, measuring me. "There are simply some things that stretch your ability to believe, aren't there, Deidre?"

"Most things about you, big guy, shake what little faith I have," I admitted.

He nodded. "I'm going to borrow some armor. We'll meet out front by the marquee."

"See you there." I smiled.

His lips brushed my cheek, a kiss so soft it was like the tickle of a feather. To my surprised expression, he said, "For luck."

Despite myself, I laughed. "What kind of luck am I going to have with a kiss like that?"

I pulled him close. My fingers prickled against his short, nubby hair at the back of his neck. Though his lips were cool, they didn't lack in passion. I shut my eyes, feeling the fire deep within the shell he wore. There was something there, something I could touch, after all. When we separated, I was smiling. I ran my hand along the sharp line of his jaw. "Much better."

"I never want to leave you."

I put my finger on his lip, hushing him. "I appreciate the sentiment, Michael." I tried to ease the harshness from my words with a smile. "But I should warn you, I don't go for that kind of devotion, even from men who aren't angels."

With a frustrated laugh, he shook his head. "Okay," he said around my finger. Taking my hand in his, he kissed my finger. "I'll see you in ten minutes."

"Ten." I smiled after him.

From his place in the buffet line, Raphael watched Michael go like a jealous lover. Then, our eyes met. Raphael stepped out of line and headed for me. I quickly gathered up my plates and tray: I had a sense Raphael had questions for me I didn't want to answer. I could feel Raphael's eyes on my back as I pushed my way to where the Malachim were gathering up dirty dishes. I dumped the contents of my tray in the bins and headed for the door. A hand on my shoulder stopped me.

"Deidre." Raphael's voice was loud in my ear.

"Raphael." As I turned, I put on a friendly smile, which faded when I saw the stern look in Raphael's eyes.

"What's going on with Michael?"

I considered batting my eyelashes and playing the fool, but as fire flashed in Raphael's eyes, I reconsidered. "Well . . . Michael's in a kind of crisis, I guess. He's doing a lot of thinking."

"Michael? A crisis?" Raphael's tight anger softened into concern. "What kind of crisis?"

"I think I'm pregnant."

Raphael's dark brown eyes widened, and his frown deepened. The sun-cracked lines of his face drew in tightly around his mouth. "I see. Congratulations, then."

"You're surprised, too?" A sense of relief filled me. Maybe I wasn't part of the divine plan, after all. "Michael says the child isn't necessarily the messiah. What do you think?"

Raphael's jaw flexed, and the Christmas lights in the ceiling reflected in the silver in his hair. "What do I think? I think this is crazy, and you must be some kind of woman to pull Michael from the path."

"I'll take that as a compliment. What about the baby, Raphael? Is it possible?"

He shrugged. "In the beginning, there have been other children with the Sons of God, none of whom became 'messiahs.'" His eyebrows drew together fiercely. "But no archangel was involved in that."

"What about Jibril and Mary?"

"Ah, the great exception." Raphael shook his head and smiled. "But, even though he talked about his father in heaven, if you recall, the only title Jesus claims for himself is 'Son of Man.'"

This conversation was getting away from me. I could feel my pulse quicken. "Wait a minute. 'Exception'? Are you telling me there are messiahs other than Jesus?"

Raphael shrugged. "Finding messiahs and angels is the

easy part, Deidre. Truly listening to them and discerning the truth? That's what's difficult."

The Gorgons being mostly nocturnal, Michael and I managed to avoid running into any of them on our way through the glass city. I shifted my backpack, so that it stopped rubbing my shoulder blades. I'd packed Danny's Bible, a water bottle, some food, and a few barter items in case of trouble.

"The city is beautiful in the daylight," Michael said.

I nodded as we paused a moment on the bridge into Harlem and let the sun wash over us. The sun warmed me, dancing on the waves beneath the steel-and-glass trusses of the bridge. I held my breath to the stench of the river, and savored the sensation of leaving behind the glass for the concrete of the city.

In another ten blocks, we could enter the relative safety of the skyway system. I headed down Fifth Avenue, toward Central Park. Michael followed, now dressed in an Israeli uniform. He was really beginning to look the part of a warrior prince. The blue-screen blue brought out the olive in his skin, and the sunlight caressed the soft curls framing his hard-angled face.

In a matter of blocks, people began appearing on the streets. The ON switch of the holographic armor sizzled as I flipped into virtual invisibility. Despite a noisy start-up, the holographic defense settled into a quiet operating hum, clearly more happy mimicking concrete than glass. We stuck close to the walls to avoid conflicting my over-taxed armor.

Harlem had achieved another kind of renaissance, this one of a more scientific bent. Because of Harlem's proximity to the glass city and lack of law-enforcement presence, many rogue scientists had taken up residence among those too poor to move away. I'd heard about the street culture that had emerged here, but, as a cop, I'd never been privileged to witness it firsthand. Indians, Asians, Blacks and the occasional white face sat on stoops and congregated just outside of bustling street cafés, talking. Regardless of nationality, white lab coats were the fashion. Along with the mussed hair and dark-framed-glasses look, men and women proudly strutted in their professional regalia. Unable to discuss certain sciences on the LINK, like geography and biology, which might clash with Biblical interpretations, those living here had reverted to an old-fashioned forum—the coffeehouse. There were hundreds of restaurants, cafés, coffeehouses, and bakeries up and down the street. By the looks of the crowds, the restaurants were open twenty-four hours. Everywhere I looked the conversation was heated. People gesticulating in the air on the corner. Inside one storefront, a group was hunched over someone drawing frantically on a paper napkin.

Bicycles and battery-powered vehicles filled the streets. On the roof, someone experimented with gliders. The constant movement and activity around me made me jittery.

The skyways had been built to absorb human noise, but here every action had a reaction, and the buildings bounced every noise back onto the street. The chaotic energy frightened me. As I slipped past a bakery filled with shouting voices, I made the sign of the cross. It was these sorts of people who created the Medusa bomb and brought about the end of hundreds of lives. Yet, there was undeniable energy here. Every excited voice echoed a primordial heartbeat that filled the streets.

As we approached the entrance to the service tunnel, I noticed a commotion. Just in front of the tunnel's opening, a ragged man stood on a crate. His hair stood on end, and he wore pin-striped pants and a terry-cloth robe. His gestures were more wild and frantic than those of the Harlem residents, but his shouts were evenly paced, almost rhythmical. Most of the scientists on the streets ignored him, but a couple of interested people had gathered around to heckle.

"You should accept Jesus Christ as your personal savior," the preacher shouted. "Science is sin, and you will rot in hell for your injustices against humanity."

The crowd let out a muffled laugh. "And what of

Kali?" someone asked. "What does She say about science?"

Invisible, Michael and I slid along the wall. I moved slowly, as my helmet's sensors informed me that the holographic armor was approaching overload. The processors' hiss sounded loud to my ears, but no one seemed to notice us creeping forward toward the door.

"Jezebel."

As if someone had called me by name, I froze.

"Jezebel." The name slid from between the preacher's chapped lips like a lover's caress. When I looked up, his bulging eyes stared directly at me, pinning me to the wall. The people who had gathered stared in our direction as well, though less focused.

I recognized the preacher. This was the same man who'd set up shop outside my office every day like clockwork since the excommunication. I'd never really looked at him before, but his whiskey-scratched, rasping voice was familiar enough.

"Morningstar," Michael said.

Excerpt from the *New York Times,* August 24, 2076. This transmission was recorded at 1500 in Colorado. It is available on the *Times'* main page. The *Times* recommends Virtual Reality replay for best results.

GREY CALLS FOR AN INVESTIGATION

The press conference was set up in a makeshift tent outside the front lawn of the sealed and gated home of Reverend-Senator Etienne Letourneau. Though wind and rain buffeted the gathered members of the press, hot coffee and chocolate was served. More than fifty representatives from competing stations attended this impromptu conference, which was the largest of its kind since before the war.

Mingling was encouraged before the event began, and this reporter met some virtual colleagues for the first time in the flesh. (Enter here for full-body experience.)

Once Grey arrived excitement could be felt in the air. At first proper protocol proved difficult as reporters shouted out questions simultaneously. Grey's aides, however, were prepared to deal with the chaos and managed the event with ease.

Rabbi-Senator Chaim Grey called for an investigation into the identity of his opponent. "A recluse cannot properly run this country. Letourneau is too much of an unknown. With me, I'm WYSIWYG, what you see, is what you get. Granted, I'm not as fancy and slick as my virtual opponent, but I am real, solid, present, and willing to be accounted for. Where is Letourneau? Why won't he face me? What does he have to hide?"

Grey announced that he has requested that an outside agency investigate the nonvirtual life of Letourneau, as, Grey said, "Did you know? The Senator doesn't even have a single parking violation?" Grey gestured to the house behind him and the gravel road that wound up the mountain. "How does he leave here without a car? Yet he has never applied for a driver's license."

John Taylor, reporter for the *Chicago Sun,* remarked that it was possible that Letourneau had drivers to take him where he needed to go.

"Yes," Grey responded, "but his whole life? Anyway, I searched for other things and found no college records, medical records, nothing."

Though a Letourneau supporter in the audience pointed out that Letourneau lived a healthy life and had an advanced degree from Columbia, Grey retorted that it was awfully convenient for Letourneau to have gone to college almost exactly twenty-one years ago, and to be one whose records were destroyed in the Medusa blast.

"I want to know if my opponent is real or imaginary," Grey said bluntly.

CHAPTER 20

"I should have recognized that brimstone stench when we first met," Michael said.

"I am a humble servant of my Lord," the preacher insisted, his gaze shifting to Michael.

"That was always your excuse," Michael said. Switching off his holographs, he materialized out of the bricks. The gathered crowd shouted in surprise. "And to think I complimented you for giving Deidre solace. What were you doing there every day? Trying to break her spirit?"

"I . . . I . . ." The preacher's whole body trembled. His knees wobbled, and his eyes rolled up into his head.

"Leaving so soon?" Michael asked, as the preacher stumbled and fell off the crate. "The fun was just starting."

"We'll meet again." A hiss, like air escaping a punctured tire, carried the words to my ear. With that, the preacher collapsed.

"Please tell me that wasn't demonic possession," I said, as I accessed the LINK to place an anonymous call to the hospital. I knew Michael would scoff at my compassion and tell me, "he'd live," but in the last year I had grown attached to the Revelation preacher, whether or not Satan possessed him.

"Sorry, Dee, it was. That's why I didn't recognize him earlier. Morningstar was hidden inside that body, like wearing a mask."

"How is that different from what you are?"

"This body was forged for my use alone. It's the one

I always use." Touching his wrist, Michael engaged the holographic armor. I watched a hole open in his chest and sky poke through. Then his legs faded into the sidewalk. "Let's go."

"You seem more yourself," I said.

"It feels good to be moving, doing something. It's how I'm meant to be."

I nodded. The sky darkened to a greenish tint as we approached the edge of Harlem and traffic tunnels began to sprout above us like green-gray arms of a millipede. "What was the preacher, er, Morningstar doing here? Do you think he was following us?"

"Hard to say. It's possible that Morningstar just invested the preacher with a bit of his spirit and sent him on his way like a windup toy."

"Can he do that? I thought miracles were too costly."

"For me," Michael grunted fiercely. "Morningstar is *yetzer-ha-rah*; he is a dark angel, turned away. He has all his angelic powers, but no moral restrictions."

"It doesn't pay to be good, eh?"

Michael's frown smoothed out. "There are rewards . . . but they're rarely earthly."

We entered the abandoned subway at the edge of Harlem. Since all of the traffic and pedestrian tubes had moved to the upper levels for safety and comfort, the old public transportation tunnels had fallen into disrepair. I walked down the concrete stairway toward a dark, gaping hole.

Our flashlights revealed a turnstile at the bottom of the stairs. Michael vaulted over the steel bars easily, while I crawled much less gracefully over them onto a large concrete platform. The remains of antique vending machines stood along the walls, their glass fronts smashed and the contents robbed. The curly steel holders inside the machines cast strange shadows on the wall as the beam from my light passed over them.

Across a chasm, I could see a faint light where another set of stairs led to the opposite side. I whistled lowly under my breath.

"Subway cars must have been huge," I said, pointing to the expanse between the two platforms.

Michael jumped down onto the rails. I peered over the edge nervously. My flashlight revealed a jumble of rails and dust, three feet down.

"Come on," Michael said, "I'll catch you."

Unable to bring myself to jump, I sat on the edge of the platform and lowered myself. I scraped my back and butt on the concrete as I slid to the ground. Michael steadied me as I tried to find footing on the rails. Slick with dampness, the cavity stretched ahead for miles. Ahead, in the distance, I could see the twinkle of Christmas bulbs dancing along the side of the wall where emergency lights must have hung.

I looked up, surprised that there was no rail at the top of the tunnel, like there was in the traffic tubes.

"How did they used to get electricity to the cars?" I wondered out loud.

"Something called a third rail, if I remember correctly," Michael said.

"Huh," I said, checking my compass and map. Finding the right direction, I headed along the underground passageway. Long ago, someone had started the process of removing the tracks. I stepped cautiously over the pile of rotting ties, moving deeper into the shaft.

Some Gorgon gang had marked this territory as theirs with a slash of color on the wall. I let my fingers trail along the rough surface, avoiding a makeshift camp in the center of the tunnel.

"It's hard to believe people live here." Pulling off his helmet, Michael appeared to grow out of a broken crate.

"I suppose it's better than the glass," I said. I switched off my armor; we were unlikely to run into anyone here. I shrugged out of the confining helmet. The air held a wild, almost swamplike odor. I took a deep breath of cool air and tried not to taste it.

Michael nodded, running fingers through his curls to shake them loose from his forehead. He fell into step beside me. "Why did you agree to meet Mouse alone?"

I stretched my neck until I could feel my muscles pull

slightly. "I didn't want to bring any more trouble to the Malachim."

Michael nodded. "You think Mouse is dangerous."

"I'm just not sure."

"Go on," Michael said encouragingly. Our boots made a sucking sound as we walked.

"Daniel said when he . . . killed the Pope, he felt disconnected, like a place on the LINK, but not. That sounds a lot like Mouse's hub."

"You were there. That's when you found Phanuel?"

In front of us, a small section of the tunnel's ceiling had collapsed. Tentacles of rebar coiled from the wall, and shafts of sunlight cut through the darkness like knives. I leaned into Michael for support as I clambered over the slippery debris.

"Yeah," I said, once we'd picked our way through the mess. "Phanuel was acting as Mouse's guardian. Even though I was in read-only mode, he blocked me. I was almost caught."

"I don't know very much about the LINK, but . . . is that possible?"

I shook my head. "It shouldn't be. Unless Mouse found a way to trap consciousness remotely." A shiver ran up my spine at the thought, and I blew a snort out my nose to hide my discomfort. "Again, though, that should be impossible. Despite advances in biotechnology, we still know so little about the soul, consciousness, or how the brain works. No one even knows if the soul is something separate from the body . . ." I looked at Michael apologetically. "Well, I suppose someone knows. Is it, Michael? Is our soul eternal?"

He stared at me with that same uncomfortable look that he gave me when I asked him if Daniel was in heaven. He shrugged almost imperceptibly, and said, "I have been here since the beginning. My soul is certainly long-lived if not eternal."

"You're an archangel, Michael. What about the human soul?"

"Millions of people of a thousand different religions think it is," Michael said, quietly.

"Is that your answer?"

The tunnel narrowed and split in two. From my guess, we'd reached Central Park. We headed down the left passageway. Here the tracks were in better condition. The ties were set at a distance uncomfortable for walking, and my stride alternately hit the gully between the boards or on top of them. When I shortened my step I hopped along at a slow, awkward pace. I lurched forward like that for a while, then gave up in favor of doing a balance-beam act on the rails near the wall. Even though it was long dead, I carefully avoided the third rail.

"If . . ." Michael said, glancing at me out of the corner of his eye. "If it is possible to separate the soul from the body, does Mouse have the tech to do it?"

"Are you telling me it is?"

"I'm asking a hypothetical question."

I smiled. "Ah-ha." I slid off the rail, but recovered my step smoothly. "Well, even if he did find a way, Mouse would need a computer the size of . . ." I trailed off.

"What?" Michael prompted.

"Mouse has a computer the size of the world; he's in every hard drive in existence. Plus," I told Michael what Dancer had said about the black boxes, pointing up at one. Thoughts formed as I spoke. "If Dancer is right, and those boxes do belong to Mouse, well, I think he might be siphoning off power from the main city grid. That, combined with the LINK's power, could be the energy LINK-angels needed to perform their miracle."

"What do you mean? How is he part of the LINK?"

As we continued deeper into the channel, I explained the mouse.nest virus to Michael. "I'd always wondered," I added, "why Mouse's name was in English when he's from Cairo. Mouse, the computer mouse, is one of those words imported whole, to distinguish it from the native language's furry version."

"He's a clever adversary," Michael muttered, almost disappointed.

"You were hoping things would point to Morningstar?"

He shrugged. "I know how to fight Morningstar."

"True enough." I nodded. "I still don't want to believe it's Mouse behind the LINK-angels, but I can no longer deny the possibility. Still . . . Why? Why would he do it? What does he get out of it?"

We'd reached another section of tunnel illuminated by flickering Christmas lights. In the weak light, I could see Michael's tired smile. "Besides power?" He shook his head. "We should also ask ourselves why would a Muslim work to prop up a Christian belief in the Second Coming?"

"Yeah," I said, extending my arms for balance as I walked along the rail. "Letourneau has a reputation as a right-wing fanatic. I just can't see Mouse and Letourneau conspiring together."

"You've met this Letourneau guy?" Michael asked. Moving smoothly, Michael didn't seem to have the same trouble walking along the tracks as I had.

"No. Well, not in the flesh. He conducts most of his business via the LINK. Rumor has it he's holed up in Colorado on a fresh-air farm."

"He does everything via the LINK?"

"Yes, you Luddite," I said. "Most people do. Politics is especially easy to conduct virtually."

"So, Letourneau could be anybody," Michael said, as we passed a poster announcing the upcoming debate between Rabbi-Senator Grey and Letourneau. Some Gorgon or, more likely, a politically minded Malach must have posted it for the benefit of others that might pass this way. The poster showed the usual picture of Letourneau's avatar, with a red "no" symbol slashed over his face. The words said, "No more virtual vitriol. Real-time debate: 7:00 EST, August 30, 2076!"

I stopped in front of the poster. "Today," I said. "I guess people will find out what Letourneau really looks like today."

"Do you think he's been a pretender this whole time?" Michael said, as we started walking again. "Some teenage girl in her mother's basement playing pretend senator?"

"There are rules against that, but if you're a good enough hacker you can run under an assumed name . . . for a while. LINK-vice usually catches up with people who do that." I shrugged.

"If they commit crimes under the assumed name," Michael said. "Right?"

"I suppose. But, if that's the case, Letourneau has been running a tight scam for a long time. He's a public figure."

"But, it's possible."

"After meeting you," I said, "I'm beginning to believe anything is possible."

Flecks of light shimmered on the planes of his face, but Michael's eyes were swallowed by darkness. Only the tips of his eyelashes shone in the dark hollows. Michael's mind seemed far away.

The Christmas lights twinkled against the ceiling like stars. I wondered what people would do to celebrate my baby's birthday. "Michael, Raphael was surprised."

"Hm?" Michael blinked away his thoughts, as if having to consciously focus on me. "By what?"

"That I was pregnant."

"Deidre!" Michael stopped walking and put his hands on his hips. "Why did you tell him that?"

I let him fall behind and kept trudging forward. "I didn't know it was supposed to be a secret. I guess I figured he would already know."

"How many times do I have to tell you it doesn't work that way?"

I stopped walking and hopped off the rail. Straddling the ties, I faced him. "Are you telling me Jesus wasn't planned?"

Michael stood motionless, like a stone. The lights danced around him, twisting his shadow against the wall. "I'm not always privy to the divine design, but this I know for certain: messiahs are an earthly concept."

"I don't believe you."

Michael nodded, a small smile playing at the corners of his mouth. "So you have some blind faith after all."

"I guess I do."

"Deidre, you've met three archangels. A Christian." He laid his hand on his chest, to indicate himself. "A Muslim, and a Jew. If one messiah was the only true messiah, how could that be?"

I remembered the funeral, and the ease with which my Christian angel had donned a yarmulke and spoken Hebrew. "Michael, you're a Jew, too."

When I looked back to Michael, my breath caught. The same gray eyes stared back at me, but Michael had transformed. Bearded, turbaned, and darker-skinned, I barely recognized him. He held a curved sword in his hands, which gleamed wickedly in the bright light.

Wings, like peacock feathers, shown an iridescent blue-green, and in each "eye" a human face was visible. With each gust of air that swelled at the tiniest flutter, I could hear the moans of a thousand souls.

The discordant voices groaned in unison and swelled. I made out the words: "I am also Muslim."

"Oh . . . okay." I stumbled backwards over the rails until my shoulders pressed against the wall. I screwed my eyes shut and reminded myself of the necessity of breathing. I drew slow, ragged breaths, one at a time, and tried to banish the terrible vision from my mind.

"Deidre." The screeching souls were gone from his voice. I heard only the gentle bass I'd grown to expect from Michael's lips.

A hand on my shoulder made me jump, but I kept my eyes shut. "Was that your true face, Michael?"

"No. Wings, like messiahs, are a human invention."

Slowly, I opened my eyes. The Christmas lights had returned to their normal, dim flashing. Michael, too, had assumed a form I felt more familiar with. I brushed my knuckles along the strong planes of his cheekbones, feeling the rough warmth of his olive skin.

"Did you pick these features because you knew I'd be attracted to them . . . feel safe with them?"

"You're looking for guile where there is none." The

gray eyes that earlier, and in my dreams, haunted a monster's face implored me to trust them. "I hadn't met you before, Deidre. How would I know what you'd like?"

I nodded, letting my hand drop. "I . . . I'm having a hard time with this, Michael. I'm finding that at the core of my being I do have a shred of faith, and that faith tells me that if God is going to take the time to send an angel, He doesn't do that without a plan . . . despite what you've assured me."

"Very well." Michael nodded. "I am a defender of faith, not its destroyer."

"You sure about that, big guy?" I was tempted to remind him he wasn't doing much for my faith—a moment ago he implied that Jesus wasn't the messiah, one of the core tenets of my belief system. However, I didn't especially want to dwell on that revelation myself. I pulled a smile out of somewhere, and said, "Come on. We're wasting time."

I hobbled along on the tracks until the frustrating pace forced me up onto the rails again. Balancing on the narrow steel beam, we moved more quickly through the tunnel.

"What are you going to tell Mouse?" Michael asked. His voice steady, he anchored me in the present. "Are you sure you're not walking into a trap . . . that you don't need me?"

I smiled at him even though I doubted he could see me. "Of course I need you. Who couldn't use an angel at their side? But Mouse is expecting me to be alone."

"I don't like it. I'm worried about you."

"I know. But we need proof that he is involved with the LINK-angels."

Michael grunted his assent. Discarded food containers, pop cans, and the increased profusion of Christmas lights revealed that we were moving deeper into the city. We traveled like this until we reached the Lower East Side. There we parted ways, with Michael promising to watch over me.

* * *

As I approached the office building, Mouse waved from the stoop. I'd turned off the holographic defense a block away when I was certain he was alone. I could hear the whiz of cars in the tunnels above, but here on the Lower East Side we were the only people on the streets.

Mouse pulled himself to his feet and began walking toward me. It was strange to see him in the flesh again. His skin was darker than I remembered, and his hair more unkempt. Dark sunglasses hid his eyes. Several layers of mismatched clothes hung off his short but lanky frame, and though I could see the shadow of stubble on his chin, he looked like a perpetual teenager.

"Hey, you." Mouse smiled, pulling the sunglasses down to give me a rakish once-over. "Looking different, definitely more wicked, but I like; it suits you."

I came here for a confrontation, but I found myself smiling in return. "Did you ever find your page?"

"Nah. Must've gone rogue on me." He shrugged, thumbing the glasses back in place. "He'll stumble back when he wants to come home."

"Huh. I suppose he will," I said, thinking of Michael's similar situation. I wondered if, right now, God was shrugging off Raphael's questions with similar unconcern.

"Yeah. . . . Say, could we go inside? I thought I saw a cop car a while back, and well, honestly, I've got to pee like nobody's business."

I laughed. When he talked like that, I had a hard time perceiving Mouse as much of a threat. "Sure," I said, leading the way. "The toilet is down the hall from my office, but it works."

I stood staring at the heavy oak door and the brass lock. The keyhole dripped with an oily sheen, and I smelled the light tang of lubricant. On the other side of the door, someone coughed. I'd started to put my eye to the keyhole to confirm my suspicions, when Mouse put a hand on my shoulder.

"What's up?" Mouse said, "I thought you'd be in by now, starting some coffee. I'm dying for a cup."

"No wonder you've always got to pee," I smiled, but the warmth had gone from my voice. Returning my attention to the lock, I shook my head. I couldn't take a chance if Mouse was intending ambush. "No keys. I left my keys at Eion's church. I wanted a change of clothes, but . . . Well, now that you've gone to the bathroom I guess we can talk anywhere."

Mouse nodded. His eyebrows twitched, and he chewed his lip.

I started to back down the hallway.

"Nah, it's okay," Mouse said. Reaching into the pocket of his jeans, he knelt near the lock. As his hand removed the thin oddly shaped metal bars from his pocket, his shirt stretched to reveal the butt of a gun. "I've got tools."

"Mmm-hm." I agreed through thinly pressed lips. Slamming the helmet on, I touched the button to engage my holographic armor. "If you've got the tools, Mouse," I asked, even though I knew the answer, "why didn't you let yourself in earlier?"

"Who's to say I didn't?" Lockpicks in his right hand, he grabbed the pistol with his left. He spun around.

I inched along the wall, heading for the door.

"Stop right there. Don't think I can't see you, girl," Mouse said. The gun was pointed right at me; his finger rested on the trigger.

"The sunglasses." I said. "Shit. Of course. Infrared?"

"Give the woman a medal." Keeping the gun flawlessly trained on me; Mouse tucked the lockpicks into the front pocket of his shirt.

"Ambidextrous, as well," I said, pulling off the helmet and disabling the armor. I was careful to leave the LINK filament in place against my temple. "Seems I forgot a lot about you."

"I have many gifts." He inclined his head slightly, and splayed the fingers of his right hand, a gesture of modesty.

I nodded, with a defeated sigh. I pressed my back

against the wall, letting the helmet rest against the curve of my elbow. "Are you planning to gun me down here? It doesn't really seem your style, Mouse."

"It's not really, and, honestly, Dee, I don't want to kill you. I'd much rather you were safely tucked away somewhere until everything is settled." He eyed me through the combat sights. "Speaking of people I thought safely tucked away, where's Daniel?"

"Daniel? Why does everybody want Daniel?"

Mouse perked up and gave me a wide-eyed look over the gun. "Who else wanted Daniel?"

"A transvestite named Ariel."

Mouse laughed. "You're kidding."

I shook my head, while carefully testing the weight of the helmet in my arm. If I aimed just right, I could knock the gun out of Mouse's hand. Problem was, I only had one chance. If I missed, I was dead. I needed another distraction.

"What's so hot about Daniel?" I asked.

Mouse cocked his head in lieu of a shrug. "Just tell me where he is."

"Yankee Stadium or the police morgue." I tried to sound flippant, but grief snagged my voice. "He's dead, Mouse."

His eyebrows raised in surprise. "Really?"

I nodded.

"Huh. Really?" I nodded again. He sighed, "I tell you, I'm off-line for eight hours and the whole universe changes. When did that happen? How?"

The image of Daniel's ashen face threatened to blur my vision. I shook my head and clipped my voice in order to keep my emotions in check. "Police sniper. Last night."

"No shit," Mouse breathed, standing up. "So it's over."

That sounded bad. "Over? What's over?"

"My archnemesis is dead."

"Daniel?"

Mouse frowned. "Of course, who else? He's the one who tripped that first alarm. He's the one who nearly brought me down a year ago. He's the bastard who broke into mouse.net last night." Something in my eyes must have made Mouse question his train of thought. He stared at me and then added, "Right?"

The barrel of the gun dipped toward the floor. Taking a quick half step out from the wall, I tossed the helmet at Mouse, underhand. My luck was off, but the helmet managed to knock Mouse's arm to the right, across his body. A bullet exploded from the gun. I felt the ejected, hot brass casing smack me in the arm.

A cascade of plaster dust and wood splinters fell around us. Though my ears were ringing, I rushed toward Mouse. He recovered quicker than I, and I'd only managed to take two steps before I was looking down the barrel of the gun.

"Oh, Deidre," Mouse said sadly. "I really liked you."

"I like you too, Mouse," I said.

The gun trembled in his hands. Mouse was sincere when he'd said he didn't want to kill me. I decided to call his bluff. "Do it already."

Mouse's mouth hung open at my taunting words. *What the hell,* I thought, *either God wants me alive or dead.*

"Come on, boy, pull the trigger," I said. "And do me a favor, will you?" I pointed to my abdomen. "Aim right here."

"You want to die?" Mouse's voice was a whisper.

"Live or die, it doesn't matter. You and your little cronies think they started the Second Coming, but yours is a hoax. I am the fucking Holy Mother." I let a hysterical laugh bubble up out of the tight place I kept my emotions.

Mouse's eyes were wide. I stepped forward until the gun pressed up against my chest.

"Stay back. I'm not afraid to shoot you," Mouse squeaked.

"Good. I'd hate for you to miss the mark, like so many of the other boys in my life."

I stood close enough to smell the leather and patchouli that was Mouse's scent. There was something oddly familiar about it: dangerous, but comfortable.

In a minute, I could put my hand on the gun . . . or he would shoot me point-blank, either way the crisis would be resolved. I honestly wasn't sure which I preferred.

"You're crazy," Mouse whispered through clenched teeth. His eyes narrowed as he took aim.

I nodded; oblivion was a pleasant option. I shut my eyes, and waited.

Excerpt from Letourneau's main page. August 25, 2076

CLASSIC!

I'm not surprised to find Rabbi-Senator Grey resorting to character assassination during these last few months of the presidential campaign. When this campaign was focused on the issues, Grey's popularity was in the toilet. Seeing this, he began to systematically attempt to tear down my good name.

Let me take this opportunity to remind the people what the Letourneau platform stands for: we support the expansion of the LINK. Those of you who have toured the Letourneau future have seen what our nation can become if we release restrictions on LINK-businesses. We have supported American businesses by opposing a direct union with Christendom. However, we would like to forge an economic tie to the Vatican that would strengthen the Free Credit and encourage the flow of Christendom and Islam credits into the American free marketplace.

The Grey platform is a bleeding-heart platform. My opponent wants to funnel US money to those godless ones who are outside of the LINK. He is obsessed with real time to the detriment of the foundation that our economic power is based on—the LINK. I want to concentrate on the issues that will strengthen us in the global economy, Grey wants to turn inward and gaze at our collective belly button.

I refuse to be goaded by Grey's immoral behavior.

Secular presidential candidates often employed these kinds of mud-slinging tactics before this great nation saw the light and became a theocratic republic.

I do not need to prove myself to anyone. It is clear that I exist. I am a duly elected senator from Colorado, and for the last two years I have been the Senate Majority Leader. Moreover, God has chosen me.

Grey has pointed to my lack of need for human trappings such as a dentist or a doctor, and I say, this is further proof that I am what the LINK-angels have said I was . . . My body is a temple, a spotless, flawless temple.

Open your hearts. Pray for guidance. God will answer: Vote Letourneau.

CHAPTER 21

"Martyrdom, Deidre?" A familiar voice drawled, "Doesn't really seem your style, somehow."

I opened my eyes to see Morningstar's hand over the hammer of the pistol. Mouse's brown face looked gray, but he still held on to the gun with whitened knuckles.

"Allah protect me," Mouse said.

Morningstar said something in another language—judging from Mouse's expression, it was probably Arabic. Though I didn't understand Morningstar's words, the tone was clearly a warning.

Mouse's eyes narrowed. Straightening his back, he asked, "Oh yeah? And who the fuck are you?"

"My *deus ex machina,* apparently." I sighed, my shoulders relaxing. "Interesting timing, Morningstar."

"Morningstar? The Mafia guy?" Mouse asked. The two of them were a study in contrast: Morningstar in his Armani suit and Mouse in his ragged street clothes.

"I'm surprised the two of you don't know each other," I said.

"Do we look like we hang out in the same circles?" Morningstar said, wrestling the gun from Mouse with a sudden jerking motion. He pointed the barrel at Mouse, "Run back to your hole, little rodent. The lady and I have things to discuss."

Having regained his composure, Mouse's eyes narrowed as though he were considering the merits of Morningstar's demand.

"What are you waiting for?" Morningstar flicked the gun in a shooing motion. "Get your tail in gear."

"Okay." Mouse shrugged. He rested one hand on the doorknob to my office. "Just let me get my things."

"There's someone in there," I said, certain.

A cold smile spread across Mouse's lips. "An ambush? You must really think the worst of me. I just want my duffel bag."

Morningstar snapped his arm taut, and the gun hovered inches from Mouse's face. "I don't remember offering you a choice," Morningstar said. "But, I will now: go or die."

Mouse raised his hand off the doorknob and lifted both arms in surrender. "No problem," he said, backing up. "I'm gone."

"Good," Morningstar said with a sneer. "I never liked rats."

Mouse nodded. His lips pressed tight, as though he wanted to trade insults, but thought better off it. To me he said, "We'll finish what we started, Dee."

"I don't think so, Mouse," I said flatly. "Apparently God has other plans for me, and He wants me alive."

"*Insh'allah,*" Mouse said, reaching the door. Our eyes stayed locked until he slipped behind the oak panel and out into the street.

I glanced at Morningstar. "Michael was supposed to be close at hand. How'd you end up here?"

"Michael is afraid of power. Power corrupts, don't you know? If he was willing to use a miracle or two now and again, he could have known you were in trouble." Morningstar cocked his head at me, curiously. "So, you see me doing God's work, do you?"

I shrugged, picking up the helmet from where it had rolled during the scuffle. "Aren't you?"

He nodded, but kept his mysterious smile. "Sometimes pain is a good teacher." Jerking his chin in the direction Mouse had fled, he asked, "Should I have killed him, you think?"

"I don't know," I said, honestly. Shaking the plaster dust out of my hair, I added, "He doesn't seem like much of a threat, does he? But he might just be counting on that, you know? That no one takes him seriously."

"Well, I take ambush seriously." Morningstar waved the gun in the direction of the office. "You said there were others?" I nodded. His chestnut brown eyes flashed with mischievousness. "Then, we should take care of them, shouldn't we?"

Edging along the wall toward the door, Morningstar held the gun pointed toward the ceiling with his finger, I was glad to notice, off the trigger. When he stood in front of the door, he raised his foot.

"Wait. It's open!" I shouted, as the force of Morningstar's blow sent the door swinging back against the wall with a bang. I shook my head. Between the bullet hole in the hall and the smashed door, there was no way I'd be getting my security deposit back for this place.

Morningstar leapt dramatically into the room, swinging the gun this way and that. I peeked around the edge of the doorway in time to see the last of Mouse's heavies, who looked preteen, scurry out the open window onto the fire escape.

"Damn." Morningstar sighed, dropping his arms. "I was so looking forward to a fight."

"You could always run after him," I said dismissively, half-hoping he would. I walked over to my desk, laid my helmet down, and shrugged out of the backpack. Everything seemed to be where I left it. I straightened the picture of Eion and smoothed out a few of the hardcopy sheets that poked out from under the blotter. I looked up from the inspection of my desk to see Morningstar eyeing me curiously.

"What are you doing here, anyway?" I asked.

"God's work, as you said." Morningstar tucked the gun in his waistband. "We can't have angel-baby splattered all over the wall, now can we?"

I froze. My heart ticked against my eardrums. I looked up from my desk to see Morningstar grinning broadly at me. "You know about the baby?"

Morningstar leaned against the window frame. "God and I are still very tight. Unlike some."

"Liar," I said through clenched teeth.

Despite my accusation, he seemed unflustered. "So many people call me that. I suppose it's because it's easier to think of the painful truth as a lie." Morningstar arched a thin, red eyebrow. "But, I'm curious. Which part do you imagine incorrect: the fact that I'm still allowed in heaven, or that Michael is not as close to God as he once was?"

I took a deep breath and shook my head. "Everyone has assured me that God isn't involved with this baby."

"I see." Morningstar sighed patiently. "I suppose, instead, those angel boys have been going on about free-will. Did anyone use the archer metaphor? I love that one."

My forehead felt hot. Hoping the chair was behind me, I sat down without looking. I lucked out, and my butt connected with the hard wood with a smack.

"Ah, I see they have," Morningstar said. "You do know, don't you, that Jibril was the father to your favorite prophet? Did you think the parallel was mere coincidence?"

My throat was dry, and I tried to swallow. "Everyone," I managed to say, "everyone told me that it wasn't important. That there were others who weren't messiahs."

"Yes. That bothersome reference to the 'Sons of God' in Genesis 6:2-4 taking mortal wives." Morningstar nodded reflectively. The greenish glow from the street made a sickly nimbus around his head and shoulders. "As in the later reference in Enoch, I'm afraid that's just my boys up to no good. We're still sons of God, even if we aren't his current favorites, you know. But, perhaps you can see why a certain bias was placed against the idea of their children becoming prophets."

I shook my head; I had no idea what he was talking about. My mind focused on one thing. "Why would Raphael lie to me?"

"It's not really a lie not to tell all the gory details."

"The sin of omission. Michael said he found it easier."

Morningstar nodded his head, and his eyes glowed warmly, compelling me to believe what he was saying.

I raked my fingers through my hair. I was beginning to feel like Morningstar was the only angel who didn't try to keep the truth from me. I rubbed the bridge of my nose with my finger. My instincts rebelled at the idea of trusting Satan. After all, hundreds of stories warned about allowing yourself to be seduced, and here I was falling for his act. I had to try to think this through. I shook my head.

"But, I don't get it," I said finally. "Why would they let me think that my baby was an accident? Wouldn't the archangels want me to know the pregnancy was part of God's plan?"

"Aren't you feeling betrayed? Used? Suckered?"

My lips thinned. With all of Michael's talk of freewill, I'd forgotten how angry I'd been when I first thought I'd be the new Holy Mother. All those feelings boiled to the surface at Morningstar's prompting. I took a deep breath trying to push down the bitterness, but a little bit slipped past my defenses. "No one asked me."

Morningstar pounced on my weakness. He stood up slowly, unfurling like a wing.

"Of course they didn't. It's passé. The whole 'appointed by God' shtick went out in the Middle Ages. Anyway, I suppose my dearest brother figured you'd be more pliant if you didn't know—less likely to do something rash, like throw yourself in front of a loaded gun."

"Ha." I didn't even pretend to find his quip funny, because my heart was sinking fast. "Why are you telling me all this? If it is all part of God's plan, there's clearly not much I can do about it."

"No, there isn't. I'm telling you because I want you to suffer the knowledge that God used you."

Used by God. I let the words penetrate me, fill me. Air left my lungs in a long, emptying sigh. From the moment I forced myself to realize that Michael was an angel, I'd feared this revelation. Pressing my forehead against the knuckles of my hand, I leaned heavily into the desk. Everything was out of my control; my whole life was reduced to being a pawn in some cosmic game.

Yet there was something strangely comforting about that concept. I felt a weight lift off my shoulders. Lifting my head out of my hands, I looked at Morningstar.

"Of course," I said slowly. "If I believed that, I have to believe God really does have some grand plan in mind. That would be more faith than I've had my whole life."

"Would it?" Morningstar asked, with a curiously serious expression on his face. Holding his body very still, he said, "Tell me, Deidre, do you? Do you believe? Are you a reverse Job? Are you willing to believe the worst and not the best? But, believe nonetheless?"

"You know what? I think so. Yes."

Morningstar stared into my eyes, saying nothing. His face still held an unnerving seriousness. The muted green light of the outside grew brighter, as though a storm were brewing. Cool wind kissed my cheek gently, and, from somewhere, I heard a rhythmical flapping. A white flash of paper flew past my face. Startled, I jumped.

The wind increased. The pile of tickets stacked neatly in the tray beside the wall fluttered and spilled everywhere. Made of heavy paper, the tickets crawled along the floor to swirl beneath Morningstar's feet.

"What's going on?" I shouted over the now howling wind.

My work here is done, A voice in my head said.

Shutting his eyes, Morningstar opened his hands, palms up. He looked like a supplicant. Wind battered him, whipping coppery hair around his head. His trench coat snapped in the barrage of air. The papers on my desk broke free of the blotter and swarmed around him like a miniature hurricane, with Morningstar as the eye.

In a thunder crash, Morningstar exploded. His body shattered into thousands of pure white pieces. The light stabbed my eyes, and I turned my head. Paper flew everywhere, slapping against my back ineffectually.

When I turned back around, Morningstar was gone, and my office was a mess of paper. I stared at the spot where Morningstar had been, incredulous. He was gone, just like that.

Moving out from behind the desk, I sat cross-legged in the spot Morningstar had stood and started cleaning up the debris. Residue warmth tingled beneath my legs. Collecting a stack of overdue tickets, I tried to decide if his disappearance was a good sign or a bad one.

I could interpret his last words in two ways. Either his work was done because I had been corrupted to his evil ways, or Satan really was an agent of God and was sent to bully me into some tattered semblance of faith. Forming a pile of all the papers I could reach, I concluded that I preferred the irony of the second option. An angel is still an angel, whether his message is pleasant or hurtful. Satan simply had the misfortune of always being the bearer of bad news.

The truth was, I did find it easier to believe the bad things about God, and my religion, than the good. Evil seemed possible and rational. It was not in the least bit fanciful to feel that dark powers lurked under the surface, ready to soil and destroy humanity. During secular times, Satan had remained a popular figure in the media despite the proclamation that "God is dead." Yet, Satan only exists if there is a God.

I had faith all along; my faith was just twisted, focused on evil. I, too, had fallen victim to the idea that goodness was just a myth, but that evil was powerful and real. Michael had been obvious in many ways when he first appeared to me, but I refused to see him for what he was. I had no faith that my life, or any life, was important enough to warrant the attention of an archangel, of God. So much so, it took the Devil to convince me that there was a God after all.

Pulling more papers toward me, I laughed. Michael was right about one thing. The problem with goodness was that it wasn't nearly as flashy as evil. Evil had the advantage of being dramatic and spectacular. It was easy to discount the goodness that wandered into your life wearing blue jeans and looking like something out of everyday life.

Too energized to be able to focus on the rest of the cleanup, I pulled myself to my feet. I wanted to talk to Michael. Tell him everything I'd realized.

As I reached for my backpack, my peripheral vision registered movement outside. A buzz vibrated at my temple, where the filament connected my LINK receptor to the armor. Strange, it was almost as if the uniform was trying to call me. But that was impossible, so I ignored the tingle.

I crept over to the window to look outside. A car sat conspicuously parked on the street. That a car should be on the street was strange enough, since no tunnel exited anywhere near my building. I always had to park in the lot connected to the second-story walkway, but that tunnel didn't exit out onto the street. A car would have had to travel for a kilometer from the nearest street-level traffic tunnel to park directly outside of my office. Once out of the electrified traffic tunnels, you had to rely solely on your battery. Most cars didn't have the power to stray too far. That is, except cop cars.

My temple ticked again. This time I decided to answer it. I mentally flipped the "go" command. A window opened in the right-hand corner of my vision.

I ought to kill you, Mouse said.

Excerpt from the *New York Times,* August 30, 2076.

GREY RELENTLESS

DENVER NODE. The real-time presidential debate took another step toward becoming a reality today. Though still in Colorado camped outside of Letourneau's mansion, Rabbi-Senator Chaim Grey responded to the recent virtual attack. When asked to comment, he smiled. "Letourneau said that God has picked him to be the next president of the United States. Who am I to argue with God? But, I say, if the outcome is predetermined, then Letourneau, chosen of God, has even less to fear from talking to a New York rabbi for a couple of hours in front of the people of the United States."

Popular opinion seems to be behind Grey. After this statement, Grey's standing in the polls rose another ten percent, giving him a slight lead in the race.

Tyler Wong, who has been a strong supporter of Letourneau from the beginning, logged on today to announce that he will be voting for Grey if Letourneau does not agree to debate in real time. "It's a real disappointment," he said. "Letourneau should kick Grey's butt, but he looks like a wimp hiding up there in the mountains. If he doesn't agree to come out, man, I'm gonna vote for the Jew."

Others have expressed similar sentiment. Hirohito Smith, presidential candidate for the Islam party, agreed. "Even though the party of Islam did not have enough of a majority to compete for this office, I encourage the faithful to challenge this prophet Letourneau. Remember what is written between the eyes of the great archangel Jibril, he who dictated the Koran, 'There is no God but God, and Muhammad is the Messenger of God.' "

CHAPTER 22

You nearly did, I told Mouse. I kept my attention focused on the car outside. I tried to discern if there was anyone still in the car, or not. *Are those your henchmen here to finish the job?*

Who? What? Mouse asked. *What do you mean? I've been in your armor hiding from Phanuel, since you and that Kantowitcz character broke into my hub.*

I focused on the LINK window. I tried to figure out which Mouse I was talking to. The image had the same dark, ruffled hair and round ears as the real-time Mouse. It was impossible to tell by looking. *Page?*

You know someone else who can live in your uniform? The page smiled with Mouse's face. *This, by the way, is a rocking sweet home away from home. Those Israelis have great tech. I'm thinking about converting. Do you think they'd let an AI be a Jew?*

I have no idea, I muttered. *I don't have time to chat, page. I've got some possible company here.*

Hey, the page said. *I'm not some companion software programmed just for your entertainment, I called for a reason. I wanted to warn you about Mouse.*

Thanks, I said, as I looked around the room for something to prop the door shut with. *But, I already figured Mouse was out to get me when he pulled the gun.*

The page looked hurt. *He did? I take it the body went to New York?*

Yeah. In the closet was a piece of plywood I was using as a makeshift shelf. I quickly brushed my shoes off it into a pile and pulled the board from its brick supports. Pushing the board under the doorknob, I tested it for strength. It would hold for a while. With that, I commanded the uniform's holographic defenses to ON and headed out the window onto the fire escape. I started down the ladder. Even though I knew I was invisible, I kept twisting around to check that no one in the car noticed me.

Bummer. The page's voice startled me; I'd forgotten he was there. *Dee, whatever you do, don't access the LINK. Phanuel is after me, and Michael. . . .*

Michael? What, is he okay?

No, the page added. *I found out he's going to be unleashed tonight at 0:00 GMT.*

The LINK-Michael? Why didn't you tell me this before? I'd reached the last rung. I stopped to catch my breath and stared at the window floating in the corner of my vision.

The page looked sheepish. *When I'm on the LINK, it's difficult for me to separate my feelings from Mouse's. He was off-line . . . and, then, when I was here . . . well, I had time to think.*

I let go of the last rung, leaping down to the street level. I landed awkwardly and knocked into a garbage can. Sprawled on my butt, I groaned softly. The pavement was uneven, and sharp edges poked at me through the tough exterior of the armor.

Deidre, you have to warn people. Mouse means business with the LINK-Michael. Serious business.

What's so special about the LINK-Michael, Page? Haven't we already seen him?

The page shook his head. *Not this version.*

What's this version? I asked, dusting off my knees.

Ever hear the story of how the angel Michael singlehandedly slaughtered 185,000 Assyrians in one night? Well, this is that Michael.

I stood up to assess the situation. Apparently, the noise of the garbage can overturning alerted someone in the car to my presence. The car door opened, and a man in a dark suit stepped out to get a better look. He was wearing sunglasses.

Shit, I said, crouching down quickly.

I held my breath; I could hear shuffling footsteps approaching. My back pressed against a Dumpster, and I watched the street for any hint that the man was within range.

When a long shadow came into view, I tightened my muscles, ready to spring. The second I saw a foot, I threw my whole body into a punch aimed at the knee. My fist connected solidly. The man went down with a yelp of pain. I stood up quickly. If he had a gun, I intended to wrestle him for it.

Luck was with me, and the man's fall had knocked the sunglasses off his face. A shoulder holster was visible underneath his suit coat. I grabbed the gun. The pistol slid into invisibility as soon as my hand wrapped around the butt.

Fingertips brushed my ankle as I stepped over him, but I squeezed past. I ran toward the car. Cops and criminals were notorious for leaving keys in the ignition.

I could see heads craning out of the window of my office as I slid into the driver's seat. They all wore sunglasses, despite the muted outside light. My hands wrapped around the wheel, and I felt for keys. Smelling stale coffee in the upholstery, I decided this was, in fact, a cop's car. The engine revved as I put my foot down hard on the go pedal. I pulled the door shut, and the car sprang forward. Securing the safety belt, I just had to hope that they had left enough juice in the battery for me to make it all the way to a traffic tube. I was feeling confident. So far all my prayers had come true.

You know, this is pretty serious stuff, the page said, his face still scrunched into a pout. *I don't know what you're doing that's more important than talking to me.*

I checked the rearview. No one was in pursuit so far. I flipped open the fuse-box panel under the dash. Feeling with my fingers, I pulled out the third fuse from the left. I smiled, twirling the small glass tube in my fingers. Unmarked police car manufactures have always understood the need for cops to drive occasionally with the homing beacon disabled. *Sorry, Page,* I said, finally, *I was just trying to save my skin . . . and yours, since you're in my uniform.*

Like I care what the body does.

Maybe, in this case, you should. I'm not LINKed to anything but the uniform, so you don't have anywhere to go if someone blows a hole in me. The page looked unsatisfied, so I added, *Tell me what this Michael can do?*

Um . . . the page hesitated, and checked over his shoulder.

Page, I already know about Jordan Institute. You have the tech to access any LINKed person's pain and pleasure centers. That's how you pulled off the LINK-angel "miracles."

The page's eyes were wide. *You knew?*

I nodded. *Well, I figured it out, anyway.*

Mouse always said you'd remember eventually. No wonder he's come to kill you.

The ground-level road was bumpy. The wheels weren't adapted for the broken concrete of the street level. I had to get in a tunnel fast. Spinning the steering wheel with my palm, I swung down the street. There was access to a traffic tunnel near the old library. The battery light was steady for now.

I continually checked the rearview for other cars. There was nothing, but the battery light had started blinking a warning a block back. I could see the traffic tunnel above. The plastic tubing curved ahead and angled toward street level. I was nearly there.

Flashing lights appeared above. The police figured out my only possible route. I hit the accelerator. I might be able to make the entrance before they could block both lanes with their vehicle.

The cop car swung around the exit curve; we were face-to-face. Nearly standing on the go pedal, the car shook beneath me. My teeth clenched, and I braced myself for possible impact.

A pop and a spark tore off the side mirror. Metal scraped against metal with a groan. My car fishtailed when I slid past the cops, and I had to struggle to regain control of the vehicle.

In the rearview mirror, I could see the cop car had swung around to cross both lanes. It bounced on its frame. I was satisfied it would take them a minute or two to recover.

What's the new LINK-Michael going to do, Page? I asked. Now that the electrified rail was beneath the car, the battery light was safely off. I took a deep breath and scanned the tunnel for options.

He's an assassin program, the page said. *Mouse intends to get rid of all competition.*

He's going to take out other hackers? But why? He already has a corner on the market.

I don't know, the page said sadly. *I'm not even supposed to know this much. I just happened to come across Mouse's files while he was off-line. Then, when you were in the hub, you woke up Phanuel. He's been trying to capture me ever since.*

You were with me in the hub?

I was there . . . I left with you.

Suddenly, lights illuminated the rear window. I ignored an entrance ramp to an upper level. I'd have to move into heavier traffic soon, since it was only a matter of time before Traffic Control isolated this lower tube and cut power. I grabbed the gun from where I'd tossed it along with my backpack in the passenger seat. I checked to make certain the safety was on and tucked it into one of the pockets of the uniform.

To my left, I saw an up-tube. Heaving hard on the wheel, I headed into the tube without letting up on the go pedal. The tires squealed in protest at the sharp turn. I decided to try a move that joy riders called the "stone-skip." Moving as fast as possible, I took the first exit one level up. The car bounced on its frame, moving through the tube like a pebble over water.

How can we stop Mouse, Page?

The page shook his head fiercely. *I can't. He's my maker, Dee. That's seriously bad karma. Besides, he knows how to pull my plug.*

All right, I said, *how about the LINK-Michael? Do you know how to destroy him?*

Mouse's page was silent. When I hazarded a glance away from the road, I could see his lips were stretched into a thin line.

I don't know, Mouse said finally. *He's too scary, Dee. Better to just stay off the line, you know?*

I shook my head. *You can't hide forever, Page, and neither can I.*

Sirens echoed in the tube. Dropping down from somewhere, the cops had picked up my trail again. Lights flashed behind me. I pumped down harder on the go pedal even though it was already pressed to the floor.

I passed through a holographic advertisement for today's upcoming presidential debate. In a blur, Letourneau's face slid through the passenger side of the car. With a fizzle, the image became a snow shower. Ahead, I could see lights flicking off. Control was shutting down power to this area. Scanning desperately for an escape route, I saw nothing. The cop was close enough on my tail that I could no longer see the headlights in the rearview. So, I did the only thing I could do: I slammed down hard on the brakes.

Link update, August 30, 2076. This site is now updated every 30 seconds as news reaches us! Political history and commentary by H.C. Yoeh:

LETOURNEAU MAKES A SURPRISE REVERSAL

In a reversal of his previous stance against a real-time debate, presidential candidate Etienne Letourneau agreed to meet with his opponent Rabbi-Senator Grey and the public at Carnegie Hall at 7:00 EST today. This debate will also be simulcast on all the LINK political channels. However, the public is clamoring to witness this event firsthand. Carnegie Hall staff say they are already filled to capacity, having issued the final standing room only pass a mere twenty-three minutes after Letourneau issued his statement.

"It's unreal," said the Carnegie Hall box office manager, Rita Morose. "There hasn't been this much interest in live performance since the Taft-Henderson debacle." The event that Morose refers to was the Democratic Convention held in 2064, in which a fist-fight broke out between then presidential hopeful Sister Alice Jane Henderson and the Democratic nominee Representative Elias Taft. It has been much speculated the embarrassment that Taft faced after being knocked unconscious by a nun weighing less than one hundred pounds cost him the race. Returning to office, Taft (also of the infamous Taft-Pallis Act) began the "Right to Electronic Representation Reform," which, among other things, abolished the traditions of real-time campaigning and political conventions.

One of the reasons the Right to Electronic Representation Reform (RERR) met with such success when it was introduced was the belief, which had continued until today, that the American public was more interested in spectacle than political content. Taft's reform was based on studies dating back to the 1960s and the first televised debates in which it was shown that Americans tend to vote based on the "image" (physical attractiveness, poise, etc.) that a politician gives off at live and recorded events. Taft's reform intended to reduce campaigning to its purest form—text and content—in order to "purify" the political process. Though the complete absence of image was never approved, Congress did pass much of the RERR, as the reform was called.

Until today, few would have argued the soundness of the ideas behind RERR. It seems that the public has, in fact, been following with much interest the content of Rabbi-Senator Grey's recent accusations against Letourneau. Perhaps it's the personal nature of Letourneau's unstated political platform (ie: that he is the Second Coming of Christ) that has roused the concern in the American people that he is, in fact, an actual human being. The nature of his being has become the focus of this debate, and the average American is clamoring to see him, live. People have started to camp out along the streets in front of Carnegie Hall hoping to catch a glimpse of the Reverend-Senator as he passes on his way to the debate. We'll switch now to Bob, who is standing by . . .

CHAPTER 23

The impact shattered the back window. Glass cut the back of my neck. My hands and head crashed into the steering wheel, while my knees banged against the dash. The air bag deployed, which cushioned my whole body, but I was thrown backward and pressed hard into the seat. When the jostling stopped, I held my breath. My neck hurt like a son of a bitch, but I was still alive. The padding of the Israeli armor likely saved my life.

Thinking of the armor reminded me of the page. *Page? Are you okay?*

Opening the car door, I fell out from under the airbag. I scrambled to my feet. I knew it wouldn't take long for the cop to do the same, if he was alive.

What are you doing out there? Your systems are going crazy. I'm sure you can see the warning light, but you're going to lose invisibility in a matter of seconds.

I could see the warning light the page talked about; the red letters filled the screen and threatened to blot out everything else. The only problem was if I switched off the armor, I'd have to remove the helmet. Without the systems operating properly, I'd be blind. Minus the helmet, my head would be a perfect target for some gung ho cop.

I decided to take the chance and flipped the OFF. Even if I somehow managed to salvage the uniform's invisibility program, all the cops seemed aware that I had armored gear, anyway; no doubt any I encountered would

be as prepared as the ones I had met earlier. I removed
the helmet and took a deep breath.

Pulling myself upright, I leaned heavily on the hood
of the car. The cop car's front end was mashed. Wind-
shield glass littered the tunnel, and its air bag had bal-
looned on impact as well. Wails from the siren filled
the tunnel.

More police could not be far behind I knew, yet I
hesitated. I hated myself for even thinking about leaving
behind a cop who was injured and could be dying. I had
to remind myself that it was me that caused the officer
harm, and that I'd done it to buy myself time—all of
which I was wasting, standing here feeling morally corrupt. My feet betrayed my brain and started moving
closer to the driver's side window of the cop car.

I've got to get out of here, I told myself, but my step
quickened as I moved up to the door. Inside, I could
see the officer slumped back in the seat, pinned by the
air bag. Blood smeared her forehead. I checked for a
pulse at her throat. I found it—weak but steady, thank
God. I knew better than to try to move her; her back
could be broken. She'd been lucky, and so had I. At
least vehicular manslaughter wouldn't be added to my
long list of crimes.

Now what to do? There really wasn't anywhere to run.
The traffic tunnels went on for kilometers. I only had
two options if I decided to try to make it on foot: forward, or back the way I came. The cops would know
that and close off both ends. Without a crowd to blend
into or a working invisibility suit, I'd be an easy target
to trace.

The wreckage of the car I'd stolen looked like a crumpled wad of paper. The bumper hung off the frame at
an odd angle, and the lid of the trunk had popped open.
Suddenly, an idea hit me.

Without opening the car door, I reached between the
cop's legs and pulled the trunk release. Thankfully, despite the crash, the mechanism worked, and the trunk
opened with a pop.

I quickly made my way around to the rear end of the

vehicle and crawled inside. Pulling the trunk lid down, I wondered how the hell I was going to get out once the lock latched. I reached into my pocket and pulled out the slip of paper that Michael had written his LINK address on.

"Well, he said I should use this in the case of an emergency," I muttered. Putting the paper carefully on the latch, I pulled the lid down as far as it would go and held it there. Now it would look closed, but I wouldn't be trapped. I should be safe, and remain undetected as long as I could hold the lid tightly enough.

Without the helmet to show infrared, the darkness in the trunk was absolute. I had to forcibly remind myself not to let in even a sliver of light. The air smelled like rubber and oil, and I could feel something wet where my cheek pressed against the scratchy upholstery. Shifting my legs around, I tried to find a comfortable position. This was one time I was glad I wasn't overly tall. I settled down to wait.

Deidre?

At the sound of my name, I knocked my head painfully against the rim of the spare wheel. *For heaven's sake, Page. I forgot you were there.*

I know. His pout was evident even in the darkness. *You really know how to make a boy feel appreciated, you know that?*

I shut my eyes and let myself go deeper into the connection with the uniform. Making sure I could still sense my body enough to keep track of how tightly I held on to the latch, I called up the image of the page. Behind my eyes, the page looked battered. His hair was mussed, his usually pristine clothes were stained, and his collar was akimbo. The page even went so far as to bruise his cheek. I chuckled under my breath; only a bodiless AI would think of wounds as an affectation.

Page! I decided to give him what he wanted. *You look terrible. Are you okay?*

No thanks to you, he said, his bottom lip out, arms crossed across his chest. *You take crummy care of your equipment.*

I'm sorry, I said, as I adjusted the LINK filament pressed against my temple. My neck was twisted in an odd angle. Holding on to the thin wire, I tried to get comfortable in the cramped space of the trunk. *But I'd be nicer to you if I thought you'd help me fight the LINK-Michael.*

Mouse's page looked taken aback. *You think kindness can be bartered? You're worse than Mouse.*

Stop pouting, Page. You know I'm teasing you.

Hmph. He recrossed his arms in front of his chest.

However, I said, *time is running out. If Michael is going to be released at midnight Greenwich Mean Time, that's*—I did some mental calculation—*six o'clock in the evening here. Prime time. A coincidence?*

Knowing Mouse, probably not, the page grumbled.

Outside, I could hear the siren joined by another. My stomach lurched in fear; they would be here soon. I tugged on the trunk, gripping it tighter.

I have to get a message to Michael. Can we risk going on-line for a microsecond?

Mouse's page pinched his lips together in disgust. *If it were really a microsecond, I'd say yes. But you humans can never process anything that fast.*

I smiled. *Are you volunteering, Page?*

The siren cut off. Someone outside had flipped the switch. That could only mean that the police were on the scene. I held my breath and strained to hear the sounds of approaching footsteps.

Okay, the page said. *I'll do it, only because I can open up a connection, send the message, and get out before you could even finish flipping the go-ahead.*

I lifted the latch a hair and removed the paper Michael had given me with his address. A thin shaft of bright light sliced through the darkness. Squinting at the swirling script of Jibril's handwriting, I read off Michael's address to the page. Then, I added, *If everything goes well, tell him to meet me at the impound lot.*

The page nodded, and the window closed. Pressing the paper back into the latch, I slowly lowered the lid again. The trunk was plunged into absolute darkness.

I heard more voices outside. The sounds were muffled and strange, but I thought I made out the word "dogs." My heart pounded in my ear, and I risked a short, thin breath.

The paper crinkled as someone leaned against the trunk. I held my breath, hoping the lock wouldn't punch through. Then, a heavy clank shook the car. As the back end lifted up, I banged against the sides of the small space. When I felt the wheels moving, I started to relax. They were towing the police car; I'd be in the impound lot in no time.

The familiar window began to open in the corner of my vision.

Took you long enough. I smiled expectantly at the screen.

Opened all the way, the window was blank. The empty screen glowed a deep blue.

Page?

Like black ink injected into a pool of clear water, the edges of the screen started to swirl and dissolve into the darkness that surrounded me.

FEAR. The hairs on the back of my neck prickled. The trunk was too small, too tight. The page's window had gone completely dim, blending with the blackness of the space. Darkness surrounded me; I was trapped. Blind, I could feel the airlessness of the confined area bearing down on me. I took shallow breaths, and, despite the stuffy warmth of the trunk, my muscles shuddered involuntarily. Sweat beaded on my forehead and tickled under my armpits.

A ghost of a form slithered through the window. I leapt back from the vision, banging my head on the backseat. The sudden dull pain brought me to the present, and I realized what was happening. Shutting my eyes, I concentrated on breathing slowly and steadily. "You can't scare me, Phanuel," I whispered hoarsely. "I know this is just one of your LINK parlor tricks."

FEAR. Like a physical blow, the emotion hit me. I curled into a tight fetal ball. A whimper escaped, unbidden, from between clenched teeth, and I started rocking

back and forth. Involuntarily, I let go of the latch, the
paper slipped out, and the trunk began to open.

I tried to reach for the lid, but fear immobilized me,
and spiders scuttled along my nerve endings. I hugged
myself tightly as another wave of the shakes racked my
body. Part of my brain knew that the LINK-angel was
not real, that it was just a sophisticated program searching out my fear center, but that didn't make it any easier
to resist. Overcome by a desire to run, my feet kicked
out blindly.

A sharp turn shook the frame, and the trunk bounced
open wider. Light streamed inward, and dispersed the
darkness, waking me. I clamped down hard on my teeth;
the pain distracted me from the emotion that gripped
me in its icy clutches. I had to gain control before the
tow-truck driver noticed that the lid of the trunk had
sprung open.

But what could I do? I couldn't run, and Phanuel was
too strong for me simply to shut him out. I had to face
him. I bit my cheek to give me sharper focus. Then,
squeezing my eyes shut, I expanded the page's window
until it filled the space behind my eyelids. With all the
courage I could muster, I called out into the darkness.
Where are you, Phanuel? I'm not afraid of you.

Inside the window, smoke slithered at my feet like
snakes. The tendrils grew up from the floor, and wisps
of mist crawled along an invisible form. They twined
upward until they reached a height of seven feet or
more. Growing dense, the skeletal lattice of holes filled,
and I saw the murky outline of a winged beast.

The sound of dry autumn leaves shaking in a Novem-
ber wind whispered, *Be afraid.*

The LINK-angel had completely materialized. Dark
robes waved, as if in a soft breeze. Crow black wings
extended fully behind him. In his bony hand, he held a
scythe, the symbol of his office. A rotting death stench
blended with the sickly-sweet smell of funeral incense.

The tingle of fear fluttered in my stomach, but I bit
the inside of my cheek until I drew blood. Lights blinked
behind Phanuel in the haze, and I knew they represented

the open gateway to the LINK. Apparently, the page
had left the LINK access open, and that gave me an
idea. With deliberate patience, I circled Phanuel
cautiously.

*You're just a ghost in the machine . . . a machine I am
master of,* I said, moving closer to the blinking lights of
the open LINK port. *You can't frighten me, construct.*

Phanuel raised his cloaked head sharply at my words.
His bone white forehead glowed in stark contrast to the
murky twilight that surrounded us. Empty eye sockets
glared at me.

I felt myself hesitating, wanting to run. Though the
metallic taste of blood was already in my mouth, I bit
down harder, superseding the fear with pain.

The twinkling lights intensified. The open LINK port
was just behind my back. Phanuel stood inside the uniform's space, and I between him and the freedom of the
LINK. I stopped my slow circling—ready for the kill.

Help. A desperate squeak came from inside the form
of Phanuel. Something protruded from the LINK-angel's
stomach. No bigger than my fist, the shape pounded at
the material of the robe, like something trying to get
out. Originally, I'd thought Phanuel's abdomen squirmed
with maggots, but looking at him now I wasn't so sure.
A tiny white paw emerged from the twisting folds of the
robe. For all the world it looked like a . . . Mouse.

Page?

Deidre? Help me get out of this thing.

I will. But be ready, I said, quickly amending my plans.
I started moving again, regretfully leaving behind the
open LINK portal. *Let the page go, Phanuel.*

Unbelievers must cower in fear, the angel hissed, flapping his wings to accent his point. A cold wind pushed
at my avatar, and my feet felt heavy, as though I were
walking through clay. Phanuel's eyes followed me, pulling into their grave-dark depths. Like the kiss of death,
a whisper of wet breeze caressed my ear. I could feel
myself slowing, succumbing to Phanuel's spell. I bit my
lip again, but it didn't seem to help.

Dee . . . The page's voice was insistent, hopeful. A

bony claw pushed at the mouse image, shoving it deeper into the angel's bowels.

I had to make my move now, or the page would be lost in the LINK-angel's code. The LINK portal glittered behind Phanuel's dark wings. I took a ragged breath to steady myself. Back in real time, I jerked my head backwards until I collided painfully with the tire's rim. The self-inflicted blow brought sharp stars behind my eyes, nearly overwhelming the LINK-landscape.

The intense pain vanquished the debilitating fear, and I sent my avatar rushing toward Phanuel. My vision was riveted to his skeletal face. The angel's slack jaw widened in a howling cry.

As my avatar passed through the LINK-angel's construct, I grabbed for the page's code. I felt the mouse's tail in my grip. Coming out the other side of the LINK-angel, Phanuel dissolved around me, dripping from my avatar like ink. The black liquid of Phanuel's image pooled around my feel and began to re-form. I tossed the squirming page out the doorway to the LINK. Quickly, I closed the door, cutting off the uniform to the outside.

Behind me, I could feel the torrential wind of Phanuel re-forming himself. In real time, I opened my eyes to bright light streaming into the trunk. With cramped fingers, I pulled the LINK connection from my forehead.

"Going to hardboot you into the great beyond, you creepy son of a bitch," I told the LINK-angel trapped in the armored suit.

Pulling open the jacket's magnetic connectors, I cut the power to all of the uniform's functions. With a wicked smirk, I said, "Ha!"

Grabbing for the bobbing trunk, I held the latch slightly open, as the paper I'd used as a wedge was gone. After counting slowly to ten, I reconnected the jacket and waited as the uniform rebooted itself. I placed the LINK filament on my receiver and tentatively opened the uniform's window. The screen was blank: no trace of Phanuel. Now if I could retrieve Mouse's page . . . Opening an outside channel to the LINK, I waited. The lights pulsed steadily beyond the door, and I strained to see the page's avatar among the swirling colors.

"Please come back to me, Page," I whispered to myself. After my run-in with Phanuel, I worried that the other LINK-angels might be on the prowl. I didn't want to leave the LINK door open for too long, but the page could be damaged or confused.

The LINK glittered coldly. If I gave up on him now, I told myself, I could check back for him in a few minutes. Just as I reached to close the connection, a white mouse scuttled in between my feet. I closed the door once he was inside.

Thank God you're okay, I said, kneeling down to inspect the rodent.

Oh, Dee . . . I hadn't known you cared, the mouse said, rubbing against my outstretched hand. *Especially after the way I treated you.*

I pulled back my hand. *Mouse.*

The one and only, and I do mean "one and only."

What have you done with the page? My avatar stood up. I opened the doorway, intending to kick Mouse back onto the LINK.

The mouse sat back on his haunches to peer up at me with beady eyes. With a flick of whiskers, he said, *Nothing yet, but when I get my hands on him, I'm going to strip him apart . . . line by line.*

Despite myself, I chuckled. *Mouse, if you're going to make threats like that, you really ought to choose a different avatar. You have no idea how silly you look.*

The mouse's black eyes narrowed, and he darted up my leg. His claws, like needles, scratched my thigh. I tried to bat him off me, but he was too fast. Finding the exposed flesh of my hand, he bit down with sharp teeth.

Opening my eyes, I cried out in pain and grasped at the virtual wound that throbbed far too realistically. I pulled the LINK connection from my temple. The snap of electricity arched between the filament and my receiver, as I severed the active connection, but it was nothing compared to the sharp pain in the soft flesh between my thumb and forefinger.

I could have killed myself disconnecting like that, but Mouse's bite surprised me. Subconsciously, I'd gambled on the fact my connection, though open to the LINK, was more with the uniform. Though I could feel a head-ache starting, I was lucky.

"He bit me; Mouse bit me." In the light streaming into the open trunk, I inspected my hand. Turning it over and over, I checked for some mark. Of course there was nothing, but, as I wiggled my fingers experimentally, I could still feel the phantom teeth marks.

Pulling the lid into place one more time, I frowned. Stretching the aching muscles of my hand, I began to understand the seriousness of the page's warning about the LINK-Michael. Before now, the LINK had been ex-clusively virtual. Jordan Institute must have come up with LINK technology that not only could access emo-tions, but also exact pain centers. Having stolen that technology, Mouse had the ability to do real-time dam-age to his enemies. But, could he kill?

The damage I had done to the FBI agents was slightly different. After all, they were completely cybernetically enhanced; their entire body pulsed through complex in-terconnects of biology and computer technology. When I had "stopped" them, I had severed the line of commu-nication between computer and synapses. I still wasn't certain how I'd done it; apparently, Jibril's biotech came with a few built-in miracles.

As a kid, I'd heard stories of people who had scared themselves to death or died of loneliness. After my bat-tle with Phanuel, I was beginning to believe that was possible, at least in part. I could have stayed caught in his web of fear until my heart burst or I starved to death. If the LINK-Michael's purview was violence, perhaps Mouse intended to send enough anger over the LINK to cause a riot, or worse.

I shook out my hand. The soft flesh still throbbed. Clearly, since Mouse had the precision to send pain to specific nerves, the LINK-Michael might be able to tell the brain to shut down its involuntary functions, like breath and heartbeat.

"Damn," I whispered under my breath. If Mouse could send the LINK-Michael to stop a person's heart, he could kill anyone on the LINK. I had to locate the page and find out whom he thought Mouse might target . . . besides me.

One answer sprang to mind. Mouse was clearly in league with Letourneau, and, right now, Letourneau's greatest enemy was his opposition in the presidential race—Rabbi-Senator Grey. From all the advertisements I'd seen, the public outcry for a real-time debate was high. If Letourneau was in fact a virtual personality as some people suspected, then he would need a distraction tonight. LINK-Michael was scheduled to wreak havoc tonight at prime time. Not a coincidence, obviously.

The tow truck slowed. I moved the latch as far down as it would go without connecting to the lock. Loud clanks and clunks signaled the car being released from the tow truck. An engine revved, and the truck sped away.

When I felt that I was alone, I released my death grip on the latch and opened the trunk a sliver. Bright, artificial light stabbed my eyes. I blinked away the watery tears and strained to hear voices. The impound lot appeared quiet and empty.

I stretched out my back, only to recoil quickly in pain. The ride had been rough, and my body protested every bump and tensed muscle. Pulling my legs over the lip of the trunk, I swung them back and forth. Pins and prickles danced along the pinched nerves.

As I'd hoped, the tow truck had taken me to the district police impound garage. Cars, most of them old and battered, stretched along the floor. Fluorescent bulbs snapped in the rafters. Somewhere up there a number of electronic cameras buzzed near the light like flies, sweeping the garage for activity.

I had to hide from them. Letting gravity do most of the work, I let myself stumble to the ground. Ignoring the pain, I shut the trunk and wedged myself under the car. Plascrete was rough and cool against my cheek. The thick, warm smell of old batteries mingled with the scent of rubber tires. I barely fit in the space between the tires and the electric rail connection, but tightness felt oddly comforting.

I shut my eyes and opened my connection to the armored suit cautiously. I ran a diagnostic and swept the area for any sign of Mouse. The LINK access door had been closed, and the uniform's interior appeared completely blank. As the search program completed, my avatar slid to a corner of the uniform. The search program illuminated the body of a mouse, lying flat on its stomach. I knelt to get a better look.

Closed, dark eyelashes stood out against the white fur. The little furry body was racked with deep, shallow breaths.

Page? I was certain Mouse would not leave an avatar behind inside the uniform. Since the LINK-door had been open when I off-lined, it would have been easy for Mouse to escape without being damaged. Besides, a non-AI avatar cut off from its host normally dissipated. Yet, Mouse had surprised me in the past, so I remained careful. *Page? Is that you?*

The little rodent shivered, and its eyes fluttered open. *Dee?*

It's me, Page. You're safe inside the uniform again. My hand stroked the fur on the image's back. I couldn't feel anything, as the action was virtual, but I hoped it gave the page comfort. It seemed to, as he stopped visibly shaking.

Mouse betrayed me completely, he said with a ragged breath.

You and me both, I assured him. *You said the LINK-Michael is a killer. Who does Mouse want dead?*

I . . . I don't know.

Do you think it could be Grey?

I . . . The page couldn't finish his thought; he was obviously strained. I felt bad for trying to pressure him.

I stood up. *Rest here, Page. I'll figure it out. Just take care of yourself.*

The page didn't respond, but I could see his breathing even out. With one last caress, I disconnected.

The next thing I heard was an urgent, hushed noise.

It took me a second to recognize the sound of my name. "Deidre."

I opened my eyes to see Michael crouched low, peering under the car. His hair was only slightly mussed, as if pulled askew by a slight breeze. On my body, I could smell the sweat and wet trunk. With a snort, I realized the worst aspect of keeping the company of angels: compared to them, you always looked like hell.

"You okay?" he asked.

"Why do I always have to ask: where were you? I thought you wanted to tag along to the meeting with Mouse to watch out for me. Instead, Satan came to my rescue."

Michael smiled. "I distinctly remember you saying you were tired of me rescuing you."

"Hmph. That's not much of an excuse." Even though I scraped painfully along the rough floor, I let Michael pull me upright.

"I'm sorry," Michael said. "I was on the roof. I saw the cops approach and was headed back toward you to warn you, when you came barreling down the road."

I smiled. Looking around, my eyes caught sight of a roving camera. "What about the security cameras?"

"We'll be all right."

"I thought miracles were too costly."

He smiled. "They are. I took care of things the old-fashioned way—I bribed someone."

We headed for the exit, and Michael held my hand. I shook my head, but gave him a smile. "My hero."

Michael squeezed my fingers tightly in response. Calluses I hadn't noticed before rubbed against my palm. There was something more solid in his grip, and I thought I felt sweat tickling between our entwined hands.

As we slipped through the gate, I caught a whiff of the smoldering smell of scorched metal. Someone, Michael I presumed, had cut the lock with a laser. The area where a guard normally stood just inside the doorway was conspicuously empty, and through the window I could see the blank screens of the video recorders. I wondered how Michael's friend would explain his absence and the destroyed chain.

"Where are we going?" Michael asked.

Pushing through the double doors, we entered an enclosed walkway. "To the Grey-Letourneau debate," I decided. "The page told me that Mouse is going to unleash your nemesis tonight at 0:00 GMT. That's when the debate is scheduled. Since the page told me that this Michael was a killer, my guess is he intends to assassinate Grey."

Checking his watch, Michael said, "It's after five o'clock now. That give us less than an hour."

I started to log on to the LINK to confirm, but, remembering the page, I stopped just in time.

"This is it then," Michael said quietly, sadness deepening his tone. Before I could ask him what he meant, Michael handed me a bundle of brown material he'd picked up when we passed the guard booth. "Put this on," he said.

Unraveling the cloth, I realized it was a trench coat. I shrugged into it, happy to be covering the stained and dirty uniform. One swish of the hem proved that the long material easily covered the bulky armor. "You've thought of everything haven't you?"

"Not everything. If we're going to save Grey from the LINK-angel, I'm going to have to contact the other archangels." Michael gave me another mysteriously sad smile as he pushed the button for the elevator.

"Okay," I said. "What's wrong?"

The door slid open with a ting. With a mock bow, Michael held the door for me. "It means I'll have to go back."

"Why?" I asked, stepping into the elevator.

"To assemble all of the archangels at once we need a miracle. If I go back, I can do that."

Cringing at the slight drop when Michael added his weight to the car, I held my breath as the doors swooshed shut. Michael pressed the button for the sixty-first floor, the public transportation level. From there we could catch a taxi, ride a bus, hop a bicycle, or take the El to Carnegie Hall, where the debate was scheduled.

"Can't you use another miracle without going back?"

"I could." Michael agreed, a sneer tightening his handsome face. "And become a dark one. I don't really think this is the best time for me to be switching sides, do you?"

"No." I watched Michael, who glanced patiently at the numbers scrolling on the display. The elevator slowed suddenly, and my knees buckled a little. "But, I don't get it. I thought your whole reason for being here was to stop this LINK-Michael. Why can't you use your powers to that end? Why does God make it so difficult to be good?"

"To make it worth it."

I rolled my eyes. We reached the sixty-first floor, and the door opened up to the public-transportation tube. The light was brighter here, augmented by fluorescent strips along the upper curve of the tunnel.

Shops lined the narrow walkway, and a crowd of people flowed around me. I was constantly amazed at the bustle of the city. Despite the fact that most people carried their offices in their heads, New Yorkers seemed to have an innate need to be on the move. After fighting our way to a city bus shelter, I plopped unceremoniously onto a bench and grumbled, "If being good means having to take the city bus, I can see why Satan is so much more popular."

Michael slid a credit counter into the ticket dispenser and punched in our destination code. His fingers jabbed at the keypad, and his face held a tight grimace. The machine spit out the tickets. When he moved away, other bus riders moved in to use the dispensers. Standing over me, he shielded our conversation from the gathering crowd. "I have struggled this whole time to be normal, human, mortal; all you seem to want is empty drama and quick fixes."

"That's not fair," I said. "I never asked for the LINK miracle or the one that healed me. What I want right now is to save Grey and come up with a way to stop Mouse. This is the first miracle I've asked for."

Michael's eyes watched the tips of his shoes, and the muscles of his jaw flexed. Shoving his hands into his pockets, he glanced up at me. His eyes were full of guilt. "Deidre. I'm afraid to go back . . . I think it would mean the end for me. . . ."

A thrum reverberated in the shelter. I felt a pressure against my back and spun around to see a woman throwing herself against the shatterproof plastic. She was shouting; the muffled sounds were filled with incoherent rage. The woman stood in the middle of the walkway. Her hair was a mass of tangles, and her face crumpled into a tight frown. I would have thought her a relative of the Revelation preacher, but, despite her wild expression, her clothes were neat and trim. She wore a power suit of bright blue, but there was blood from her nose on her blouse. As she ran at the shelter again, I backed away.

"What the hell is going on?" I asked. People around me stared in horror and confusion.

I caught a businessman's eye, and said, "You, call the police."

Michael gripped my shoulders protectively. The woman crashed headlong against the plastic again, leaving a smear of blood. The plastic began to buckle, and this fueled her anger. The woman scratched and tore at the indentation she'd made like a wild dog.

People in the shelter screamed and scattered. A mother and child huddled in the farthest corner.

"Where are the police?" I muttered, looking around for another exit. "She's going to hurt herself."

An angry roar erupted at my side. Turning I saw the businessman I'd talked to clutching his head. Then, lifting his fingers from his eyes, he glared at me with pure hatred.

"I'm going to kill you!" the businessman screamed, spittle flying from the corners of his mouth. He launched himself in my direction.

With a rush of air, Michael stood in front of me. One

strong punch sent the possessed businessman sprawling backward. Another thrum echoed in the confined space, as the woman continued to beat against the bloodied plastic shield.

Ignoring his rapidly swelling jaw, the man in the business suit staggered to his feet. His eyes stayed locked on mine.

Michael pointed to the ticket dispensers. Catching his meaning, I scurried to the protected alcove between the two machines. I slid sideways between the humming dispensers and rested my arms against the cool metal.

The bus shelter erupted with noise; shrill screams of terror turned to guttural cries of anger. Around Michael's bulk, I could see all the eyes around us filled with dark emotion. The woman who'd been huddling in the corner with her child leapt up. The child, too young to have a LINK implant, looked bewildered.

"Michael," I said, "it's the LINK-angels. We've got to get out of here."

Turning to face me, Michael's arms were around me in a second. "I will do it. For you. Shut your eyes, Deidre."

"Why? Wha . . ." My words were swallowed by a torrential wind. Lightning stabbed my eyes.

"Shut your eyes, Deidre," a calm voice intoned, as I. felt myself rising, as if separating from my body. I had the distinct impression that if I were to look "down," I would see my body crumpled in the bus shelter. "We're going back."

" 'Back'? Back to heaven?" Panic made my voice tight.

Bob Courtland reporting in real time from Manhattan, in front of Carnegie Hall:

Bob: "Thanks H.C. The crowd here is enormous. There are people stretching in both directions for kilometers on the pedestrian tube near the main entrance to Carnegie Hall. Police have had to arrest an unconfirmed number of adults who were attempting to gain foot access to the vehicle traffic level apparently trying to be the first to witness what type of vehicles in which the presidential candidates will arrive. To say the mood here is chaotic and exciting is an understatement.''

H.C.: ''Tell us a little bit about what's happening down there, Bob.''

Bob: ''Well, it's amazing. People have unplugged in a serious way. I've been talking to some of the crowd and several have said they joined the crowd just out of a need to be with other human beings on such a historic moment. Let's talk to this young lady. Hello? This is Bob Courtland from LINK-politics, can I ask you a few questions?''

Woman: ''Wow. *The* Bob.Courtland.polLINK? You look so much shorter in real time. Do you think Letourneau is shorter than he seems in VR?''

Bob: ''It's hard to say. Is that why you're here today?''

Woman: ''I guess. I heard about all the people gathering here and I thought maybe it was some kind of sign or something, you know? I mean, if Letourneau is the Second Coming, then, maybe this moment is like the whole sermon on the mount/bread and fishes thing. Who would want to miss a thing like that? I mean, I want to be able to tell my kids I was there, you know?''

Bob: ''Thank you. Let's ask someone else. Ah, here, excuse me, sir, I'm Bob Courtland from LINK-politics, can I ask you a question?''

Man: [waves] ''Hi, Mom.''

Bob: ''What brought you to Carnegie Hall today, sir?''

Man: ''I'm a big Grey supporter, see?'' [points to tee shirt bearing slogan ''Grey in 76—REAL people's choice!''] ''I've been to every one of Grey's talks. It's kind of an event, you know, getting out and meeting real-time people. I used to be this total plug-head, and I've had this epiphany, see? It's time to unplug and experience real-time real life . . .

Bob: ''Uh, right. Moving on . . .''

CHAPTER 24

Flames licked and danced along the deep green bay leaves without burning through them. I found myself on a rocky desert plain; various hues of browns and yellows extended to the horizon. Above, the sky was cloudless. Heat brought prickles of sweat to my body, and the air was still. The crackling snaps of the fire were the only sound.

Michael stood in the center of the shrub. Like wax, flesh dripped from his body, sizzling and spitting in the fire. His expression was sad, yet peaceful. Michael's hands stretched open in supplication; his posture reminded me of Joan of Arc at the stake. Light, as sharp as a laser beam, punched through the skin over his heart. Tears of pain and joy evaporated in the heat. " 'I am, who I am.' "

"No," I cried, watching Michael's body tumble into seven pieces. "Don't go!"

Swallowing his flesh, the fire popped with joy. A hiss from the bush seemed to say, "We love you."

"No!" The coolness of the air startled me, and I blinked. The houselights were up, and people moved through rows and rows of plush seats. The curved vaulted ceilings bounced the sound of voices around the hall until the noise jumbled together into a pleasant and excited thrum. Carved columns supported the proscenium arch of the stage. A crew of people were busily setting up podiums and positioning LINK-sensory camera connections.

I blinked again. Even though part of me knew I wouldn't see him, I whispered, "Michael?"

"Deidre, darling!" A tall Asian woman waved at me from the central aisle. Her bobbed haircut bounced around heavy dream-catcher earrings as she made her way up the row of seats to where I stood under the balcony—blinking and bewildered.

Reaching me, the woman gave me a measured look through long lashes. Her dress was tie-dyed and shimmered under the houselights. Putting her hands on her narrow hips, she frowned at my trench coat. "You're a little underdressed, honey, but it'll have to do."

"I'm sorry, do I know you?" I looked past the woman to the stage, where workers were adding velvet drapes to the podiums. The chill of the theater's air-conditioning reminded me of the absence of a hot desert sun; even the bright stage lights lacked heat.

"I'm Ariel," the woman said, startling me by dropping her voice an octave. "The archangel Uriel. I'm here with some boys I think you know."

She pointed to the edge of the stage. In a turban and tux, Jibril's dark features stood out in the crowd. Raphael nodded in agreement to something Jibril said. "Where's Michael?" I asked.

"Oh, the poor lost lamb. He's . . ." Ariel's smile crumpled at the edges. "Let's just say, karmically, he couldn't make a return trip . . . just yet."

"Karma?" I looked Ariel up and down. "So, what are you? Buddhist or something?"

The tips of her black bob swished, and her earrings shook to and fro. Her smile showed crooked, masculine teeth. "Honey, do I look like a *bodhisattva* to you?"

I shrugged, moving out of the way as a couple stepped into the hall to find their seats.

"Well, I am. In the flesh, as it were," she said with a broad wink.

I nodded, but I wasn't really listening to her. "Michael is gone for good, isn't he?"

Dark lipstick became a sharp line. "I like to think positively, you know, PPT: 'Power of Positive Thinking' and all that," she said. Lightly taking hold of my elbow, she herded me into the hall. "The boys like to obsess on the Old Testament—all that flooding and Sodom's destruction—but don't listen to them; it'll only raise your blood pressure. I believe, ultimately, that whatever higher power there might be is a forgiving, loving entity. You have to trust in it."

I made the appropriate uh-huh noises, but I was thinking of Michael consumed by the holy fire. I would never see the Michael I knew again, I was sure of it. If there was one thing Michael forced me to appreciate, it was that our flesh defines us. Even if he came back, he would not be in the same form; I had lost him.

The boys, as Ariel had called them, seemed to know it, too. Raphael's eyes watched mine warily, sympathetically. Jibril shook his head sadly, and said, "It's the final hour, Deidre. Are you ready?"

I nodded solemnly, not trusting myself to speak yet.

"Spirit never dies," Ariel said, her breezy manner abandoned momentarily. "Like energy it can neither be destroyed nor created, only transformed."

I turned away to watch the stage. The podiums and cameras were in place, and the crew had left the stage. A hush permeated the concert hall, which was filled to capacity. Nearly everyone had taken a seat. "Do you know what time it is?" I asked Raphael.

"Six on the dot," he said.

The lights dimmed, and a young man stepped out onto the stage. Clearing his throat nervously, he said, "Reverend Letourneau's plane has been delayed."

The crowd rippled with disapproval.

"It should only be a matter of minutes," the nervous aide assured the audience. "Rabbi-Senator Grey has nobly offered to begin with his opening remarks."

From where we stood, I could see the senator standing behind a heavy velvet traveler curtain. Like his name, his hair and beard were a steely gray. Though his body was trim and athletic, he looked at least sixty, perhaps older. Even from a distance, I could see the sharp glitter of his eyes; he looked meaningfully at the four of us, as though he understood the significance of our presence.

The crowd rumbled again. Like a roll of thunder, the noise started in the far end of the hall, growing louder and angrier as it moved up the rows.

"It's starting," I murmured, watching as the back row staggered to their feet. The maliciousness of Letourneau's plan made me laugh. "That bastard. LINK-Michael will cause a riot, and then some stand-in for Letourneau will show up just in time to pretend to calm the beast, making it look like Letourneau saved the day. Clever. Evil, but clever."

"What should we do?" Raphael asked.

"Keep the rabbi from physical harm," I said, pointing at Grey. "I'm going to see if I can distract the LINK-angel before any damage gets done."

The angels leapt up onto the stage as one. They made a strange sight: Muslim in turban and tux; Israeli Jew in full military uniform; and Asian New Age drag queen striding purposefully toward where Grey waited in the wings. To his credit, Grey seemed unafraid.

Security met the angels halfway across the stage, but was quickly distracted by the possessed audience swelling toward the podiums.

I settled into a crouch in the corner where the stage met the wall. Attaching the filament to my receiver, I entered the uniform.

Page? I scanned the uniform's contents for the AI.

Here, the page said, popping into view. Still the small mouse, his avatar looked rested. His whiskers quivered, testing the air. *What's going on out there?*

Michael has . . . I choked at the mention of his name, my mouth drying like a desert plain. I swallowed my grief, and started over. *The LINK-angel has been released. I'm going to try to stop it.*

The mouse shook his head, and this tail quivered in fear. *What are you going to do, Dee?*

I sighed, but squared my shoulders. *I don't really know. I'm hoping it will come to me.*

The mouse icon blinked. A shake of its furry head

transformed the mouse into a human image, with a face full of bewilderment. *That's your grand plan? 'It'll come to me'? Great. We're screwed.*

You have a better idea?

The page's face scrunched up in thought. He was silent for mere seconds, and I wondered how many scenarios the page was able to run in that time. *How about a blackout?*

Can you do that?

I have access to Mouse's power connections, but I can't affect anything in the physical world.

An idea sparked, and hope surged briefly in my heart. *So, what you're saying is that we need some terrorists. Someone who could, say, physically smash the black boxes in the subway system.* I was thinking of Rebeckah or even the Gorgons.

The page frowned. *If LINK-Michael has been unleashed, it might be difficult for me to get a message to anyone.*

I'll worry about that. You do what you can to screw up Mouse's system.

The page beamed with pleasure. *Okay. Sounds like now you've got a plan.*

I nodded, even though the page couldn't really see the expression. We opened the connection to the LINK. Darkness subdued the usual glitter of the space. The angel's presence oozed around us, dampening the normal vibrancy of the space.

Shit, the page whispered beside me. *This is worse than I imagined.*

Go, I said. *I'll get the message to Rebeckah.*

With a cascade of light, the page disappeared into the ether. I stepped out into the LINK. The LINK-Michael had infected the crowd through the entertainment and news channel. My avatar interpreted the sensation by showing thick, slimy tentacles undulating through the ceiling of a tunnel and disappearing into the floor. The air held a charred smell, like wet burned toast. I grabbed the nearest feeler and yanked hard. Moist flesh slithered through my fingers.

You're not going to make this easy for me, are you, Mouse? I said. This time I punched at the waving palp. Continuing to pull and punch, I danced through the narrow band, calling him out. *Are you afraid to fight me? Are you scared I'm going to kick your ass just like I did Phanuel's?*

That got a reaction. Rearing out of the floor, two tentacles reached out. Their slippery wetness enveloped me. Curling around the body of my avatar, the feelers hugged me tightly. At first the feeling was welcoming and warm—dark, but not threatening, like snuggling under a feather comforter at night. Suffocating heaviness descended next. Panic rose in my throat, but the pressure in my skull squeezed tightly, pushing my consciousness deeper and deeper. I fell back into that place that I watched myself from when I was a practicing wire-junkie.

The distinct, floating part of my mind became aware of my body shifting in real time. The LINK-angel twitched my muscles, as if testing out the controls of a new machine. Through the angel's senses, I felt a familiar heaviness in my breasts. Observing my body in this way, I understood what had happened to Rebeckah's male sysops. Most men were still socialized to be able to distance themselves from their bodies—wire-wizards even more so. The more into the machine you could go, the faster your interface was. Thus, the LINK-angels were able to devour them whole.

On the other hand, most women were brought back, once a month, like it or not, to the sensations and needs of their bodies. That's why Sharron had been able to function where Rebeckah's male hackers had not.

Feeling the heaviness in my womb, my body was telling me I was pregnant . . . pregnant with Michael's child. Michael had sacrificed to get me here, and I refused to let me down. No matter how hard and how deep LINK-Michael pushed on my consciousness, part of me stubbornly clung to the physical realm. I used that to my advantage now. Opening my eyes in real time, I thrust my back firmly into the corner, resisting the angel's command to stand. My body twisted with the effort and flopped hard against the floor. At the same moment, I sent out a plea for help to Sharron, Rebeckah, or any Malach on the web. As double insurance, I sent out a message to Dancer via Michael's credit counter. I told her that if she could gather enough friends to smash Mouse's boxes in the tunnels, I'd find a way to get her in the front door of some restaurant.

Before I could get a response, I was yanked away by searing pain.

Curse you, McMannus, Mouse said, with LINK-Michael's deep echoing voice. *I don't want to hurt you—not really.*

Pain cut like a knife across my abdomen. I wanted to disconnect, but I was too far out on the LINK for that move to be safe. Curling around my stomach, I gasped in pain. I tried to stay focused on my body, to think about breathing, the baby, but the pain centers the LINK-Michael manipulated were part of me as well.

Switching tactics, I tried sending another message to the Malachim on broadband.

No one hears you, the LINK-Michael informed me. *I can block your pathetic attempts at communication.*

The page is headed toward the hub, Mouse, my avatar hissed through clenched teeth. In real time air escaped in bubbles between clenched teeth. *We're going to pull your plug. Expose you like Oz behind the curtain.*

Bullshit, Mouse spit, cramping the muscles across my back.

I cried out in pain, shinnying along the floor like a crab. *You think he won't betray you?* I sputtered, *You . . . you should have told him about the Pope.*

Mouse hesitated. I sensed other ears listening intently; the octopus tentacles of LINK-Michael projected our conversation into the minds of the others he possessed.

Using the angel technology to kill the Pope was a stroke of genius, Mouse. Proto-Michael possessed Daniel, didn't he? Feeding his anger . . . moving his body like a puppet. Did you attack me just to see if it could be done—directed at a specific person . . . ?

My accusations stopped. Prone, I could feel the weight

of my back pressing down on lungs that suddenly stopped working. I no longer took in air on my own. Mouse had upped the ante, and I was out of chips.

I'd always hoped to think of something clever at moments like this, but all I could think was: *Fuck. Breathe, damn it, breathe.* Despite my pleading, my lungs refused to obey my commands. My muscles spasmed as I tried to flop onto my back to relieve some of the pressure. Veins stood out on my neck, tight with lack of oxygen. My head felt light.

My eyes opened, and I saw flames licking at my flesh. The tongues danced along the material of my trench coat, but there was no pain. I smelled the spicy scent of crushed bay leaves, and I knew I was dying. My mind whispered a prayer, my first in years, *Let Rebeckah or Dancer get my message.*

A year ago, the idea of dying would have frightened me, but Morningstar had kindled the ember of faith left in my heart. I felt myself moving upward, floating toward the surface. The sun-speckled surface of the water Michael's archer shot through glowed above. The dark haze that shrouded the LINK lifted, and glittering stars shone in the sky. Tentacles receded, and I surrendered.

Your faith is admirable, Deidre, but this is an exceedingly bad time to die, a warm, familiar voice said.

Michael? Then, I asked, *Morningstar?*

The voice didn't answer. I felt something akin to a push, and then I buoyed upward toward . . . Consciousness. A harsh gulp of air brought the pain back to my body. My lungs heaved with the effort to make up for lost breath.

I opened my eyes, surprised to be alive. I lay facedown on the polished wood stage. Though the stage lights shone in my eyes, I could see the gathered crowd. They continued to push against the security guards, and in a moment they would overwhelm them. Lifting my head, I could see the angels standing in a tight guard around Rabbi Grey. By nearly dying, I had escaped the LINK-Michael, but, from the blank looks on the faces of the angry mob, he was not gone from the LINK.

I'd escaped, but my plan had failed. I struggled to my feet, just as a collective roar came from the crowd. I ran toward Rabbi Grey and the angels, just as the mob broke over the security guards like a flood over a dike.

"Get him out of here! To the trade tunnels!" I shouted, but I doubted I could be heard over the din. As I was swept up in the flow of bodies, I opened my LINK connection. I wasn't sure what I'd do, but I hoped to reason with the crowd. Before I could hail a broadband channel, an incoming message icon filled my vision.

Who could possibly get through all this noise, I asked, as I flipped the go-ahead. I wondered if someone, some angel, had answered my prayers with a miracle.

It's us. A double vision of Rebeckah and the page filled my screen. *We got your message and are in position,* Rebeckah's avatar said.

We'll do it for chocolate, piped in Dancer and a frightening multiple image of a gaggle of Gorgons.

Do it now! I told Rebeckah and the page.

Around me the crowd pressed to where the angels guarded Rabbi Grey. I could hear a rain of fists and the tearing of clothes, as the crowd pummeled the angelic defenses. Though they were angels, their flesh was real here on Earth, I reminded myself. They couldn't hold off the crowd forever.

Then, through my LINK connection, I felt a popping sensation. It shook the foundation of the LINK. High-pitched sproings, like suspension-bridge cables giving way, ricocheted through all the channels of the LINK. I felt my feet begin to drop out from under me.

Before my eyes, the LINK-angel crumbled to dust.

PolLINK feed, back on-line.

"MOUSE" ARRESTED

In a scandal that nearly brought down the LINK, the hacker known only as "Mouse" was arrested today for impersonating political candidate Etienne Letourneau. Mouse will be transported to the New Jersey State

Penitentiary while awaiting trial. He has already made claims of diplomatic immunity. The United Nations, however, in light of current events, has disbarred mouse.net from its customary status as a sovereign "nation." Russia, whose entire network operates via mouse.net, has petitioned for Mouse's release. [Hotlink here for more on that political debate.] "You won't keep me behind bars," Mouse shouted as he was taken away from Carnegie Hall late yesterday evening.

"Even if he's not guilty of perpetrating the myth of Letourneau and the LINK-angels, Mouse is certainly responsible for the LINK-outage that happened during the prime-time debates," alleged Captain Allaire Morgan of the New York Police Department. "We can keep him locked up for a while for that."

It is unknown, at this point, whether or not Letourneau ever was a real person, but sources believe it is highly unlikely. More likely, Mouse managed to create the entire persona of Letourneau electronically.

"What is most disturbing," says congressional colleague Pastor-Senator Dwayne Smith, "is that I feel like I knew the guy. He attended several of my online parties, and, well, I'd thought we were friends. Now I find he's completely constructed. It's unreal."

Smith's reaction is not uncommon in the Senate and elsewhere. Many people still don't believe that Letourneau may have never existed in real time. Neighbors of the Colorado ranch where Letourneau supposedly lived said, "I still say he was a good neighbor—real or not. I guess I just figured the man was a recluse. Ain't nothing wrong with that."

"In a way," said one friend who wished to remain anonymous, "he was as real as he needed to be. I had more meaningful interactions with him than I do with friends I know exist in real time. Honestly, I'm going to miss him. I intend to have a funeral in his honor."

A "funeral" for Letourneau will be held in his hometown at the church where he preached. When asked how they felt to discover their reverend might be a construct, one member of the congregation had this to say. "I think he was a fine preacher, and I still say he might have been a messenger from God about the Second Coming. Angels are supernatural, which means they don't exist in nature, yet good Christians believe in them, don't they? So, there's no reason to discount what Letourneau said just because he's not real in our usual definition of that term."

CHAPTER 25

The glass shattered beneath the spade. Underneath the sheath of Medusa poison, I could see sandy soil. Since I was six months pregnant, Rebeckah forbade me from doing any of the shoveling, so I held the thin trunk of the sapling. Rebeckah hadn't even wanted me this close to the remaining glass sections of the kibbutz. But I'd kicked up a fuss, and, more practically, promised to wear the heaviest radiation armor we had.

Leaning into the shade from the hot sun, I could smell the bay leaves. I had to be here. After all, we were dedicating this tree to Michael. Looking across the compound I could see the other trees the kibbutz had planted, each dedicated to a fallen soldier. Daniel's sturdy oak had been our first experiment, and it was recovering nicely from the shock. We'd miscalculated how much extra sun and heat the glass would reflect, but now each of us took turns checking the soil and watering diligently. It would survive.

As would we. Rebeckah had formed the kibbutz at the edge of the glass city. Most of the complex was surrounded by a domed radiation shield, and we were slowly breaking up the glass perimeter. For every section of glass we broke, we added trees.

A red flash at the corner of my eye informed me the page had a message. I flipped the go-ahead switch.

Hey, home, I greeted the image of the page that popped into view. He affected his feminine aspect today, and wore colored robes that covered everything but a slit for the eyes.

Hey, girlfriend. Tell Rebeckah we've got company. Travelers at the door.

Tell her yourself, I said with a smile.

You're the sysop for the compound, Dee. You do it.

Sweat rolled off Rebeckah's back as she heaved another spadeful of dirt out of the glass, oblivious to our conversation. The muted light from the nearby plasti-shield cast strange-colored shadows along the curves of her muscles. *We're planting a tree,* I protested feebly. *You know she hates being interrupted during a ceremony.*

Believe me, I know. That's why I'm telling you to tell her. Anyway, these guys can't wait. They're demanding religious asylum.

I stood up straighter, nearly dropping the tree. The leaves shook noisily, and Rebeckah looked up from her work.

Asylum? I repeated. *Who are they?*

You've read about the prophet, right? the page asked me. Lately, I'd been notorious for not scanning the news. After Mouse's arrest and since the *Times* had run the article exposing Letourneau as another of Mouse's constructs, I'd stopped LINKing to the news and entertainment band altogether. Truth was, watching the 3-D replay of the police hauling Mouse away had filled me with guilt. I hated feeling that way, so I stopped watching the news.

News about the prophet, however, was hard to avoid.

After everything that had happened, Americans were skeptical about any talk of a messiah or a Second Coming. The LINK raged with debate. No one wanted to be duped again, and so the prophet had been branded an outlaw.

Though I'd never seen a vid of him, I'd heard all about his philosophy. From everything I'd learned from Michael, it hadn't been too far from the truth, as I understood it anyway. Still, no one liked to hear the truth, and everything the prophet said managed to piss off one faction or another. No wonder he was seeking asylum here; our kibbutz, like the Malachim before, was known for its open-door policy.

Let him in, Page. Rebeckah and I will meet him in the mess.

Rebeckah leaned against the shovel, eyeing me suspiciously. "Who was that?"

"Page. Apparently, a prophet is at our gate."

Rebeckah nodded and wiped the sweat from the back of her neck. "I hope you let him in."

"We're meeting him in the mess."

With a gesture, Rebeckah handed the shovel to another. Even though she no longer led the Malachim, she continued to have the ability to command with a look. It took me longer to find someone to relieve me of my burden. Finally, after handing off the tree to a disgruntled volunteer, I trotted to catch up with Rebeckah.

"You know, most people wouldn't make a pregnant woman scramble after them."

"Have you seen him speak?" Rebeckah asked, ignoring my whining.

I shook my head. "I stay away from newsvids, remember?"

"You've never even seen a picture?"

"Sure, I've seen a picture. I'd have to be dead not to have seen at least some things. You ask me, he looks like any other scruffy-looking Jewish guy claiming to be a prophet." I didn't tell Rebeckah, but the prophet's gray eyes had struck me. Even in the holos of him, they'd seemed deep and intense.

Rebeckah laughed. "I guess so. He's got an interesting group of followers, though."

We reached the mess hall. Most of the kibbutz was carved out of the glassed remains of the city. We had destroyed most of the taller buildings, but this section of brick row houses was too beautiful and too historic to bulldoze. Patiently, people had been chipping away at the radioactive glass to reveal the perfectly preserved woodwork and stone. Some of the bricks had enough sand content that they were permanently transformed to glass, so the sun caught squares here and there along the tight line of buildings.

He stood up as we entered, those piercing gray eyes raising to meet mine. He'd cleaned up from the last vid I'd seen. Dark curly locks were cut in a martial style that took my breath away. A shaven face revealed the planes of his face, sharp enough to cut.

"Michael," I breathed.

As he looked at me, his gray eyes not quite comprehending, a wind shook the air between us.

I felt the baby kick.

Look what we have for you to read next...

☐ **THE DARKEST ROAD: BOOK THREE** by Guy Gavriel Kay
In a world of extraordinary imagination, a final battle is waged against a power of unimaginable proportions.
458338/$13.95

☐ **RESURRECTION** by Arwen Elys Dayton
In 2600 B.C., the first ship built by the Kinley race capable of travelling faster than the speed of light, the *Champion*, is sent to explore a tiny blue planet called Earth. But the *Champion's* first mission would also be its last...
458346/$6.99

☐ **SILVER WOLF, BLACK FALCON** by Dennis L. McKiernan
The final novel in the bestselling world of Mithgar "blends lore and prophecy with vivid battle scenes and emotional drama to create a tale of high fantasy that should appeal to...fans of epic fiction." (*Library Journal*)
458036/$6.99

Prices slightly higher in Canada

Payable by Visa, MC or AMEX only ($10.00 min.), No cash, checks or COD.
Shipping & handling: US/Can. $2.75 for one book, $1.00 for each add'l book;
Int'l $5.00 for one book, $1.00 for each add'l. Call (800) 788-6262 or
(201) 933-9292, fax (201) 896-8569 or mail your orders to:

Penguin Putnam Inc.   Bill my: ☐ Visa ☐ MasterCard ☐ Amex _____ (expires)
P.O. Box 12289, Dept. B   Card# _____
Newark, NJ 07101-5289
Please allow 4-6 weeks for delivery.
Foreign and Canadian delivery 6-8 weeks.   Signature _____

Bill to:
Name _____
Address_____ City _____
State/ZIP _____ Daytime Phone # _____
Ship to:
Name_____ Book Total $ _____
Address _____ Applicable Sales Tax $_____
City _____ Postage & Handling $ _____
State/ZIP _____ Total Amount Due $ _____

This offer subject to change without notice.   Ad # JanROC (9/00)